June 18.45

Mrs. Heaton's Daughter

Mrs HEATON'S DAUGHTER

By
Dorsha Hayes

ZIFF-DAVIS PUBLISHING COMPANY · CHICAGO · NEW YORK

THIRD PRINTING

To
FLORENCE *and* RICHARD

1

IT WAS a glorious gift. Mother would be astounded. Diana sensed the quality of gay delight with which her gifts were all received and then impatience came that Mother had not yet returned.

From the front porch one could watch, could see a figure walking down the tree-lined street, growing bigger and bigger, the moment coming to make a dash forward and be lifted high, shouting high, into the air.

Hurry came into her. The child was in motion, wriggling down from the nursery chair, backing from the table where her creation lay, a rose made of bright paper, green and red, cut and twisted, a very special gift. She skipped out into the hall, went warily down the front stairs, one step at a time, warnings of disaster held obediently in mind, and came out upon the porch.

Roddy was there, playing some game of his own imagining. She stood watching her brother, fascinated. "I want to play too." After she had said that several times he took notice of her and explained. The game was 'Boat.' The upside-down chair was a wheel that steered. There was ocean all around. *All* around, he said shrilly, you would drown if you left the porch.

But it was not fun. She did not like being 'passenger' and sitting still. She leaned against the porch rail and looked out into the yard. A slow hot breeze that came and lapsed shifted quivering patches of sun and shade beneath the big tree on the lawn. A black and yellow butterfly wandered through vibrant sun-drenched air. All at once she spied the whirligig sprinkler turned on beside the flower beds. To edge close enough to get wet but not really wet. . . .

"Sis! You can't get off now!"

Halted in the act of going eagerly down the steps, she was dismayed by recollection of his game. For one unhappy, yearning moment she clung to the rail, eyeing her brother, dubious, then a turn of her head—and there was Mother coming. With a shriek of joy she went scrambling down the steps, galloping toward the woman. A trip and she lay sprawled, wondering if the pain was bad enough to cry.

Mother's hands were lifting her, Mother's face was on a level with her own. "Oh darling, are you hurt?" Mrs. Heaton looked anxiously into the child's face. "You aren't hurt, are you? Not badly?"

Diana decided she was not and held out smarting red palms for sympathy. Mrs. Heaton, kneeling before her, wiped and kissed them both and smiled, coaxing a smile from the child. Then Diana knew the contentment of being lifted, carried, everything bouncing to the spring of Mother's step.

Rod looked on, sulking. "Sis spoiled my boat."

Mrs. Heaton, coming up the walk, cocked her head at him, not thinking that report important.

Her mother loomed up at the screen door. "Hattie! You're not carrying that heavy child! Why, she's near on six! Put her down."

Too breathless to answer, Mrs. Heaton toiled up the steps before she set Diana on her feet and inspected the cut on her knee. Trivial, but of course it must be taken care of at once.

"Enough to bring on one of your indigestion attacks," fretted Mrs. Fletcher, and righted the overturned chair with a decisive switch. "Landsakes, you'd ought to know better! All fools aren't dead yet. How'd choir practice go?"

Mrs. Heaton took Diana's hand and passed into the house, speaking over her shoulder. "I needn't have gone. I'm singing a solo."

Injured, needing sympathy too, Rod trailed his mother. "May I go to church with you on Sunday?" Permission gained gave a measure of relief; Sis was only a baby who went to Sunday school.

The cut washed and doctored, both children followed Mrs.

Heaton into her bedroom, stood close about her as she un-
buttoned her dress, stepped out of it, sat down at the dressing
table.

"Sis spoiled my boat."

How he could harp on a thing, like his father! Rod was
not her favorite; in the honesty of her own thoughts that was
admitted, along with the guilty awareness that to have a
favorite was wrong. But Rod wasn't at all the dashing little
fellow that Mrs. Heaton would have expected a son of hers
to be, she couldn't help wishing there was more man-stuff
in him. Clever, talented—his chalk drawings were unquestion-
ably exceptional—but too nervous, too set in his own mold,
while Diana—oh, there was no comparison! So responsive, so
affectionate, so eager and intelligent—and beautiful too—a
treasure of a child.

She removed hair pins and sidecombs and unwound the
thick coil of her hair. Diana reached for the sidecombs and
Mrs. Heaton handed them to her absently, trying to think
of something to divert Rod from his lingering sense of injury;
she could not bear sulking. Nodding at him with a smile and
a wink, she asked, "How would you like to sit beside me in
the choir loft Sunday?" Rod's eyes blinked and shone. With
a swift welling up of tenderness, Mrs. Heaton reached out to
tousle his bright red hair. Now he was happy and her conscience clear.

How hot it was, sickening! The sun poured heat through
thick motionless air, the frame house was like a heated box.
You grew up in a prairie town, thought nothing of the blaze
of summer, but once you had been east, known sea-air and
fog. . . . An old restlessness stirred her. She did not belong
in this place, she had no part in it. The big cities of the east
called to her. Get away, get away. . . .

Diana tugged at her mother's starched petticoat. "See! Now
I'm a grown-up lady!" The combs had been worked into a
mess of updrawn golden-brown curls.

Mrs. Heaton gave a touch to a comb here and there and

3

drew the child before the looking glass to gloat over the effect. "My, what a beautiful young lady!"

Rod asked, "You're beautiful, aren't you, Mother?"

Mrs. Heaton chuckled. "I was called a beauty when I was a girl. What do you think?"

"You *are* beautiful," he assured her, wanting that comforting fact established, and then in order to be truthful, admitted in his own mind her one flaw, 'all but the hair under you arms.'

Diana chanted happily, "Mother is beautiful, Mother is beautiful, it said so in the paper!"

Puzzled, Mrs. Heaton asked, "What paper, Dicky?"

Diana crowded, dancing beside her, remembering it all. "When you were a girl. You sang. You had your picture in the paper. It said you were beautiful."

"Why, how could you remember that! You saw it only once!" Mrs. Heaton slipped an arm about Diana, drawing her close, gazing sad-eyed into the mirror, memory coming with a swift, moody ache. That one picture, treasured, that one time, so long ago. "I wonder if anyone else remembers."

The face in the looking glass was pretty, young. The thick, loosened copper hair framed the small even features and the white skin of throat and shoulders. Beneath dark eyebrows that were surprisingly level, that levelness surprisingly attractive, clear eyes of amber-brown looked out, true and straight, yet with a wistfulness that gave a quality of mystery and added to their beauty. The mouth was full and sweet and carried no hint of petulance or sadness. Mrs. Heaton thought, why, I don't look old! I don't look thirty-five!

She stood up and at once Diana asked, "What are you going to do, Mother?" with an air that told of glad expectations, games, stories—anything might happen.

A momentary realization of heat-worn lapsing strength held the woman irresolute; she was not strong and the day had been exhausting. She would have liked to send the children from her, lie down, rest in quiet before supper.

"A story, Mother, a long story."

4

For Diana there must be no denials, no disappointments, no failure on her mother's part. The eager clamoring set in flow the life-giving sustenance of love and Mrs. Heaton answered brightly. "Come along! Three-on-a-bed and I'll tell you a story."

While they were there Mrs. Fletcher came to the door, sniffed disapproval; the three of them with their shoes on and the cover not turned back! "Supper's nearly ready. Your father's come home, Hattie."

Luke Fletcher trudged into the house with the slow, plodding steps that marked him as a farm-bred man. He hung his hat on its accustomed peg and went down the hall to his den. There he washed at the closet basin and poured out his habitual, measured drink of bourbon; medicine; that stemmed back to days of malaria picked up down south in Civil War time. Marching through everlasting dust clouds, dreaming about watermelon . . . cholera balls they called them then. And now America was in another war and Wilson was sending the boys overseas. Ah well, it had to be and duty can't be shirked.

His wife came to the door, querulous, complaining. No good would come of it she knew right well, but he should speak to Hattie all the same. Diana had again gone into the flower beds, trampled them; the child should get a whipping. Luke listened in silence while she talked; he need say nothing for she knew he shared her thought on this. A child should be punished for disobedience, that was plain common sense. It wasn't right the way that Hattie raised her children; she'd speak to them like equals, let them answer back, get down on the floor and play games same as if she was a child herself; it wasn't natural or proper. But he had talked with her without result, she had her own ideas and stuck to them, plain willful. Diana had never been spanked, Diana never would be spanked, she would not have Diana's spirit broken with a whipping. 'Teach her discipline through pain or fear? The only discipline that she shall know is love

5

and reason.' He had warned, 'Diana only obeys you because she wants to,' and, head flung up, triumphant, she had retorted, 'Could there be a better reason for obedience?' No, no sense to argue. And they were good children mostly, well-behaved; Hattie was fortunate in that.

Left to himself, Luke drew out his suitcase, laid it on the desk, began packing for a business trip. Papers from the desk drawer were stowed inside the bag. The Bible went along, a copy of Shakespeare beside it. Into a side flap went a revolver; no use for that these days, but habit sticks; it had come in handy, years back, just having it along, seemed right it should be there though there was no violence these times, nothing like the railroad strikes in '94. He set the suitcase by the door, ready to be taken upstairs, some clothes put in.

His wife's voice sounded through the house, announcing supper. He stood a moment thinking again on Hattie, knowing how heat wore her down. He turned to the closet, poured another measured drink and bore it to the dining room where they were all assembled, sitting down. His daughter was bizarrely ornamented, a gaudy paper flower in her hair. Some foolish child's play; he took no notice. "Here, Hattie, do you no harm. Reckon the heat has you tuckered out."

"Hattie oughtn't drink that on an empty stomach," warned his wife from her end of the table, eyeing the absurd paper flower in Hattie's hair. But Mrs. Heaton smiled thanks, drank it off and followed the breath-cutting stuff with ice water.

The man ate silently and his mood of abstraction, not unusual, was respected. He carried work problems in his mind; he might be figuring out new ways to benefit the railroad, devising signals. It was not until dessert was finished, the children excused from the table and the hired girl settled down to her own supper in the kitchen that Luke spoke, dark eyes under white-tufted brows fastening on his pretty daughter. "Alf's in town."

"Alfred!" News of her husband surprised Mrs. Heaton. "Is he—sober?"

"Says he's not drinking. Been taking some new-fangled

6

cure." The man chose his words, wanting to be just. "Seems steadied up. Came in today on the 5:17. He's at the Grand Union."

"He oughtn't to go to the hotel," Mrs. Fletcher fretted, "no use advertising these things."

The man joked grimly. "Wants to make sure of his welcome. Says the last time he saw Hattie she threw a book at his head."

"A book? No Papa, everything I could find."

Her mother was shocked. "Why, you didn't!"

"But I did. What did he say, Papa?"

Luke pushed crumbs into a square. What hadn't Alf said. A slick talker, always was. "Reckon you better hear him for yourself if you got a mind to. Only don't go gittin' upset over it."

"He couldn't upset me now! Why, he doesn't mean—" Mrs. Heaton snapped her fingers "—*that* to me now."

"Harriet," admonished Mrs. Fletcher, "After all, he's your husband."

Mrs. Heaton looked at her, the enemy. Nagging, nagging, always making out that everything is my fault, always trying to turn Papa against me. That thin-nostriled aquiline nose in the pale fleshy face, the thin pursed lips; aristocratic looking, the best that could be said for her. But early farm life in Michigan had left its mark; courtship days, when Alfred came calling, Mama might be out in the front yard rooting for dandelion greens the same as a servant.

"You had your heart set to marry Alf," the older woman reminded. "You would have him." She sensed disapproval from Luke and hurried on, exasperated that he would not back her up. "You wouldn't give that nice steady fellow Merck a thought. No, it had to be Alf."

"Would it have been any different if I married the man you picked out for me?" cried Mrs. Heaton. "I'd have been just as miserable! I didn't want to get married at all—you know that! I wanted to sing! You let me go to Boston and study in

7

the Conservatory and then when you heard I might be famous you stepped in and stopped it!"

The man intervened, his voice grave, kindly, a power in it. "This don't git us anywheres. What's done is done, and Hattie, 'twas meant for the best. Might be a lot of good women singing in opera, but that's not what most people figure. A nice young lady doesn't git mixed up with stage folks. We thought you'd forgit all about it when you settled down in a home of your own. Why, young folks always git wild ideas. First time I saw Booth I was all set to be an acting fellow myself." Memory cut in, of players moving on a stage, the sonorous beauty of majestic, noble speech. He shook his head, getting back to what was on hand, his tone persuasive. "There's your mother, real sweet natural voice, used to sing in church even after you were born, but we settled down like we'd ought to, like we figured you would."

Mrs. Heaton flung herself back in her chair with a sweeping gesture of repudiation. "There's no comparison! No one ever told Mama her voice was good enough for opera."

"No one was darn fool enough to throw away money sending me to singing school to get my head stuffed with crazy notions," snapped Mrs. Fletcher.

Her daughter's stare was cool and taunting. "Maestro wasn't talking through his hat when he said my voice was good enough for opera and you know it."

Luke rapped his knuckles on the table. "Stop it, both of you. No sense to quarreling. It's not right."

His wife folded meek, complacent hands, but Mrs. Heaton's words rang out. "No, there's no sense to it—it's too late, too late! I was meant to be an artist! What a little fool I was to take orders! Why didn't I run away and do as I pleased— why didn't I steal the money if I had to!"

The silence was heavy, ominous of shocked feelings; then the man said gently, "You don't mean that, Hattie," and she knew that she had hurt him. "No, Papa, I don't, not the way it sounded. I know *you* meant well. There, I won't say any more." She was up, moving restlessly to the sideboard, fin-

8

gering the silver fruit dish. "Oh, but it'll be different with Diana, you'll see. She shall do just as she pleases. She's going to *be* somebody." She checked herself, made secure, victorious by the prediction. From the morning when the girl-baby had first been laid in her arms, purpose had formed; the frustration she had suffered would never blight her daughter; whatever talent Diana possessed would be nurtured and developed; Diana would know all the active joy that she had been denied. Spinning the silver dish upon its circle of embroidered linen, she lapsed into dreams, thinking happily of the child's response to music, of how, ever since the trip to Chicago to see Duncan, the dance had come into that well-formed, beautiful little body. Some day. . . .

Luke's voice came at her. "Now about Alf. Better sit down, Hattie, don't wear yourself out."

Luke spoils her, always did. Mrs. Fletcher folded her napkin with a hard precision, a woman long tried. Spoiling her right now. Unnatural, that's what Hattie was, unnatural. Talking about being an artist. A woman ought to be a good wife, look after her family and her house and be thrifty. Landsakes, I wish she had a home of her own and would stay where she belonged. Mrs. Fletcher spoke cautiously, feeling her way. "Might be Alf's sown his wild oats by now. I don't know anyone can make himself more agreeable when he's a mind to."

Mrs. Heaton strayed back to her chair. In through the open window came the faraway hooting of an engine at a crossing. A young girl hearing that had dreamed of fine, dangerous, starry things beyond the ways of ordinary folk; beauty and freedom and art, a career in far splendid cities. . . . Rebellion came up fresh, the old sense of injury strong. Stuck back where I started, Frostburg, middle of no place. My girl shan't grow up here. Alf meant Chicago, anyhow. "Oh, tell him to come up for inspection. Maybe. . . ."

Luke replaced the watch he had drawn automatically at the engine's whistle and lifted himself out of the chair. "If you could see a way to make a go of it, Hattie. A woman needs a husband and a home of her own." He trudged from the room.

Out of the house, he cut tobacco, chewed as he walked by comfortable frame houses sitting back from the sidewalk, each in its own square of well-tended lawn. Hattie troubled his heart. He sighed, not understanding that rebel spirit, that variation from the normal, that somehow he and Lucy had produced. A sweet woman with odd, pretty ways, light-hearted, gay, but fragile, high-strung, flighty; somehow he had always feared for Hattie. The years hadn't steadied her; still looked like a girl and acted like one. The suspicion that it might not be all Alf's fault that the marriage didn't go came to bother him; might be a steady woman could have taken Alf in hand. But Alf would be a handful. No proper husband at all. Luke spat without relish. Black sheep of a good family; sound and well-to-do, the Heatons were re-spected people in Chicago—all but the one Hattie picked. Couldn't stop her, couldn't tell her anything, headstrong. And not a grain of ambition in the dandy. Luke's thought turned on his son and comfort filled him. Nothing shiftless about Nyrum, down in St. Louis now and working his way up.

Diana and Rod were playing in the hall when Grampa came in, a man with him. The little girl looked up, confused by her brother's glad cry of "Father!" Roddy was older, he could remember far back. . . . Strange people had a way of appear-ing out of nowhere and saying playfully, 'Don't you remem-ber me?' This man had the look of one of them. Mother and Granma had come into the hall; Diana went to stand beside her mother.

Alfred Heaton, dapper, upright, his narrow shoulders giv-ing him the appearance of being taller than he was, kissed his wife's cheek with an appropriate suggestion of restrained emotion, and bowed to Mrs. Fletcher with a courtesy foreign to Frostburg. He pulled Rod's head against his side and smiled down on Diana from behind glittering pince-nez. "Gad, how the children have grown, Hattie! Son, you must look to your laurels, Sis is catching up with you. That's your

10

fine cooking I'm sure, Mrs. Fletcher, best pumpkin pie I ever ate was in this house."

Luke had gone on to the cherished privacy of his den; no call on him to sit around entertaining.

"Why, there's nothing to cooking, Alfred," beamed Mrs. Fletcher, hands folded on her stomach.

"Nothing to cooking!" Alfred exclaimed as the group drifted into the parlor, "You remind me of the joke about the two Irishmen looking at Niagara Falls. 'Isn't it a grate wondher entoirely' says Mike, 'all that power of water rushing over the idge.' 'Arrah, what's wondherful about it?' says Pat, 'Shure and what's to hinder it?' Hattie my dear, how do you manage to look as cool and fresh as a daisy?"

"Look, Father, Diana's not as tall as I am. Please look, Father."

From the horsehair sofa, Mrs. Heaton watched her husband, a smile fixed to her lips while slowly her heart sickened. Alfred again? Oh, no, no, it would not do! This man had not changed, this man would never change. There would be winning spells of charm, and then the drinking, the gambling, the wasting away of the money he had inherited which rightfully should be preserved for Diana and for Rod—that would all start up again. And there would be the horrid, senseless quarrels and he would fuss and fume and bite his nails and grow nasty in exasperation. No, not again; to go live with him as his wife now—why, there was something indecent in the thought!

Diana had drifted toward the man, making acquaintance with him. Mrs. Heaton started up, crossed the room, drew the child away. "It's past their bedtime," she made excuse, "Children, say good night. You'll excuse me for a few minutes?"

Alfred stood up, puzzled by this abruptness. "Let them stay. Why, I haven't even seen—"

"They need their rest." She spoke coolly, putting distance between them.

He was flustered, his dignity in disorder. Was this a trick, one of her damned witch spells to fuddle and to bind him? He caught the hard fixity of her smile, a glint in her eyes. No, by gad, it was dismissal, imperious. He continued to make protestations, helpless, surrounded, unable to lash out, to hit upon the adroit, cutting things that could be said.

Mrs. Fletcher and Rod had joined in the protestations; to Mrs. Heaton it seemed an uproar from which she could not escape quickly enough. She conceded to Rod, he could stay, and made off with the wondering Diana.

Mounting the stairs, she answered Diana's questions as best she could in the distraction of her thoughts, loving the child anew for her sweet-tempered compliance, making no fuss at having been swept off so hastily to bed. In the bedroom her thoughts ran on swiftly as she helped the child undress. Suppose—suppose Alf set himself to win Diana's love, establish an influence upon her! He could do a thing like that, just for spite, and what did he actually care about the children? What real affection had he ever shown them?

She fetched Diana's nightgown and sank into a chair while the child, engrossed in her own competence with buttons and buckles, went on undressing.

And to think I was infatuated with Alf once! It was an amazing, shameful recollection. No, there would be no more of these recurrent attempts to make a go of it that had gone on almost from the beginning. Finality calmed her. For a moment longer her thought played over the life that she had known as Alfred's wife, Mrs. Heaton, one of the Chicago Heatons, mistress of her own beautifully-appointed, well-run home. . . . But with Alf? Better to be a woman without a husband, without a home.

Still, something must be done. One decision led to another; the strong rebellious feeling that she did not belong in Frostburg in her father's house, a part of ordinary, small-town life, came back and all at once she was resolved—she would take the children and go east to live; Diana must have better than Frostburg. Papa would just have to understand, give

12

her the money. Go at once—escape this heat—Maine, the sea-shore for the summer. . . .

Diana stood before her, waiting for the nightgown. Mrs. Heaton dropped it over the naked little body and held out her arms. "Oh, come to Mother, Chick!" She took the child upon her lap and rocked her with the fierceness of possession. Here was what meant most in life, here was solace for all fret and failure. "Sweet little pal. We *are* pals, aren't we, Dicky?"

"Pals!" Diana was delighted. "But then—shouldn't I call you something beside 'Mother'?"

"What would you like to call me?"

Diana cuddled closer, considering. "Sue is my favorite name."

Mrs. Heaton laughed, hugging her tight. "All right, I'm Sue, and you and I'll be pals always." She reverted to her happy purpose, instilling it into the child. "And you're going to be somebody when you grow up. You're going to be famous. You shall do just as you please."

Deep in content, enfolded in her mother's love, Diana announced, "I'm going on the stage. I'm going to be a dancer."

"There isn't going to be anybody saying that you can't." Mrs. Heaton sensed the moment as a turning point in life, an old hateful pattern broken, swept into the past. The chair rocked rhythmically. She began to sing a lullaby. The warm, quiet dusk had deepened; heat lightning flickered in through the windows. Happiness was in the room.

2

VACATIONING IN Maine, just the two of them, and they
were pals . . .

Diana entered into this new life with a rapt intensity.
Days of gay wind and friendly sun; magical days of fog, a
streaming white density, walking through it like walking
through a cloud; nights of myriad stars and nights when
Northern Lights waved pale bands of violet and green
across the heavens; tumbled rock-strewn fields where wild
flowers grew among long, tangled grasses and no one raised a
prohibition on their picking; woods of silent, odorous pine
with a yielding floor of fallen needles, and the hermit thrush
giving out his song at twilight; the sea with all its wonder of
tides and surf, the great waves rearing white and booming
on the craggy rocks; and days upon the sea, out in a lobster-
man's boat—lie flat on the prow, sidle up one heaving glassy
swell of green, go whack down another, crackle of salt spray
rising up in a thin shining, silver wall to collapse with a
swish-slap, and the salt wind blowing strong enough to taste
it; come home hungry in expectation of lobster stew and fried
clams and hot blueberry pie. And in the evening there were
books read aloud and music, always music, Sue singing in
the parlor after Diana went to bed, and the song easing the
drift into slumber.

Sitting up alone after the child had fallen asleep, Mrs.
Heaton would muse contentedly. True, she had not managed
to win Papa over entirely; he was so old-fashioned. . . . No,
Hattie couldn't go off and live alone with the children, she
belonged with her folks, or people might get to talking. But
to this he had consented, summers in the east, and this was
an opening that could, in time, be widened; later, when
Diana was old enough to go to a girl's school in New York.

Mrs. Heaton accepted the compromise and the pattern was established, winters in Grampa's house, summers in Maine. Though she was, at first, a little dubious about leaving Roddy behind, but there too her father had his way, saying one child was enough to be looking after far from home, and maybe he was right; Rod could be trying.

Mrs. Heaton had no regrets over her decision; Alf vanished from her mind, Diana filled it. There were brief spells when she felt her womanhood and knew a pang of loneliness, and thought wistfully that some women had husbands loving them whom they could love in return. But such moods were rare. The union between mother and daughter deepened and the intimacy was sweet. Diana had no secrets unconfided, there were no questions Mrs. Heaton would not answer. The woman went far into the child's world and shared it, quickening the girl's perception, hastening her growth, delighting in the quick responsiveness her love evoked, seeing beauty and talent and precocity beyond her most daring hope, so that she was awed, wondering how much of this could be her doing.

And then, when Diana was twelve, change came.

It began with Christopher, Christopher Meredith.

Diana found him. She was playing Indian, a scout roaming alone in the vast wilderness, having identity with the silence of pine woods, traveling through them lightfooted and alert. And there was an unknown paleface sauntering ahead of her along the trail.

Who was he? Where had he come from? Diana knew every one of the summer people on the small island, but this man was a stranger. She trailed him, still keeping to the game of Indian, flitting behind tree trunks, scouting from the shelter of one lichened boulder to the next, until at last he glanced back, saw her, warpaint on her face and feathers in her hair.

Ordinarily, with grownups, that would have put an end to the game and Diana would have walked away, suddenly sedate, pretending there had been no game. But this grownup did exactly what Sue would have done. He played back. He went down on his knees, holding out imploring hands and begging for his scalp.

It was wonderful. She circled in a war dance before consenting to palaver. And then she let him join her tribe and they went down on the shore and lit a fire and got acquainted, the game left off. His name was Christopher Meredith. He lived in New York City. He had a boat and he had a cottage on Hokomok Island where he came every summer with his sister. But this summer his sister had stayed in New York. He was a school teacher, but he begged her not to count that against him, and he really was a lovely person so Diana assured him that she wouldn't. Then she told him all about herself and that she was going on the stage one day to be a famous dancer, and about Sue who was not like other mothers, and about Grampa and how Grampa always said 'Look after your mother' so that really Diana was not like other little girls for she had a responsibility imposed upon her, and she did look after Mother all the time the way Grampa had told her to, and that was fun because Sue and she were pals and Sue was wonderful only she couldn't climb big rocks because she was delicate—"Come and see her. Oh, you must meet Sue before you go away!"

They went back through the wood and came into the field where the cottage stood, and Diana called out as they approached. Mrs. Heaton appeared upon the step, blue dress and copper hair vivid against the white paint of the house, the sun full on her face.

"Sue, this is Christopher Meredith and he's—he's really awfully nice!"

Man and woman shook hands, laughingly.

"I'm sure he is, Diana! Won't you come in, Mr. Meredith? It's rather primitive here but we could manage tea."

"I'd love to, but I've got to take the tide into account, you've got a sandbar in your harbor." He still held the woman's hand and looked into her eyes. "May I have tea another day?"

"Of course!" Diana cried.

Mrs. Heaton, flustered by the prolonged handclasp, the man's unmoving eyes—he was astoundingly good-looking—smiled her answer, nodding.

"He played Indian with me," Diana told her, "He's Chief Firelighter."

The man released her hand, glanced approvingly at Diana and looked back at Mrs. Heaton. "The only child I've met with real imagination. We had a grand game. We'll have to have another."

Mrs. Heaton was now smiling with a fond pride. "You must come back."

"I shall. Good-by. Good-by, little Indian."

An arm about Diana, Mrs. Heaton watched him go down the worn grass path that led into the harbor road, and down the road that wound between open fields and came out upon a spit of sand where fog-silvered shanties stood in a row and fishing gear was scattered on the beach. He passed out of sight behind the shacks and then the chug of a motorboat started up; the boat came into view, setting out upon the wide expanse of sparkling, sun-paled water dotted with small rocky islands, darkly fir-capped, the smooth knobs of Mount Desert rising in the distance, a mottled lavender.

Christopher Meredith. . . . He had looked at her with some quality of recognition; he had admired her. There was no room for doubt. He had roused a self long slumbering, forgotten; it was alive and quickened now, making her all new to herself. His look had told her that she was a woman, lovable. It had told her that even with Diana's love, she was lacking, unfulfilled, wanting the admiration and the interest of a man.

Stunned, she stood silent, unaware that Diana was beside her, that the girl grew restive. What did this upsurge within her mean, what could it mean? Why was she now without reality, the sense of wonder and amazement thrilling her with

17

joy, setting up commotion beyond her power to put in order? Could this happen?

A handsome, intelligent face with glowing, ardent eyes, their look intimate, possessive; a fine handsome figure of a man. Such a man as could be loved. . . .

But—it was preposterous, incredible. Besides. . . .

What age was he? Why, he might be only thirty-five.

And she was forty.

Diana saw the level brows upslanted in distress. "Sue, don't feel bad, he said he would come back."

Mrs. Heaton started at the sound of her voice, gave an odd laugh, her teeth biting on her lip. She turned to her daughter with a sudden blithe intensity, shot through with yearning. "Ah, he'll come back! But Dicky—there's so little left of summer!"

Chris came back, came early and stayed long, but this time they did not stand on the doorstep watching him set out alone, no, they piled into the boat, bag and baggage, and sailed off along with him to Hokomok! Why not, said Chris, and why not, said Sue. Oh, what a lark it was adventuring like that! Diana was quite certain that no other mother was as gay and free and fine as Sue.

It was much, much nicer on Hokomok; that was what Sue told Dicky and Dicky told Sue. *So* much nicer—Chris, the place, the people. There was the dearest little hotel that had really no right to call itself a hotel at all. And their room, all white and dainty, looked down upon a tiny crescent beach where quiet harbor water lapped; from the windows you could look out over a jutting arm of pink granite rock and see Christopher's cottage in the next cove.

So much fun, the three of them, laughing and joking and talking together, walking in to the village or through the woods, going to a party at the cottage of one of Christopher's friends . . . But then it began to change.

"You won't mind, Chick?—once in a while we like to be by ourselves."

18

Oh, of course she wouldn't mind . . . Only it was strange that they would not want to have her come along. But Mother was very happy, and there was the beach, the woods, the fields for company. Games made up and played alone would pass an afternoon; one could be Peter Pan or Launcelot or Florisande. And there were books to read, a whole lending library of books, and when the girl behind the counter questioned, Mother said, "Grown-up books? It doesn't matter, let her take anything she pleases; she won't understand what she's not ready for." And so there were a lot of books, though some of them were dull.

No, it didn't really matter much, with Sue so happy. Except that sometimes when Sue came back to her from Chris it did not seem that all of her was there; Mother would just sit and think and think and hardly hear a thing you told her.

Mrs. Heaton's need was great to sink into absorption, to brood over all that Chris had said, ordering it, estimating, putting this remark beside that, counting in the look in his eyes, seeing what it all came to. And behind this need was the overwhelming desire to relive every moment in memory, to sink into a trance of rich, sensual happiness.

She lived in wonder, scarcely knowing who she was. That years could have slipped away, that she could have let them go, drifting into a dull placidity, asking nothing of life for herself but motherhood; a woman traveling on toward age, believing love was over—and this could happen. Love, real love, love as she had never known it; the love a young girl dreamed of and then forgot, accepting substitute, believing that was real.

Alf could be divorced; that was simple, plenty of grounds. But for the present, until Chris asked her. . . . She told Diana urgently and more than once to make no mention of Chris when she wrote letters home. Mrs. Heaton quailed at the thought of what that stern old puritan, her father, would say to all of this, for she had been most strictly reared. As a girl of sixteen she had once dared to loiter with a boy, coming home from a party; she would never forget the whipping he

19

had given her for that. Dear Papa, so good and kind, but vigilantly moral.

"Oh Dicky, Dicky, I'm going to *sing!* Chris asked me to—in the church in the village on Sunday and Hans Kindler is going to play the cello and the minister from Boston is giving the sermon—it's for the Widow's Fund in the village—and Mr. Gambier will be there—he's the big music critic from New York—and Chris says that it might lead to something! Oh Diana, what if I could get back to singing and *be* somebody after all!"

She had come into the bedroom radiant with happiness, but she had no sooner left off than she began again, this time dismayed and gloomy. "But how can I, I'm so out of practice for anything professional! And it's this coming Sunday. Oh dear, Diana, what shall I do? I want Chris to be proud of me, men like to be proud! If I should do badly!"

Then, before that could be answered, "Diana, do you think that you could dye my hair if I showed you how? Just here, at the side, a few strokes. You see? I keep it covered, but there *are* grey hairs, and I sent to Portland for a bottle. Could you, dear?"

This was much easier to deal with than the things Sue said; Diana assured her that she could of course. So they plunged into the task at once, and this too was a secret Diana must not tell.

The imminence of event brought Diana to wakefulness the moment her eyes opened on Sunday morning, and a moment later the warning bell for breakfast burst into a racket of clanging in the hall below. Mrs. Heaton was instantly awake, sitting up with a jerk, no smile, no greeting. "I've overslept."

"No, Sue, that's only the first bell."

"I hate to hurry." The woman tossed back long thick hair and clasped her knees with a groan. Alarm in the child's face forced her to a sickly attempt at a smile. "Stage fright. The thing that hits you right in the pit of the stomach when you're up against doing something in public. Diana, I should have refused, I'm not in practice." She flung back the covers with startling haste. "Get dressed. Hurry, Ah, it's years since I've really sung." She was across the room, the china pitcher caught up, pouring water into the basin, not minding that it splashed on the flowered wallpaper.

Diana slipped to the floor and pulled on socks. Mrs. Heaton, moving to the bureau, knocked the hairbrush to the floor and said, "Oh, darn it!" She waited for Diana to pick it up, stared at it stupidly when the child put it in her hand. "Why should I be rattled singing in a country church! I've sung in churches all my life, big ones, too, in Boston. What are you standing still for? For goodness sake, get dressed!"

Startled by the queer, abrupt tone, Diana dropped down on the floor, thrusting on a shoe. Her pal was acting very strangely.

"I didn't mean to sound cross, sweet." Mrs. Heaton made another quivering smile for her. "Oh, now!—where's my chemise—I've got it—don't bother—I was the best coloratura in the Conservatory Maestro wept when I sang hand me those shoes the mad scene from Lucia at graduation the dressing room crowded with chrysanthemums and American beauty I can't find the button hook never mind a hair pin'll do Maestro gave us champagne before we sang—"

Diana struggled with hurry; Mother was dressing fast.

"I *can* sing." The woman pouted angrily. "After all, today's not the only chance in the world! Button me up." She flounced into a chair so the child could reach her back. It was the princess dress of white batiste with twenty-six buttons, but Diana went nimbly at the task, knowing it was important to look after Mother now.

Finished, she asked, "Will Chris go with us?"

"Don't mention Chris," her mother said, "it makes me nervous to think of him!"

The church stood at the end of the village street, a white wooden structure of a severity of line to content the Puritan spirit. Old elms flanked the walk to the door, a decaying shed at the back had once tethered horses. People grouped about the

21

steps, dresses, white and colored, bright in morning sun. With a nod and a smile and a greeting for those she knew, Mrs. Heaton went straight in, turned to one side and led Diana up a circular staircase to the empty loft. She settled her blue wrap on the bench beside her and leaned forward to peer down into the slowly filling rows of seats. "I like singing in church. Most people don't know how, they make it sad and dreary. I'm sure the angels must be joyful." She leaned back, opened her handbag, took out a card with the words of her song penciled on it. She hemmed, hummed, made certain that there were no stray wisps of hair at the nape of her neck, settled her leghorn hat. "I knew it! Now I've got to go to the bathroom. You stay here."

"You can leave your wrap, Mother."

"No, I can't. Oh dear, I wonder where it is."

Diana continued to stare down into the congregation while her mother was gone, but excitement blurred her vision, snarled her interest; the woman's nervousness had been communicated to the child. It *was* long since Mother had sung in church—not since the early days in Frostburg. And then Grampa had been there, and Roddy.

Mrs. Heaton came back, flushed and breathless. As she took her seat an aroma came from her, something alien yet familiar, something that made Diana think again of Grampa.

When the time came for Mrs. Heaton to sing, she stood up, shook her skirts free of the seat, grasped the rail with both hands, head flung up, eyes shining; she seemed to look beyond the walls to some far splendid recognition. As soon as she began, Diana knew it would be all right. She's singing for the angels, the child thought, and a tingle went over her, skin creeping to gooseflesh. Sensible of the honor of being in the loft, she sat primly, eyes straight ahead. But below in the congregation heads turned, remained fixed.

Pure and sweet, ringing with a strange, sad exultance, the soaring, nimble melody went on. With the last note held and finished, Mrs. Heaton sank back on the bench, spent and happy. "That's showing them!" she whispered, "That's singing!"

There was something strange in the glitter in her eyes, the aroma of her breath, the clutch of her icy hand, that made Diana gaze at her. Mrs. Heaton swayed back in her seat, wrenched herself straight, looked restlessly about her. "I can't stick it. Come on." Gathering her wrap, she pushed the bewildered child before her. The cello solo had begun, its velvety music too hushed to give promise of muffling their steps, but they tiptoed across the loft, crept downward.

All at once there was a rackety thud-bump-thud of something falling downstairs. It came from behind Diana, passed her, rattling to a stop three steps below. A whisky bottle . . . That, falling from her mother's wrap, had surely betrayed them. The child's eyes flashed back at her mother in scared wonder.

"Pick it up!" snapped the woman. "Hand it to me quick!"

Footfalls creaked below, someone coming to investigate. Diana scampered after the bottle, handed it up; it disappeared under the blue wrap just as a strange man gaped around the corner of the staircase.

Again Mrs. Heaton pushed the girl on. "I feel faint," she whispered to the man and gestured weakly to make the point clear. "Air. I must go." She gathered Diana close, stealing behind the backs of the congregation and out the door. She began to laugh; she tried to muffle it, the church windows open, the solemn cello music close, but the more she tried to stifle laughter, the more persistent were the giggles from behind the handkerchief.

Chris stole out of the church and overtook them on the walk. They went on briskly, Mrs. Heaton still shaking and bowing into her handkerchief with odd breathless little snickers, the white daisies on her hat aquiver. It was not until they had gone on up the street and turned into a lane and laughter need no longer be suppressed that it escaped with a sigh.

And now she began to talk, very fast and brave and gay, and she was all confidence, glittering and beautiful—and yet. . . . Diana looked at her and felt a strange presence and wondered, feeling odd and lonely.

Chris settled things. His arm linked with the woman's, he addressed Diana, and she saw that his mouth smiled and his eyes did not. "May we run off by ourselves? I'll bring your pal back by dinnertime. What do you say, Sue? Shall we walk over to the surf side?"

"Oh, let's!" cried Mrs. Heaton, ready to start out at once. "What a delicious day! Isn't the air bracing?—like champagne. Here, Dicky, take my wrap, will you? I shan't need it. And my hat."

Diana stood holding the hat and the wrap, feeling the weight of the bottle in the pocket, watching her mother stride off in step with Chris. She did not know why, but the lonely feeling was heavy on her. Chris looked back and smiled at her. But her mother did not; she was still talking, and the laughter bubbling with the talk.

Lots of clever women marry younger men. . . .

But was she clever? Chris's friends were so different from any people she had ever met; in contrast, the world that she had known was stupid, stuffy, mildewed, the Heaton clan ridiculous in their scrupulous adherence to the pattern of the past, and Papa positively archaic. These people of the island summer colony were moderns, smart, lively and amusing. But in such a mocking, shocking way. They all talked so fast that conversation was like ping-pong; only it wasn't really conversation, it was a rapid random kind of chatter that stayed on no subject and settled nothing. And nothing seemed important to them, worth the respect of discussion; any topic, God or sex, was fair game for outspoken raillery. Yet somehow what they said was clever and accurate so much of the time that she felt a fool for not having thought of it herself. Indeed there was a lot of hypocrisy in all the things that people were brought up to believe in; once pointed out you couldn't help but see it, and such things should be, as they said, 'debunked.' But sometimes she thought they went too far. They might

24

laugh at marriage all they chose, but she wanted Chris to marry her—why, he must marry her of course . . . . But she laughed with his friends, made smart sallies of her own in keeping with the rest, and hoped that none of them would ever guess how much like a Louisa M. Alcott heroine they made her feel, or know how relieved she was to get away and have Chris to herself.

Diana was a help, oh such a help. Diana reflected credit on her; a mother who could have a child like that! She drank in praise of Diana as a further accomplishment of her own, rejoicing in it. And how unself-conscious the child remained despite all the fuss that was made over her! Mrs. Heaton could thrust her daughter forward, draw her out, and know Diana would not fail to be herself.

Diana entertained with dances, her mother at the piano. They were dances that, as Mrs. Heaton explained, Diana had composed; but it was improvisation that most delighted the onlookers. And the girl, face serious and dreaming, barefoot and in the short Greek costume that left most of her slim twelve-year old body nude, could always improvise, following the mood of anything that Sue would play.

But alone in their bedroom, Mrs. Heaton worked to help her. "You could put *more* expression in it, Chick. I know you feel it, but art is exaggeration. They taught us Delsarte in the Conservatory when I was a girl—things like this—" She flowed into a pose tense with checked emotion and came out of it to say, "That was Fright;" flowed into another, "That was Horror;" and went on through "Joy" and "Grief" while her daughter watched in fascination. "Do you see, dear? Whatever you feel, make your gestures big and clear."

And Diana danced at Mrs. Austin's chowder party and everyone said what a beautiful, wonderful, gifted child, what a great dancer she would be. Chris said it. And Hans Kindler praised the child's feeling for music. . . . Yes, Diana was a help.

But dances and parties and boat trips and strolls, with Chris every day, sometimes from early morning until late at night—it was a strain since she must always be at her best and lively as the youngest of them. Mrs. Heaton stood before her mirror hunting anxiously for signs of wrinkles and thanked God that there were none, only the vaguest suspicion of softness in the throat line, and not even that if she remembered to carry her head high. She practiced walking with books balanced on her head and sat up late reading *Freud* and *Why I Am A Socialist.*

But it was a strain. She took little nips out of the bottle steadily. Very careful little nips, just enough to give her sparkle. He must not see her tired or dull, there must never be a lag.

Days melted away, she grew aware of summer's end rushing upon her and still Chris had not said Will you marry me. . . . But there was love in his eyes, love in his voice, love in his caress, of love itself there could not be a doubt. What then?

The strain increased. She had to talk about it, she had to have a confidant. She told Diana, swearing her to secrecy, "I am in love with Chris."

Diana understood. Love was in all the books. She was stirred to think that this was like a story, that Sue and she herself were like the people in stories; she was proud to be coming nearer to that grown-up world that held the full of understanding. "You're glad that I'm in love?" Sue asked. Of course Diana was; it made Sue happy.

But walking alone on the small curved beach, not Peter Pan or Launcelot or Florisande but just Diana, the child knew change had come, big change, and how would it be with her when Chris and Sue were married? Would she and Mother still be pals? Would it be *just* the same between them?

The tide was going out, stranding jelly fish upon the pebbles. The cold slimy touch of the things was horrible but it was more horrible to see them evaporate in the sun, only a wet circle where opaque grey entity had been. She went up and down searching for them and flinging them into the water. The splashes emphasized the silence and all at once she knew that she was lonely.

She longed for Roddy. She recalled girls at school, games

played together. She remembered dolls, lost in the past. Grampa's image came up strong and close.

The sun had gone. A spatter of rain made her look up. It was only a dainty, passing rain, there was sunlight on the wooded headland on the Point. Still, she wasn't supposed to stay out if it rained. She went up across the lawn, stopping to give the apple tree a hug, and then went on unhurried. Only a dainty rain, cool on the face, softer than cobwebs.

Surprise awaited her in the bedroom. Mother was lying on the bed, her dress a bright blue splotch against the white cover. The woman raised her head from the pillow and her smile was thin, hastily put on.

"Why, I thought you were at Christopher's house! What happened?"

"I was, Dicky, and nothing happened. That's just it, nothing happened."

Troubled, probing at mystery, Diana sat on the bed. "What ought to happen?"

"He ought to say, 'Will you marry me?'" Mrs. Heaton propped her head on her fist. "Diana, doesn't he love me?"

"Why, of course he does."

"Why doesn't he say so then?" She let her head fall back upon the pillow. "Why does he look at me so soulfully, admiring, tragic? What's tragic about it?" She stopped short and sat up, arms about her knees. "I'm too old, that's what it is."

"But isn't Chris old, too?"

"No, he's young, young! What's thirty-four to a man! Oh Lord, if I only knew I had him I'd stay young forever! It's this being up on my toes all the time—I'm not strong, I never was. Jumping about in boats and climbing over rocks!" Alarmingly, a sob broke from her. "Anyone might get tired once in a while, but good Lord, I've been so careful!—the teeniest nip for sparkle, never a drop too much!"

Diana stroked the rounded back. She did not think sparkle so important, she thought sparkling made Sue fidgety and strange. "Don't feel bad."

"I know, sweet, for your sake—but don't mind, I can't help

27

it." Head dropped on knees, the woman wept, letting herself go. Diana put both arms about the shaking body, miserably helpless, but certain things were not as bad as Mother thought. Chris was nice, he wouldn't want her to cry.

Abruptly the sobbing ceased. "There! That won't do. He's coming tonight. Fine thing if he saw red eyes." With a forlorn smile rewarding the child's sympathy, Mrs. Heaton rolled off the bed and searched the bureau for a handkerchief. She dabbed at her eyes, peering intently at her reflection. "Now honestly, I *don't* look old, I don't." She laid a palm against her cheek and pressed gently upward tightening the dread suspicion of softness in the flesh. "I could have my face lifted when I was really old." She became aware of the silent watcher on the bed and alarm gripped her. She came swiftly to the bedpost, clasped it. "Diana, don't tell Chris what I said. Don't tell him that I cried. Don't tell him that I'm forty. I know you wouldn't mean to, but—"

"Oh, I *wouldn't,* Sue!"

"Oh, I'm not old, I'm not, I'm not!"

The woman sank into the rocker by the window. The mosquito netting was beaded with moisture; it was like looking toward Chris's cottage through tears. "I can't understand. Maybe it's his sister Addie. She's always writing him, he's always mentioning her . . . I can't understand."

"Would you like me to brush your hair, Sue?"

"Yes, anything. Hand me the nail file. He wants us to go to New York and visit with Addie in Astoria. He talks as though Addie were his mother! Does he need *her* permission? Oh Diana, what if he's only a philanderer? Oh, I'm distracted, I can't stand it!" Mrs. Heaton tossed the nail file toward the bureau and folded her arms, staring gloomily across the rain-dappled water toward the roof top. . . . She let him go too far. Did he think her a fast woman? He had no right to kiss her if he didn't mean it; he had no right to take her in his arms. The agonizing wrench of will to tear away, to keep her head. She closed her eyes, seeing a pagan world deep in still woods, the filtered light falling on the moody savagery of a flushed, handsome face with heavy-lidded eyes, and in her ears that insatiable murmur, 'kiss me, kiss me,' the kiss given and the murmur going on. . . . Beastly, carnal. No, the right passion of real loving. I love him, I want him. I never thought to know such longing. Desire frustrated goes out of all proportion.

"My, your hair is long! Oh, what made you jump? Did I pull?"

"No—oh, maybe just a bit—it doesn't matter. Oh Dicky, what will I do? I love him so!—everything about him; the way he plays with you, his humor, yes, even his melancholy, it's all Chris and I love him. But—summer's ending—only a few days! My nerves are taut. I'm getting thin. I'm drinking too much. A woman shouldn't *drink!*"

"Sue dearest, I'm—I'm sure he loves you. Why, how could he help it? Look—I've braided your hair. You look just like a little girl!"

Mrs. Heaton's smile was wan. She nodded at her daughter, confiding with a wistful charm, "Maybe that's all I am, Chick, just a little girl without any sense."

Diana mothered her at once. "There now, you mustn't be sad. Why, it's nearly suppertime and you're not dressed at all! Why don't you put on the pretty white dress with the frilly ruffles?"

The smile deepening in affection, Mrs. Heaton hugged Diana close. "Do you think I should?"

"It's most becoming. I'll help you dress."

After supper Diana sat on the veranda steps while in the darkening parlor Mother sang, waiting for Chris. The rain had stopped; there were high-up clouds, rippled like tide-sand that holds imprint of waves, and here and there clear sky. Breeze ruffled the apple tree, shadow lay solid beneath it; night gathers under trees first, pours out slowly, pools of darkness grow and merge and then it is night all over.

Songs My Mother Taught Me. . . . Listening, the sense of beauty grew in the child and with it, the sadness of beauty, the knowledge of all things passing away. This contenting moment would fade; generations moved into oblivion, a song a mother had sung was handed down to a child.

People die.

It was a personal realization. Not ugly, not scary, but big, awesome, immense and distant like the stars. Stars last forever. The ones you love, you yourself. . . . The living moment grew intense. To be sitting there, seeing the evening star, feeling the wind, hearing the song and knowing that there was death. The knowledge had become personal; it would remain, a part of selfhood, imprinted. Talking with Mother would not alter it, shake it off. For awhile it seemed Diana had the power to sit on, alone, knowing this. And then it all faded, the intensity, the newness of realization, the power; she was a small girl growing chilly. She went into the parlor and leaned against her mother.

Mrs. Heaton stopped singing. "What is it, dear?"

What could be said of all this? And this was not the time to try. Diana asked, "Shall I light the lamp for you?"

"I want him to find me in the twilight. You'll leave us alone, won't you?"

Going away when you don't want to is being chivalrous; Sir Launcelot rode out upon a prancing charger to guard the castle walls. From the steps Diana called, "Chris is coming," and maneuvered an unruly steed about the corner of the house.

Her mother had begun another song—*Drink To Me Only With Thine Eyes*—and that, floating out into the twilight, had meaning, too, a meaning that overtook Diana and put an end to her imagining, so that she went to stand beside the apple tree, smitten again with the growing pain of newcome knowledge; 'Drink to me only with thine eyes, and I'll not ask for wine.' If Chris would say 'marry me' Sue would not take nips out of the bottle. . . . That smell, like Grampa's, was on her breath right now. And Sue had said 'a woman shouldn't drink.' Oh, if only Chris would say it, so Sue would be happy and things would be the way they always had been. Only . . . they wouldn't be the same. . . . Now nothing would ever be the same. . . . Knowledge came in like a smashing wave and then broke and all was disordered, and understanding was harder than before.

Mrs. Heaton went on singing as the man's steps sounded on the veranda, as the door darkened. Chris came to stand beside her, leaning an elbow on the piano. She left off, lips tremulous, her smile appealing and uncertain.

He bent to her on impulse, wanting that fragile sweet woman in his arms—and as he drew her up and their lips met, caught the scent. But she was lovely, yielding and desirable. Passion glowed in the kiss, mounting swiftly, the once slumbering desire now quickly roused, with each curbing grown more fierce, temptation no longer a thing to play with, but a savage, intolerable compulsion, outraged nature rioting against the frail pretense of will.

She broke away to stand, back turned, waiting for the words. They must come. This was love.

"Sue—you'll come to New York? Come to Astoria, to Addie's house."

Astoria indeed! Was the man a fool? He hovered close, his arms reaching out. Words broke from her, got away, as she spun about, backing from his embrace. "No. Go 'way. Oh, Chris, I can't stand any more of this! I—" She covered her face with her hands. Fool, fool, couldn't he understand—why didn't he say. . . .

"I'm sorry, Sue."

The tone was somber. She felt somber eyes upon her, willing surrender as he drew close again, came to a stop before her, and she fought desperately with herself, fearful of turmoil breaking into riot, not daring the risk of words. Didn't he know?

A horrid gulf of silence spread, widening.

"Forgive me." It was a mournful, repentant sigh. "I'm sorry."

He was going.

She stood frozen, hearing his steps, the screen door opening,

31

shutting, steps crossing the veranda, descending, lost in grass. My God, is this the end?

What did I say?—do? Panic took her. I can't lose him.

She went after him. The screen banged, high heels clattered, then grass underfoot and ahead a man walking away in the dusk. "Christopher!"

He stopped, faced about. She ran blindly, stumbling, skirts whipping heavily about her legs, came up against his breast. Startled arms caught and steadied her.

"Chris—you fool! Don't you know I love you?"

Caught and steadied but did not clasp. Concern in his eyes. He heard me. I spoke. Leading me back. Oh God in hell, he doesn't love me.

In sickening unreality she walked by his side, head up. Shame and hatred clawed at her, to breathe was hard. She was in the center of ruin and she must hold to walking steadily, head up.

The steps were gained. Diana appeared close by. Mrs. Heaton freed her arm, stabbing at him powerfully with a cruel smile. His face had altered, he was going to speak. There was nothing to say. She went up the steps, Diana gathered close, swept into the dark parlor and stood panting; the child pressed tight, the imprint of the small body against her loins, her shaking legs; that kept her upright.

Diana was silent, frightened, made small by this swift unknown impact from the grown-up world. It was a long time before she felt slackness come into the woman's body and dared ask, "What is it?"

"I told him I loved him, and he walked me back without a word." Mrs. Heaton's voice was flat.

They toiled slowly up the stairs. Inside their room, purpose came into the woman. She went to the closet, took an armful of dresses and threw them on the bed. "Help me pack, we're going."

"Now?"

"Right now. Tonight." Mrs. Heaton threw shoes toward the trunk.

"But Mother, we can't. Your check hasn't come yet. We haven't any money."

The woman answered recklessly, defiant. "I've enough to hire a motorboat to get us away from here tonight! Empty the bureau drawers." She took more dresses from the closet.

Diana moved to obey. "But where shall we go?"

"Go?" said Mrs. Heaton, frowning, puzzled. "Think. Help me."

Diana thought. "Well, I suppose we could—" She left off; Sue was crying, crying passionately without restraint, settling down right where she stood, letting an armful of dresses spill, and sitting in the center of that confusion on the floor.

"Oh, don't, Sue, don't!"

"I can't, I can't let it end like this! Never, never see him again—No—I can't do it! Oh, how can you go on loving a man who isn't worth it! I'll die!" Diana was beside her, holding tight, but she cried on, taking no notice. "I can't give him up—I won't—no, he—he loves me! I'm not old, I'm not old!" She broke Diana's clasp and rose unsteadily, assisted by the child. Fumbling, tear-blinded, she began picking up the dresses. "Help me. Put them back. We'll go with Chris to Astoria."

3

As the afternoon wore on, interest in her book grew harder to sustain, pulled away by the mounting oppression of that silent, intent figure in the bed. Mother was thinking of Chris. But how could she lie in bed all day just thinking? It was a part of that grown-up world Diana could not understand. She did not know why they had come to this dreadful boarding house to live, why they stayed on in New York, why they did not go home. Chris did not love Sue; it was all over. They should go home to Grampa.

She looked restlessly about the dreary darkening room with its ugly wallpaper and its stuffy clutter of worn ornate furniture. Mother did not even notice that she had stopped reading. Soon it would be dinnertime and Mother had made no move to rise. It would be hard to go alone again into that dining room to sit among strangers. Diana wanted to go to her mother, rouse her, beg her to get up, but she held back, worry fixed lest Mother, rising, should turn to whiskey for a wanted strength; it might be only a nip, it might be one nip after another, and then Diana would be more alone than ever, for it would not be really Mother who would be in the room with her.

She gazed into the back yard where a lone young tree stood in a square of beaten earth tormented by gusts of October wind and rain and the backs of other buildings pressed in, shutting out the sky. The rain came like mist, aged mist.

Aged mist . . . Words formed, fitted together, she chanted them in her mind, making a pattern. . . .

"Dicky, are you *crying?*"

Tears were rolling down Diana's cheeks, sweet comforting tears loosened by the beauty of her poem. Confused, she hurried to her mother, snuggled close, rejoicing in the touch and smell of soft warm flesh, the notice taken of her.

Mrs. Heaton cuddled her remorsefully. "I'm not much of a mother."

"Oh, you are, you are!—the best in the world!" She forgot caution, urging, "Get up, Sue. Come to dinner with me."

"All right, turn on the light."

Diana slid off the bed and scurried to switch on the light. But, the light turned on, she was dismayed to see that once again Sue lay flat, unmoving, eyes upon the ceiling. Had she lost her? "Aw, you said you'd get up!"

The disappointment in the child's voice made Mrs. Heaton sit up briskly. "Well, if the ship's to sail she must be rigged! Where's my stockings?"

Diana helped, but dressing wasn't easy. The trunk had to be ransacked for a fresh chemise, a button was missing and safety pins were already in urgent use; corset strings were elaborately tangled and at the very moment of unknotting them the string of the silk petticoat retreated into the gathering band. The girl sat down to retrieve it with scissors.

In the short chemise, long hair hanging down her back, Mrs. Heaton wandered aimlessly, looking like a dainty elfin child. She paused before the piano, rented when they first moved in, and touched the keys in changing chords.

Diana's eyes shone. "Sing something, Sue."

Uncertain, the woman sat down. She enlarged the chords, added an arpeggio, a singing exercise. A melody emerged, faltered, was searched out, reconstructed. The drawstring captured, Diana took up the brush and came behind her mother, wielding it gently. Lilting, timid, Mrs. Heaton's voice took up the melody, swelled, charged with feeling. The child listened, rapt, the brushing stopped. All at once the song broke off, hands lay motionless upon the keys, thin white fingers spread, inanimate.

"Oh, why did you stop? Go on."

"I could have been a singer."

"But you are! A beautiful singer!"

"I haven't any heart for it. I haven't any heart left to sing with." The woman turned on the piano stool. "I hope you're a heart-smasher when you grow up. I hope you break all their hearts. But you won't. You'll be like the rest of us, you'll cry your eyes out over some long-legged stroller. I hope it hits you when you're young, Chick. It's cruel to be forty when you fall in love."

The dinner bell rang. Diana laid a hand on her mother's arm, urging her to the bureau.

"No, I must wash first." Mrs. Heaton went to the wash-stand in the alcove, and Diana searched the closet for a dress. One of these days it would be impossible to find anything that could be worn and then what would happen? The hem of the suit skirt was ripped and the collar on the blue dress was spotted. The black dress needed pressing but it would have to do.

Mrs. Heaton came from the alcove and moved to a seat before the bureau. Diana, following, caught the smell of whiskey. The woman looked into the mirror and saw the frightened eyes. "That's medicine to me, you don't understand." She twined a coil of hair and thrust in pins. "Don't look like that because I take one little drink to give me strength!" The coil was not satisfactory; she took out the pins and laid them aside, her body slumped. "Go down without me," she pleaded, "I can't go. You don't mind those dreadful people the way I do. I'm not in a mood to put up with them. You can bring me a tray."

"All right." But the child did not move and the worry on her face was an accusation.

Mrs. Heaton's voice came out quick and sharp. "Why don't you go?"

In agony lest the words give offense, Diana blurted out, "I'm afraid you'll take another drink while I'm gone."

Mrs. Heaton reached for her hand and pressed it tight, not looking at her. "I promise I won't. Go ahead."

Halfway to the door, Diana looked back. Mother was watching with a sad face. "I'll hurry, dearest."

36

"Don't hurry. Enjoy your dinner." Mrs. Heaton tried to smile.

The boarders were all at table in the long basement dining room. Diana meant to slip in unobserved, but as usual, everybody stared. They weren't real people, only imitations; Mr. Albright talked pompously about The Market, pretending to be important; Miss Hansen went into horrible falsetto giggles, pretending to be a young girl; Mrs. Jenkins wore glittering black beads all over her disgusting bosom, pretending to be a lady; Mr. Hodges was the nicest, but he would use a fork like a dagger, tempting her to forget that staring was rude. Fortunately he was describing a new musical comedy and they had forgotten her, she could forget them. It was like being in disguise to sit there, silent, unnoticed, knowing that one day she would be on the stage and famous. She ate hurriedly, looking out at the dark street, seeing the lower halves of people passing by. A burst of laughter made her look about, curious.

"You didn't get that one, Diana," Mr. Hodges said archly, and when Diana smiled, pretending that she understood, everyone laughed harder than ever. They were laughing at her. They were not nice people. But some day she would be famous. . . .

When she carried in the tray Mother sat just where she had been sitting, in the same position. She rose, moving to the table where Diana set the tray. "Beef a la mode again." She sat down, pecked at this and that, but before the food was half eaten she started up like one summoned and stood tautly as though listening, and then strode to the window, staring into blackness.

Diana followed and took her hand. "What is it?" Mrs. Heaton did not answer. Tears were filing down her cheeks.

Her words came abruptly. "I've got to have another drink. I kept my promise while you were downstairs, but Dicky, Dicky, you don't know how I'm suffering!"

She was sobbing now and the sound uprooted Diana's

whole being. "But Mother, it'll make you more unhappy."

"You don't understand, child, how could you?"

"You'll cry more and you'll talk more—"

As if a mask had slipped over the woman's face a sudden ugly look changed all that was familiar and the girl winced back, aghast.

"Do I have to explain everything I do?" The strange woman strode savagely into the alcove.

Diana braced herself against the window, waiting. She could only wait, not knowing what would come or how to cope with it or even if it could be coped with. And Grampa had said, Look after your mother. . . .

Mrs. Heaton emerged from the alcove and flung herself into the nearest chair. The movement had a wild grace about it that made Diana think of Delsarte, the coaching in expression, the flowing poses, each with a name.

"You don't have to stand in the corner, silly."

Diana slid onto the nearest chair.

Mrs. Heaton announced, "I'm going to Astoria."

Astoria? "But Chris has gone, Sue."

"Chris has gone." The woman said the words over so that their full tragic value rang out. "Chris has gone."

Diana squirmed. "He's in Buffalo." That was better, more matter of fact.

"I know that! Do you think I've lost my wits? Ah, that's the worst of it—I can't forget, I can't." She made another large Delsartian gesture and again something in the grandeur of the movement stirred the child; this was life, this terrible scene; her mother's heart was breaking. Mrs. Heaton stood up, looking helplessly about her. "Where's my coat?" Her eyes were wild, blind and hard. "Get me my coat."

But Diana still tried to look after her. "I think it's raining—"

"I don't care if the sky falls." She went to the closet, pawed over hangers, her teeth gritting. The child hurried, picked out the coat, shook it free of the hanger. Mother's hat had fallen to the floor; a straw hat; it was disgraceful to be wearing straw in October. She wriggled into her own coat. Her mother faced her, demanding, "Have I got my hat on straight or do I look mad?"

"There's a wisp of hair—"

"Fix it! I don't want to look like a hag!"

Diana poked the wisp under the hat and then was following out into the hall and down the stairs. Oh, what a trail of whiskey smell there was! Mrs. Heaton paused to survey herself in the hat-rack mirror by the front door. "You did *not* fix my hair." Mr. Hodges came running lightly down the stairs, passed them with a polite "Good evening." Had he noticed? Mother had only bowed her head, haughty. Mrs. Heaton sailed out the door, down the brownstone steps and along the street in a straight course. To Diana, the very precision of her movements revealed change. The rain had stopped; the air was fresh with a gusty wind.

"How do we get there?" Mrs. Heaton stopped short, facing her daughter.

"We can go uptown on the Sixth Avenue car, or we can—"

The woman stamped her foot in anguish. "Don't bother me with details! I don't care *how!* Take me there!"

In the half-filled street car Mrs. Heaton sat sideways, elbow on the window ledge, chin in palm. With horror, Diana saw that tears had formed in her mother's eyes and were about to fall unchecked. Two young women across the aisle stared and whispered.

"When do we get there?" Mrs. Heaton asked, too loud.

"Soon," Diana said softly and smiled at her.

"What are you smiling for?" Mrs. Heaton demanded, still too loud.

Agonized, Diana murmured, "I was hoping you'd smile too."

"I'll never smile again." She twisted about and looked fixedly at the young women without seeing them; leaning on her palm, her hat had been shoved sideways. "When do we get there? Why don't you answer me, you little goose?"

"Six blocks." The child's face flamed heat, blood beat in her temples. Everyone in the car was looking now. Suppose

—suppose a policeman came in—intoxicated people are arrested. "Fix your hat, Mother, it's crooked."

"I told *you* to fix it. I distinctly told—"

"We get off here."

"Let go of me. I can walk!"

They stood on the sidewalk, waiting to transfer. Diana reached up and straightened Sue's hat. But in the crosstown car it was no better, Mother talking loud, people looking. Cruel people. If they knew that Chris had broken Sue's heart. They shouldn't look, they shouldn't whisper, they shouldn't smile. How *could* they *smile*. . . .

At the end of the line they got out and walked onto a ferry. Mrs. Heaton headed for the front of the boat. She leaned on the rail, looking down into the water. The sheen of green light from the pierhead wriggled over oily blackness and pale lumps of color-tinted froth. The water smell and the sour smell of wet wood mingled together.

"That's where I'll be some night. In the river and make an end of it."

The shock of the words, the immediate awful vision, Mother floating, hair loosened, face staring blankly, broke Diana. She cried out, clutching the thin body. "Mother! Mother! You've got me!"

Mrs. Heaton clasped the child to her. "I've got you, you're mine. But some day I'll lose you. You'll fall in love and leave me."

"Never, never!" They were both crying. A deckhand strolled by, gaping at the two who took no shelter from the wind; he went into the cabin to stare out through the glass-topped door.

"What good are old women!" Mrs. Heaton wept, "Oh Chris! Chris! Chris!"

By the time the ferry docked, Diana had wiped both their faces, and though her knees still shook, she knew a return of heart in the sureness of her mother's love; Mother wouldn't drown herself, she wouldn't do it, Mother loved her. There was another streetcar ride ahead of them, but the people in this car were different, laborers with mud-caked shoes, shapeless women without hats; they looked once or twice at the pretty woman with the solemn little girl and then forgot them. The car traveled on and on past gas tanks and empty grass lots and rows of identical small houses with here and there old mansions set back from the street, grandeur assertive even in decay.

"Two more blocks, Mother."

Mrs. Heaton came out of bitter-sweet reverie and followed Diana down the swaying car, held to her uncertainly as the car jolted to a stop and they got out; Diana was hopeful, seeing in this unsteadiness a return to Sue's right self.

The house was before them, Christopher's house—or was it Addie's?—dark save for light streaming from back parlor windows. Addie would be in there with her strange friends who never stopped talking. Did Mother mean to go in?— give Addie a piece of her mind? Diana flinched. "What are you going to do, Sue?"

"Nothing. I just wanted to be here."

There was a flight of stone steps, four of them, and then a gravel path that led to front steps between old pillars holding up a roof. Mrs. Heaton turned off the path, walking through wet uncut grass, skirting the dark side of the house. Big trees loomed about them, they scuffed through dead leaves.

"Up there," said Mrs. Heaton, "that's Chris's room."

"Yes."

The woman stood silent, unmoving. Looking toward the hedge at the back, Diana thought of Jane. Why had Jane, in her gruff man's voice, said 'Give me a kiss, Diana,' and why had Sue been so furious when told that she had swept into Addie's room, slamming the door behind her, and for a long time there had been the mutter of hushed angry talk. Jane was a strange woman; so many queer people 'visiting' in that house. 'Bohemians.' . . . Mother had sniffed and run her finger the length of the grand piano, leaving a trail in the dust. What had gone wrong? Wild quarreling, one voice coming fast on another, Addie and Chris and Sue, but mostly

Addie and Sue, and Sue wild and strange, taking one nip after another.

Wind stirred in the big tree close by. Diana glanced at her mother; she hadn't moved. The grass had wet their shoes, it was cold. The child shivered. What if Chris could see them standing there? Why *were* they standing there? It was strange and somehow beautiful, like listening to an orchestra; perhaps there *was* music, music that could be felt, not heard. She lifted her face and saw stars through racing clouds. She gazed until her neck grew stiff and the cold wonder of the stars faded. Still Mother hadn't moved. It was growing colder. The child huddled close to her mother.

Mrs. Heaton felt the shivering body and drew her closer. "You're cold. We must go home. If it weren't for you I'd lie down in the grass and die."

Diana felt her mother's hands. "You're cold, too."

Arms about each other, they walked back across the grass. When they came to the four steps, the woman said, "Go ahead of me and give me your hand. I'm stiff. My joints are stiff. I'm old."

They had to wait a long time for a streetcar. Across water the spires of Manhattan rose high. Mrs. Heaton took her daughter's hands and chafed them. "Poor Diana, poor child. This is dreadful. What am I doing to you, what am I *doing?* Oh Lord, my Diana, my beautiful, wonderful girl!"

"No, no, Sue, don't feel bad!" Diana did not want her mother to be upset and now everything was right, Mother was herself again. Besides. . . . How explain that there was pride in being lifted up to heights of tragedy and beauty? How explain the noble solace of that strange unheard music, or the star magic? Still. . . . "Mother, don't you think we should go home to Grampa?"

It was the thing to do of course. She would have to pull herself together, stop drinking, forget Chris. This was no way to treat Diana. And Diana meant more to her than anything in life, yes, more than Chris. Mrs. Heaton gazed at the distant spires. "There's your city, Diana. Some day it will be

42

yours. Then my life won't be all failure. Yes, Chick, we'll go home to Grampa, but we'll come back again—for you. You belong in New York where there are theaters—fame."

The streetcar came clattering along. After she had paid the fares, Mrs. Heaton straightened her hat, tucked Diana under her arm, pressing the girl's head on her shoulder. All the way home she fondled the child, babied her.

Luke was pleased with promotion. Getting on in years, it was good to have the pattern of his life sustained, to know his work in harness still had pull. Promotion marked the years, milestones along the way; deserved rewards, his just due. He was pleased too that promotion meant working in headquarters, living in Chicago. Not for his own sake; he liked Frostburg, his own house, neighbors he had shared the years with, men who stood for something in the town, men who had built it up and could think back along with him to when the prairie ran right down to Main Street, when the first paving put an end to mud, which house first had electricity, and who drove the first automobile.

No, not for his own sake, but for Hattie's; she was always talking about wanting the children to have advantages, saying all Chicago had to offer. Well, now they could have advantages and a good home too.

He missed talk with known men. Missed church, too; Lucy couldn't seem to get the hang of going to church in Chicago, just went now and again. And he missed his son; Nyrum still in St. Louis, and so busy making money he hadn't time to see his folks. Might be a shade too much drive in the boy; earned money wasn't good enough for Nyrum, he went in for speculating, and that wasn't like money worked for, nothing grown, nothing built, nothing invented, no industry or contribution; money come easy on a smart trick can't be like money earned.

Growing older, memory shifts, what happened five years back stands out less clear than what took place a half century ago. Walking with Diana on a Sunday afternoon, Luke talked of boyhood back in Michigan, of the first dollar earned, of Lincoln seen in Illinois. Sometimes Rod came along, but the boy was strange to the man, not understood and not admired; a good boy, religious, intensely so, but at that he just lacked grit and common sense. Diana should have been the boy only it would have been a waste of looks. Luke loved the girl, though it wasn't right the way Hattie reared her. All this talk of going on the stage, and calling her mother by a nickname, and speaking out pert, same as a grownup. But for all that, a good girl, my yes, dutiful and loving and a joy to Hattie.

Ice filled Lake Michigan, massy ice sculptured the rock-filled breakwaters, the wind blew sharp and biting; heavy snows fell and the gutters were heaped with soot-covered snow banks that stayed high, growing grimier, not enough heat in the rare pale winter sun to melt them down. Days were dark and cold and black wind-swept night came early. The children away long hours at school, Mrs. Heaton sat alone in her room, lost in her thoughts.

Forget Chris? That was not possible. She could not go back to being what she had been before he came. But even so, the pain of memory might have been endurable had it not been for those hideous ten days in Addie's house. She had let Chris see her go all to pieces, drinking, quarreling; he would remember her so. That thought was torment; she was not actually that kind of horrible person. There was pride's need to efface the memory, to set up the true image of herself, establish it; a woman poised, heartache hidden under a serenity of manner; a woman, charming, gracious, well-behaved; a woman with a stake in the future, mother of Diana. Good Lord, it must not be thought that Diana's mother was a *drunkard*.

And if he saw her so . . . her true self . . . thought she had stopped caring. . . .

To see him again. To look straight into his eyes. To challenge him by the assertion of the being that she truly was.

Return to Hokomok? Oh, was it mad, disastrous folly, or the brave, right thing to do?

Addie might be there. . . . But Addie could be ignored. Mrs. Heaton and her daughter could have a little cottage to themselves, an appropriate background, tasteful, cosy and attractive, a place to entertain the smart and lively people of the summer colony. It would take spunk to go back, meet him, carry it off. . . . Well, she *had* spunk.

Besides, she and Diana belonged in that other modern world that Chris's friends had opened to her, a younger, smarter world, quick and alive. How grim, dreary and dull Papa's way now seemed in contrast; the nineteenth century was in his home; she was suffocated and oppressed by it. Mrs. Heaton played her role of Mr. Fletcher's daughter in his presence, conforming to his expectations, but she had gone far out of his world and no return to it was possible. Besides, for Diana's sake, she did not want to settle down, grow old, become a stick-in-the-mud. Diana's mother should be modern, lively, up to date.

They would go back to Hokomok when summer came.

A fantastic figure strutted through the sunlight, singing. Diana, gay in gypsy costume, skirt of red and blouse of yellow, bedecked with beads, wild roses in her hair, went forward barefoot, light and supple, ready for encounter. The day was fine, tonic in the breeze, the aspect of the world of fields and hills and woodland sheer delight. Diana's spirit moved in the surge of nameless joyful power, the sense of destiny was on her; life lay ahead and all things could be done. . . . To be a dancer, go upon the stage.

She had come free of worry over this return to Hokomok; it was as Sue had said it would be, quite all right, and the little rented cottage on the Point held high spirits, song and laughter. The unexpected is always happening when one is young; Diana did not marvel overlong that Sue could be so glad and light of heart when Chris was frequently encountered, yes and Addie, too. What fun it was to be giving

45

parties and going to parties, and Mother so pretty, so attractive, so admired!

Where was Diana off to now? No place in particular, just a gypsy wandering along a road, singing, keeping step with song, having an afternoon to spend alone, Mother gone to tea at Dolly Austin's.

The warm, powdery dust underfoot grew cool as trees closed overhead. What a different feeling came upon you, entering a wood, grave, secret, silence-demanding. The song left off, the rhythm of her stride slowed, Diana stepped from the road and went uphill among the trees, walking on the cushiony prickle of pine-needle covered, body-warm earth, her nostrils widened to the strong pine fragrance. A crow lifted from a high branch and beat away, cawing, leaving silence to close in. What silence . . . not a void, but living. Solidly happy, the girl stood quiet, enjoyment swelling into emotion; she was uplifted with a sweet sure strength that was the doing-power for turning into dances; that music of motion was in her. It began to flow, raising her arms, arching her back, lifting her head.

Uphill a branch snapped, something stirred. What? An animal? No houses that way. Voices; a woman's chuckle, a man's low-toned response; two people approaching, coming into sight, the flash of a white skirt in a spot of sun, a man's legs moving in white flannel, a forked thing. . . . Sue and Chris! But—what were they doing in the wood? Diana called, "Hello!"

Man and woman started guiltily apart. The girl heard Chris mutter, "It's Diana," and her mother's murmur, "Well, not the first time she's seen *us* together." Mrs. Heaton raised her voice in a blithe, "Hello yourself, gypsy!"

High heels made the descent precarious, the woman leaned on the man's arm, dainty and small beside him. Coming close, she exchanged his support for Diana's and let Chris go first, parting the branches. They watched the ground until they came out upon the road, and then Diana saw her mother's face. It was wonderfully beautiful; it was alight with a serene radiance; there was singing in her eyes. Sue looked at Chris and owned him. She was asking, "Would you like to come to supper with us some night?"

"Tonight?" His face was red and he had no look for the gypsy girl.

"Not tonight. Bob Hoffman's coming. Tomorrow? Seven?"

"I'll be there."

Chris and Sue were looking into each other's eyes and it seemed as if talk flowed between them. Then Mrs. Heaton felt for Diana's hand, backed away, turned, Chris left behind. They came out of the wood and went along the road, going home. Across meadow, the distant purple-patched slopes of Mount Desert rose above a line of deeply blue sea.

"Why Sue, you've got pine needles all over you!" Diana brushed her back. "I thought you were going to Dolly Austin's."

Mrs. Heaton stole a quick side-glance at her daughter. Did Diana suspect? But even if she did not now, later, upon reflection, suspicion might arise, conclusions be formed, and those conclusions might be condemnatory. That must not happen. Nothing must ever come between Diana and her mother. Caught red-handed, it was better to tell the truth and keep Diana's confidence. Mrs. Heaton confessed. "I went with Chris. I love him. I always will. You mustn't think me bad."

"*Bad!*" The innocence in the girl's eyes, her frank amazement at the word, threw Mrs. Heaton into confusion. It was so hard to know what should be said or left unsaid. If only Diana had not come so suddenly upon them and there was time to think! But if Diana ever suspected, condemned—Mrs. Heaton backed the truth and went ahead. "Most people would say I *was* bad, old-fashioned people. But of course nowadays people are advanced, intelligent; they take a different viewpoint, more broad-minded, modern. They know there is a lot of hypocrisy in the conventions. If a man and woman love each other it's not wrong."

Diana could not understand why this speech was so earnestly delivered. Why, she knew Sue loved Chris! "Of course it isn't wrong!"

The woman was dismayed that what she had set herself to do was still undone. She came to a stop, facing the girl, tall at thirteen, as tall as herself. "I want you to understand. We're pals. You must never condemn me." Words balked, she had to thrust them out. "Chris and I have done what men and women do when they're in love. It's not sin. It's beautiful and natural. Now do you understand me?"

What Sue was trying to convey leapt at Diana, coming suddenly, large and sharp and clear. She stared at the woman, dazed. The fact was understood, yes; yet somehow not the meaning of it. For all Mother's quiet, reasonable explanations in the past, this mystery of man and woman life remained a mystery. And here the mystery had actually been performed, and by Mother, and it was a fact, spilled out there, standing in the sunlight, Sue talking to her. . . . But even stranger than what had been said was the way it had been said, Mother pleading, anxious, making a demand for love and comfort. The girl put her arms around the woman, not knowing what was the expected thing that she should say, but only that Sue had need of her love.

Mrs. Heaton knew a vast relief in that embrace, everything straightened out, no barriers allowed to form. Diana was so mature, so understanding! They stepped on together. She took the girl's arm and tucked it cosily beneath her own, talking not to her child but to her pal, her confidant, the one being in the world who mattered most. She must be certain that Diana understood this thing intelligently and realized just how silly and stupid the conventions were. Love, beautiful and natural, stood above all man-made laws. Marriage sacred? Why, half the marriages were hell on earth, no minister could sanctify them! There was freedom for women in the modern world, old taboos broken down. Clever people laughed at the old-fogey beliefs; these were the debunking years. "I love Chris, I always shall, no matter what. I fought against this, I wanted him to marry me, I wouldn't give in

48

to him last summer. But now—I'm not sorry. Whatever happens, I've had this. You'll be a woman some day and then you'll understand."

Diana walked straightly, close beside her, not child or gypsy but woman-soon-to-be, accepting all her mother had to tell about this adult world she soon would enter, giving attention and response. "Yes, Sue, of course . . . I do understand . . . and if you're happy now. . . ."

There was no thought of censure in her. What Mother said to her was always true. Her thought was set in the mold of trustfulness; this woman she adored, who gave back adoration, had never told her lies or been evasive or unkind; she brought a gentle reasonableness to every question that the girl put to her. This talk going on now was a deepening of that intimacy they shared apart from all the world.

And yet. . . . It was not talk Diana wanted. The revelation was too big and it had come too quickly, too unforeseen, upon her. But for Sue's need of her companionship, Diana would have run fast, over the ridge of a hill, far into the woods, out of sight, out of call, girl alone and having a girl's need for slow brooding over the mysteries of oncoming womanhood; the craving was strong for fast physical movement to ease the pressure of that difficult alteration in being at work within her.

They came up a rise of ground, nearing the small cottage in the daisy field, so white, so decisive in outline against the dark wall of somber pine woods. Breeze brought them the faint tolling of the bell buoy off the Point.

Mrs. Heaton paused in her steps and faced her daughter, stricken with a sudden thought. "Diana, the family must never know—none of them. Papa—good Lord, Papa would kill me if he knew! Chick, don't tell on me. Promise."

Diana gave the promise readily.

They could not get out of each other's way, both hurrying to get dressed at the same time in the small attic bedroom. Side-stepping collision with Diana, Mrs. Heaton bumped her head against the sloping rafters. "Good Lord, will you hurry and get out of here!"

Diana struggled into her dress. "I'm through, Sue dear. Can I help you?"

Mrs. Heaton confronted dresses hanging in a row upon pegs. Which one to wear . . . for a celebration, his first supper in the house. . . . "No. Go downstairs and stay in the parlor. Someone ought to be there when he comes. You might help me—no, never mind. Go away."

She chose the white dress, dropped it carefully over her head, not mussing her hair. Getting to the bureau, she bent close to the mirror, working skillfully with lipstick. Five past seven—Christopher was late. Running the buffer over her nails, she thought her hands looked thin, and went to the trunk for her engagement ring, seldom worn. The diamond flashed even in the darkening room; yes, the ring looked well. She hesitated beside the open trunk, knowing what was hidden there, close to hand. She had not intended . . . but tonight was special, and even with Diana's help—impossible to get a servant on the island—the cleaning and the cooking, the last minute hurry, had left her worn and jumpy just when she should be fresh and poised and sparkling, with never a hint that she had once run down a lane to cry 'I love you.' And especially after yesterday . . . tonight must be successful, a precedent for nights to come. Her hand stole guiltily into the trunk, drew up the flask. . . . I don't mean to do this very often.

The drink carefully measured and tossed off, a last glance in the mirror, and she was ready. She stole a moment to stand like an actress about to make an entrance, indulging in a rich, secret gloating, yesterday recalled. . . . Ah, to be a woman, desired, fulfilled. What was a woman without the love of a man? But—ten after seven! He oughtn't to be late.

She went swiftly down the stairs, ran a critical eye over the parlor. The chintz curtains made it jolly, wild roses in a blue bowl upon the piano were a nice touch, Diana was

growing more beautiful, and that picture hung straight at
last. "Light the lamp, Chick."

"Listen, Mother."

"What?"

"The bell buoy. The wind is rising."

Mrs. Heaton went to the door. There, of all people, came
Bob Hoffman! Boor, he hadn't been invited. Invitations were
another thing these moderns gave no heed to. Still, did it
matter? Show Chris that someone else was interested, someone three years younger than himself and not a bad-looking
fellow at that, even if he had been dubbed 'The Minister'
for his sober mien. "Hello, Bob."

He was cheered by the cordiality of her greeting; he hadn't
been sure but that he came too often. Not that she stood on
form or anything like that. Son of a missionary, he had trouble
sometimes with his conscience; after all, she was a married
woman. But damned attractive and she knew it. Well, he
was a writer—or trying to be; his agent told him that his
stories lacked love interest.

"Look at Diana in mufti for once! No costume tonight?"
Bob dropped into an easy chair.

Mrs. Heaton still stood by the door. "You didn't happen
to see Chris?" She spoke lightly. "I'm holding supper for
him."

Bob was surprised. "The Merediths were having supper
when I passed their cottage."

She faced about, eyeing him levelly and the moment's silence
seemed to stretch. "Oh. I mean . . . are you sure?" The same
lightness of tone did not deceive Diana. The girl rose slowly
from her seat, watching her mother.

Bob Hoffman shrugged. "They had candles lit. I could see
into their dining room."

Mrs. Heaton began pleating her handkerchief methodically, giving that her whole attention, her face working, eyebrows raised, drawn together, lips pouting, sucked in. If
Chris did not come. . . . She let her hands fall, looked out
the door and back at Bob. "Did you see Chris?"

51

Bob got it now; still, he didn't know what to say and blundered on with the truth. "Chris? Yes. He was there. He was at the table."

Mrs. Heaton turned in a flash and whipped out of the room. Her feet struck hard, quick blows on the stairs, pounded into the room above. A door slammed.

Diana appealed to the man, wringing her hands. "She'll feel *awful* now. He said he'd come."

Overhead, bedlam broke loose. The ceiling shook with a violent crash, there was the bang of furniture overturned, the smash of breaking china. Diana reached for Bob's hand and started for the stairs, tugging.

The bedroom door was locked and Mrs. Heaton cried, "Go 'way" when the girl rapped, calling to her. The noise of smashing had left off; there was the stealthy rustle of skirts and then the evil chuckling of liquor coming out of the neck of a bottle. Diana told the man, "We must get in. I've got to look after her."

Bob knocked on the door. "Mrs. Heaton, if you won't unlock the door I'm afraid I'll have to force it open."

A sobbing, derisive laugh came back. "Break it, do! Break everything in the damn house!"

Bob scratched his head, perplexed. Diana nudged him. "Go ahead and break it." He thought of his key-ring and got it out. The girl squirmed beside him in impatience while he tried one key after another. Then the lock turned, the door swung open.

Mrs. Heaton faced them, copper head flung up, glass in hand, smiling. There was a spurious gaiety about her, a tremulous sheen overlaying fierce, defiant pride, a shimmering, fragile, opalescent beauty with the sparkle of cold fury. Bob thought, she's magnificent.

Diana stepped over fragments of the china pitcher. "Sue dearest, don't."

The woman held the man's eyes, defying his approach. As he stirred forward, she finished off the drink in a gulp, retreating under rafters, the bottle swung behind her skirts.

Bending low, he followed, took the bottle from her in a sudden tussle and set it on the bureau.

Her anger leapt out. "Go 'way—go 'way!" She tried to get to the bureau but he caught her wrists and held them. The glass fell, shattering. Sobbing with fury, she wrenched this way and that, trying to be free of him, and then all at once was quiet. Bob let go of her. She stepped clear of him with an icy bow of dismissal. Her hair had come loose and fell looped and tangled on her shoulders, her dress had torn and the whiteness of one bare shoulder shone in the gloom. It was a second before Bob realized that she was heading for the door.

He caught her arm. "Where are you going?"

She gave him a hateful look. "Take your hands off me. I'm going to Christopher."

Diana cried, "Oh Sue—no!"

"Mrs. Heaton, I can't let you, you're not yourself." He held her fast and she began to cry brokenly, pitifully, face averted.

"He told me he'd come. He promised. Oh what do you know of this—let me go, let me go!" She grew excited, wild, struggling to be free and Bob had to put both arms about her. "Chris, I tell you, I want Chris! I've got to see him, I've got to know why—" Her voice rose in a long-drawn call with all her singing strength. "Christopher Meredith! Christopher Meredith!"

It was growing dark in the room and the wind was moaning. Diana got the lamp lit and shadows sprang upon the rafters. She set the upturned chair upon its legs and kicked the broken china to one side. She went close to Bob. "Maybe you ought to let her go."

The man was exasperated. "She doesn't know what she's saying. She'd be sorry afterward."

Mrs. Heaton wriggled free of him; imperious, she strove to stare him down. "I was never more sober in my life. I've got to see Chris. I've got to know how he can treat me this way. I've got to know why—I've got to see him—Oh, Chris, Chris—"

Her control shattered into a wretched heartbroken sobbing.

The man took her in his arms. "Sue, Sue dear—"

Another violent tussling began, another calling cry to Christopher. Diana could not stand this any longer; if Mother wanted Chris then she should have him. The girl slipped from the room and down the stairs. Suppose Sue died, her ghost wandering along the road, seeking Chris. . . . Diana headed out the door, running through the night, hitting a smart clip she knew she could keep up all the way to the Meredith cottage, grateful for moonlight showing the road. She went over the swells of ground and into the dips, skirted rock ledges, pace unslackened, the night wind moist and cool on her face. Chris's cottage was brightly lit, smoke coming from the chimney. Still running, she turned into the lane, thudded along the porch and pulled up before the knocker.

Christopher opened the door and forced a smile over obvious surprise. "Well! Here's Diana come calling!"

He pressed her hand affectionately as he drew her in. A fire crackled in the grey stone hearth, Addie sat on one side and Jane on the other and a bearded man lolled on the sofa, his legs stuck out; if you didn't look twice you'd think they were all men, the way Jane and Addie were dressed. Addie didn't speak. Jane, gruff and hearty, said, "Hello, stranger."

Diana gave them an inclusive bow, holding tight to Chris's hand that showed an inclination to be free. She looked up, telling him, panting, "Chris—you said you'd come to supper —I heard you."

There was soft worry in his eyes, he seemed both distressed and amused.

"Chris, you promised. Please—just for a minute."

He freed his hand and groped along the mantle for a pipe, his head dark against the bright oil painting over the fireplace, flames vivid behind his long legs.

Addie stirred. "Sit down, Diana." She was very like Chris save that what was handsome in the man was harsh and coarse in the woman, and her eyes were paler, like blue glass. Jane said, "Aw, sit down, you're sweating."

54

But Diana remained on her feet, braced against them, the feeling growing that she had plunged into a hostile camp among foes who held unknown weapons. "No thanks, I've got to go. Chris, please come."

He chewed on his pipe. "I don't know if I should, Diana."

Angered by the failure of her sociability, Addie drawled, "You don't know what your mother wants of Chris."

Diana declared, "Yes, I do."

"You don't. She wants to sleep with him."

Diana hated Addie. She fought back, defending Sue. "Well, then, why shouldn't she?"

The bearded man guffawed and Jane snickered; it was one on Addie, the avowed liberal. Chris kicked at a log fringed with fire, muttering, "You shouldn't have said that, Addie."

He wasn't like the others, he was nice, he cared. Diana took his hand. "Bob Hoffman's there. Just for a minute, Chris, she's liable to die."

The man knocked coals from his pipe. Addie spoke out sharply, "If you go you'll be at that woman's beck and call for the rest of the summer. Diana, your mother's not dying, she's probably drunk."

Chris was angry. He moved with Diana to the door. "I'll be right back. I told you, Addie, I should have gone." He opened the door, wind swirled in, fire roared in the chimney, Diana followed him out, not looking at the others. He walked with quick strides, gloomy, wondering what this long-legged precocious child with the beautiful face actually knew. A fine mess I've made for her, he thought. But Sue—spellbinder with the red hair and the yellow eyes and skin as white as a fish's belly, made for love and demanding it so that a man would have to be made of stone. . . . But how could you marry a woman who drank, drank all the time, made scenes. No. Addie was right, stay clear of Sue, she's plain dangerous. The child beside him tripped and caught at his hand. He took and held it, loving the girl, repentant. Moon passed under clouds, they had to pick their steps. Diana was wondering why it was she felt no hatred for him. And Sue could

55

not hate him either. He *seemed* so nice. But he had broken Mother's heart.

"You're growing up with some queer notions, Diana. They won't do you any good. It's all right for older people to lead any lives they please, but you shouldn't be talking about people sleeping together. Don't think about all this man-and-woman stuff until you're old enough to know what it's about. You know too much already."

Diana pondered this, not thinking much of it. "I know Sue loves you."

Chris answered savagely, "She shouldn't."

Why . . . if she could tell Sue why. Diana gathered courage to ask, "Do you love her?"

Just as savagely, he answered, "I shouldn't."

That was no explanation that gave help. Perhaps Sue would not like her to be asking questions of him, but if only —"Why?"

The cottage came in sight, yellow lamplight streaming from the windows. The wind brought them the long-drawn singing cry, "Christopher Meredith! Christopher Meredith!"

Drunk. The man hurried his steps. "That's why."

Entering the house, Diana fell back, letting Chris go up alone. Had she done the right thing in fetching him? She listened, fearful. A sudden joyous babble broke out in the room above, Sue's voice in tumbling, incoherent words and sobbing laughter. Diana drew a deep breath, relieved.

Bob came down, mopping his forehead. He sat on the sofa making no talk, avoiding Diana's eyes. The girl went to sit gratefully beside him. Bob's sleeve had been torn; she stared at the long red marks in the dark flesh of his hairy forearm. Sue had clawed him like a cat. Bob's flesh under Sue's nails . . . she gave a little shudder. The man saw what she was looking at and twisted his arm so the scratches didn't show. They managed a smile, as though that didn't matter.

Chris came down, quick of step, his air defensively jaunty. "Just wanted to say hello. Well—" He waved and went out.

Diana said, "I'll see if she's all right," and ran up. She

56

came back in a minute bringing pleasant news. "Lying down. Resting. She'll be all right now."

"Say, you didn't eat." Bob rose heavily. "Let's go out in the kitchen and help ourselves."

The table set, the cold supper laid out, daisies in a vase in the center, brought to mind the miscarriage of plans. Diana put the daisies in the sink before she took her seat. The clanging of the bell buoy went on, the distant boom of the surf on the headland sounding when the wind lulled. Bob preferred silence and his smile was shy.

They sat at table, their supper finished, Mrs. Heaton, Bob and Diana, allies against Chris, bound together in their ignoring of so much as mention of his name. Rain droned on the roof; a nor'easter had set in, the wood fire snapping in the kitchen stove was cozy.

Mrs. Heaton related her triumphant news, sending a playful smile across the table. "We'll be living in New York this winter. Come to see us, Bob?"

"Sure. I'm often in New York. But I thought your home was in Chicago."

Mrs. Heaton made a face. "My father's. But it's preposterous that I should go on living in his house! I'm grown up now, I should hope." She pulled a daisy from the center bowl and twirled it idly. "Besides, Diana belongs in New York, she must see all that's going on in the theaters. Do you know I had to coax and argue and lament? But at last I have my way! Oh, I could never go back now!"

Diana was thinking of Roddy, wishing he would be with them. He would feel bad about this. They had always shared the winters with him and he loved Mother so.

Mrs. Heaton fell to plucking the petals. He loves me, he loves me not . . . . She stood up, restless, tossing the stalk upon the table. "This gloomy storm! Did you bring some poetry to read? Let's go upstairs, I'd like to lie down. My, I tire so easily! Diana dear, will you wash the dishes? And when

57

you finish, work on the nautch costume, won't you? I want you to do that dance at the clambake."

Diana had the lamp for upstairs lit. "Yes, Sue."

Bob followed Mrs. Heaton from the room, the lamp in his hand. "I don't know if you're familiar with T. S. Eliot—"

The dishes washed, Diana stood at the window. Beyond glassy beads rolling down the pane she could see only blackness. At night the woods marched closer, unfriendly, mysterious and primeval. Rain struck the house in squally gusts; a bad night for a man out in a lobster dory . . . .

If Sue would only consent to finish the summer in some other place. Why did she feel that she must stick this out? It was a strain on her, she was only pretending to be happy, and the nips were growing bigger and more frequent. She might laugh and toss her head but unhappiness was in her eyes, plain to see. How could Chris make her suffer . . . .

The costume, the sewing. Why must it be done tonight? Tomorrow would do as well. She did not want to go sit alone in the parlor, bent over stitching, she wanted to be with Sue; besides, it would be nice to hear the poetry.

She mounted the stairs, her steps muffled in the steady drumroll of rain upon the roof. Halfway up, eyes level with the floor above, she halted, seeing what was queer: no light came from the crack under the door . . . but Bob had taken the lamp . . . . She went on faster, troubled, not knowing what could be wrong. Then, as her hand reached to the knob, she checked, rigid, informed by a brief secret whispering, a rustling stir, the creak of bedsprings.

Not to be there—to be instantly someplace else—get away—

She was traveling backward down the stairs, hurrying frantically, one hand sliding along the rail, one hand pressed to the chill plaster of the wall. Get away—out of this—

She gained the kitchen and stood stupid.

Chris, yes . . . but Bob, too? 'Beautiful and natural.' . . . 'What men and women do when they're in love.' . . . But . . . did Sue love Bob? How could she love Bob when she loved Chris?

58

Draft swept in under the back door, sparks snapped in the stove. Storm beat about the frail house, shook and rattled it. It was a night when to be sheltered, cozy, a house held comfort. But it was as though the enemy storm with all the wild black fury of the night had got inside. There was no comfort in the house.

4

ER OWN breakfast swallowed down, Diana waited while
her mother's tray was being prepared. Last in the
boarding-house dining room, she sat alone, staring
gloomily at nothing. Mother had been awful when she came
home last night, awful. And anyway—*Hodges*. Bob was all
right, of course, Sue had explained that; besides, Bob made
Sue happy; it was too bad he wasn't in New York all the time.
Mischa . . . well, at least he had been a violinist and not alien
in spirit. But *Hodges*—a fellow boarder, not even a nice person. Sue having an affair with *him*. Why, Sue didn't seem to
care what happened to her any more.

Life had gone all askew and something was terribly, terribly
wrong. Diana knew that, although her thinking followed
quite naturally and unconsciously along the pattern of her
mother's. Sue was always explaining things. The trouble now,
Diana reflected, wasn't really the affairs into which Sue had
plunged since coming to New York, for, as Sue said, a woman
had a right to lead the life she chose, and modern women did;
Dolly Austin was openly living with a man she wasn't married
to. But even so—Hodges. . . . Well, it wasn't actually the
affairs, of course; it was the drinking. 'A woman shouldn't
drink.' . . . Sue had said that. Sue knew she shouldn't. But
Sue drank because she was unhappy, because of Chris.

How wrong it all was . . . that Mother, so beautiful, so fine,
so good, should suffer heartache, should live on in a dingy
boarding house, should drink, go out with Hodges. . . . No,
it should not be, it must be ended somehow.

I've got to look after her. . . . If there was something—yes.
The career. That would bring Sue the redeeming joy! Of
course it would. And that rested with Diana; it was a decisive,
purposeful action that could be undertaken which would

re-make their lives, hers and Sue's, and set things right. Diana brightened, full of hope, impatient to begin. I shall go on the stage at once.

The landlady entered with the tray. "There, I fixed it myself so she won't have nothing to complain about this time."

Diana was on her feet, taking the tray, murmuring loyally, "She doesn't mean to make you any trouble, Mrs. Hilton."

"It's you she's making trouble for, dearie." The grumbling woman followed Diana to the door. "I'd turn her out of my house if it wasn't for you, 'deed I would."

But the girl was hastening up the stairs out of reach of talk.

Sue was still asleep. She looked very small and childlike curled up in the big bed, her face in repose strangely youthful, innocent. But as Diana set the tray on the chair beside the bed, the woman's eyes opened and filled with instant misery.

"Here we are dearest, nice strong coffee, piping hot."

Mrs. Heaton wrenched herself up and sat, head drooping. "I can't eat. My head is spinning. I ache all over."

"You'll feel better after coffee."

The woman looked up, meek-faced. "You're so sweet, Dicky. For your sake."

She let Diana place the tray on her lap, but she couldn't take anything but coffee; even a cigarette was not wanted. She waved food away. And when she spoke it was in a thin voice, morose. "Dicky, I'm frightened."

The girl laid the tray outside the door and came back to the bed. "What is it, dear?"

Mrs. Heaton smoothed the sheet with nervous fingers. "I mustn't drink."

Diana's heart bounded. "You can stop, Mother. You've stopped lots of times. You've got will power." Diana sat down close beside her.

Mrs. Heaton curled a strand of hair over her finger. "You don't know what I went through last night . . . Diana, he brought me home in a taxi and just because I was crying he—he was rough to me." She bit on the strand, her distress rising. "He told me to shut up. He put his hand over my mouth.

And then—oh Dicky, put your arms about me!—he slapped me!"

Arms clasped tight about the frail body, Diana gasped under the stab of horror.

Mrs. Heaton leaned against her daughter. "So I screamed more. I wanted to get out, to run away from him, and he wouldn't let me. It's enough to make you crazy when someone pins you down and you can't move. So I put my foot through the glass."

"Oh Sue! You might have bled to death!"

"The chauffeur stopped and he and Hodges got out on the street and argued and I climbed out—oh, this is the worst part! I wanted to run home to you, and Diana, I couldn't remember where we lived."

The girl groaned, her face buried in Sue's hair.

"I had to crawl back in the taxi and huddle in a corner like a scared rabbit and I don't remember how I got home."

Diana spoke sternly. "Sue, you must make up your mind not to drink ever again."

Mrs. Heaton pulled free of Diana's arms to face her. "I'm not a drunkard, Dicky, I'm not. I'm not one of those torpid, sottish creatures who drink because they like it. I've never drunk for fun in my life. I'm like Papa, I've turned to it like medicine to give me strength. Dicky, I'm really a nice person."

Such a childlike, pleading face! Diana's heart was wrung. She drew the loved woman back into her compassionate embrace.

Mrs. Heaton rewound the strand of hair about her finger; wistful, she confided, "I get lonely sometimes, just—empty, scared. You're away at school so many long hours . . . Chris . . . Oh Lord, it's a shameful thing to go on loving a man who isn't worth it! Is he alive or dead? Wouldn't you think he'd let me have a word from him, be friends at least—just a little bit? It wouldn't hurt him to call *once* in a while. He could send me Christmas cards."

"Forget him. You just make up your mind to stop drinking."

" 'Stop drinking.' . . . How horrible that sounds. Oh, don't think I don't realize what I'm doing to you, don't think I don't. Why, when I think of that it nearly drives me crazy and I *have* to drink! My beautiful girl, my glorious Diana!"

"Now Sue—"

"Suppose it's got a hold on me and I can't stop."

"Yes, you can."

"Oh, you're so good, so sweet. I couldn't live without you. But I ought to be dead. I ought to kill myself."

Diana stood up and went to the end of the bed and gripped the rail. "Look here, Sue, we've got to change all this. There's no sense my going to school any longer. I'm going on the stage. Now."

Mrs. Heaton gazed in astonishment. "But—you're still a little girl."

"No I'm not. I'm fourteen and a half. If you get me the duds I'll look eighteen. I'm taller than you are. I'm grown up. Sue dear, you always said I could do as I pleased. I want to go on the stage right now."

A shine had come into Mrs. Heaton's eyes. She propped cushions, sitting straight, pride and admiration coming for this serious young girl who spoke with such a confident air. Ambition for Diana, long cherished, bred out of her own defeat, had been stored up waiting for this day to come. That ambition, a strong, fixed desire, had grown more urgent as her spirit met fresh defeat in loving Chris. Could it be that now— "But—Why, I don't know, I can't think—hand me a cigarette. *Now?*"

"Now." Diana assembled the cigarettes, the matches, the ash tray. Yes, now; an end to hurrying home from school and toiling up the worn carpeted stairs never knowing what waited you inside the room, Sue herself or Sue gone strange in drink; the never-knowing a blight that made the happy interludes without validity because of haunting worry. She only drank in spells but that spoiled all the rest. And why should this go on? Why, when uptown, only a few blocks away, a fabulous new world waited, a world that would remake their lives?

"You're not getting much from school," Mrs. Heaton admitted, faintly bitter. "You're not making the friends that most girls make at school; you've no home to invite them to. And they're all rich, they probably look down on you." She frowned, trying to think clearly on this. "It's such a big decision."

"But we always knew I was going on the stage, Mother."

Mrs. Heaton studied the figure standing in the center of the room, pleading so eagerly. Diana was smart, precocious, no ordinary young girl. Properly dressed she could pass for seventeen at least. A young lady . . . why, a stunner! The slender active body, rich with vitality and youth, the slim pretty legs; the beautiful young face with the steady, thoughtful, blue-green eyes, the full curved lips, so amiable they seemed to smile in repose; the sunny glints in the brown, silky, curling hair, the sunny glint in the tawny, satiny skin. And that confidence, that priceless, enviable confidence. Why should I hold her back, interfere, act as Papa did with me? Mrs. Heaton brushed ashes into the tray, frowning over the decision.

"Sue, why do you hesitate?"

Mrs. Heaton answered honestly. "Because I want it so much I'm afraid of being selfish. You know I want it."

"So do I. Well then?"

The woman smoked in silence. Now that Diana's career had come suddenly close she felt her own inadequacy to give advice, direct procedure. What did she actually know about the stage? "Sit down, Dicky. We must talk it over. They say it's a hard profession. They say—oh, I don't know, but you hear stories. About how actresses get ahead. Being 'nice' to some stage manager. And you *are* young."

Diana took the chair beside the bed, prepared for hard, reasonable talk. This was certainly a new consideration and one she had not foreseen, but she was silent for only a moment. "Well, all right, if it turns out to be like that, then that's the way it is."

Mrs. Heaton was horrified. "Why, Diana!"

The girl was surprised at this response; it did not fit in at all with Sue's talk about the freedom of the modern woman.

"Well, after all, it's my profession, isn't it? No matter how hard it is—"

"But you mean to say—"

"You said I might find I had to be nice to some stage manager to get ahead, didn't you? And I say if that's the way it is—"

"Oh, you don't know what you're talking about! You're only a baby!" Mrs. Heaton snubbed the stub of her cigarette with quick agitated jabs, folded her arms and shook her head.

Diana was perplexed. "Why, Sue, I don't understand you. You've said yourself that conventions are silly and there's a lot of hypocrisy about sex. *I* don't know what it's going to be like, I only say *if* it turns out that a woman has to sacrifice herself to get ahead, well then she has to. But at least a woman with a career is doing something fine and splendid with her life, isn't that so?"

But Mrs. Heaton continued to shake her head. "You don't realize what you're saying, you're—"

"Mother," Diana interrupt i, impatient, getting to her feet. "Are you going to say *now* that I can't go on the stage?"

The woman looked at her, not knowing what to say. Of course it had always been taken for granted that Diana would go on the stage. "But Dicky, you're so young, your whole life lies ahead of you—"

The girl strode up and down. "The quicker I get started the better. Lots of actresses began when they were babies. Think of the years I've lost already! Why, Mother, I can't understand you! You've always said your life was spoiled because Grampa wouldn't let you do what you wanted. Sue, are you going to say that I *can't*?"

Challenged thus, Mrs. Heaton conceded. "No, Dicky, I'll let you go. It's only—"

But Diana cut her off, plunging upon the bed, smothering her in a hug. "Sue! Dearest!"

"Well, maybe nothing will happen to you, and we'll always talk things over like pals, won't we?"

Diana lay sprawled on the bed beside her. "We'll be so

happy now, you'll see! Everything will be all different, won't it? Sue, you must buy me duds. Today? Will you feel well enough today? So that tomorrow. . . . "

The future had been caught up with, brought into the present. All the years of saying 'someday' and now. . . .

Mrs. Heaton stroked the young, excited face, proud and fond. Diana, a winner, stuff in the girl, spirit, ambition. Here was promise coming to fulfillment, all of life's bitter failure canceled and atoned. Tears of joy came into her eyes. She bent forward and kissed her daughter, grateful and adoring. "Oh Chick, I love you so!"

Diana had not the slightest idea of how one started in. Go on the stage . . . but how was it done? There were stage managers, men to be seen who would have an eye open for a new star. But where were these men? How did one find them?

She went to a box office and told the man who sold tickets that she wanted to see the stage manager. Faintly curious, he asked what about, and Diana explained. So he told her to go to the producing offices and ask for the casting director, and it was really simple after all. She wondered why people said that it was hard to go upon the stage.

The offices that she went into were singularly drab and matter of fact and the people waiting in them were an odd assortment; none of them looked famous and some were old, yet they came to ask for a place in the theater just as she did. But most unexpected were the casting directors themselves, men coolly brisk and quite disinterested, not the least bit anxious to discover someone new. They asked if she had had experience and turned away. And often she was not even admitted for their consideration. Going from place to place on that first day, dressed in the smart grown-up clothes that Sue had bought her, it began to seem that there was still some mystery to the thing she had not fathomed; it might not be so easy after all.

But it was different in the Block offices right from the start. Riding up in the elevator the Negro operator was friendly with advice. He told her to ask for Mr. Mowbray, and told her how he could be recognized. "He speak like he makin' out to be an Englishman."

Stepping into the corridor, Diana saw a door open and three men come out, two taking leave of a third. And the third man's speech was clipped and sing-song! She would speak to him before he had a chance to retreat inside the door.

Mr. Mowbray was old, fifty at least, short and paunchy. His face was grey-toned, even his lips, flesh pouched and wrinkled under his eyes, pouched and wrinkled under his chin; there were so many wrinkles about his mouth that it looked as if it were on a gathering string, loosened now in the joviality of talk. Diana wondered why casting directors were never young, handsome men.

The two departing men moved off. Mowbray called after them something about 'box office' that made them laugh. Diana moved forward.

Mr. Mowbray's eye caught her, wandered over her in quick appraisal.

Diana smiled at him. "I want to see Mr. Mowbray, please."

He liked what he saw. Lips pursed to an inaudible whistle, he stepped back, holding the door open. "You've winged your bird, my dear. Step in."

Guided by a wave of his hand, she went triumphantly through a swinging door in a low wooden railing and by a girl at a desk and on into an inner office. She had won consideration. She was rosy with hope.

The man, following, closed the door behind them and took a seat in a swivel chair back of an enormous desk as big as a bed. He picked up a cigar, lit it, tilted back in his chair, his stumpy legs clear of the floor. "Well, my dear, let's have it." Again he waved his hand and she sat down in the chair indicated, vastly relieved that he had not kept her standing; she could not imagine Sue standing while a man sat, and for a moment she had dreaded lest he think her only a child.

"I want to go on the stage, Mr. Mowbray."

"First time out, eh?" His sharp eyes went wandering over

her, not meeting hers for longer than a glance, his lips loosened in a held smile. "Well, what can you do?"

He was interested, friendly, and no doubt very smart. She returned his smile happily. "Oh, I'm a dancer. But I could do anything just to get started."

Young, in her teens, rosy cheeks and lips, not rouged; a pretty bit. He swung his heels, puffing the cigar, still looking her over. "A dancer, eh? Let's see your legs."

Without a moment's hesitation Diana stood up and lifted her skirts above her knees. Dancing in the short Greek costume at parties she had heard people praise her body, speak of sculpture; though now, eager to make a good impression, she did not think her legs looked well, the line broken where her stockings stopped and her garters began. She looked back at the man, hoping he would approve, nevertheless. She let her skirts fall, waiting .

Mowbray tilted out of the chair and came toward her. He put his hands on her arms as though to judge the muscles, and now his hands did what his eyes had done; they wandered over her body while his eyes stayed on her face, watchful, the smile held.

Diana stood passive, accepting this as a part of the routine of consideration. She was so used to having her body spoken of that it did not seem so very strange that this man should make an estimate of it; still, she did not quite like this handling; strangely, it disquieted her, and all at once she was aware of breasts budding, round and hard as unripe fruit beneath her dress, secret things that he was finding out. She grew flustered and heat came up into her face.

He had no mind to startle her away. He thrust his hands into his pockets, standing close. "So you're a dancer, eh?"

He was certainly friendly, he was considering her with interest. She knew that she should answer brightly. But the confusion that had come upon her stayed and she was gawky and tongue-tied as a child.

Mowbray reflected. "I might place you. Suppose you could do a bit of a Chinese dance in with six girls?"

Her hope came uppermost. She clasped her hands in delight, assuring him, "Oh yes, of course I could!"

He went back to the swivel chair, a busy man with other work on hand. "The dance is simple, very, a bit of atmosphere. Come tomorrow, on stage at The Royal. Bring a practice costume and we'll give you a try." He puffed at the cigar, nodding, dismissing her. She moved to the door, thanking him, thanking him again, ardent and excited, grateful.

It all came true in such a dizzy, jumbled hurry. One minute she was actually going in through a stage door, the next she was with girls in a dressing room, changing into practice costume, then she was following them out upon the stage itself and there was Mr. Mowbray, a different Mr. Mowbray, not smiling, calling out clipped orders in his squeaky sing-song; and the five girls—young women, really—moving quickly, silent, alert to orders, and there she was, in among them, straining to catch on to what they did and do the same. And there wasn't time to understand what hidden danger lurked in this place that made them all so tense, so quick; there wasn't time to gloat, to look about, to say 'I'm in a theater, backstage,' there wasn't time for more than a hazy impression of the mysterious gloom of the vast bare stage, strange without scenery or lights, overhead a confusion of hanging things, beyond the unlit curve of footlights, the dark yawning cavern of the empty auditorium.

And then, abruptly, approval. "You'll do. You can go on tonight. Miss Jackson, come early and give her a hand, make-up and all that."

And she was swept along in the hurry of the girls, back to the dressing room, out into the street.

It was evening, *the* evening, and hurry still going on. She was climbing up a staircase at Miss Jackson's heels, a wide circular staircase, a gigantic iron corkscrew. She was following Miss Jackson along a cement corridor, going into a dressing room, looking at a long shelf littered with make-up, a long mirror framed with light bulbs, six chairs drawn up to the shelf, and on the opposite wall, the splashes of color where costumes hung, yellow and sky-blue against white cement.

In a theater. Part of it. I'm on the stage. Tonight. . . .

"Hang your things here, this is Mae's place." Miss Jackson was unfriendly. "You a friend of Mowbray's? Or a relative, perhaps? He shoulda held Mae's place open, she's sick. Go on, take your clothes off. You step into it easy, joining a show that's running. Live with your folks?"

"With my mother."

Miss Jackson eyed Diana's clothes. "She rich?"

"Why, no."

"Who's the boy friend, then?"

"Boy friend? I haven't any, Miss Jackson."

A shrewder searching of the young face softened Miss Jackson's tone. "Maybe you're real, I dunno." She sat down beside Diana at the shelf. "Call me Babe. Now cold cream your face and then wipe it off, then grease paint over that, see? If you're as green as you look I'll give you a few tips might come in handy. Look out for Mowbray, he likes 'em young. He's got bad hand trouble and I wouldn't trust him in the dark. Mae coulda done with a little advice. She ain't sick, she's knocked up, and some people say Mowbray knows all about that."

"Knocked up?"

"Caught," Babe explained tersely.

But still Diana was puzzled. "Caught?"

"You being funny? Don't you know? I said Mae was in a family way. Aw Jesus, don't you know where babies come from?"

Shocked, Diana murmured, "Yes, I know. You mean she's pregnant."

"You know a lot, using doctor's words. Well, let me tell you it don't pay being kind to the men. Keep both your legs in one stocking. Now—blue over the eyes."

The strange talk went on and time was passing; excitement swelled, a slow deadening of perception. Other girls came in, undressed, sat at the make-up table, jabbered. Time was moving in a quickening flow, carrying Diana Heaton on to that

70

moment when for the first time she would step out upon the stage, and Diana was slowed up, numbed. Getting into costume, her fingers were clumsy with large hooks, her chest rising to a deep-drawn breath pushed against a weight, and all at once her stomach fluttered and sank. Babe was smirking at her queerly. Diana tried to smile. Her lips twitched, out of control.

"Come out in the hall and walk through the dance."

Diana opened her mouth but no words came out; her tongue lay swollen, muscleless. She followed Babe with legs that jerked queerly, she leaned dizzily against the wall of the corridor. The floor waved underfoot, the walls swayed; before her a young man ran down corkscrew stairs, revolving with sickening speed and crying loudly, "Fif Teen Mints! Fif Teen Mints!"

Babe's face came close, leering. "Buck up. Everyone gets stage fright. You ain't got nothing to worry about." She patted Diana's shoulder and instantly Diana loved her. "Go on, walk through the dance."

Dance?

Babe showed her. It came back to mind. The jerky legs would take orders. But. . . .

"Come out in the flies, get an idea of the set." Babe moved off along the corridor, Diana following, not knowing where. They stepped out into a dark place, solid floor giving way to metal grill, and Diana lurched giddily for a railing. Through a tangle of ropes they looked down at the stage, thirty feet below, now swarming with activity. "That's the entrance we go on—where that bunch light is—don't bump into it, it's hot. There's the tormentor downstage, framing the wings. Beasely—that's our stage manager—stands there, giving the cues and ready to jump on your neck. Remember, we move down on the apron when we enter—that's off the groundcloth and it's slippery. Those is flats they're steering into place and lashing together—mind you don't trip on the braces. That's the backdrop coming down—see the sandbags riding up to balance it? If one of those ever drops on you it's blackout and finaly."

71

So many things could happen to you in this strange place, so full of bustle. If only the routine of the dance would not fade from mind. . . . Babe was rambling on. Diana tried to cling to her words, stay with them, but the sickening waves of excitement came, overwhelming her with fright. This, she believed, was very, very wrong—to be scared now when she had her chance; she ought not to be *scared*—and she was. Black, unthinkable disaster was right before her and time was racing. Any minute now. And there was no escape, she could not get out of this. Somewhere in the audience sat Mother.

The call-boy's voice echoed out from the corridor. "Overchure!"

"Come along. We go on first you know."

Babe was leaving her, Babe must be followed. Now, in a few minutes . . . Thought drowned in a swirl of shameful, cowardly, black agony. What followed was a blur of movement, meaningless, disconnected as though a light flashed on and off. She was one in a stream of people going downstairs for a long time, round and round; strange, jostling people with inhuman painted faces that chattered and grimaced, costumes vivid as parakeets; shrieking color, orange by green, yellow by pink, swishing and flashing. Babe disappeared—where? The archaic terror of a lost child in an unknown place struck at Diana and when Babe's voice said, "Right in back of you," Diana clutched her new friend's hand shamelessly. The stream of people came out on the level, poured along, spreading and thinning in the shadows of the wings. Babe pushed, then pulled her to a stop. Music was playing someplace, a long way off.

I've got to do it. I've got to.

A man's voice hissed a warning, "Curtain rising." The music swept closer.

I've got to. . . .

A girl in front of her began a shuffling movement. A prod struck her sharply between the shoulder blades. Diana moved forward, dancing, passing into a brilliancy of blinding light— and nothingness.

72

And Babe was squeezing her arm, saying, "Okay, sister" and they were back in the wings and it was over. . . .

But what. . . .

"Babe, I—I don't remember anything—what did I do—"

"You didn't miss a trick. You even smiled. Sort of stiff, but okay. Hey, where you think you're going? We gotta hang around and walk on with the mob in the finaly of the scene. Want to watch Fleurette's solo dance?"

"I—could I—just for a minute—sit?"

"Sure. See the prop-box up there, backstage in the corner? I'll call you."

Sitting alone in the dim corner, Diana considered the miracle and came slowly to herself. She passed into heartfelt rejoicing and from that into feeling quite cocky. I did it. I did it somehow. I even smiled. Sue saw me. Tomorrow night I'll really smile.

A man was walking toward her on short stumpy legs. She stood up, eager. "How was I, Mr. Mowbray?"

"Missed it, my dear, came in as the dance ended. But that chap Beasely says you'll do. Come up to the office tomorrow and the girl will have a contract for you."

This was the friendly man of the first meeting. Diana answered with a prepared speech Sue had suggested, "I'm grateful for the start you've given me. Some day I'll be famous and you'll be glad you helped me."

He cast a look downstage; no one was looking. He moved closer, pinched her cheek. And there she stood, unflinching, with the same doll-happy smile. What an intriguing, tempting innocent this young bit was. How far can I go. Mowbray shot another guarded glance to where figures stood by an entrance, looking out upon the set. Quickly, he slipped an arm about the young slim body, pulled it up against his own and squeezed it there. Just for a moment; someone might look; this was not the time, the place. He released her, purring, "You're a pretty thing."

She knew now. The talk of how actresses became famous flashing into mind, Diana gaped at him. It had not occurred

73

to her as possible that anyone so old, ugly, flabby, would attempt a lover's role; even when he had pinched her cheek she had only thought he liked her; most people did. But he meant something else . . . this old man. . . .

Her amazement intrigued him more, a verification of her innocence. He wanted another feel of the virginal body squeezed against his own, but downstage a figure stirred, looked his way. He stepped back, assuming the impersonal, told her "See you in the office, my dear," and stumped briskly away.

Diana sank down on the box, weak-kneed. Everything was coming at her so fast she couldn't think. What was going to happen next? It was true then, how women on the stage got ahead. And she had been picked. Surely Mr. Mowbray did not fall in love with everyone, he would not pinch and hug Babe, certainly. But he had chosen her. It was a sign. Fame would follow. But . . . what did it mean. . . .

Ideas and sensations seethed together. The ambition Mrs. Heaton had so nurtured saw in this the imminence of fame, a cause for jubilation. But there was no joy. The physical memory of that man's body pressing upon her was an assault that roused abhorrence.

And still there was no time to think. Babe was walking up, stony-faced.

"I seen you giving Mowbray the come-hither. Jesus, I didn't think you was that kind. I oughta known they don't make virgins anymore. Come on, make this finaly so I can wash my hands of you."

"Babe—you've been so kind—I hope—"

"Aw shut up. You're just like all the other bitches in this burley-cue, just one more, that's all."

5

DIANA HAD gone on the stage.

The Heatons talked about it, lowering their voices. It was just what you would expect from Harriet, an unstable wife, a flighty mother. This was family disgrace perpetuated into another generation; this was a severing of ties. Discussion brought decision; a letter must be sent, registering disapproval, making severance quite clear. Obligation of any sort was canceled by this violation of family integrity.

"Oh, it is?" laughed Mrs. Heaton, tossing her head and throwing the letter to the floor. "Who cares? Diana, you're going to rise to heights the Heatons never dreamed of! Wait until you're famous and then they'll be wanting you to recognize them!"

Alf was enthusiastic. This defiance of the family made him laugh and slap his leg. It set him up considerably. He took to crowing about my little girl who's on the stage in New York. He managed to escape from the watchful eyes of the family and maneuver a binge that went on for days in every speakeasy he could win access to, and he wept joyfully into his potion of rot-gut at this resurrection of his own wasted talents.

He wrote quite a touching letter to Diana, the first one he had ever written her, and after several drafts the handwriting looked fairly steady; he had a unique and distinguished handwriting ornamented with many flourishes, and he signed his name Alfred Harrison Heaton.

The letter amused Mrs. Heaton, though really there should have been at least a line of congratulation addressed to her. She pointed out the omission to Diana and so Diana did not answer.

Luke marched up the room, wheeled, marched back again, up and down, up and down.

At last his wife dropped her darning to her lap. "Well, why don't you put your foot down? Why don't you stop it? Tell her to come home and stay where she belongs. Stop sending her money to do as she pleases. Hattie's no sense about money or anything else. Landsakes, I sold eggs at two cents the dozen and thrift is good. Diana on the stage! It's not right."

Up and down, reply considered, words weighed and gravely spoken. "Mightn't do any good telling Hattie what she'd ought to do, Lucy." His tone was mild. "Sometimes I figure we were wrong in stopping her from singing. Hattie's set to have her own way in this and there's no sense making things hard for her."

Stubborn, same as Hattie and a woman might as well save breath. "That child's only fourteen and Hattie hasn't got the sense of a three-year-old. They'll get into trouble, see if they don't."

That was what Luke feared. And yet. . . . "Diana's smart, Diana's a good girl. She'll look after her mother. She'll come out on top."

What nonsense—a child looking after her mother! Mrs. Fletcher shook her head and sighed audibly in disapproval.

Luke continued his trudging. Yes, Diana was smart; a steady head on the youngster, a good girl, obedient, loyal.

Rod walked alone in the park after school, seeking comfort in the solitude of trees and sky and water. Matted grass underfoot gave off a stiff crunch, the ground frozen hard. Ahead, a row of trees, evenly spaced, starkly artificial, cried out for summer foliage in the way wild growth never would.

One must be patient; nature is patient, nature too is waiting, waiting through the long hard winter for spring's coming. Someday I can be with Mother always.

Patient, yes. But reconciled? No. Sis does as she pleases. She has Mother all the time, does anything she likes.

Bracken, ungroomed brush, less accurate trees, gave the eye

reward. Fretwork of dry branches, withes of yellow and red and olive against grey-dark trunks, color soothingly softened in a world of wintry grey. He passed through underbrush fending tenderly with a mittened hand. Wind met him on the promenade, lashing sharply. Above grey tumbling water, Lake Michigan smoking with frost, a slate-grey sky with fast flying whitish scud. The biting cold, the lashing sting of the wind, was flagellation of the spirit, sobering, so much to be endured, and God is with the meek, the humble.

A gull tore by, sliding up the wind. . . . Mother stands in the loft in Frostburg, radiant, angelic, mouth sprung wide, throat pulsing as the hymn pours forth. . . . He squeezed his eyes shut, clearing them of the film of tears.

Why doesn't Mother want me with her? That was the wounding, recurrent question.

He began to shiver in the raw east wind and turned homeward. Not be late to dinner; show obedience and a meek spirit. . . . What kind of lives do they really live in a New York boarding house and Sis upon the stage. . . .

Granma met him at the door. "My, you're froze by the look of you! Got a good appetite?" She was fond of the boy; she liked him best.

He knew that, and put an arm about her thick middle, pressing thankfully, answering with cheer. "I'll eat everything you've got, Granma. My, something smells good!"

He hoped God watched, noted and approved. Patience, humble in spirit, devout.

Mr. Mowbray had not been in the office when Diana called for her contract. Then word went round that he had gone to England to do a production there. Diana settled down to a rapturous enjoyment of this new life, the being in a theater, part of a big, artistic spectacle, the all-too-short moment of actual work upon a stage. Mother was so proud, so happy, and it was such fun to bring her home the salary, to buy her presents. They had moved to a different boarding house; there was no more of Hodges, no more of drinking; it was the way Diana had known it would be. Her ambition grew; she practiced dancing for hours, Sue sitting at the rented piano playing for her, helping with suggestions. Long happy weeks went by. And then—

The production was closing, going on the road. Word spread that Mowbray had come back to whip the show into shape for the tour. There would be cuts in the scenes, changes in the cast. The solo dancer was not going on the road.

"Mr. Mowbray, Miss Heaton wants to see you."

He couldn't place the name.

"One of the dancers in *The Lotus* show."

Ah, the rosy-cheeked child. "Send her in. And tell me when old man Block's out of conference. Come in, Miss Heaton."

Diana entered; the secretary closed the door, shutting her in. She came pluckily to stand before the desk and ask, "May I do Fleurette's solo on the road? I can do it, Mr. Mowbray."

In the swivel chair, tilting back, legs dangling, "The solo? We were thinking of cutting that out, my dear."

"Oh, please don't, please! Please let me do it!"

"Sit down, my dear." He reflected; the solo was a pretty bit, helped the scene; she would do it for half Fleurette's salary. Plans were not going smoothly, Block was uncertain what he wanted; *The Lotus* might end up in the junk pile of Cain's warehouse instead of going on the road.

"Please, Mr. Mowbray, please!" Diana sat forward, begging.

Had she been fooled with in his absence, had some man got at her? He slid out of his seat, his lips held in a smile, advancing, laying his hand upon her shoulder. She did not flinch; her eyes wide, intent upon his face. His hand stole lower, touched her breast. The girl's head dropped; there was a faint shiver in her body, that was all. His hand moved to her chin, lifted her head. Confusion in her eyes and blood in her face, she tried to look at him, lips wavering, striving to smile. He drew her to her feet and pressed the young, unresisting body against his own. "Be nice to me if you get your dance?" He squeezed her cautiously, not wanting a scene

78

in the office. "Be nice to me, eh?" It was a playful purring.

Helplessly, Diana watched his face, finding no words with which to answer. Having come this far the rest was fate, and a solo and fame waited just a little way ahead.

Mowbray squeezed a little tighter and ran his tongue along his lips, moistening the held smile. "Don't be afraid of me. I won't hurt you. You show me that dance in rehearsal tomorrow and if you can do it you shall have it. That's what you want, isn't it? And if I give you what you want, you give me what I want, eh? Fair enough? You and I'll run off by ourselves some afternoon this week to a hotel. What do you say?"

Diana could say nothing.

"If you want the dance, my dear," he purred, warning.

A knock came on the door and Mowbray stepped away from her. The secretary looked in to say, "Mr. Block's out of conference now."

He was brief, business-like, dismissing Diana. "Very good, my dear, we'll see the dance tomorrow."

Diana drifted to the door, got away.

"Preposterous!" Mrs. Heaton sprang out of her chair and came to a tense stop, staring at her daughter. "Do you mean to tell me—? Oh, out of the question! What are you talking about!"

Sue was going to be unreasonable, hard to handle. Diana was dismayed; she had been hoping for her mother's support in this, she badly felt the need of it. But if Sue was going to make it harder still. . . . Diana pumped up courage and stood her ground, prepared to fight for Sue's own good as best she could. After all, Sue wasn't always consistent, she was temperamental and that must be taken into account. But wasn't this thing that she proposed what Sue actually wanted her to do since it led on to fame? Diana had thought it out and reached what seemed to her a sound if difficult decision. "Now Mother, we knew it would be like this, you said so in the first place. This was all settled when you said I could go on the stage."

For a moment longer Mrs. Heaton continued to stare at her daughter with the stunned look of one seeing metamorphosis take place, then covering her face with her hand she drooped, shaking her head. Let my Diana sleep with a man I've never even seen? It was overwhelming, incredible, and there Diana stood, as cool as you please, blandly proposing— Oh, it had all sounded so different talking of a vague future, but that future had skidded into the present with fantastic speed. Oh Lord, the career only just begun and so promising, such an artistic production and already the chance of a solo. And the family had been told. . . . Distraught, she made fitful moves about the room and fell back gloomily into her chair.

"There, dearest, you'll make yourself sick fretting over things you don't need to. Can't we talk this over calmly? You know I'll do anything you say."

Yes, they were only talking and Diana would do as she was told. But the comfort of that thought was canceled by the responsibility it imposed upon the woman, and Mrs. Heaton's foot tapped irritably upon the floor. Such a decision—so much at stake. Still, this was as it should be, the girl confiding everything, wanting to talk it over. Her mother should think for her; so many mothers of famous people had the credit coming to them. She granted Diana's plea for reasonable discussion and answered quietly. "You're so young. You're only a child."

Her mother's calm brought needed reassurance to the girl. Diana sat down on the bed, asking with a show of cheer, "What difference does that make? I can't waste time if I'm going to get ahead."

But Mrs. Heaton's calm was brief. She drummed her fingers on the arm of the chair. "Diana, did that beast say you had to?"

Her daughter got up and walked over to the window. Why couldn't Sue see it wasn't as though she *wanted* to, and make

80

it easy? She drew again on resolution, knowing the supply had limits. "Yes, he did. It's—conditional."

Still drumming, the woman snapped, "You can get a solo some place else."

Diana turned to face her. "No, Sue, I might not, not right away. You know how people are about artistic dancing. There aren't many openings for it. The theater was half empty at Ruth St. Denis's performance. I've got my chance now. Why should I throw it away?"

"You're terribly anxious to throw yourself away!"

Shocked and hurt by the irritable, unjust words, Diana retreated to her seat on the bed, silent. Mrs. Heaton swung one leg over the other, her hands gripping the chair arms, her head sunk. Silence lengthened, each thinking back and ahead, each profoundly disturbed by this first threat of disagreement between them.

Diana rankled under the unreason of Sue's attitude; Sue was no ordinary mother who believed in the conventions; why should she now, all of a sudden, behave like one? She thought of Sue in the taxicab with Hodges, drunk, having her face slapped. . . . That was the awful past that must be fled at any cost. Maybe Sue didn't realize how bad it had been, seeing that degeneration going on. I've got to look after her, the girl reasoned, that's my duty. Of course it isn't easy to be famous but I can make her happy if I am. Go on the road now doing a solo, prove I can do it, and Mr. Mowbray will give me a solo in New York when I come back. . . . The girl held as resolutely as she could to this line of thought, approving it as sensible; thought that put a stop to imagination and shut out the unwanted intrusion of Mowbray's image that could come so woundingly upon her if vigilance relaxed. If Sue thought her anxious! Oh, he wasn't at all what she had so vaguely imagined when they first talked of sacrifice; then it had been loftly somehow, on a noble plane. But Mowbray—he must not be dwelt on for a moment, no, only on what he stood for, a being who held open the door through

81

which she must surely go to win that fame which would bring such immediate happiness.

Yet. . . . She would have liked to tell it all to Sue, just how she felt; to have the solace of Sue's perfect understanding and her counseling. The girl looked across at her mother, yearning for her help, half of a mind to give way to that strong impulse. But there had been so many times when Sue was not herself, when Diana had been forced to take on responsibility; more and more the girl had come to shelter the woman, sparing her what worries could be dealt with single-handed. Now that Sue was so distressed, was this the time to burden her further? To do so seemed selfish and unkind.

Diana had no clear idea of what it would be like to go with the man to a hotel; she was not even sure of what he meant to do to her, confused by his talk of not being afraid. But, high-minded, innocent, by nature confident and full of trust, she could assume that at the worst the experience could be endured, and once done, effaced from mind. That it was wrong did not enter her head; right and wrong in this modern world she shared with Sue were not fixed by standards of conventional morality; right and wrong to Diana were clearly seen as what was good or bad for Sue. Her dread of Mowbray was instinct, not reason; that dread came up from the depths of her being, rising in recurrent waves of abhorrence so that even now, arguing with Sue in favor of this proposal, her courage shook and her intention wavered.

Mrs. Heaton was torn between two worlds, the one in which she had been reared, and the one she had come into, knowing Chris. At one moment, consideration of this thing her child proposed was monstrous, sinful, and in the next she wondered if she were being weakly sentimental, old-fashioned. Diana must be somebody, that was imperative. Yet, when it came to this, her own daughter, her loved baby. . . . Diana was too young, too innocent to realize what this meant; Diana's whole life might be ruined by such a step. But would it not be ruined if her career was interfered with? Wasn't that exactly what Papa had done to her with all his prating talk

82

about 'nice young ladies' not getting mixed up with stage folk? Mrs. Heaton did not want her daughter to be a 'nice young lady' and undergo the bitter and corrupting heartache she herself had known. No, she wanted freedom for her daughter, freedom and a career—that was what counted, that alone could bring the rich, rewarding happiness. It *was* stupid to hesitate, to make a fuss; if this were circumvented now what was it but postponement; surely this very situation would arise again, and this, right now, this might be Diana's chance. But still . . . her baby. . . .

It was so hard to think. Had there been a time when her mind worked smoothly, making clear and accurate decisions by a precise measurement of right and wrong? That time was gone; her thoughts were in a muddle, and beneath them lay the fierce, urging desire; Diana must be famous.

The short February afternoon was waning. Diana, glancing across the room, a fugitive from her own thoughts, saw how shadows hollowed her mother's cheeks, deepened the lines of worry, aged her. The girl went swiftly to her, knelt before her chair. "Sue, if you think it's wrong—"

At that moment Mrs. Heaton was angry with Diana for making her decide; if only she did not have to know about this! "Wrong? I don't know what to think! Who does? The whole world's mixed up, people debunking everything! I used to go to church and believe in that, I used to think a woman should obey her father and respect her husband, I used to think a woman who had affairs was bad—and it's all toppled now. I don't know what to believe!"

Diana pinned her down. "But you do believe that I should have a career?"

"Yes," Mrs. Heaton admitted, still vehement, "I do. But when it comes to this—!"

Diana lifted responsibility from her mother. "Then let me decide. I'll do what I think is right."

The woman gathered the kneeling girl into her arms in a rush of love; she wanted the communion, the reassurance of embrace, the hard pressure of her child's head against her breasts. They were pals; whatever happened, this must endure. But as though flesh had its own wisdom, out of touch came augury of evil, and guilt grew strong upon her. "No, you're too young to make such a decision! I should forbid it." She turned her daughter's face up to her own. "Diana, do you *want* to do this thing?"

The truth came out. "No, I don't. I—I just think I should. No. I don't want to."

That was not the answer Mrs. Heaton had expected; she had hoped Diana's reply would set her conscience wholly at rest. Out of this unpleasant surprise, a new train of thought started up—suppose, suppose it was Diana who decided to back out of this, let the chance slip. . . .

She rose abruptly and fell to pacing back and forth, fingers knotted together under her chin, thinking, thinking. The decision must be hers; that could not be escaped. Oh, this was suffering, a suffering Diana could not guess until she had a daughter of her own! Not many mothers would go through ordeal like this to save a girl's career.

But was there anything more wonderful in life than to be able to do the thing you were cut out to do? Diana was made to dance, that had been in her from the start. The day would come when she would realize what it meant to have a mother who pushed her forward, helped her. . . . If I could stand in in her shoes, spare her—

Stand in her shoes? Have a career to fight for? I'd be the happiest woman in the world! I could face anything for that.

The end justifies the means. Of course it does. Success is for the bold, for those who dare defy convention. Once on top, who will question? Could any woman with a successful career fail to be happy? Success. . . . She saw it all in swiftly passing visions; Diana's name in lights; Diana coming through a stage door, flowers in her arms; Diana in a stunning evening dress, the center of a smart salon; Diana sailing for the capitals of Europe. Ah yes, and Chris—Chris would read of this, he would come to the stage door, send in his card. But there would be no time for Chris; he would stand

84

in a crowd looking on from afar at the radiant, glorious, triumphant being who was Mrs. Heaton's daughter.

She checked her pacing, her eyes went back to the girl. Diana was still on the floor beside the chair. Huddled there, the girl looked spiritless, ambition gone out of her. It was a frightening aspect. "Diana, get up off the floor! My goodness, you're a young lady now!"

Diana stumbled to her feet, perplexed by the nervous rasp in her mother's voice, apprehensive for the woman; Sue was all upset. "Mother, let's not talk about—"

Mrs. Heaton came up close to her. "Do it. Go ahead and do it. You said you thought you should. Then why do you hesitate? How can you ever be anybody if you waver?"

Diana looked into the bright eyes, the set face, and knew there was an end to talk. She drew a deep breath and answered softly, slowly, "All right. I will."

Mrs. Heaton turned away from her.

"After all," Diana said, still speaking slowly, "I'm sure Grampa would approve."

Mrs. Heaton spun about crying out in horrified consternation, "Papa! Are you mad?"

"Oh, I didn't mean literally, Mother, of course not. Just the idea. A person being ambitious, aiming to get to the top, not giving up when the going gets hard—"

The woman cringed away. "Diana, you said not to talk about it!"

"All right, I won't." She cast about for some activity. "Let me dye your hair. Isn't Bob coming to New York this week end? You want to look pretty, don't you?"

Diana's quick resumption of the normal, her cheery air, made the woman stare again. How strong Diana seemed, how grown up. It was comforting to have a fearless, strong young woman for a daughter. She fell in with the suggestion, removing hair pins, releasing tumbling hair as she walked toward the light switch. Her hand upon it, she hesitated, holding back the light, reverting to the topic. "Diana—*no one must ever know.* Don't tell. Do you understand?"

The girl nodded, smiling, and went into the alcove to fetch the dye.

It was a mistake. A ghastly, hideous mistake.

Diana came back to her from that man, calamity in her face, speechless, so shaken that you would think the girl had barely managed to extricate herself from the wreckage of some frightful explosion. Diana was in a state of hysterical collapse and she behaved like a terrified child. Mrs. Heaton had to put her to bed and there she lay, moaning and tossing, her face covered with her hands, unwilling or unable to say more than 'It was awful,' and she said that over and over and over again. Mrs. Heaton nearly went out of her mind. What could that man have done to her?

For two days the girl stayed in bed, not caring what happened at the theater. But with the ceaseless, penitent, nursing care her mother lavished on her, she grew gradually more responsive, her spells of silent, stricken brooding lightened; and with youth's resiliency, she even made attempts to smile at Sue. On the third day she was up, dressed, and moving about the room.

Yet, bad as all this was, an even more astounding blow fell. Diana did not get the solo.

There was no solo. *The Lotus* was not going on the road. It was closing in New York. And there was no word from Mr. Mowbray of another engagement.

This news came on the fourth day, just when Mrs. Heaton had decided to broach the matter of Diana's work, for after all, the girl must think of that.

But now this—

Mrs. Heaton was stunned, infuriated. Why, what Diana had gone through could not be for nothing! Only success could justify what had been done. Success? Where was it now? She turned upon her daughter. "What does it mean? You told me he said—Oh God in hell, I'll never understand this! He had you—and it didn't mean a thing."

Diana was huddled in the chair, legs tucked under her,

curled into a ball, withdrawn and silent. Eyes down, she did not follow the movements of the distracted, raging woman. Her thought was separate and traitorous to Sue's. She could not help it, she was glad, glad; relief was an expanding and ungovernable flood of feeling. It was over; she would not ever have to see that man again nor hear his voice nor dread his touch. Over. . . . But it was not over; still the memory came, possessing her, she was back in that experience, again living through it. . . . A strange hotel room, green shades pulled down, white daylight leaking in, too bright, too bright; the horror of that ugly naked man gone crazy; no escape; eyes shut, his breath remains, his voice goes on; ears plugged, his hands go free; assault, pain, nausea. . . .

"Diana, you must have botched it from the start. I thought that you were smart. You had your chance—he *was* interested —and you made nothing of it. Any clever woman would know how to handle a man, get what she wanted—and you got nothing. There must be some other solo, something he could offer you! Or maybe he's nobody at all and you should have known that in the first place." She stopped short, turning searching eyes upon her daughter. "Maybe you're not smart. You used to be. Maybe you're not anymore. They say precocious children peter out."

"Don't look at me like that." Diana began uncurling from her chair, rising slowly. "Mother. Don't. I'll get another engagement."

"Not that way, you won't!" Mrs. Heaton clutched her head, galvanized in a pose of furious despair. "You haven't sense enough to play the game. Oh God, it's all my fault, you're only a child, a stupid little child, I should have known, I should never have consented! This will haunt me all my life!"

"Don't Mother, *don't!*"

"Why, you're crying! Oh no, Dicky, don't cry! Oh, I've done wrong, terrible wrong!"

They were both weeping. They went into each other's arm and moved together to the bed, sat down, still crying.

Mrs. Heaton was the first to stop. She drew out her handkerchief and dried her eyes and wiped Diana's face. But then she again turned puzzled eyes upon her daughter. "I can't understand . . . if you had been smart. . . ."

Diana scrambled to her feet. "No—you mustn't look at me like that! Mother, Mother, say you love me!"

The passionate violence of the demand startled Mrs. Heaton. "Why, Diana. . . ."

"Say you love me! Say it!"

The woman moved to caress, to quiet the girl, but Diana backed away, crying out her demand. "Say it, say it!"

Mrs. Heaton was alarmed. "I love you, Diana, you know I do!"

With that, Diana consented to fondling, but her abject weeping continued. "You're only saying it to please me. You think I'm stupid."

"Oh Chick, no. I only meant in this. Not *love* you? Why, you're out of your head!" She reverted quite easily to the role played back in nursery days, the guardian mother who kept all evil from her child, asserting that tranquil authority as though nothing had come to trouble their lives. "Sh, dear, kiss Mother."

Responsive to that familiar tone, Diana quieted, the kiss given. But uncertainty still lingered. She asked, "We're pals, aren't we?"

"We're pals, Dicky."

They made tea on the sterno stove. They decided they would go out to dinner and then to a concert. They were going to forget. Nobody would ever know. Diana would find another solo. Everything would be all right. Of course it would.

But Mrs. Heaton had to talk to someone. Things were in a disastrous state, Diana hunting about, not finding an engagement, getting nowhere, no salary coming in, the bill to the landlady mounting, and Papa had the audacity to write suggesting a return to his home. If only she had never written him about that solo on the road! But who could have foreseen—? How could Diana blunder so! The calamity preyed upon her; she could not comprehend just what had happened. She had to talk of it. And Bob, of course, would sympathize, would understand.

Mrs. Heaton found the place that Bob had taken her for dinner quite intriguing—such a cute, sophisticated little restaurant, Greenwich Village, candles on the tables and such amusing, wicked drawings on the walls—and the mood seemed perfect, warm and intimate; yes, she could confide in Bob.

But it was a blunder. Bob did not sympathize, he did not understand, he was simply horrid.

"You let that child—? Well, now you've done it. You've spoilt the lovely thing you made. She's through. You might as well throw her on the dump heap."

Mrs. Heaton gasped. "Why, how can you say—"

"I'm only saying what the world will say. Who'll give a damn for the girl now? Do you think any decent man or woman will respect her, take an interest in her? It'll mark her. And I'll tell you another thing—the day will come when you'll wake up to what you've done and you'll come to hate the sight of your own daughter."

"Why, how can you—"

"We hate those we've harmed, and you've done harm to her."

Mrs. Heaton gathered purse and gloves and mustered dignity for a withdrawal. "I'm glad to know what you actually believe. Then I suppose our intimacy is a sinful affair? I thought that you were modern, broad-minded!"

Bob was sputtering. "If you can't see the difference between an affair that's based on mutual attraction, two adults, old enough to choose for themselves, and letting an innocent child sell herself for profit—"

Mrs. Heaton rose, holding beautifully to dignity. "Good night, Bob."

She would never, never see *him* again. She told herself he was a hypocrite and a fool, and she wept the hot, scanty tears of anger when she was alone. That he could speak so brutally of Diana, that he could prophesy—

But Mrs. Heaton was scared. If Bob could talk like that, Bob who was intelligent. . . . He had pierced through her new modernity. The old self in her answered him, granted his right to condemn, revile. The sense of guilt which it had hitherto been possible to lull, now grew into a torment that could not be endured. No, it could not even be admitted; she walked away from it, blotted it out. When Mowbray came to mind, her thought swung instantly in another direction, caught at something else. That calamity had never happened.

It had begun again. Now there was no knowing when you climbed the worn, carpeted stairs, when you laid your hand upon the knob, pushed open the door, what waited there inside, Sue drunk or Sue herself.

It was to be expected. Diana took the blame. Of course Mother was unhappy now.

She sat on the hall steps outside the door listening to the racket of Sue's wild crying-talk die down as the stuff the doctor gave to quiet her began to take effect. He was a good doctor, he seemed to know what to do.

An idea came to her; she was astounded that she had never thought of it before. As the thin, tall man with the black beard came out into the hall she rose with an anxious eagerness. "Dr. Minelli, isn't there some cure, some treatment you could give her? She's not a drunkard, she hates drink, she only drinks in spells when she's unhappy. Months go by when she won't touch a drop and then she begins again and it creeps up on her and gets bad and then she stops again. She always wants to stop. It isn't that she likes to drink."

The man's dark eyes were sad. "I cannot cure her."

There was a chill finality in the simple answer. Diana protested. "There must be something you could do!"

"She is a periodic drinker. I can give you my opinion—she will never be any better."

Long after he had gone down the stairs and the street door

had shut behind him, Diana stayed motionless in the dim hall that smelled of cabbage and of furnace heat, hearing the doom that had been spoken; 'She will never be any better.'

A lie. He had no right to say it. He doesn't know my mother.

Diana leaned against the wall, grief-burdened, without tears. Oh, Mother, Mother, Mother!

They were poor. Figured out on paper, what Grampa sent should have been enough and undoubtedly he thought it was, but there was an expenditure he did not know about in the bottles that accumulated on the closet shelf. But it would never do to ask Grampa for more money; he might tell them to come home.

They moved to a cheaper boarding house. The place depressed Sue and the food gave her indigestion. Sue could not buy the pretty clothes she wanted for herself and for Diana. They could not go to a theater or a concert when they pleased. Often toward the end of the month there wasn't even carfare. They had no friends. Mrs. Heaton would have been ashamed to see them.

And it lay with Diana to change all this, to get a solo dance, be somebody; to toss a pay envelope into Sue's lap, to bring the shine of hope back into her eyes and brighten her step.

But there was no solo to be had on Broadway. It was sought for daily in every office, in every agency; sought for at first with such a fierce resolve as to be almost joyful, but with summer merging into fall, resolve shifted to desperation; with fall drifting into winter, resolve became a shamed doggedness.

Broadway looked very different to Diana now, it had an ugly aspect. Resolved to leave no stone unturned, she hunted everywhere, going into the unsightly old buildings plastered with signs, traveling along the dingy rat-runs of inner corridors leading to agency doors, attending auditions in unswept rehearsal halls littered with cigarette butts. She heard queer honky-tonk jargon about classy flash-acts with fast-stepping girlies and a lot of flesh. She moved among a strange assortment all going the same rounds, brazen-faced girls with baby voices, men too nattily dressed who spoke in bland falsettos and ogled other men, imperious dowagers who rustled feather boas of a bygone age and talked with imitation English accents, shrill-voiced brats of five or six with permanent waves and indecently short dresses revealing scrawny legs. The world of make-believe, carried over into the actuality of getting a job, was tawdry, sordid, in the mass.

She encountered agents, casting directors; paunchy pale-faced men who leered, cautiously obscene, unwashed hands giving off the sporty flash of diamonds; men with dead-pan faces and the furtive, suspicious look of those who live by their wits and have only a limited supply; men who tried to stand too close, men with hands that had to be watched, men who tried to get you to step into an inner office. All men were suspect, she lived in hidden terror of them, even in the better offices where a man might seem to be a gentleman, speaking with courtesy; she shrank from everyone at the first hint of an advance upon her, and nervous, apprehensive, shrank where no offense was meant. No man could touch her, no man could come within a foot of her; panic stayed alive within her. Mowbray's image pursued and overtook her time and again, the revolting visual memory coming sharp and clear . . . the horror of that ugly, naked man gone crazy. And he had said he would not hurt her, he had said she need not be afraid. . . .

Time passing, she knew the increased misery of growing doubt. Was she indeed a fool? 'Precocious children peter out.' Mother was disappointed in her. The disappointment was big, it overlay their lives, altering them; it ate into Sue's heart, wearing her down like a physical affliction. The weight of guilt bore heavily on Diana; she was the cause of her mother's suffering. Sometimes Sue tried to give encouragement, saying gentle, patient things, but more often the woman eyed her, not saying what she thought. Worse still were the things Sue said when she was not herself. Well, of course what Sue said then should not be heeded, except that. . . .

Diana had heard it said that truth comes out in drink. To be called a fool over and over again. . . .

Oh, of course Mother loved her. But—not the same, not just the same. Something in the old intimacy had gone. There was no more of the gay, proud talk of Dicky, the winner, my girl who's going to be somebody, and what will Chris say. A rich undercurrent of sustaining belief no longer flowed from the woman to the child, and Diana felt as some shelled creature might from whom the protecting shell has been torn leaving raw flesh exposed and quivering with a hideous new sensitivity.

The hurt that she had suffered and was suffering worked upon her. Diana lost ease and serenity of manner, the happy confidence which Mrs. Heaton had so prized; she became afflicted with agonizing spells of shyness in which she felt that everything she said or did was wrong; dejection could come down upon her with a crushing force. With mounting intensity she came to hunger after belief, approval, love.

Why was it no one picked her out? Why was it that when she did get a job in some second-class night club it never lasted? How could it be that the very dances—yes, and better ones—that had so delighted Chris's friends on Hokomok were subjected now to ridicule? Why was it something to sneer at that she danced barefoot, or that she wore a Greek costume, or that she used classical music? The greatest artists of the dance had done the same.

The months were going by her, one by one. Diana saw them go with shame. But, scared and shy and wretched, she stuck at it, being Luke's granddaughter, bolstered by her memory of his iron strength and by the counsel he would have given; never say die; shiftless, no-count folks git nowheres, but if you got the will to do. . . . Voice out of the nineteenth century, it helped her somehow. And self-belief lived on, too deep-set to be extinguished even now. Feeble as it was, it came to flame in rare spells of lonely exaltation when her spirit stirred upward and she knew a high, moody, secret triumph, a brief certainty of destiny. A day would come when she would

93

dance upon a stage, dance gloriously; that power was in her.

But it was hard; to go on meeting insolent stares, bawling talk, suspected intentions of assault, the flat rejections that meant failure; worst of all were the bright spurts of hope, the long-sought interview with a big producer, the Come-back-on-Monday-I-can-use-you. . . . And Sue saying, Well, what happened? Why didn't something come of it? And not knowing the answer.

One day an agent, giving a negative shake of his head at sight of her familiar face, had a kindly impulse. "Say, why don't you wise up? No one's going to give you a solo when you only done one bit of line-work in a show that went to Cain's warehouse two years ago. No one wants that arty barefoot stuff. Why don't you get into the chorus with a big producer like Shultz? If you got any talent he'll see it and give you a bit and then you're started. I'm just telling you for your own good, girlie."

Diana walked home considering the advice. She knew how Sue would feel about it, horrified that her girl had sunk to this low level, but it might be true that this was a way to get ahead; then too there would be a salary and even a small one was better than none.

But stronger than all the reasoned arguments was the longing to be at work inside a theater, privileged to walk through a stage door, sit in a dressing room making up, to experience that exquisite tingle that came with the call-boy's cry of Overture, to be out upon a stage lifted up in the life-giving current of performance.

Diana walked in on her mother announcing, "Sue, I'm going to start in all over again, start at the bottom. I'm going in the chorus."

6

O F COURSE it was only chorus work and, as Sue said, that was about as low as you could go. You punched the time clock coming in and going out, and you were jammed into a crowded dressing room with a lot of brainless, excitable girls who had reached the height of their professional ambition in being in a Shultz chorus. Girls whose real ambition lay outside the theater in a world of men and money, who talked shamelessly about sex in a way Diana had never heard, who told dirty stories, who could swear like men and thought that smart; girls who thought her a fool for blushing, for being shocked, for not going with a man. In among all that lively and incessant chatter Diana's loneliness was acute.

Still, it was theater, it was being on the stage, having the barest toe-hold on a career. And it had the good and solid feel of active work; you rushed from one number to another, scrambling to make a costume change, muscles toned and springy from the fast routines. In the moments of a lull, a wait between numbers, you could stand in the dim, disciplined quiet of the wings looking out upon the stage, all flushed with the glory of luminous color, scheme of costumes against design of set bright as a painted illustration, hearing the rousing music of the orchestra, the swelling, gargantuan mob laughter from out front and the quick spatter of thickening applause; hearing along with that the brief, low-voiced orders given backstage, seeing the solitary figure of a strolling stagehand moving in the shadows, stepping over the cables that lay along the floor, feeding the bunch lights; seeing too the excitement of those privileged ones who held the stage alone and came off ecstatic after encores.

It was only chorus work of course, and it was tormenting to be one unit in a line of mechanical figures doing meaningless steps while in your heart the longing grew and grew to go out there upon the stage alone and dance, dance beauty and joy and hope—fine things that must not, must not be lost.

Would Shultz notice her? Would he pick her out from all the others? Would her chance come? If she worked hard, hard . . . . Ah, if only he would notice her.

Nick noticed; assistant director, kept on temporarily as stage manager while this show was but newly opened, there was nothing going on backstage he did not see. The running of this show through each performance was in his charge; Nick Allingham saw to it that it ran smoothly with speed and accuracy and sparkle, no letdown anywhere. He sized up the new kid who had come into the show since it opened. A-1 on looks any way you judged, face or figure, and a swell worker, digging right in, catching on quick, holding her own. But shy, shy as they come, shy and strange.

He saw how she slipped into the theater, slid along the passages, retreated into dark corners, backed away at an approach, striving to be invisible. And he saw the transformation that occurred the moment her line moved out before the audience; then she was a girl who tried in every way she could, outside of breaking rules, to attract attention to herself; a girl come suddenly alive, radiant and poised, a girl who never, matinee or night, let the work sag. Standing in behind the tormentor, alone and hidden in the shadow, it made him grin to watch her work.

Diana never looked in his direction if that could be avoided. She was so scared of him she hoped he wouldn't notice her. She heard the chorus girls speak of him with spite; they hated him; they said that he was mean, that he was hard, that he wouldn't let you get away with a thing, that he could bawl you out so it hurt. And Diana heard him for herself the time he caught a girl smuggling gin into the dressing room; she thought that she would die if she were ever spoken to as he had spoken to that girl—not shouting, not loud, but with such a cutting power of cold, furious contempt that the girl, one of the sauciest of the lot, had been reduced to tears, begging for her job before them all. But the begging hadn't done her any good; Nick said it wasn't the first time and fired her on the spot. Even in little things, in some chance slip, he was quick with reprimand. Diana moved backstage in consternation lest an unlucky moment come when she would be the one who forgot a headdress, put on the wrong shoes in a quick change, failed to step lively getting into line. Mr. Allingham was a dread figure; the power to take your job away was in the hands of this decisive, harsh young man.

And then one night he became a different person in her eyes. He was lounging beside the time clock when she came in, standing slack with that deceptive air of relaxation he could assume, out of which, she knew, could shoot a startling sharp call down. She gave a scant, hasty nod and was quick about slipping her card into the clock. She was scared when his hand reached out, took away the book that she was carrying. She had seen him take packages, examine them, but this—was there anything wrong with taking a book into the dressing room? Some rule she didn't know?

He merely wanted to see the title; *Crime and Punishment;* he handed it back and his eyes met hers, friendly; he even seemed to smile at her, pleasant-faced. "Good book." His attention left her, darting to a troop of girls entering in a noisy band.

Diana went lightly up the stairs, her face bright. It was approval. Yes, approval. And interest. He had wanted to know what sort of book she read. He had admired her taste. He did not think she was a fool.

After the long spell of loneliness and hurt and doubt kept hidden in her heart, this brief gleam of friendliness was enough to send her spirit soaring. Nick became a new being for her, wonderfully discerning.

Her make-up hurried, she came down into the wings ahead of time to stand at a distance, stealing glances at this person who had seen something in her to admire, making a study of him.

97

He was not reassuring to look at; now, giving orders to the crew, working along with the men, he seemed so much one of them, the fact that he was a man emphasized. He was tall and strong and lithe, quick in movement; black-haired and yet his eyes were light. She thought there was a dark look about him, as though anger could blaze out, and she thought pride would dominate, direct that anger, giving him a fearsome power. His dark suit was smartly cut and had a Broadway look, and he carried himself with the hint of a swagger. To be as strong and sure as he was . . . .

She was awed, disturbed, realizing what sort of being had bestowed his notice on her. It was a relief when the performance started and she could plunge into work. But the next night she came down early again, drawn to him. This time he was nowhere to be seen. She wandered toward the prop-room, meaning to stand against the wall out of the way of the last minute sorties of the stagehands.

The prop-room door opened smartly and Nick was right upon her, advancing. She side-stepped, expecting him to pass. He swerved toward her. "What else you like beside books?"

He was a man. He stood close. He had come upon her without warning. Her eyes were on his hands, the panic live within her. There was no time for intelligence to take control, inform her that there was no danger here, no intention of assault. A long struggling moment passed before she could summon wit enough to force out one word in answer. "Music."

"Music, huh? Play an instrument? Sing?"

She yearned with a swift, passionate desperation to make herself known to him, to look up, smiling, speaking with fluency. But the fright was too deep-set. He was a man; he stood close; she could not raise her eyes. It was an effort to say, "I dance."

He saw her confusion and that she was made miserable by it. Boy, was she shy!—made her turn red in the face even to speak. Well, he wasn't going to bother her if that's how she felt about it. Good-natured, he said, "Don't let it get you down, kid," and moved briskly off about his business.

'Don't let it get you down, kid.' Mockery, deserved. Now he knew she was a fool, a stupid, gawky fool. Diana remained standing where she was, head down, suffering. He hadn't meant any harm, no harm at all; he had again shown interest; friendship was possible between them. But not now. Now he knew. To have had a friend . . . . Yes, even if it was a man; someone to talk to, someone who thought that you were nice. And she had lost the chance of that. He would never speak to her again.

But the next night and the next, hope still lingered and longing made her daring; she put herself in way of notice, her courage screwed up to meet his eyes if he should choose to speak to her.

Performance after performance went by and Nick took not the slightest notice of her.

A week went by, and then rumor ran backstage which blotted out all thought of Nick—Shultz was out front, watching the show.

Was this the chance she had been hoping for? Would he single her out, come backstage, ask for her? She knew what Shultz looked like though she had never had a word with him, since one of his innumerable assistants had given her the job. Excitement racing through her veins, she flung herself into her work, knowing her worth lay there and not in any cleverness of talk, and in the intermission she hung about the wings, waiting to see that short, bulky figure, head thrust forward on a thick neck, come through the door that led in from the audience.

He did not come . . . .

The second act began. He might still notice, it was true, but it now seemed more unlikely than it ever had. Her hope had been so wild, so high, that disappointment very nearly broke her self-control; she had to bite her lips to keep tears back. But, numbers passing, disappointment veered into abandon; she didn't care; one day she would be famous, yes, one of these days.

The curtain slid down for the last time, the performance

over. It was such grand, sad confusion the way the show came to pieces after the curtain struck the floor, discipline broken, everything pulled apart. In the scramble of the assembled cast to get off the set at once, wedging through narrow entrances, ducking under braces, tripping over cables, Diana moved passively in the crowd, borne along by it. The brilliant lights went out in a wink; stagehands, uprooting bunch lights, unleashing flats, bearing off pieces of the set, ploughed through the crowd with warning shouts. Nothing was left of beauty or illusion or order, there was only a chaos of movement in dull lights, the music over. Diana remembered that it had come on to rain, cold, windy, March rain, and she had no umbrella.

Joe, the doorman, baggy and rheumatic, stood just inside the stage-door passage, giving a message to one or another of the cast as they went by. His eyes picked out Diana. "Miss Heaton, your mother's here."

Sue! Why, she never comes!—and in this rain . . . . Deviation from the normal could mean only one thing; in drink Mrs. Heaton was unpredictable. Diana bounded up the stairs, unfastening her costume as she went. Get out of here quick, get her away, no one must see. The costume dropped from her as she entered the dressing room and snatched up clothes; make-up came off in one hasty scrubbing smear. The girl moved so fast that she was running downstairs dressed for the street while stragglers were still coming up.

Mrs. Heaton sat on the chair Joe had vacated for her. Wet and bedraggled, water dripped from her hat, wisps of mahogany-colored hair had been whipped loose by the wind; her eyes glittered too brightly in a thin flushed face. At Diana's approach she smiled sentimentally, head dropped to one side, crooning, "My baby."

Diana thrust her card into the clock. "Hello, Mother." She had but one intense desire—get Sue away quick.

Joe shared Mrs. Heaton's sentimental mood. Leaning against

the wall making use of his spittoon, he told Diana, "You got the best stage-door Johnny any girl can have."

Couldn't he *see?* "Yes indeed. Ready, Mother? Let's go."

The woman rose reluctantly with a sweet smile for the nice old man; they had been having such a homey chat.

At that moment Nick's voice sounded right behind Diana. "Mr. Shultz wants to see you on stage."

The girl spun about, her breath drawn in a gasp, her eyes wide and shining.

Nick was looking at Joe. It was to Joe that he had spoken . . . .

And Joe was lumbering forward to the summons. And Nick had looked at Sue before he turned away, Nick who took in everything in a glance.

Why were they standing there? "Come on, Sue." Diana took her mother's arm.

But Mrs. Heaton had heard the magic name of Shultz. Mr. Shultz here? With an adroit wriggle she had freed her arm and was mincing in upon the stage where no outsider ever was allowed.

Horror-stricken, Diana felt herself towed after Sue, responsible for her, involved in God only knew what was to come. She shot one look ahead and saw how the group stood, Nick and Shultz and Joe, and dropped her eyes to Sue's heels.

Mrs. Heaton sailed right up to them. "I'm Diana Heaton's mother, Mr. Shultz." Her tone was playful, intimate. "I want you to keep an eye on my girl. She's going to be somebody, you'll see! She's going to make you all sit up and take notice!" With a shred of gay, unstable laughter and a toss of her dripping hat, Mrs. Heaton switched about, collided with her daughter, thrust an arm through the girl's and made jauntily for the stage door.

Diana felt as though the clothes had been torn from her back, as though she walked naked. The distance to the passage was a nightmare length, it did not seem that they would ever reach it and pass out of sight. This was the end of her, this was worse than bringing a bottle into the dressing room.

However had they both escaped immediate and blasting destruction? Sailing right up to Shultz—*Shultz*. Why, even stars, big people, waited for him to speak first! And Nick had seen it all. Oh, would he think her mother drunk or mad? Never a thickness of speech, never a reeling gait—drink didn't affect Sue the way it did others, she just acted crazy.

"I told him! You wouldn't think to introduce your mother in a thousand years. All *you* do is get in my way and bump into me. Awkward, gawky thing!"

Wind and rain met them on the sidewalk.

"Why didn't you introduce me, silly? Why did you hang back like a stupid nobody?"

There was no use explaining now how awful an act Sue had committed. Diana answered through clenched teeth. "He's a hard man to approach, Mother."

"I approached him, didn't I? You chicken-hearted ninny! No wonder you don't amount to anything."

Diana steered grimly for the nearest subway.

"Afraid of Mr. Shultz! You're no good, you're a fool. Where are you dragging me?" Mrs. Heaton baulked, coming to a stop.

People were hurrying by bent against the raw, wet wind. The sidewalk ran with water, glittered with the reflection of the bright lights. "Sue, it's raining. We can't stand here."

"*I* know it's raining—I can tell that for myself. I'm not going home. You might inquire before you start yanking me along with your brute strength. Home. I haven't any home." She stubbornly resisted the pressure on her arm, her face set in sulky grief.

At any moment Nick might come from the stage door, pass right by them. Diana choked down exasperation, trying to speak pleasantly. "Come on, Mother. People are looking at us."

Mrs. Heaton affected a biting incredulity. "My, you a famous dancer, afraid of being looked at!"

"You'll catch cold—"

"And die. Hurrah. Wouldn't that be fine? I'm going to Chris."

Chris! Oh, what next. "Sue dear, it's late, you don't know where he is."

"I do so, stupid. I called up his home. And where do you think—on Staten Island at a hotel called the Marine House. So there."

One of the stagehands ran by, coat turned up about his ears. "All right. We'll take a taxi to the ferry." Diana moved her mother to the curb and waved at passing cabs.

"We can't afford taxis. We're poor, we haven't any money." Fresh cause for grief brought tears; Mrs. Heaton wept bitterly without restraint. "Mama hates me. Mama won't let Papa send me a decent income."

Cab after cab went by, occupied, and then one swung in, throwing up a sheet of gutter water. But the woman held back, suspicious. "Where are you taking me?"

Diana was savagely sweet. "Wherever you want to go, dear. Get in."

Mrs. Heaton addressed the driver plaintively. "I want Christopher."

"Yes, Mother, Christopher." Diana told the man, "South Ferry."

Mrs. Heaton crept in and huddled in a corner. Diana took her place beside her, falling back with a stifled groan of thankfulness as the cab spurted forward. What blessed privacy to be in the dark, jolting cubicle! She was drenched; water dripped down her neck, her coat had the smell of wet wool, her skirt was clammy, her shoes sopping. But what did that matter? Her job was gone. It only remained to face the bawling out from Nick, the actual firing.

And he had seen her mother drunk. . . .

She was wishing that she could have denied her mother in that dreadful sortie, that she could have walked away, disowned her; the wish went further—if only Sue would be like other mothers, grow old, behave sedately, be respectable.

With a shock Diana awoke to the treachery of the thought.

Ashamed of her own mother? Ashamed of Sue? Sue, whom she adored with all her heart? There was no one in the world finer than Sue, no one more sweet or wonderful. And no one more in need of love and pity. To judge Sue on what she did when she was not herself was neither kind nor just. That was what the world did, smirking, condemning, thinking a drunken woman fair game for all the cruel inhumanity of ridicule and censure. Ashamed of Sue? No. If right now she had to go through that ordeal again, she would walk head up, defiant, meeting Nick's eyes or Shultz's. I love my mother. I know the beauty of her soul, I know the pathos of her life. Who dares condemn her? She's my mother and I love her and I'm not ashamed.

But this was no way to look after her. Sue was soaking wet. "Mother, we should be going home."

"I want Chris."

"I know, dear, but you can't have him."

"Ah, how cruel you are to say that to me! You don't know what love is."

The cab sped on, going fast through darkened streets, once freed of theater traffic. After a time, a small obstinate voice announced. "I want to get out. No air in here."

"I'll open the window. . . . Better, Sue?"

"No air I tell you."

"Yes, dear, I opened—"

"I want to get out!" It was a willful shriek.

"Sue—you can't. You're better here. You might get into trouble in the subway."

"I'm in trouble now with a fool for a daughter. Cheap little chorus chippy! So happy because she's in the chorus— all she wants in life—all she'll ever amount to. Let me out!"

"We're nearly there."

"I want to get out!" The words were screamed.

Calm. Calm was necessary. When Sue got into a tantrum— "Dearest—"

"No one ever bossed me!"

Diana caught a small, hot hand reaching for the door. "You open that while we're going, you'll fall out and be killed. Dearest, you're drunk."

"I'm not!" shrieked Mrs. Heaton, "I'm driven crazy with misery with a fool for a daughter! Ah, ah, ah, God in hell, let me out!"

Go on like this, she'll be arrested. Sue was plunging violently, struggling for the door. Something had to be done, done quickly. Saying "Stop it, Mother, stop it," Diana, distracted, tried to hold the necessary calm. Make her stop, make her behave, you've got to look after her.

The crazy screaming, the almost uncontrollable tussling, rattled her, loosened impulse. Her flat hand falling on her mother's cheek informed her instantly of wrong; even as her palm struck, flesh rebelled, trying to pull back.

My God I slapped her.

Sue staring, mouth wide, the fingers of one hand crawling up her cheek, verifying, her face twisting, and the whisper, "Dicky, you hurt my sore tooth."

What have I done what have I done plunge into oblivion never come up oh God I hit my mother. The reeling panorama of dark glistening streets, oncoming pillars of the elevated, green sparks from a thundering train overhead, dissolved in a void and there was nothing but that whisper, Dicky you hurt my sore tooth.

A lurch of the cab threw them together. They were clinging, saying incoherent things, both crying, Diana's hands, soothing, caressing, futile with guilt. A jolt and the cab was standing still and the driver's voice—"South Ferry."

"Chris." . . . Wavering, uncertain. "I want Chris."

"Yes, darling, Chris." Diana got out and paid the fare. Not waiting to be helped, Mrs. Heaton clambered out and headed for the ferry. Spilling change, Diana hastened after her, reeling, while Mrs. Heaton's walk was straight. A boat was leaving; running, they made it, hurrying down the slanting gangplank to the rattle of gears and chains.

Mrs. Heaton veered from the warm, brightly-lit cabin. "No air in there. Make me sick."

They walked fore and aft on the lee deck, wind meeting them bow and stern. The woman was silent, lips down-curved. Diana, looking again and again into her mother's face, began to believe Sue's thoughts were fixed on Chris and not on what had happened. Maybe she didn't realize, didn't actually know, and thought the slap an accident. Oh God, don't let her know I ever did it, please God let it be so she doesn't know. How could I. . . .

Their sodden skirts hugged their legs, whipped by the wind. Diana's teeth began to chatter. Seeing that Sue felt no chill, the girl bore discomfort with a fierce, penitential gloom. If Sue had said, 'Let's end it all, let's jump overboard,' Diana would have held her hand and jumped. How can you face life when you have hit your mother?

The ferry, lumbering into the wide dark of the bay, creaked and waddled in the wind. Drift ice shone palely on the black choppy waves. They passed Liberty, looming vaguely in the murk, tankers lying at anchor, bows to the tide; the white hull of a United Fruit boat, up from the tropics, slid by like a ghost. The Robbins Reef bell buoy warned of the approach to Staten Island, a melancholy, disordered raving in the night. . . . . The pines come down close to the shore on Hokomok Point, their roots wind in among pink granite rocks where brown seaweed is cast up to dry and wither, and the salt wind blowing brings the bell-sound; go home through the woods to a sunny parlor where a beautiful woman sits at the piano singing for the angels. . . .

The boat shook to the pulse of reversed engines, sidling in between jewel lights of emerald and ruby, nosed deeper, lurching, crushing gathered ice.

"Sue, I'll have to look up the address of the hotel."

They got off and Diana hunted for a phone booth. Mrs. Heaton stood quietly beside her while she searched the listing. "It's way out on the south shore, Sue."

"Maybe. . . . Call up, see if he's there."

106

Diana rang the number. It was slow to answer, and then a man's voice said, "Marine House."

"Is Mr. Meredith there?"

"Yes, Mr. and Mrs. Meredith."

"*Christopher* Meredith?"

"Yes, Mr. and Mrs. Christopher Meredith."

"Thank you." She hung up and turned to Sue.

"What is it?"

It would have to be told. "He's married, Mother. The clerk said 'Mr. and Mrs.' He said it twice."

Mrs. Heaton looked down at her skirt and smoothed it. She looked back at Diana; communication of suffering was in the look, and knowledge that Diana understood; in that moment they were two women knit together, sensing the mystery of heart pain. Mrs. Heaton reached for Diana's hand. "Take me home. I feel sick."

They went back on the same ferry. They held hands all the way. Toward the end of the ride Mrs. Heaton began to shiver. They had hot coffee on the Manhattan side, but still she shivered. She was shaking violently when Diana put her to bed with a water bottle at her feet. But by the time Dr. Minelli, roused out of sleep, arrived, the chill had gone; he said she would be all right.

Sue moaned and talked in her sleep, but it was Chris's name she said and not Diana's; she didn't know that her daughter had struck her. God had spared her that; Diana thanked Him for it.

Diana stole into the theater, nerved to face whatever came if only by some miracle she was not fired. Nick was not laying in wait for her beside the time clock; she checked in and hope bounded. There seemed to be a point in getting into make-up and costume as speedily as possible, a claim asserted; but all the time she was in the dressing room, she waited for the summons that would pluck her out and cast her adrift. It did not come—and she was out on the stage in the opening number!

107

Still, it was best to keep out of sight as much as possible; Nick might have overlooked his duty. After the second number she was aware that he was watching her. She became a fugitive from his gaze, taking cover every chance she could, but still his eyes followed, sought her out. And at last he came walking deliberately toward her. She braced herself and lifted her head.

"What you hiding from, kid? What's scaring you?"

Being prepared for disaster, she could not grasp the friendliness of the tone, believe, in it. "Please don't fire me, Mr. Allingham. I love my work."

"Don't get ideas in your head. Snap out of it. Your work's okay." It was an order, calmly spoken, no whiplash in the voice. He turned, going back to his place. A few yards distant, he looked back, saw the change in her and smiled.

Her joy was instant and complete. The two things together, her job secure and his friendliness, sent her soaring through the rest of the performance. He had smiled. She had never seen him smile before.

The next night and for several nights she was again bold, coming early on the set, lingering in conspicuous places, making herself accessible to any conversations he might choose to begin.

But Nick left her to herself.

Mrs. Heaton's cold had turned into a lingering bronchitis cough. That, and the fact that she was going through one of her periodic spells of recuperation and was dejected, fretful, and besides all this, melancholy over Chris, would have made it heartless to ask her to sit playing while her daughter danced. But Diana wanted urgently to dance, to work on a new solo. She suggested, "I could practice in the theater," and the woman, listless, agreed.

It was a change Diana welcomed, though to admit as much savored of disloyalty. But for no reason she could fathom, practicing at home had come to be a nervous business. Plainly, it was her fault, for if she would only do what

Mother told her, all would go smoothly. But that Diana was no longer able to do; when it came to making up a dance Sue's promptings irked and nagged her. She did not know she had outgrown her mother's help, she only knew a compulsion to shape the dance as she felt it must be shaped. Often they would fall into disputes that left both of them depressed, wondering what had gone wrong that they should quarrel.

No doubt she should have asked Nick's permission to make use of the stage in the afternoon, but Joe assured her it was quite all right if the one pilot light left burning on the stage would be enough. So she worked in the dim, eerie silence of the empty theater, dressed in her short Greek costume of pale yellow silk and her barefoot sandals. She missed the music and wished she could afford to engage a pianist, but she had the new dance pretty well set, it was possible to work on it without music. And the joy of being able to make changes without explaining why!

She finished warming up with vigorous preliminary exercises, tucked her towel into the tormentor brace and set to work on the dance. It was different from anything she had done before, full of varying moods, more complex, more brilliant. Pausing to catch breath, she exulted, knowing it was good. Why had she never tried a Hungarian gypsy dance before?

All at once her heart leapt and thudded—a man's voice was coming out of the dark auditorium. She sprang about, peering into the gloom, hearing the words, "Wouldn't it be better with music?"

Nick! He had been watching her. He stood at the back of the orchestra seats, his arms crossed on the low partition that ran behind them. As she stared, he moved briskly, approaching, coming down the side aisle, leaping to the rim of a box, springing across the wide space to the apron, going on over to the rehearsal piano by the prop-room. He swung the stool down from atop the piano, tossed his hat in its place, and sat down, prepared to play. "What music you use?"

It was as though the wind had entered. His strong presence filled the place. Something in that swift, animal grace of movement dazzled and electrified her.

He ran his fingers over the keys, his touch skilled, and scowled at the tinny sound. He asked again, not looking at her, "What music?"

The sound of the piano roused her. The realization that he actually meant to play for her was so astounding that it was a moment longer before another thought could form— he would not be able to and it would be embarrassing to tell him so; he evidently assumed she used some simple composition he would know, could play from memory. The constricting, miserable shyness took hold upon her. "I'm—it's— I'm afraid you wouldn't know it."

He glanced up, still scowling, demanding direct answer. "I said, what music?"

She answered hastily, "Brahm's First Hungarian Dance."

He shook his head. "You pick concert stuff. Wait till I see. . . ." He began to play the music, pulling it out of memory.

This was even more breath-taking than his sudden appearance. He could play *that*—and without the score? Why, then he was a pianist, a fine pianist, and not a stage manager! But even so, how many pianists could attempt a piece like that from memory? He was rehearsing it, repeating a difficult section, getting it right. Diana drew closer, marveling.

"Can't do a good job on it," he still shook his head. "But here goes. Tempo as written?"

She blurted out her amazement. "How do you know—how can you—"

He eyed her coolly. "I know a lot if the memory holds and it's a pretty good one." He jerked his head toward the center of the stage. "Take the dance."

He was the stage manager, giving an order; Diana moved quickly to obey. But the strangeness of the whole proceeding, this sudden and novel intimacy, the two of them alone, and the force of his personality so strongly felt, combined to

110

rattle her. Ready to begin, she hesitated, nervous. "I—it's a new dance. I still don't know it very well."

He gave another order. "Forget me. Imagine you got an audience out front."

Forget him? But he had used a word that was a part of her world, 'imagine.' She lifted her head, looking out into the dark, high up where the second balcony would be. . . .

"All set?"

She nodded. The music sounded, carrying her into movement and she was in the dance and it was good. She was aware that he watched, following her tempo, that the music came out rich and full and sustaining, but that was in the background of her thought, the joy of the dance strong in her. How marvelous to dance, to know this brief, intense celebration of joy and beauty and bravery, unconfounded, rising pure and free out of all that was worrisome and sordid and frightening and ugly in life. She could dance; this power was hers.

She came out of the final pose renewed, no longer nervous and insecure, the moody triumph of the dance still holding. She went toward the piano, eager for his comment, having at that moment no apprehension, all the cheap, sneering ridicule she had endured in her search for a solo effaced from mind.

He saw that unguarded, innocent joy in her and wished she would keep to it, not lapsing into her strange shyness. He told her honestly, "Not bad by a long shot. You got the makings." An elbow on the keys, cheek on his hand, he appraised her impersonally, approving. "Set the dance yourself?"

She was in the middle of a wonderful experience. Out of elation, she answered easily, "Oh yes, I always do! And that's such fine music for a dance."

"Know what you need on that? A wow finish."

The expression jolted her. Some of her elation dropped away. She regarded him doubtfully.

His lips twisted, smiling. "Sure I'm talking Broadway, but that's where we are. To sell a dance you need a punch ending

111

to pull a hand, some of those things ballet dancers do, whirling in a circle."

She hugged herself, her whole body swaying in negation, doubt still in her eyes. "That wouldn't be artistic."

"You working for a living?"

She confessed as much with a nod of her head and added shyly, "But for something else too."

"What?"

She hesitated, rocking her body, dreading a wisecrack retort, and then she braved it, murmuring. "To be an artist. Like—St. Denis, Duncan, Pavlowa."

"Sure." He accepted the statement as a reasonable one, thereby giving her immediate relief. "But those dames pulled a trick or two on their way up. Not counting in the promotion."

She assured him earnestly, "They don't do 'wow' finishes."

He had a ready answer. "They aren't working Broadway. Think Solly Blotz's agency would give one of them a job in a night club? If you got money enough to hire a hall you can do as you please, but the concert racket takes promotion that runs into money or it's a wash-out. Go to work, earn the money, do what you please when you've got a wad. And to earn Broadway money, don't kid yourself, you need a wow finish. Say, you've got enough to buck trying to sell something artistic and staying clear of tap and acrobatic. Stick in some fireworks and you've got a chance." He paused, smiling again, friendly, but some hint of irony in the smile. "Don't let it throw you if I steer clear of the snob talk. I got a particular hate for snob stuff. But I might know what I'm talking about just the same. What I'm handing you in the way of advice isn't a cheap line. A wow finish can be artistic, kid. Brilliant technique is no handicap to an artist." He stood up, took out a cigarette and lit it. On second thought, he offered her one.

Nick smoking! Nick, who if he caught a girl in a dressing-room—but this was different, no performance on, just the two

112

of them. Just the two of them. It was wonderful. She had found a friend. "Thank you, I don't smoke."

"And you don't drink and you don't go out with men, no stage-door Johnnies hanging around for Miss Heaton." He spoke smoothly, matter of fact, his manner pleasant. "There's some chorus girls like that but not many, and not in this show. Outside of being a dancer, you seem to be a damn nice kid."

Ease left her, constraint came. She twisted before him, bothered by his scrutiny.

"Say, what's wrong with you?" Cigarette held between his lips, eyes squinting through the smoke, he reached out to lay a friendly hand upon her shoulder. And at the movement she ducked out of reach, eyes intent upon his face, eyes bright with fear.

He was offended. "Say, you think I'm trying to make you?"

The harsh accusing query shocked her into awareness of what she had done and she was completely demoralized, wretched at her blundering, stupid fright that had given him offense. Despite all that was formidable and alien in him— his sharp commands, the flashes of cold hardness, the dark scowls, and his talk in the Broadway vernacular—she sensed a fineness in him, something clean and forthright, a warmth and friendliness she hungered for. Friendship had been there but a moment ago and now he glowered, hostile and remote. Oh—was he going to walk off huffy? She stretched out a hand to him, clutching at amends. "Please—I—"

He accepted her hand and held it between his own; eyes still squinting keenly, he waited for her to continue. But though she met his eyes, the words would not come.

Nick asked her quietly, "What you trying to say, kid?"

She made an effort. "I just mean, I mean I don't want you to think—It isn't that—" Speech died; words were of no use. He was holding her hand, turning it over in his own, looking down at it. She knew surely this was only friendship, that he waited for her to go on with what she had to say, that in some miraculous fashion she had won his interest and

113

his sympathy. But he was male; the strong, slim body standing close, half a head taller than herself, the touch of his hands, disordered her completely. She knew in one and the same moment that she wanted to be in flight, running from him at top speed, and that she wanted to go on standing there, close to him, letting him possess her hand, the sense of dream stealing upon her.

"What's wrong, kid?" His voice was new to her, low and gentle. She was silent, the more shaken by that tone.

He pressed her hand and dropped it. "Do what I said. Get a wow finish. Stick in some of those turns."

Back on the subject of dancing, she could speak. "Do they teach them in dancing schools?"

His glance was quick and piercing. "Don't you take lessons?"

"Why no, I never did. I go to see all the famous dancers. I learn from that and then I work at home."

He estimated her afresh and decided she was not lying. "Then you're more of a marvel than I thought. But that's crazy. If you can do this well without lessons, think what you could do with training. Don't you know you have to study? It's an art, not just a gift. Think a guy can learn to play the fiddle just by ear? You go to ballet school and get all the technique you can."

It sounded reasonable. "All right. As soon as I can save some money for it."

He twisted his wrist, bringing his watch into sight. "Want to work on the dance some more? I got twenty minutes, I'll play for you."

It was friendship, real. She gave him a shy, thankful smile. "You play beautifully."

"You're easy pleased. I'm missing half the notes." He dropped his cigarette to the floor, stepped on it and slid back on the stool. "All right, take it again."

She would have much preferred being left alone to dream over all that had transpired; this time she could not forget him while she danced. She did badly and finished feeling

114

disgraced, knowing certainly it was flight at top speed she wanted. But Nick rapped out the order, "Take it again," and then, "Take it again," and kept her going until she steadied, until, dripping wet, the yellow silk darkened over chest and back, she leaned against the tormentor, panting for breath.

He sauntered over to her. "We'll have another go tomorrow. Three? I got an idea for you. Shultz is putting on a new show and there's a Roman scene in it with a specialty bit that calls for a soloist and twelve dancers doing classic stuff right down your alley. They didn't start to pick the girls yet. I'll get the dope on the audition and pass it on to you tomorrow."

"Oh—you really mean—?" Her delight was intense. "You mean—I might be picked for it?"

"Pull yourself together." He frowned, and still frowning, smiled. "Sure you're good enough. Don't you know it?" His hand moved to give her a bucking-up pat on the back. And again came that quick wince away, touch eluded. Nick stared. Then, moving with deliberate intention, he stepped after her and carried out his intention. He informed her with a hard ring in his voice, "I don't bite, I haven't got leprosy, I'm not trying to make you. I don't paw girls just to feel 'em up. Got that straight?" His rigor broke and he was grinning. "Oh boy, are you dripping! Got me all wet. Serves you right, says you. Pass over that towel and let me wipe my hand." He took the towel, made use of it, tossed it back to her. "Three tomorrow. It's a rehearsal, not an assignation or a murder."

He left her, catching his hat from the piano as he passed and clapping it on his head, disappearing into the passage with his quick swagger.

Diana stayed motionless, welcoming the inpouring silence, the solitude, wanting the whirl of emotions to subside so that she might find herself.

Find herself? But who was she?

A nice kid, he said. . . .

A strange hotel room green shades pulled down white daylight leaking in too bright too bright and the horror of that ugly naked man gone crazy. . . .

No. Oh no. No.

I did it.

But because of—

The girls in the chorus sleep with men.

It's not the same, it's not the same—

Yes it is. They go with men for what they can get out of it. That's what you did. You know it now.

But not for clothes, diamonds, a good time—

It doesn't make any difference. They want one thing. You wanted something else. You sold yourself to a man to get something out of it.

For a career—beauty—fine things—

Tell it to Nick. You've heard wise talk up in that dressing room. You're not a green kid now.

But I was then. I didn't realize. I didn't know.

Tell him. You have to. You can't let him think you're a nice kid. Be honest, anyhow.

But Mother—she's modern—we're different. Is Nick a virgin? Well then, I don't think so—

Oh, what's right, what's wrong!

Mowbray was wrong. That was wrong. You know it was wrong.

Yes. . . .

If it had been Nick instead of—

No never never no man touch me leave me alone no man ever—

Oh, why, why. . . .

She threw herself into movement, striding back and forth on the apron, head up, defiant.

I can dance anyhow. I can dance. That's what counts. He saw I can dance. I know I can. I'll dance, I'll dance, I'll never stop.

7

M^{RS. HEATON} was not elated. Only one of twelve girls when admittedly there was a solo to be had. But some other girl would do it, not Diana. And Diana expected rejoicing over that? Where was the girl's spirit, ambition? Why didn't she walk up to Mr. Shultz and tell him what she could do? And this new talk of studying ballet—going into a class with a lot of empty-headed girls to be taught how to dance! Had anyone taught Duncan, St. Denis? No, they were creative artists who composed their own art forms. Pavlowa, yes, she studied. But was Diana going to become a toe-dancer? Oh, what was wrong with the girl!

And Nick!—stage manager in a girly-girly show. Why, Diana would be making a pal of the call boy next! Bringing home *his* slang, *his* cheap comments! 'Wow' finishes indeed. He certainly wasn't a gentleman, now was he?—no educated person would use such speech. So he composed music? What kind of music? Popular songs, musical comedy tunes. Of course, just what you might expect, wasn't it? Composer, indeed! That trash. Well then. . . . Nick does this and Nick says that. . . .

Suddenly Mrs. Heaton, musing alone, sat bolt upright, smitten by a horrid thought. Suppose—suppose the little goose should become infatuated, throw herself away on some worthless puppy of a fellow?

That would be the end.

Diana—the one being—why, Diana—precious—why—

She seemed to wake horribly out of long nightmare, to come back from some place a long way off. Diana was the only thing in life that mattered. Diana, yes, and now—

Was she all right? Was Diana all right? Supposing even now—all lost, destroyed. Dear God, no, no.

117

I'm to blame for this. Yes, I am. Distraught, she rose, wringing her hands.

It was at that moment that quick, light steps sounded on the stairs. Mrs. Heaton had barely time to compose herself before the girl came brightly in, swinging her hat in her hand. A glance at that joyful face and the woman pulled herself together. This had to be dealt with cleverly. "Hello, Chick. Where were you?"

"Why, at rehearsal, Sue."

"But—" smiling, fond and intimate "—what time did rehearsal finish?"

"Four." Diana gave back the smile, responsive to her mother's mood, grateful for it; Sue was herself today.

"Four! Why, that's what I thought. And now—" Mrs. Heaton glanced at the clock, the hands standing at a quarter to six.

"I walked home, dear." Diana tossed her things on the bed and crossed over to the window. "It's lovely out . . . you can smell spring even in a city. There's a fragrance in the air."

Mrs. Heaton, playful, teased, "I'll wager Nick walked home with you."

Diana turned about in honest surprise. "Why, how did you know?"

Her mother was smiling in the friendliest fashion. "And you probably stopped for a bite."

"For a soda," said Diana, coming over to sit on the arm of her chair. "Sue, are you a mind-reader?"

"I don't have to be," the woman answered merrily. She was relieved. It wasn't serious, the girl's honesty was so complete. Oh, Diana would be truthful, of course, that could be counted on, but if this had actually been love, that naïveté would not be there, no, there would have been the brooding look of secrets in Diana's eyes. Mrs. Heaton drew a long breath, recovering from the scare. Diana was only a child. Still. . . . "Hand me a cigarette, Dicky. On the bureau—? Where did I. . . ."

"Here they are. But you shouldn't dear, really, they do make you cough."

So considerate, so sweet, Diana, mine. The woman shrugged, unconcerned, though sure enough, the first inhalation sent her into a fit of coughing. When she caught her breath she said, "Sit down, Chick. No, not on the arm of the chair, make yourself comfortable. There's something I'm going to say and you're not going to like it, but do try to understand your pal. Oh, I know what it's like, being young, spring, a fine day, a boy to talk to, dawdle along the street with. But Diana, you're cut out for bigger things than that! Why, you can't afford to waste time fooling around with boys!"

The girl stared, incredulous. "Why, Mother—"

"Oh, don't you think I know? Your head is full of this Nick person, you've been chattering of nothing else for the last week. A boy like that—"

"He isn't a boy, Mother." Diana was reproving. "He's a man. He's twenty-six."

Mrs. Heaton's smile turned rueful. "Well, man, then, but that makes it worse. What is a man wasting time on you for if he hasn't got ideas in his head? And he'll be putting them in yours and then you'll go mooning about and the career will be forgotten, you won't be anybody—" She broke off coughing, edged forward on her chair and continued with an urgent pleading. "Now don't think I'm going to scold—"

"Scold?" Diana was amazed; why should Sue speak of scolding? "What are you talking about, dearest?"

"Men," said Mrs. Heaton, and crushed out her cigarette with short decisive jabs. "I want you to leave men alone."

Diana was thoroughly perplexed. Why should Sue be saying such odd things—things you could not believe she would say? The girl asked bluntly, "Why?"

Mrs. Heaton told her, "Because it's wrong. If you get mixed up with some fellow—"

"Wrong! Why Sue, you never said anything like that before!"

119

The woman bit her lips. "Maybe I should have, Dicky, maybe I should have said it long ago."

"But how can you—! 'Leave men alone?' Why Sue, you don't believe that! 'Wrong.' You've had men friends, you said it wasn't wrong. If it wasn't wrong for you, why is it wrong for me? Not that it's the same," she added hastily, "Nick and I are only friends, that's all. But still, I don't see how you can say. . . ." Peering intently into her mother's face, trying to grasp the intention of Sue's thought, she saw how that face had altered. There were tiny crows-feet about the eyes, the color of the eyes had faded, they were paler, more yellow. The lips had thinned; now, needing rouge, they looked bloodless, almost blue, and her hair, wanting dye, showed white at the roots. Diana looked away, hurt by this fresh sight of her cherished, beautiful mother, hurt by the crude thought that the slow coming of age would make Sue feel differently about men. But she had to know if this was the reason for Sue's strange talk. She asked, trying to be gentle, "Isn't it maybe, well, just that you've changed?"

"Changed?" Now Mrs. Heaton was perplexed.

It could not be said outright; but had they not always tried to understand each other? Diana hinted, "Well, you—you might not be interested in men anymore."

Mrs. Heaton understood. "Sour grapes, Dicky? You think I'm old?" It did hurt, but she kept on smiling, knowing that was not important at this time, though unconsciously her hand stole to her cheek, pressed upward, tightening the flesh. "No, Chick, it isn't that, it's you, it's thinking about what's best for you. Perhaps I've been wrong about a lot of things, ever since I met Chris, I don't know. But anyhow, when I see you in danger—"

"*Danger?*"

"Yes, danger." The woman was speaking very earnestly. "Men can become a drug, a distraction, you can lose your head. Oh, Diana, please believe me, I know! Now, when you're so young and the years count—oh Lord, with all your life ahead of you, can't you wait until you are somebody and you have all the world to pick and choose from? Please believe me, Chick. You know what you mean to me. I'll die if I see you throw your life away. You must leave men alone."

The appeal brought the girl to her, kneeling, full of comfort. "There, dearest, don't. Oh Mother, you ought to know that dancing comes first with me and I shan't throw my life away. And about men—" Diana buried her face in her mother's lap; it was hard to speak of this, but the truth must be between them, and quite evidently Sue didn't understand. "—I wouldn't have an affair, Sue, I couldn't. No, never, never, I'd die if—no, honestly, if that's what's worrying you. No, you needn't worry, I promise you." There, that was set straight; she sensed her mother's relief, it mingled with her own now that the subject could be dismissed. She raised her head, speaking lightly. "Sue, you haven't given me a chance to tell you! I've got good news, dearest. I asked for the understudy of the solo today and I got it. I know my career is going pretty slow, but after all, I'm out of the chorus now, rehearsing with a new show—and I might—I might get a chance at the solo."

It rang true, all of it, and the woman kissed her daughter's cheek, contented. Everything was all right, everything was going to be all right, Diana would leave men alone; had not the girl assured her with a promise? And Diana was the soul of honor. In a way . . . it was even a good thing . . . that experience . . . it had given Diana a distaste. That 'experience' was banished instantly from mind. "I'm so glad, Chick."

The scare was over. But the effect of it lingered in a vague restlessness, and Mrs. Heaton's eyes wandered to the piano. To turn back in time, to regain a lost something. . . . "I wonder if I could sing again. Some small church choir. I think my voice might be good enough still." She turned the question to her daughter, doubt in her eyes.

Diana saw the longing and the pathos and loathed herself for having but a moment since cast up the thought of age. "Do it, Sue. You can, of course you can. Your voice is beautiful." She rose, taking her mother's hand, leading her to the piano. She stood beside it, seeing how, seated there, Sue's back had straightened, how the small, burnished head lifted, how a wistful gallantry, delicate and fragile, came with the singing. Yes, Sue could sing. That rare quality of tone—joy and sorrow made into one thing. *Songs My Mother Taught Me.* Diana's thought went back to that far off evening on Hokomok, sitting on the steps, feeling the wind, and the sense of revelation that had come, Sue singing, waiting for Chris. The sum of all the poignant heartaching beauty in the world was in that singing, and now the beauty came again, pressing more heavily on the heart. . . . Ah, beautiful, good, good like morning air, the smell of wet grass, clear water in a tin dipper when you're thirsty, sea-wind rising and the talk of pine boughs, a lovely woman coming out of a wood on the arm of a man, and all the joy of love in her face, love, beautiful and natural. . . .

Mrs. Heaton left off, coughing. "Of course with this hacking—"

The tears were running down Diana's cheeks, coming from closed eyes. "That was heavenly, Sue, heavenly."

It would have been better, after that talk with Diana, if Bob had not called up that very week. He had been out west, Taos, an address had been lost, he couldn't write. It was strangely gratifying to Mrs. Heaton to hear him beg, yes beg, for a luncheon date. Sour grapes indeed! A lot a young girl knew! Indeed she had not the slightest intention of resuming intimacy with him, he had been much too horrid. Still, she had missed him; you lose something of yourself when you lose a lover, some part of you that has gone into the giving and is no longer yours but his; you are diminished as though the man had walked off with a bit of you. Mrs. Heaton thought sadly that a number of men had walked off with bits of her. But a lover is like a mirror in which a woman sees herself at her best, stays young. . . . My goodness, anyhow there is a difference between a woman's life and a young girl's—that was a matter easily explained, and especially a woman without a career. Why should *she* leave men alone? No, not intimacy, she did not intend. . . . But how much more graceful and contenting for a woman to make her choice about the kind of life she meant to lead, otherwise it could be said—well, sour grapes. Yes, of course she would see Bob. Nothing wrong in having luncheon with an old friend.

Only . . . perhaps just now . . . it might be best not to mention Bob to Diana.

After all, Nick was a friend. There wasn't anything wrong in having luncheon with a friend. Only . . . perhaps just now . . . it might be best not to mention Nick to Sue.

It was all in the line of work; he had offered to play the music of the solo so that she, as the understudy, would be ready if the chance came. After a snack they would walk over to the theater, rehearse.

Turn Nick down? It was unthinkable. Leave men alone, yes, she intended to of course, but this was different. To speak of 'wrong' and 'danger' meaning Nick! Sue didn't know him. Besides, Sue could be, well, erratic; that was part of this unhappy, shameful business, drinking in spells, and in between the spells, invalidish, often fretful, not actually her old self save in rare hours. Once the career picked up, happiness would come, all would be the way it used to be. And now, with Nick's help, the career was progressing. Still, for the present, there was no use in worrying Sue with talk of Nick.

Nick had to be. Beyond Diana's reasoning, the need went deep. Here was healing for the ugly hurt she had suffered and solace for the bitter groping loneliness of spirit. There had been too long a time of hungering for the very thing he gave—approval and belief. A word of encouragement from him, a kindly look, a gentle tone, and the raw, painful sensitivity was dulled, the damaged selfhood started in to heal. A few brief encounters and she had come to know some intervals of ease and laughter. Joy moved, quick and alive within her, and her spirit sang.

123

And yet she feared him; fear stayed. He was a man; in the mystery of his male nature what forces moved that she, a girl, could not hope to fathom or foresee? In his other world apart from hers, processes of thought and feeling went on of which she could not guess. It was not Nick, her friend, that she mistrusted, it was nature in him, the fact that he was male.

But Nick, her friend, was still unknown, full of variance and mystery. He said emphatically that he was not a pianist —and played beautifully. He spoke in Broadway jargon—yet never ridiculed her dreams. But often what he thought remained unknown; you could look into his face and it would tell you nothing. That face could be dark with held anger and sweet with a smile. The voice that could lash out with a whip-sting could be gentle, actually gentle. This was someone to marvel at and respect.

No, she did not know him. Only that he was her friend and truly that. It was enough to bring her into a new growth of selfhood, blooming.

Nick saw the change coming in her and at first he told himself he just couldn't get it, he hadn't believed a thing like that could happen. But it wasn't an act, it was real. He studied her, skeptical, alert for any tricks or falsity, yet for all his hard-boiled habit of mind she had him wonder-struck. She walked with a swing and a gladness that made her a different girl.

And it was his doing. He was the cause, the creator of this strange innocent joy. He called himself a fool to think so, but there it was, his doing, no doubt about it, he saw her blossom at a word. And what had he done? Nothing, nothing but try to give her a hand. Because she was a good kid who worked every show like a first night and then came around to the theater to work alone, trying to get ahead. And she had the stuff, the makings for top rank. Who wouldn't try to give a kid like that a hand? But seeing what it meant to her to have his help had bowled him over. He discovered that he was tickled, that he was scared, that he was proud, that he was happy. Why if he as much as said, 'Pretty good, that time,' the girl would glow as if you handed her the crown jewels. It wasn't right to let an innocent like that go loose. To see her smile. . . . All right, she had him roped and trotting at the halter, but she was different and that wasn't a gag.

That lithe, perfect body, so flexible, so rhythmic; the happy wildness in her dancing; the vivid, changing face, the warm, eager abstraction of her dreaming moods, the searching honesty of her eyes; Nick thought that he had never seen such honest eyes in anyone. He had seen girls lie, plenty of them, experts with innocent baby stares that were a work of art. This girl couldn't lie, not if he knew anything. But something bothered her, something big. He thought of that woman who had come to the stage door, and he believed he understood. Sure, that was big trouble for a sensitive kid.

But she was a strange being, shy as a wild creature, afraid of touch. He didn't like the way she shied off, it wasn't natural, no, not even for a virgin. Someone must have told her scary stories of the wicked world and she had queer, fixed ideas about how a girl should look after herself and she was certainly living up to them. A sensitive innocent thrown in with that bunch of toughs in the chorus dressing room would get a lot of shocks that hurt and scared. Maybe she'd heard something about him, twisted around so she thought he'd do her harm. He hoped not. He didn't go in for pawing girls, but he wanted to be touching Diana all the time, he couldn't bear to have her shrink from him; she ought to get over it, he meant to win her over, to make it so—

Sure he wanted her. He wanted her the way he had never wanted any woman. And this had to be right; it had to be so she would want him too. Then it would be love, lasting and important.

Diana had roused the deep self in him; the self that he kept hidden, fought to keep down, hold under control, knowing the power it had of feeling, not wanting to be possessed by it. Now, realizing the stir of that unadmitted self, he knew his love went deep, that this was real.

They had dropped into a lunchroom on Eighth Avenue, a place that drew professionals, lights shaded over the counter, small tables set in stalls. Finished, they lingered, Diana chatting. She told him, starry-eyed, that she had never known friendship could be so wonderful; it made the whole world different.

Friendship, yeah, that was right, that had to be there, but if she thought this was just friendship that was making the whole world different. . . . He stood up, taking the small bag which held her rehearsal costume. "Want to work?"

She rose eagerly and went before him to the door. How smoothly she moved; she could turn walking into a dance. Out on the street he took her arm and felt tension come into her at his touch. Wanting her to get over that, he started talk on the subject he knew would absorb her interest, make her forget to draw away. "Know what's good about your dancing? It's not the cheese-cloth variety of self-expression."

"But I do express myself in what I dance! I pour it all in."

"You feel it, sure. But what you do isn't petty and personal. It's big enough, deep enough, to hit the universal, and that way it's art. You've got my emotion in the dance as well as yours."

She was walking easily beside him, the tension gone. "But it seems like mine. And yet, sometimes I make up the happiest dances when I'm sad. When I was a child—" Diana meant two years back and that did indeed seem a remote period "—I made up such tragic dances. Now, when I'm most miserable it seems as though I have to prove that joy is undefeated."

He wished that she would speak out about what made her miserable, feel free with him to do so, banish all constraint. But they were coming up to the stage door. He dropped his hand from her arm; no use giving anyone around the theater too much to talk about, let 'em guess—as Joe was guessing now and asking everyone to help him out.

They found the stage filled with people, a rehearsal in progress, another of Shultz's shows shifted in there for an afternoon.

"That's that." Nick led the way back into the street. "We're out of luck. Unless. . . . You keen to work today?"

She was; disappointment had distressed her. She stood by the stage door as though she could not bear to go away.

Nick offered, "You can come to my place. Right over on Fiftieth. I've got a piano and a lot of space."

She looked up startled. Go alone with him into his apartment. . . .

Nick's voice was harsh. "Say kid, I'm not pulling anything on you, I'm just saying if you want to, that's all, and I don't care, see? Sometimes you make me sick. Think I'm an ogre?"

Her look was speculative, apprehensive; she seemed to be trying to decide whether or not he was. Then, being brave, "I'll go."

"Oh, forget it. If it takes heroics."

"No, I'll go." She started along the street with a quick spurt of nervous determination.

They walked rapidly in silence. Nick thought, I shouldn't have suggested it. A girl going into a man's place alone with him, no, it wasn't right, not for a nice girl. He shot a glance sideways. The color had gone out of her face. He pulled up. "Call it off. You don't want to go."

She kept on walking. "Yes, I do."

He caught up with her. "Now you're lying."

She turned her white, set face toward him. "No. Suppose Miss Yoland didn't come to rehearsal tomorrow and I had my chance to do her solo and I wasn't ready. Besides. . . . I want to see where you live. I want to go, Nick."

He growled, "You look like you're marching to the gallows. Up to you, you know."

They went on grimly. What the devil did she think, anyhow. She's not paying you any compliments, Nicky old boy, and you're a sap to take it. Ought to leave her flat right now and let her think it over all by herself. But I was wrong, suggesting it.

They came to a row of brownstone houses, remodeled into apartments. Nick turned into one of them, unlocked the first door on the ground floor and held it open. She went in like a cat in strange quarters, looking all about her, and he stayed by the door, holding it open.

After the dreary old-fashioned clutter of boarding-house rooms that no touch of Sue's could ever redeem, it was a joy to see a room like this, so big, so dramatic in its bare simplicity, so striking and effective in its color scheme. It was unusual, the walls dead white, the couch, the armchairs and the long window drapes a stark black, but warmth and richness came in the few touches of red, the cushions along the couch, a tapestry on the wall above a long table of dark wood that held a litter of music and blank music manuscript paper. Warmth and color came from the wide bookcases that ran along the wall furthest from the windows, broken by two doors leading into other rooms. The place was large enough to be spacious even with a grand piano by the windows. You could dance in such a room. . . .

Nick, still holding the door wide, mocked, "Think it's safe to stay?"

She nodded, embarrassed by his sarcasm. He closed the door, sent his hat spinning into a chair and walked smartly to the piano. He waved toward one of the doors. "You can get dressed in there."

"Why do you have a grand piano if you're not a pianist?"

"I told you. I make up tunes, light stuff." He waited for her. "Well—?"

She was looking at the tapestry. "That's handwork, antique. Lovely. So many books! You like to read."

"Say, this is a rehearsal, isn't it? Would you oblige me by getting this over with? I'm sitting here waiting to play for you. Snap into it."

It was not Nick, her friend, who spoke with such biting

128

hostility, it was the stage manager who bawled you out if you missed an order. Diana disappeared swiftly through the door that he had indicated.

Nick had planned to go into the music the moment she stepped out, but seeing her emerge in the scanty costume of yellow silk, so much pale satiny flesh agleam, he sprang up, saying, "I better pull down the shades. If you work down this end of the room people might see you from the street."

Diana stood motionless, seeing a shade come down. And it was another room, another man, white daylight leaking in. . . . "No! No!"

It was a cry of animal terror. Nick whipped about and saw the panic in her face. There was a moment without sound or movement. "Diana, what *is* this?"

The rigid, staring fright broke. She turned, flinging herself against the wall, arms about her head, sobbing, "I can't help it, I can't help it!"

He wanted to go to her, to take her in his arms, to soothe and question, find out what the devil ailed her; put an end to it. Instead, he slid back on the piano seat and began to play, softly, improvising, knowing music had a power over her. He saw the effort she was making to stop crying. He told her coolly, "You can beat it any time you wish."

She had the sobs choked down. She bent forward, wiping her face on the skirt of her costume. She turned about and stood docile, head down, waiting.

"Take the dance." It was a professional order, and she obeyed. Once begun, he held her to the work, driving her. "Take it again. Watch your last four bars. . . . Take it again. . . . You got a repeat of a theme there you're not paying any attention to. . . . Again."

At last, wondering and breathless, she protested. "I don't need to take it again, I know it now."

"Well, get dressed, beat it." His face was dark. "You want to, don't you?"

Nick was angry with her. It was her fault. She had hurt

him. Not meeting his eyes, she murmured, "You're good to help me. Thanks."

He was silent, morose, the black mood holding. Shyly, she came close, right up close, and held out her hand to him.

That child's trick—like the first time in the theater. "What am I supposed to do with this?" He turned her hand between his own. "You're like a dog that's been taught to put up its paw." He let her hand drop and went back to playing.

She sidled closer still, breathless. "Nick, please don't be angry with me. I didn't mean to make you angry. I'm sorry. . . ." He gave no heed. "Nick. . . . I like you. . . . Do you hear me? I said—I like you."

"I heard you." He came up tall and straight, taking both her hands and holding them, looking down into her face, his eyes smouldering. He knew now. It had come to him the moment she turned from the wall, not meeting his eyes. He had been a sap not to have guessed it before. He thought if she was to lie about it, it would take everything he had to keep from hitting her; what was hidden, vulnerable, the capacity to believe, to trust, to dream, was in her hands; she could smash it, lying. "Some man had you."

She went on gazing straight into his eyes. He saw the muscles moving in her throat as she swallowed. She did not lie about it. "Yes."

"And it was a dirty business."

"It was . . . dirty."

She had never looked so young, so like a child, standing there motionless, her eyes never leaving his. He asked, "How old were you?"

"Fourteen."

"How old are you now?"

"Going on seventeen."

"Are you lying?"

"No."

"You're only sixteen now?"

"I'll be seventeen in August."

130

Could she be lying? "Was that your mother came to the stage door? Your own mother?"

Diana's head lifted a little higher. "Yes."

"Was she drunk?"

"Yes."

She was giving the hard answers straight. He looked down at her hands. "Tough break, kid." He let them fall and moved to the arch of the piano, leaned against it. She had not stirred, her eyes following him. He had never seen her stay so still, so without motion. He didn't like to go on asking questions, putting her through this, but he had to get it clear. "Were you attacked?"

Her head went higher still, her breathing quick and light, and again he saw the muscles in her throat moving. "No. I did it. Deliberately. I didn't know any better. And Mother—" Words were coming that she did not mean to say. She stopped them short.

"What about Mother?"

Diana was silent. All that could not be said was in the turbulence of her look. Her eyes talked with him, begging understanding and compassion.

The compassion came in a savage anger against a woman with a mind so fuddled in drink that she could neglect her daughter, fail to guard her, betray the trust of a child's innocence, not knowing, not caring what happened to the girl until it was too late. He didn't stir. He stayed quiet, feeling the rage come in him and willing it to go; it had no place while Diana stood there, helpless and suffering. He put her through two more questions. "Did you go with the man more than once?"

Fear flickered in her gaze. "Only once."

"Only one man?"

"Only one."

He waited, through with questioning, thinking she might speak. She did, telling him in a desperate small voice, close to whispering, "I'm not a bad girl. Don't think it. Don't, Nick, don't."

Unmoving, somber, his voice quiet, he answered, "You said you liked me. Listen kid, I'm in love with you."

Wonder widened her eyes and opened her mouth.

Nick asked, "Think you can take it?"

"You love me?" She could barely speak.

"I do, as they say in church. I said, could you take it?" His smile came, bitter-sweet, his lips twisted. "I have an idea you and I can work this thing out so you can forget about that dirty business, so you won't be scared about anything. Might take a bit of rehearsing. You've let me help you some. Will you let me help some more?"

She was taking in everything he said. She nodded.

"You got to get over being scared of me. You got to know it means something different when I say I love you. You got to know that means, so help me God, I don't want any more harm to come to you, and I'm only trying to help you be yourself. Right?"

She drew a deep breath, nodding again.

"That's set. Now before you scoot in there and change into your clothes and beat it out of here, I'm going to ask you to do one thing that might come pretty hard to you. Try and do it so we can see whether or not we have a chance to make a go of this thing, will you?"

She regarded him steadily, considering all possibilities, and he went on smiling, holding her eyes.

"I'll try."

"Swell. Now I'll tell you what. I'm going to stay here just as I am, not a move. And you're going to walk over here under your own steam and give me one kiss. Remember, you said you liked me and I said I loved you, and this is something I'm asking you to do. For both of us."

He waited, letting time go by, not taking his eyes from her. Slowly she began to move, advancing, dream-like, drawing the strength to move from his eyes. She came on slowly, smoothly, put up her mouth and kissed his lips. It was a child's kiss.

"Swell." He was smiling happily, lips no longer twisted, and staying so motionless he scarcely breathed. "You're beautiful. That took doing, didn't it? And you did it. Now suppose you change and clear out of here, huh?"

She went away with the same slow, dream-like tread, passing into the next room. After a moment Nick swung around to the piano and began to play.

THE GIRL came down Fifth Avenue, walking home from Nick's; home to Sue. She moved in a trance of joy, astounded with happiness. Nick loved her. She had kissed him. He had said So help me God. No harm would come. She would never know the stupid mangling fright again. He gave her his strength to build her own. There was no ugly secret standing in between them. He knew, and the fact of his knowing and his love had set her free of guilt. She was herself, only—a new self, a dream self.

She was borne along in a magic exhilaration, drifting through the press of active, nervous life that paced the proud street, slipping through the massed impatient traffic at the intersections, traveling across stripes of sun and shade and by the big shop windows with their artful luxurious displays. Sunlight on a tall gleaming tower was delight to the eye, the Empire State a majestic marvel. A gull skimmed high, a slender arch of blazing white floating against Atlantic blue; a faint sea smell in the cool east breeze gave reminder that the big city was a coastal town; not far out the rollers curved and broke and spilled their soft thunder on the long pale beaches.

Nick loved her. She lived it over, seeing how he rose to face her, the terrible moodiness on him, and then how the angry smoulder went out of his eyes and his voice grew kind; the grace of his figure, leaning against the piano, and the way his eyes grew warm and soft and gave orders; and the shared happiness in his look, staying there at the piano, watching her go out the door. . . . She did not want to go beyond that in time, but to stay motionless in that interval, possessing its perfection, feeding on its bliss.

But nearing home, thought came of Sue. 'Leave men alone.' Foreboding stirred; Mother would be enemy to all of this.

Nor could it be explained to Sue; the thought of explanation was as shocking as a desecration. Sue could do damaging things to this great happiness.

I won't tell her. Not right now. Later, of course. Not now.

The quick, firm resolution brought an ache of conscience. Yet how could it be conscience when there was no wrong in this? It wasn't as though Sue were herself and you could be sure that she would meet you with an open mind. You had to look after her, not let her get upset, nervous. Sue *was* nervous and easily upset and sometimes quite unreasonable. Could anything be more unreasonable than for Sue to say 'Leave men alone?'

It occurred to Diana that her mother would not know she had not been to afternoon rehearsal, or that from now until the last couple of weeks of rehearsal she, as a member of one of the specialty acts, need only attend in the morning. So, if she said nothing, Sue would naturally believe. . . .

Tricking Sue, deceiving her. Diana was appalled. Her lips moved forming the words, 'Of course I'll tell her.'

But not today. On that there was not even the struggle of a decision; the resolution came ready-made by a compulsion stronger than any promptings of conscience. A moment longer foreboding stayed and mingled with a pang of longing, regret that this wonder could not be shared, made bigger in the proud telling. Oh, to sing it out—He loves me, he loves me!

Joy swept in. Nick's presence moved beside her. She walked more slowly, holding to the precious interval of time.

Not yet seventeen. Why, she ought to be running around with pigtails down her back and school books under her arm. How can she dance like that if she's only a child? Where does she get the fire and the subtlety and the poise she puts into it? Is it all a bloody gift she hardly knows she has? But she doesn't talk like a child. Well, someways yes. But not like sixteen.

Asking her for a kiss. . . . Anger with himself grew, recurring. I shouldn't have done it. Three days ago and he was still moping.

Nick started up from the table. The score was there, but he was fooling himself, trying to stick to it, the work wouldn't go. No use fooling yourself about anything. He went to the bedroom closet searching through coat pockets for a pipe, snarling at himself. Take it easy, will you, wait till she crawls out of the cradle. Yah, you were being nice to her, getting her so she wouldn't be scared of a kiss; not so hard on you, was it? What right you got stirring up a kid like that? Suppose she was your sister—

He paused in the filling of the pipe, struck by the sentimental banality of the 'sister' line, and wagged his head in mock sorrow, sheepish. Nick old boy, you're hammy. That heart-sob stuff taken on the straight is not your style. Don't go putting that in your songs or you're done for.

He strolled back into the living room and stretched out on the couch, drawing on the pipe. No fun, this go-slow idea; lot more fun to be nipping over to the stage door, picking her up as she came out. But he had set that for tomorrow; if he couldn't stick to what he planned he might get the habit of letting a lot of things go slide.

Just be friendly; let it come along natural—from her. All right, maybe a year, two years from now; it's worth it, I want her for always. . . . She stuck to the truth when she wanted like hell to lie. . . . I'd like to know—Yeah, you'd like to know; stand her up for a little more torture, 'How'd you come to do it? Who was the man? Tell me everything.' Good old Nicky, nice fellow, wanting to pile hell on the kid, asking questions. . . . The way she held her head up. . . .

His thought loosened, words no longer forming, feeling enlarging, taking him into another plane of consciousness where thought moved too bright and swift and smooth for utterance, and Diana was no longer an image perceived but a presence felt, a quality of experience excited to a new intensity of joy.

A knock came on the door. He lay still, considering who it might be, and at once the knock came again, soft, eager.

Puzzled, he rolled up on his feet and sauntered to the door.

Diana looked up at him.

"So. I'm habit-forming. Howdy."

"I came under my own steam."

"Hard going? Bet you walked around the block three times working up courage. Walk in, take a chair. What's on your mind?"

She slipped onto the couch, sitting close to the edge, flustered, silent, pretty in confusion.

He presumed something had brought her; she wanted him to play for her or she had some news about rehearsals. "Spill it."

She fussed with the clasp of her purse, shy. "I . . . just got tired walking around."

He stood before her. "Don't get it."

"The last two afternoons."

"Still don't catch."

"Well I—I didn't want to go home because then I'd always have to go home if she knew—if my mother knew I wasn't rehearsing afternoons and I thought some afternoon I mightn't want to go home if you—I mean if you and I. . . . So I walked around instead, but then today I thought if you weren't busy. . . ."

"And if I'm not?"

She looked up, rosy-faced, "I can come see you, can't I?"

He sat down beside her and in his pleasure at her coming he forgot the fear she had of a man. He saw it spring into her eyes on the instant, he saw that she braced herself, fighting it, not shrinking away, only the widened eyes betraying her. Seeing that, stabbed by pity, he knew this thing must be cured and there was no sense planning in terms of years; consideration of her youth was canceled by the damage done to her already. Not seeming to notice her discomfort, he leaned away from her, resting on the palm of a hand, asking lightly, the pipe in his mouth, "So your mother thinks you're at rehearsal?"

His question brought a thoughtful, troubled look to her

137

face. "It's not right, is it? I've always told her everything until now."

Everything? Nick wondered. If that were so. . . .

"She's not an ordinary mother," Diana confided, now at ease with him. "She's not old-fashioned. She's a lovely person, really, and she can sing like an angel." How good it was to have someone to talk to! With whom, save Sue, had she been able to chat, confident of understanding? And with Sue it had never been the same since. . . . Diana laid her purse aside, took off her hat and settled deeper into the couch, running her fingers through the long bob. "We've always been pals."

Casually, Nick asked, "Discuss everything with her?"

Diana nodded readily, unaware of any implication. "Everything."

Could it be a literal statement? Nick bit on the pipe, smiling at her. "No secrets?"

Diana assured him, "None. That's why I feel bad about coming here without telling her. I've never done anything like this before."

Then Mrs. Heaton had known. . . .

The girl was rambling on. "We mean so much to each other. In a way, I'm all she has in life."

"Ambitious for you?"

"Ambitious! My, yes! It would break her heart if I didn't succeed. She always wanted a career and she never had one. That's why she wants me to have one."

Stage mothers were a type, he had seen a few. Smoothly, he drew her on. "Gives you advice about your career?"

"Oh yes, she wants to help me all she can." Diana paused, pursuing a thought. "I should show her that new dance, the Hungarian."

He did not want the subject changed; what he wanted to know was bound up with Mrs. Heaton. He went back over what Diana had said; he had got a lot by now. Drawing on the empty pipe, he asked, "So your mother's not old-fashioned?"

Diana followed where he led. "Not a bit. She's modern."

"Modern?"

She was puzzled that he should need the word defined. "Well—broad-minded."

"About what?"

Pinned down like that it did not seem so easy to explain. "My family is old-fashioned. Grampa is very strict. Oh, he's a fine person and I love him! But he's not broad-minded."

"Broad-minded?" Nick smiled the query.

"Well—about conventions."

"I see. And your mother is?"

"Yes. She's not conventional at all."

Nick nodded as though he understood perfectly and Diana was relieved. The attempt to clarify her statements had sent her floundering. She was glad the subject was dismissed. And then Nick asked, "And you?"

Landed right back in the floundering, the girl hesitated, seeking the answer. She picked up her hat and spun it slowly, her introspection deepening. "I'm sure Mother is right about a lot of things. . . ."

"Only?" he prompted.

"Only some things are wrong." She spoke in a low voice, almost to herself, and her face had clouded.

He risked it, being pleasant, casual, asking softly, "How'd you find that out?"

And she was telling him, vibrancy coming in the low voice, her speech quick. "That thing I did. Mr. Mowbray was a director and he promised me a solo dance if I would do that and I did it—it seemed right and it was wrong—wrong—awful—"

The pipe dropped, Nick was on his feet, striding the floor. "And she let you do it. She told you to do it. By God."

The harshness in his voice roused the girl. She saw the black anger that had come like a thunder clap and she was confused, not knowing how it was his censure struck at Sue. And Sue had said 'Don't tell.' . . . But what had she told? How did he

139

know? She got shakily to her feet, assailed with guilt. "No, no! I didn't say—Oh, you mustn't! I did it, I decided—"

"*You* decided." He spat out disgust, wheeling in his stride. "At fourteen. Don't try to shield her, you can't. No secrets, you said. Ambitious for you. Giving you advice about your career. Your own mother! I'll be damned."

His anger was terrible. Diana quailed, seeing everything blown to pieces all at once, thinking she had lost him. She hovered, beseeching, "Oh Nick, Nick, please, please don't be cross!"

"Not with you, Diana." He strode and spun and strode, boiling. That woman was a rotten stinker and she had the girl believing she wore wings and a halo.

Diana tagged at his heels. "Nick, don't, don't be angry."

He turned on her snapping, "I'd like to—" and before he knew it, he had put his arms about her.

Her fists thrust hard against his chest cooled him instantly. The quick seizure had panicked her, she was caught up in the stored terror, not thinking, aware only that a man had laid hold upon her with a strength beyond her own. The blank fright in her face, the plunging struggle to be free, sent a scare into him. Let go of her now and her fright would live on; she would distrust him, thinking this might happen any time. Nick gripped her tight and spoke levelly, his voice hard and cold, no timbre of emotion in it to excite her further. "Hold on, kid. Use your head. I've got my arms around you because I love you. Hear that? I love you. Ever hear that from a man before? That makes it different, doesn't it? There's no harm coming to you." Maybe she couldn't get the sense of what he said, pay attention to it. She was struggling still, all her strength thrown into the pressure on his chest, her face turned down and sideways so he couldn't see it. Suppose he couldn't talk her round. . . .

He went on, sharp and biting. "You're acting like a freak, like a fool, panicky child that hasn't brains enough to know all men aren't the same and this is different. Sure I've got my arms around you and I'm holding tight because you're acting like a freak and a coward and a fool. For Christ's sake, snap out of it and wise up to what love means to you and me before you spoil it all and I tell you to get the hell out of here." He was winning; the tense struggling pressure was dying away. But was there ever such a wooing! "That's the ticket. Now you're using your head. I knew you would. You're no fool, Diana. You've got too much sense to be acting this way with me. You're no coward either, when you use your head." There was no pushing now. His voice grew gentler and his grip eased. "Say, try to figure this out—how do I feel when you act as if I were a toad it made you sick to touch? How would you like it if I loathed the touch of you?" She was standing quietly, but her face was still turned away. He asked, soft and low. "You said you liked me. I figure that's on the level. Is it? Will you look at me and tell me?"

She raised her head and met his eyes. "Yes."

He held her loosely. Smiling, he went on in the low-toned voice. "That was an accident, kid. I didn't mean to grab you. I'm sorry I did. No, maybe I'm not; we've got to have things natural and right between us. See now, I have you in my arms and you're letting me hold you, and you're not scared any-more, and that's something, isn't it? You know what?—you might even get the habit and start pestering me for a hug. If you really like me."

Her eyes clear, she returned his smile tremulously, still shaken by the storm that had passed over her. "Nick, it isn't just liking, is it? Me, I mean. I'm in love with you, aren't I?"

He was so happy that he felt lightheaded. He let his arms fall, releasing her. "Why, I wouldn't know for certain, honey, unless you told me. That's your end of it."

"Don't let go of me, Nick. Nick, I don't want to be a freak or a coward. I like you to hold me. Now, I do."

He did not know what to make of this, incredulous of so much joy, and his eyes searched hers. She meant it, meant it like a child, affectionate and grateful. But seeing her so

141

gentled, so lovable and sweet, all at once he could not trust himself to take her in his arms again. She was too desirable, the male want of her came too swift, too strong. If she should feel that force—No, he had blundered once already. This thing was fragile, precious; it called for a cool head and a lot of direction. He backed away, went hunting for his pipe, and found it on the floor beside the couch. She was great the way she had pulled out of that, listening to what he said, coming round to reason. Sitting down, stuffing the pipe, he gave her a playful smile. "We got to practice up on this. It's going to take rehearsing. Don't rush me, will you?"

But she followed and sat down close and laid her hand on his. "I didn't mean to act as though you were a toad."

She made him nervous, sitting so close, and he saw the irony of it—now he was the one who shrank from touch. Well, Nicky, you started this; you've got to handle it, handle it right and do the thinking on both sides, she's a child. He lifted the hand that lay over his and kissed it. Then, rising briskly, "I didn't eat yet. Did you? What say we go have a bite?"

"All right." She was as pleased with the idea of going out as staying in, and rose at once, putting on her hat. But as they moved to the door something crossed her mind and she came to a stop. "Nicky. . . ."

It was the first time she had called him that. "What, honey?"

"Last time—I kissed you good-by."

"We aren't saying good-by."

"But I won't come back after we eat. I'll have to go home then."

"Say, aren't you rushing this?"

Over her face came a look of hurt surprise. "Why, don't you want to?"

He had laid his hand on the door knob but he hesitated. There was worry in her eyes; sensitive, she might be hurt if he just led her out. "Diana, do you want me to kiss you?"

She nodded, still anxious.

He warned her gently, "It was you kissed me the other day.

If I kiss you it'll be different because I'll mean it. You like me. I love you."

"No, we're both in love. You should kiss me too."

"You want me to?"

"Yes, I do."

There was a hint of being brave about it that steadied his will. He laid the pipe on the book end at the head of the couch. Tenderly, handling what was precious, he drew her into his arms and bent his head, pressing his lips to hers. It was a man's kiss and a lover's. After a moment, he drew back his head and sought her eyes and saw that some very small part of what he felt in the fullness of his love had passed to her and that there was marvel and dreaming in her gaze. "Do you love me, Diana?"

"Yes."

He wanted achingly to keep her in his arms, to go on gazing at her, to kiss her again and again, this joy mounting. But he opened the door and they went out. It was a small stab that she should accept the going so readily, walking contentedly beside him. His well-meant plans came back to him, her youth, waiting. . . . And this was going at a dizzy speed. There was a lot to straighten out and nothing must go wrong. That woman; he must get Diana away from her mother.

He took her arm and she accepted his touch with a quick, glad glance of pride. "Look here, Diana, I want to marry you."

The idea surprised her. "Oh, but you couldn't!"

"Why couldn't I? You could say you were older. Women have been married at sixteen."

"It isn't that."

"Well, why couldn't I?"

She thought it strange he didn't know. "Why, my mother wouldn't let you!"

Coming into the theater for rehearsal next morning, Diana stopped short. Mr. Shanley, the director, sat as usual at the table on the apron, but beside him, surprisingly, stood Mr. Shultz and Nick. Curious, she drew in by the foot of the stairs, watching, while girls came in, went by, going up to the dressing room.

Shultz left the others, came away, passing by her, ducking a surly nod. Nick stayed a moment longer, talking with Shanley, and then he, too, came away, following in Shultz's path. It looked as though he hadn't seen her, which was, after all, quite impossible. "Hello."

He shot a glance back at the director, murmured, "Come out in the alley," and went right on. Mystified, Diana followed him.

Nick stood behind the stage-door entrance out of sight of anyone coming up the alley. He pulled her in beside him. "Why did you stand there looking at me? You want people talking about you?"

Diana stared at him in consternation. It was a call down; he had spoken as he would have spoken to a chorus girl; there was no gentleness, no link of intimacy, no hint that he had ever said 'I love you.' He was giving orders, sharp and quick, demanding her attention and obedience.

"Now get this—Shanley's got a call from Hollywood, he may finish directing this show, he may not, but I'm taking over as assistant director, and inside there, that's all I am to you. Understand?"

"Yes, Nick."

His severity melted, he was smiling, shaking his head. "No-go. You spoke that line with the proper feeling for a dutiful wife. And the name is Allingham, Mr. Allingham. Go to the Automat for lunch, I'll be there. Now scoot, Miss Heaton."

Diana hastened inside. She was hurt and puzzled even though reason told her the call down was deserved; she had heard backstage gossip, she knew how little it could feed on and how devastating it could be. But how could Nick speak so harshly, become a stranger, impersonal, alarming.

There was more to trouble her when rehearsal started and Mr. Allingham stood by the director's table, relaying orders. The white work lights lit up the unwieldy mass of a large musical show in the disorder of the second week of rehearsal; numbers were being beaten into shape, scenes formed in vague outline, the tinny piano music began and stopped and started in again and directions were incessant. Everyone save the more important principals was present at the morning rehearsal; lesser principals in street clothes, still holding to rumpled scripts, chorus girls in their fresh, many-colored rompers, looking like precocious and astonishingly pretty little girls in play suits, Diana's group in the practice costumes that marked them as students of one school of dancing or another, interpretive or ballet, no two alike. Sometimes they would all be on stage in a bustling confusion, sometimes one group alone came into the center and the others dropped into the row of chairs along the back wall. In an occasional brief rest period clusters formed to chat, drifted to the water-cooler by the prop-room, went aside to practice alone.

It was no longer Shanley who gave the directions, Nick had become his mouthpiece. Often the two men conferred, called up the fellow who was setting the chorus routines or the man who had written the book, but the conferences were brief, the work drove on. And Nick drove it in a fashion the easy-going Shanley had not; Mr. Allingham had a way of giving orders, clear and sharp and coolly pleasant, but with a demand for alertness and a quick response, and if he did not think he got that, if there was any lag in execution, any hint of saucy rebellion, his voice would change, quiet still, but with such a cold, stinging lash that it did not matter what he said, the tone was enough to wither all resistance and impel effort; then, that trouble straightened out, in the next instant he was back at being coolly pleasant, driving on.

Diana watched him with increasing consternation. It had been so easy to forget that this was in him. Now it was unbelievable that this hard, dominating man could be a lover, that his ways were tender, that his kiss was magically sweet, that he had said I love you. She did not want him to be like this, it wasn't Nick, yet she saw with dismay that he was getting results Shanley had been trying for, and that seemed to justify his tactics.

She grew nervous as the time for the specialty dance approached; it was in rough shape, some of the girls weren't sure of the routine at the very beginning.

Nick saw that and stopped the dance almost at once. "What's the idea? You all got the same orders, didn't you? How come you're all doing a solo of your own?" He called up Yoland, who had set the dance, talked with her and Shanley. He told the group, "Get over in the wings, the bunch of you, listen to what Miss Yoland tells you. We're not holding up rehearsal while some of you learn your right foot from your left. We'll cut the number if it strains your brains."

Quaking, Diana moved in among the others, a resentful, shamefaced lot. 'The bunch of you!'—and she was one of them. Would he actually cut the number, take her job away? She had seen numbers wiped out since rehearsals began.

Later, that scene came again and they were up for scrutiny. This time he let the dance go as far as it was set, then, with a nod from Shanley, Nick pointed, "You and you—drop out. You ten, take it again."

Two girls had lost their places; the remaining ten went into the routine with the fervor of a team of pack dogs in harness. Nick nodded and went on to the next number.

Sitting across from her in the Automat, Nick said, "There's a lot in show business you don't know yet. Why did you look scared when I bawled out the dance number? Didn't you know you'd done it right? You ought to know, you ought to show you know. You're a better dancer than Yoland right now, but no one's going to guess that if you haven't got the nerve to keep from getting rattled. Where's the pride, kid?"

"Pride? Why, pride isn't nice!—being conceited?"

"No sir, not conceit, just knowing what you've got to give. You go out there and who are you?—just Diana Heaton? No, you're a dancer, you represent a profession, a tradition—yeah, an art with a capital A. The dignity of that is something you've got to stand up for and take a pride in, you can't let it sag. Besides which, it's my idea that you as an individual ought to take a pride in yourself; whatever gifts God gave you, you're honor bound to make the most of, you can't let them go to waste. Pride gives you standards to live up to, a pattern to follow, a tradition of your own you won't let down."

Listening, Diana had grown moody. "Maybe I'm not smart. Maybe I'm stupid."

"What puts that worm in the apple?"

"I seem to be two people, all mixed up. When I'm dancing I guess I'm what you call proud, proud of all the beauty and the joy. But other times. . . . I do get rattled, I'm not sure. Mother is clever. Oh, I don't mean she doesn't do foolish things sometimes, but she's smart in a way I'm not. And—she's disappointed in me. She wouldn't say so, of course, except when she's—not herself."

Nick snarled with disgust, settling back in his chair. "Believe in your mother or believe in yourself. And if you're going to believe her, get out of the business."

Downcast, the girl mused, "She gave me a star to aim at, she showed me beauty. . . . She always thought I'd be somebody. . . ."

"Listen, Diana, this is serious. You can't go around hanging on to nasty things Mama said and thinking maybe Mama's right. You've got to believe in yourself all the time, and keep on believing no matter how tough a bawling out you get from anyone."

Diana looked across at him, asking timidly, "Do you believe in me, Nick?"

His answer came like a slap in the face. "Suppose I say I'm not so sure?" He made it insulting, the words sneered. "Suppose I say I'm not convinced?"

She winced back, dropping her head. He watched the struggle that went on in silence. Slowly her back straightened, her head went up and she met his eyes with a steady look. "I can dance. I know that."

He wanted to hug her for the victory she had gained in

147

making that quiet declaration. "That's something, sugar. You look nice and proud right now. Stay that way. I see I got a lot of salvage work to do on you, the ego's kind of sickly. I believe in you, Diana, I've believed in you from the first day. Maybe I can see some things other people don't. You're not going to be somebody, you are somebody."

She thanked him with a richly happy smile. "Nicky, I love you for that."

The truth of what she said stung him. "Yeah," he said quietly. "I guess you do—just for that. And that's not enough by a long shot. I might be worth loving for myself. I don't mind building up your ego, kid, but you're not going to tear mine down. What are we sitting here for? Get going, honey, we can do better in my place, and this is the last afternoon I have to spend with you. And listen—" he led the way out "—couple of things you might go to work on. When you going to study ballet?"

"When the show opens and I have a salary."

"Get an advance on your salary and start now."

"Could I do that?"

"Done all the time." He steered her adroitly through the crowd on Broadway. "Here's something else—will you take your beautiful eyes off me sometime during rehearsal?"

"Why! Was I staring?—but how could you know? You never looked at me."

They ducked across a street, dodging traffic. "I saw you all the time and maybe some other people noticed. You've got a face that tells the world what you're thinking. It's an asset in your work, having an expressive face, but you might learn how to control it when the spotlights aren't turned on."

She challenged him by asking what she had been thinking.

He grinned at her, impish. "Don't like me as a director, do you? Shocking how mean I can be, huh? You wish I'd speak nicely, be sweet and kind and say 'please' and 'thank you' when I call a number. Ever think how long I'd last as an animal trainer in that menagerie if I did? I'm giving this bunch

148

what they're used to, what they'll answer to, and I'm new with Shultz, I can't take chances and fall down on the job. Don't forget Shultz's girls are mostly tarts and a pretty spoiled bunch of tarts at that, some of them with daddys who could buy out Shultz and never miss the dough. Besides which, maybe you didn't notice, I'm young—and—maybe you didn't notice this either—some girls think I'm good-looking, all of which doesn't help much when it comes to authority. Yeah, and besides all that, I hate poor work, lazy work, the kind that tries to get by on pull. It doesn't belong in a theater."

They turned into Fiftieth Street and Nick stopped talking. What Diana had said came back to him, 'I love you for that' . . . . No, not enough; I have to mean more to her than that.

They went into the apartment. Diana looked about, sighing. "The last afternoon. . . ."

"Care much?"

"Yes." Her moodiness returned. "So much. Only. . . ." She shrugged and sank into the armchair, letting her hat drop to the floor.

"Only what, honey?" He picked up her hat and laid it on the piano.

She sprang out of the chair and went into dance movement, sweeping and circling about the room with a sudden intensity, calling out to him, "Play for me, Nicky! Please! Anything!"

He leaned against the wall, studying her, not knowing what impulse drove her. "What you trying to get away from?"

"Myself!"

"Can't be done."

Thwarted, she came to an abrupt stop and stood dejected.

"What's bothering you, sweetheart?"

She walked back to the chair and curled up in it before she answered. "Coming here. Not telling my mother. I should."

He turned to the table and straightened a stack of music. "Suppose you tell her?"

"I think . . . . I think she'd say I shouldn't see you anymore."

Nick's reply was prompt. "Then don't tell her."

"But that's not right. A girl shouldn't have secrets from her mother. Oh Nick, you don't know how it feels! The first day I didn't start to worry until I was nearly home. Yesterday I started in to worry as soon as I left you."

"And today you're starting in as soon as you get here." He gathered scattered pencils and set them evenly in a row.

"It's such a haunting, guilty feeling. . . ." Diana left off. The feeling was beyond expression in words. For the last two years, brooding and hurt, she had lost the facility of speech, the sum of what she felt poured into dancing. Now that there was someone to whom she longed to talk, language still seemed inadequate, the more so since with Nick she was constantly in the turbulence of new emotions, new ideas, not yet in order and resolved. She would have liked to think of Nick and nothing else, but the pangs of conscience grew. They came without process of reasoning, up from a deep fixation, the life habit of loyalty to Mother mingling with the unknown, archaic race memory of mother-domination. "Oh, I should tell her! I keep expecting her just to look at me and see it."

Nick arranged the pencils in a square. "And if she does?"

"I don't know what'll happen." Diana's voice was full of trouble. "I only know I should tell her."

"But you're scared to." The square was broken, altered to a triangle.

"I can't bear to hurt her. I love her so."

He let the triangle stay and rested on his knuckles, putting an end to the nervous fidgeting. It was clear what this meant. He could lose Diana, lose her any day. It wasn't as if Diana were a woman, feeling love deeply, naturally, prepared to fight for it. Today, tomorrow, that woman could snatch the girl away. A fine mother she was; it wasn't safe to trust the girl in her hands. I can't lose Diana, I can't let her go and not know what'll happen to her or if I'll ever get her back.

He looked toward the young, brooding face; an emotional face with a fine sensitive intelligence; the girl would love deeply, passionately, loyally. But there was that fear in her which worked against him. . . . Love should be a thing that would grow slowly, beautifully, no forced growth. . . . But it wasn't as if things were natural and right with Diana now. . . . His purpose formed, was accepted, and his will set.

He caught her eyes, and smiling, held out his arms. She regarded him, not moving, and his heart sank. He waited, willing her to come to him, and then gradually she uncurled out of the chair and approached, but stiffly.

"Say, we're getting out of practice. You said you liked me to put my arms around you. Or was that only yesterday?"

Standing shyly close, her smile was faint.

"Don't be obliging, kid. If I'm still the toad—"

She came impulsively into his arms. "No! It's just—Oh, Nick, what's right, what's wrong?"

"That's a big one, honey. Thought you had all the modern answers."

"You're modern, aren't you?"

"Modern enough to know the old pattern got shaky because a lot was wrong with it. Now people say there aren't any answers, so what the hell. But that won't work. We have to have a code to go on, we have to be able to put trust in one another or it's dog eat dog and to hell with humanity. Honor and honesty might sound like old-fashioned words but they're mighty useful, trying to pull together and know what's what. I told you not to tell your mother, but that's not what I want to say. I want to say—go ahead and tell her. Only you're kind of messed up right now and I'm not sure you got the strength to get everything straightened out at once. You still let Mama do the thinking for you and I guess by your way of looking at it that's right, but my way it's dead wrong. You're out in the world, fighting your own fights, and you ought to think for yourself." He left off speaking seriously, became cajoling. "Now honey, I did my best for you on that. Don't think much of it, do you? Will you stop puckering that brow of yours? Suppose you give me a break and forget about Mama while you're here, you can think about her when you're home. That fair? So. Thinking about me? No. What color are my eyes?

151

Aw, you had to look to find out. Yours are sea-color, blue, green, grey—mostly green. Next time you're dancing, think to yourself 'He said my eyes were beautiful,' and you know what? —the dance will be different."

"Will it? How?"

That caught her interest. But it didn't mean anything to her to be in his arms. "Be thinking, 'He loves me, he loves me true,' and the audience will say, 'That girl's got something.' "

"Why?"

He ran the fingers of one hand through her hair, caressing her. "Love can make a woman beautiful. The women up on top in show business know love. I don't mean all this cheap wisecracking stuff about experience and knowing life and a lot of sex affairs. They know that love is something fine and they're proud and beautiful in love. They're not kids who don't know what it's all about."

Beautiful. . . . 'Beautiful and natural'—Sue said that, coming out of the woods with Chris, and now—'Leave men alone.' It was so hard to understand. "Nick, I'm not just a kid, am I?"

His smile was tender, "Someways, yes."

His answer worried her. "I'm not a freak, am I?"

"On your way to being one, weren't you?" He kissed her cheek. "You don't love me, Diana."

"Yes, I do."

He shook his head. "I have my arms around you and it doesn't mean a thing to you."

Troubled, she tried to find his meaning and failed. "What should it mean except that—that I do like you—and I trust you?"

" 'Like?' " He brought out the word as proof against her. "I'm glad about the trust part. But if this meant love to you, you'd want to kiss me."

Still troubled, she offered, "I'll kiss you."

"Most obliging."

"I'll kiss you because I love you."

152

"A punch line. And you don't know how to speak it. No inflection. That would leave an audience sitting on its hands."

"Why are you teasing me, Nick?"

"I'm telling you the truth. You say you love me and you don't know what love is."

"I do."

"Kiss me."

She gave him her child's kiss.

Again he shook his head. "Did I kiss you that way yesterday? See, you don't remember. Like a girl who can't learn a routine."

"Don't say that!"

"Hurts your professional pride? Well, why don't you kiss me the way I kissed you? Because you don't remember, you don't know how, you don't love me."

Taunted by the mockery in the gentle voice, Diana was silent and uneasy. Eyes down she murmured, "You kiss me."

"Want another lesson?"

A flush spread over her face. "I want you to kiss me."

"Sure about that?"

"Yes."

He wasn't sure; she had grown tense. He laid his head against hers, stroking her, wanting to feel that yielding quiet come into her body, stalling for time. "I don't give kissing lessons, honey. When I kiss you it's because I love you and I want you to love me in return. It's something—" He broke off. Her tense body had begun to tremble. "What is it, kid? What have I said—?" He drew back his head, seeking her eyes, but she had turned her face away. "Tell me, Diana. Something's wrong." She did not answer and her agitation grew.

"I just thought—" Her voice shook and stopped.

"What did you think?"

"I can't tell you."

He stepped back from her at once. "No, that's wrong." He took a cigarette from the table, lit it, put more distance between them. "You can say anything to me."

Deserted in the center of the room, she stood unmoving, head down; the pose might have been from a tragic dance.

He spoke sharply. "Tell me, kid."

"I got scared."

"Scared of me?"

"You were—it sounded as if—warning me—"

"And you thought—?"

Her whole body flowed into an imploring gesture, arms flung out to him in appeal. "It's true what you said yesterday—men are different? You—you won't—?"

He shot forward, the cigarette thrown down. "My God, is that what you thought—that I was leading up to something?" He took her strongly by the wrists. "Get this straight—I wouldn't have you now for anything in the world."

She blinked at him, blinded by his intensity, still contending with the unknown. "You mean—you wouldn't?"

"No, I wouldn't, you damn kid."

He towered, glowering, a hot, dark gypsy look about him, his grip on her wrists a tight, binding pressure. She could not grasp the reason for his anger. In a weak voice she struggled on, needing the truth. "You don't want me that way?"

"I do want you that way."

She could not meet his eyes. Still, mystery remained. Feebly, she questioned, "Then, why wouldn't you?"

"Because I'm going to marry you, that's why." He threw her hands away from him. "And you're going to want me to."

"No, I couldn't. Besides, Mother—"

He cut in harshly. "That'll come straight."

"Oh, I don't know, I don't know!" It was an abandoned, despairing cry. Diana flung herself down on the edge of the couch and huddled there, her face in her hands.

Nick crossed the floor to pick up the burning cigarette, bring it to the ashtray, crush it. The sight of Diana's wretchedness washed all the anger out of him. "Take it easy, honey. You're wound up so tight the spring's going to come loose if you don't look out, isn't that so? I don't blame you for getting twisted, maybe what I said sounded the way you thought it did, but you don't know me yet. Maybe I'm not modern, not what your mother means by that, anyhow. I just know I love you and I want to marry you and I want you to feel the same way about it. That's what the real thing means to me. It made me mad that you'd think I was just trying to make you after I told you I didn't want any more harm to come to you. Diana, I promise you this, you don't have to be scared of me, I'll never do a thing to you that you don't want me to. Now forget about it. Stretch out on the couch and quiet down." He strolled over and arranged the wine-red cushions for her head. "Do what I tell you. Lie down."

She obeyed the order. He sat down on the edge of the couch. "There now. Take a couple of deep breaths, relax. Everything all right?"

"But how can it be? Mother—besides, marriage—I don't want—"

"Sh. Stop fretting. You're all set for tears. Want to make me feel bad, too? Listen kid, do you believe what I promised? Do you trust me?"

"Yes."

He picked up her hands and kissed them. "Nice hands. May I do that?"

A fragile smile crept slowly to her lips. "Yes."

He bent over and kissed her cheek. "May I do that?"

"Yes, Nick."

He kissed her throat. "And that?"

Her smile deepened in affection.

"Sure about trusting me?"

"Yes, I do."

He lay down beside her. "May I do that?"

Her eyes widened, a momentary rigidity possessed her body, but her smile stayed. In a moment she answered as before. "Yes."

"Sure? I'll go over and sit in the chair if you wish me to."

"You can stay here."

He took her in his arms. "That's better, honey."

She was not afraid.

"I think you like me a whole lot, sweetheart."

"I do, I really do. So much."

"You're going to love me."

Talking softly, now bantering, now serious, saying the loverly, praiseful things that came to her so healingly, caressing her tenderly, breaking off to give her his kiss upon the lips again and again, he set himself to turn a scared child into a happy woman, to win her wholly and in such a way that she would have no foreboding of the change, so that in time the full of love might be between them; natural and right, fright eased away, desire standing in its place. It must be her desire, not his, that she would act on when the showdown with that mother came; Diana must come to love him wholly as a woman loves a man, prepared to fight for love.

Joy grew in him that he had the power of will to do this thing, that he could so cherish her that love was like a work of art, a beauty to be created with all the skill and patience and mastery that a man had in him. He could do it; the immediate, surging longing for her could be held, hoping for that union when she would come to know a joy to match and lift his own, a union that would be complete and beautiful and lasting.

9

THE LANDLADY met Mrs. Heaton coming in the street door. "There was a phone call for Miss Diana from a theatrical agency. I thought it might be important, so I called her theater, but they said she wasn't there."

"Oh, but she must be! I'll try again. Thank you, Mrs. Borden." Mrs. Heaton went on lightly down the hall to the phone booth. The call from the agency was probably unimportant, Diana's name was in so many agencies and calls came in from time to time but always for some cheap thing, work as an extra or in the chorus. Funny, Mrs. Borden had been told Diana wasn't in the theater! Mrs. Heaton, searching for a nickel in her coin purse, hummed. She had enjoyed the hours with Bob, she was not sorry that she had gone further than she had intended; life could be so bleak and lonely. Friends she did not want; she would have been ashamed to have visitors, living in a boarding house, and besides how flat and dull were friendships when one has known the heightened stimulation of affairs! Bob was pleasant, very . . . . She dropped the nickel and gave the number.

A man's voice answered. No, Miss Heaton wasn't there. Quite positively. No, Miss Heaton only came mornings. Why, since last Friday.

Mrs. Heaton sat on in the dark, close privacy of the booth, stunned. Why on earth hadn't Diana told her that she did not rehearse afternoons? What could it mean? What was the girl doing with herself in the meantime?

The answer came like a blow that sent Mrs. Heaton staggering out of the booth, gripping at the banister.

That man. Nick.

But even so, she could not believe it, Alone in the dim hall she clung to the rail for support as though she were in an earthquake with the whole world heaving and rending about her. Diana deceiving her? Diana lying? No, it could not be, not Diana. Had she not told the girl leave men alone? Had not Diana always, always obeyed? Had not Diana promised?

But it was that man, she knew it. Otherwise Diana would have told the truth.

Diana had deceived her.

The pain and shock of that betrayal came first, shutting out all else. It was betrayal she had never believed could be. She crept up the stairs, retreating to her room, pulling herself along by the rail, an old woman, her back bent and her steps slow. Stupefied, she kept repeating, but I told her not to, I told her not to, as though that fact were final and nothing else could follow.

This was disaster, utter and complete. And now guilt that had lain hidden, laying waste like a slow disease, came clear in the full anguish of remorse; Mrs. Heaton had one long blinding moment of revelation—I should never have sanctioned Mowbray; that started this.

The door of her room shut, the woman leaned against it, clutching her head with both hands, thinking, I will go mad. To know that Diana, so beautiful, so full of promise, could lie, deceive her mother, lapse into ruin, come to nothing; and to know the cause of this—

It could not be borne. One could not go on living and endure that monstrous and destroying guilt. Mrs. Heaton thrust the intolerable pain from her and in an instant remorse had changed into another shape—it came out now as hatred for the girl.

Diana was to blame. Yes, Diana. She had been told what not to do and she had done it anyhow. To go on playing about with that man was a deliberate act in flagrant defiance of her mother. The girl was bad.

Mrs. Heaton's will hardened and fixed. She shan't do it. I won't let her. I'll make her be good. She's got to be somebody.

She sat down to wait for her daughter's return. For the first time she knew what it was to wait not knowing when the girl would come or from where. Not to know where your own daughter is; to know that someplace, lost in the vast city, a strange man had her. Waiting, minutes passing, quarter hours, waiting helplessly to get her back, to gain possession, and thinking what if she never comes back, what if something awful happens to her, what if I never see her again. . . .

Smoking one cigarette after another, the filmy layers of smoke forming overhead to bend and tear and spin in eddies of air current, the craving came for the blessed soothing fiery strength that could be poured out of a bottle. But that could not help her now; this was one emergency that must be met with a clear head; if Diana came in and found she had been drinking, Diana would not take her seriously; the girl would put on that maddening phlegmatism, that provoking, goading air of 'what you say now doesn't count.' No, this great crisis would have to be gone through on her own strength.

Waiting, minutes dragging, memories came . . . . of that little girl who held to Mother's hand, traveling on rubbery, uncertain legs, and of the sunny, all-consuming happiness that sprang from gazing at that bright, trusting little face. . . . The perfection of the small naked body standing tranquilly upright in the tub to be soaped and sponged. . . . Papa's pride in the girl, the stern-faced, white haired man taking the eager child upon his knee . . . . Strangers on the street turning to look a second time, and Diana, so blithely unconscious, skipping and chattering by her side. . . . Pals . . . . The hours shared, the devotion and the patience lavished on Diana that she might grow in beauty and in promise . . . . Why, Dicky, not the loyal, loving little pal—Dicky, you couldn't do this to me! Hate Diana? No, not Diana, not what Diana truly was, not what Diana still had it in her to become. This was some changeling who disobeyed, deceiving her, some changeling brought into being by a bad man's influence . . . . Oh, but for absorption in Bob's company, this would not have happened, it would have been detected; that much of guilt could be admitted. Confound Bob and his attentions and persuasions— he had let in Nick.

Steps were coming up the stairs, Diana's steps. I've got her back. She's coming to me. I've got her and I'll keep her. No more of this, she's mine. Mrs. Heaton put out her cigarette and settled deeper in the chair, all her energy gathered, ready to drive forward.

Diana came wandering in, moving in a spell of beauty, a glowing daze upon her face, rapt dreaming in her eyes. "Hello, Sue." From habit she came to kiss her mother's cheek, the action automatic, her spirit far away. She strayed on through the room, spilling purse and hat upon the bureau, fell into a trance, staring at nothing, idled to the open window, sat upon the sill, face lifted to the sky. Wariness was not in mind; she did not know her mother looked at her. Her wits were wandering, lost in a soft confusion; the murmur of love-talk went on in memory; her spirit floated, singing.

"What have you done!"

Poignant with accusal and despair the voice came from the corner. Confounded, the girl started to her feet, staring.

"Diana, what have you done?"

Done? Done? She had done nothing. The girl struggled to gather her wits knowing with a sudden sinking of heart that this was the dreaded foreseen moment—Sue knew. "Mother, I haven't done anything wrong."

This was bold-faced lying and defiance. This was the hated changeling, not Diana. Mrs. Heaton kept her head; Diana must be brought to her senses, recalled. The woman spoke with quiet and accusing sorrow. "You don't need to tell me, Dicky. You were with a man, I see it in your face. He kissed you, didn't he? You don't need to answer. I know. And I know you have deceived me. You haven't been to rehearsal any afternoon this week, have you? Chick, how can you stand there and tell me you have done nothing wrong when you have done the thing I told you not to do, which you promised not to do, when you have sneaked away to do it, thinking you'd trick me? Don't lie to me, Dicky. I never lied to you."

Diana was lost. She had thought it could be explained when the moment came, but facing those grief-bright eyes, hear-

160

ing the grief-laden reproach, knowing the truth of what Sue said, she was cast into the full misery of remorse, helpless and without defense of any kind. She started toward the woman, needing to come close, embrace, establish love.

But Mrs. Heaton waved her off. "You're sorry now. What good does that do? I've got to know one thing I cannot understand—why didn't you tell me?"

Checked, the girl sank on her knees before her. "I thought you'd worry. I thought you'd be unhappy. I didn't want—"

"But you, my pal, deliberately went ahead and did what you knew would make me unhappy?"

How could it be explained? "I didn't want to hurt you, I just couldn't bear to. I knew I should tell you."

"Then why didn't you?"

Diana didn't know. There seemed to be no answer.

Mrs. Heaton took silence for resistance. She bent forward, speaking with energy, insistent. "You have got to tell me, Diana, you have got to or I'll die. Don't think I don't know that this is all my fault. I've put ideas in your head, thinking you had sense enough to grasp them. You know I've had affairs, you think that you can have them. You aren't smart enough to see the difference in your life and mine—you with a career, your whole life ahead of you. Don't you know it will kill me if I see you fail?"

"I'm not going to fail, I'm not."

Mrs. Heaton brushed this earnest speech aside. "Why did you do it?"

Diana sought for the words, the right words. A stupid answer now would bungle everything.

"Why did you do it?"

The answer formed, the true one. Diana stood up. "Because I love him."

It was the worst that Mrs. Heaton had dreaded; now the woman knew the force that she would have to break. Aghast, she spoke so softly that she almost whispered. "I shan't let you. You can't do this. You must promise me that you will never see that man again."

161

Diana backed away until she felt the wall behind her. Her answer came as softly. "No. Please. No, Sue. I can't promise that."

Mrs. Heaton sprang up, a small, vital, willful figure. "You *shall* promise me."

Frightened, the girl's words rushed out. "No—no—wait a minute—let me explain—Nick is wonderful, he's good, he's clever, he loves me, he wants to help, he wants to marry me, he won't interfere with my career—"

Mrs. Heaton cut her off with one word. "No."

Diana squirmed in distress. Oh, what were the things to say, the smart things that would explain and make all clear! "Mother, wait, please be reasonable—"

"Reasonable?" Mrs. Heaton's control broke. Hatred for this changeling shot loose. "You dare stand there arguing with me about a man who's got you so crazy that you'll cheat, you'll disobey, you'll break your word, you'll tell me what you will and will not do? What kind of man would see you on the sly, sneak you away, not dare to face your mother? You—married?—to some Broadway cheapskate, a worthless dishonorable nobody? Of course he wants to marry you! He can see you might be somebody! But he'll want to boss you, he'll tell you what to do, he'll give you babies, and you'll wind up nowhere! You shan't, Diana, you've gone mad!" Grief laced through her anger. "You can't do this to me, you can't! Why, you're my baby, flesh of my flesh, I made you, you're mine! Oh Dicky, Dicky, you're all I've got! Can some fool's kisses make you cast me off?"

Diana had begun to cry. "Mother, no—I wouldn't do that—"

"But you're doing it right now! Oh Lord, I'll die. I can't stand this. I tell you that I'll kill myself—I'll jump out that window. My girl, my baby that I've loved—"

The woman raged in furious, despairing grief about the room and Diana stayed flat against the wall, calling out to her, imploring, "Mother—dearest—"

"Oh, I've loved you so. My wonderful, beautiful girl.

Who sat and played for you for hours? Who took you to see Duncan? Who taught you to interpret music?" She stopped, incredulous, before the girl. "Why Diana, this isn't you! Don't you know you're bewitched? You wouldn't break my heart, you wouldn't let me go stark, staring, screaming mad!"

Diana's tears had turned to a heart-rending sobbing. "Don't, don't, I love you, Mother!"

"But you'll leave me for a man?"

"No, no, I'll never leave you!"

"Then you'll give him up?"

"No, no, I can't, I can't, please—"

"Do you want to kill me? You've got to give him up. You've got to promise me."

"Please—no—"

"You *will* promise me."

"I can't, I love him—"

"You little fool. You stupid, silly, worthless little fool. I will not let you throw your life away. You're bad, Diana, you're wicked, this is an evil thing. You'll never dare to face an audience if you do this to me. You promise me, do you hear?"

Diana slid to the floor and lay there, face down, sobbing. "No, it's not wrong, it's not evil! You can't make me promise! I love him."

Mrs. Heaton was beside herself. "Love! Lust, you mean, that's what it is. Are you the girl who told me you could not bear to think about a man's love? Why, you shameless, dirty little liar!"

Diana writhed upon the floor, shaken by her sobbing. "Don't, don't! You mustn't! Let me explain—"

Mrs. Heaton stood over her. "Yes, do. Tell me, tell me everything you've done. Tell me what he's done to you. Tell me where you've been with him."

Sitting up, battling with the wrenching sobs, Diana tried to tell her, tell her everything so that Sue would understand. She went on blindly, headlong, answering every question, piling statement upon statement. And Sue did not, would not understand; it seemed the things Diana said only made matters worse, the woman more determined. It came back to the same thing— "You have got to give him up. You have got to promise me," and Diana, plunged again in tears, "I won't promise, I can't."

It went on and on. The room darkened, steps went along the hall, lodgers going down to dinner; and then returning steps, the dinner over. It still went on, the lamp upon the table lit, the hours changing, and still the insistent, nagging demand, "You will promise me," and Diana, exhausted, clinging to refusal. Worn out, the woman drew upon a reserve of energy; the bottle brought out and set upon the table, she started in afresh upon the wretched girl and kept it up so that it seemed there could never be an end. Fighting for possession of her daughter, prepared to go to any length to drive the hated changeling out, the woman knew no pity. Pity? How could she think of pity when before her loomed the black, mad, desolation of hope utterly destroyed, life stripped of meaning, the cherished dream demolished and in ruins? Panic made her merciless. In this catastrophe that called for strength and power, she felt the inroads of the years of degeneration since she had started in to drink; seeking to hold that domination over Diana she had always held so easily, now that it met with opposition for the first time, her nerves gave way and she was scared and desperate beneath her determined assertion of authority. Pity for Diana? No, she had no thought of that, only that somehow she must keep the girl. Having the facts on Nick, she dirtied everything about him, she lashed and lashed again at the raw sensitivity, sparing no cruelty of talk to break rebellion. But Diana, groveling upon the floor, hands covering her ears, sob-shaken still, fought back, moaning the one word, no.

And Mrs. Heaton had to come to bargaining. "For one month, then. Promise me you will not see him for a month."

Diana gasped, "How can I—when he's in the theater?"

"Idiot. You can't promise not to see him if he stands before your eyes. But you can promise that for one month you will not go to his apartment, you will not let him make love to you, you will not let him kiss you. Can you do that, or are you so depraved, so full of lust—"

Diana gave the promise.

Coming briskly into the theater, Nick's eyes ran over the early-comers who were already on the stage, the more ambitious limbering up, practicing alone. But the one who should have been among them wasn't there. Nick went on without pause to the table on the apron where Shanley sat and took the seat across from him. The two men talked, reviewed the run of the work, and then Shanley lapsed into complaint—Hollywood was waiting for him, and wasn't Shultz a louse to hold him to this contract? The stage was gradually filling and still Diana had not come. Nick glanced at his watch, remarked there was time for a smoke and went out to linger in the alley, seeing the late-comers make a dash for it, but no Diana. Time up, he came back in, and there she was, off alone in a corner, not practicing; she must have arrived at the theater ahead of him and stayed up in the dressing room till now. He went on to his place and rapped on the table. At the signal for work to begin, there was the bustle of girls rising from their chairs, making a last minute rush down the stairs, pushing into places, forming lines. He saw Diana moving into her place and the way she moved—heavy, slow, dulled—informed him.

This is it. It's come. There's been a showdown. And she lost. Then, as Diana neared, not looking toward him, he saw the swollen eyes. My God, she must have cried for hours.

It cut into him. Behind his impassive waiting for the places to be taken, anger leaped and surged. That Diana should be made to suffer, that the mark of her suffering must be seen, stared at, whispered about, she would feel it, sure, a sensitive kid like that. Mrs. Heaton, you're a devil to do this to your daughter.

He rapped again, sang out an order, and the music and

the action started up, bright and gay. He did his work, concentrating upon it, keeping his thought off Diana, but as he called the Roman scene his nerves began to jump; the slim figure in the pale yellow silk getting into line still moved without life, clumsy, numbed, and instantly, thinking, Jesus, she's licked, he saw the danger right ahead. She was going to be lousy and if she was how could he spare her, pass it by? He might just as well make an announcement to the assembled cast, I play favorites and this is my sweetie. And if he bawled her out, if she couldn't take it, broke down. He wished to Heaven that he had never called the number, had found some pretext to skip it—Shanley didn't give a damn what went on. If only now, the music starting, she would come alive, save herself. He took a pencil out of his pocket, played with it, his eyes on Diana. Come on kid, please kid, snap into it.

Diana could not come alive. She was a stupid girl, wicked, lustful, she would never dare to face an audience. . . . Sometime, a long while back before this misery set in, she had been loved by Nick and had known light and radiance and music of the soul. Not now. She could not even want to dance, the music sounding. She was burdened, stupefied, and the dance was fast.

And then it happened; she blundered headlong into another girl, they both tripped, caught at each other to keep from falling, and in the split second of the impending collision, Nick had dropped the pencil, stooped, pursuing it.

A hushed malice ran through the watchers back in the chairs. Ah, there was one blunder Hawk-eye hadn't caught! But Nick had to pick up the pencil, see the end.

Diana was late in the final tableau.

He could not let it go, he had to call it. "Take it again—no—not the whole dance—last eight bars. And you there in the middle, for Christ's sake snap into it."

Brief as the call down was, he had sworn, and a resentful murmur ran through the watchers; he had his nerve, all right, swearing at a girl! Why, she was the best in that bunch and anyone could see she had been crying and was upset about something. He might have let her off, just once. Mean, all right.

Nick had sworn at her. It was public disgrace, just what would happen to a fool. She tried hard and this time the tableau passed. He called the next number.

One of the other dancers put an arm about Diana's shoulders as they left the center of the stage. "Don't mind him."

Grateful for this unexpected friendliness. Diana slipped her arm about the girl's waist, confiding, "I was bad."

"Aw, he's just nasty."

But she could not stand talking to this friendly girl, she had to get off by herself and practice; the dance would come again. He had said for Christ's sake, and there was appeal in that as well as command; it was hard on him if she did badly. She went alone into a corner and practiced diligently and when the number came again, lifeless still, no light on her face, no spirit in her work, she yet managed to move fast and make no blunders.

Nick, groaning inwardly, thought, I've got to see her, I've got to find out how bad this is. But how arrange to meet? She might go straight home after morning rehearsal. By what device slip word to her? Simple enough to call her aside as he dismissed; the company would take it as a further call down, and in a second he could arrange a meeting. But no, her face would give it all away. What then? He called the finale of the first act, still hunting for a pretext. Yes, the advance, the money for her lessons. He signaled the young fellow breaking in as assistant stage manager and Tommy came quickly to his side. "Miss Heaton wants an advance. Tell her to come out to the box office when she's dressed. I'll take care of it."

The company dismissed, Nick nodded to Shanley, walked down the apron, jumped the footlights and went up the aisle. A glance back took in Tommy giving his message to Diana. Nick got the money for her from the box office and waited in the back of the darkened auditorium.

167

"Mr. Allingham wants to see you in the box office when you're dressed." It was a business summons that might mean anything, even dismissal; the man who would swear at the woman he loved put work first and her work had been dreadful. Could she beg another chance, promising to do better? But could she promise to do better? Would she ever again know that fine elation out of which dancing rose? He had told her how to dance; 'Think to yourself. . . .' No, she hadn't thought it; it would be too painful now to think. 'He said my eyes were beautiful, he loves me true.'

Dressed, she hurried along the passage that ran behind the boxes, stumbling in the dark. Stupid, bad girl, never dare to face an audience—

Nick formed out of shadow. "Come down in the lounge. We can see what we're doing."

The stairs yawned, a black pit. He struck a match, leading the way. As they reached the lounge, the flame died and they were in pitch dark. He struck another, taking in the layout of the long room, the scattered blood-red plush seats, the location of the light switch, then, looking into her face, whipped out the flame.

Blackness closed in, thick. She was in his gentle embrace, his lips were against hers. This was so unexpected, so quick and deft, that she was amazed and unresisting. Why then, Nick loved her still, loved her despite that exhibition of stupidity; he would not take her job away. Happiness rose in a wave and broke at memory of her promise to her mother —Nick was kissing her, and that was forbidden. And because she must break away, explain, go into the confusion and misery of talk, all at once she was clinging to him, giving back the kiss, needing him, needing him, wanting to stay lost and hidden in the blind dark.

It was wrong; she had promised. She broke the kiss. "I mustn't."

Still having her in his arms, his voice was low, happy. "You love me, you want my love."

"No—don't hold me. I promised. She knows."

He was gone. There was only the dark and silence. Frightened, she groped for him. "Don't leave me! Nick—?"

"Right beside you, where I'll be every time I get the chance." His fingers met hers, he held her hand. "Diana, we've got to talk. Take my key and scoot over to my place. I'll pick up some sandwiches, we can eat there."

"I promised I wouldn't go to your place."

"You told her you had gone?" It was reproof, hurt. "What else?"

There was a moment of shamed silence. "I told her everything."

"All the things I said to you?"

"Maybe I missed some."

"How I held you in my arms on the couch?"

"Nicky, she—Yes, I told her."

"And then you promised not to see me any more?"

"No. That's what she wanted. I wouldn't promise that." His fingers tightened on hers. "Say, that's something! What did you promise?"

"I didn't want to promise anything. I tried hard."

"I bet you did, kid."

"I did. I told her that I loved you."

"Swell. Not easy, huh?"

They were unaware that their bodies had drawn together, his arm about her shoulders.

"But I had to promise. She—made me."

"What?"

"For one month. I won't go to see you or let you kiss me." She felt his arm about her and moved conscientiously away. "I promised."

They stood, not touching. His voice close, came out of the darkness. "Diana, you've got to keep that promise. I believe you're the kind that will. But listen to me—She'll do everything she can in that one month to make you hate me, and maybe she can do it."

"No, she can't."

There was silence, then bitterly. "I'll bet right now your

169

head is full of nastiness she put there—only it hasn't had time to brew. I've only had one day, one afternoon, a couple of hours with you when things were right between us and you trusted me, you weren't scared. That isn't much to stand against the years she's had you, I know that. Listen, you gave her a promise, will you give me one? When the month is up, will you walk into my place and let me take you in my arms and kiss you and talk to you, a good long talk, two, three hours? Will you?"

"I will. I promise."

"Good for you. Something else I'd like to ask—don't tell her. If she knows that you've promised that, it'll be hard on you, she won't let up."

Diana was silent. Tricking Sue, deceiving her; no, if Sue should ask. . . .

"All right, so you can't promise that, drop it. It was for your sake, honey."

"Nicky, don't you have to go? This is your lunch hour." No answer came from the dark; again she was beset by the sense of desertion and reached out, groping.

His hand met hers. "Yeah. . . . Just trying to figure out words of wisdom for the young. . . . You were damn lousy in rehearsal, and speaking as Mr. Allingham, I'm telling you I won't take it, see?"

This was the hard, professional voice. "Oh . . . you sent for me."

"To give you an advance. Tommy tell you that?"

"No."

"He should have. Well, now that you're here you can take the call down. You were lousy. Did you ever stop to think that Shultz comes breezing in every now and again to check up on whether we're earning the pennies he hands out? Suppose he saw you this morning? What chance would you have going up to the office to say, 'Mr. Shultz, I want a solo?' "

"Oh Nick, I don't know, maybe I'm no good—"

"Cut it. I could slap you for saying that. I told you yesterday—believe in yourself or get out of the business. So all right, you went through something last night, I know you did, but what right have you got to mope up there on the stage while work is on?"

"Nick, I tried, I did try."

"Then you've got to try harder. I saw a woman work a show the night her husband died. All right, you're just starting in, but you've got to learn fast. You've got to learn to be a trouper, Diana, and keep your head up. Don't forget you didn't pick an easy berth, aiming for the top as a dancer. If it was easy the world would be running over with would-be's, everyone has got some of the stuff in him the artist puts to work, but most people won't take the chance you're taking—the chance of failing; that goes right alongside of aiming high. You chose the dream and you face the danger. Well then, face it, stand up to it. Don't forget it's not what talent you have that counts, it's what you do with what you have. Now get this straight—I let you down light the time I dropped the pencil—"

"You did that on purpose?"

"God forgive me, I did, but I won't do it again, see? From now on I'll ride you, ride you hard, every time you come out there and don't give me the best you've got to give an audience. You've got a lot to give, and I'll lambaste the stuffings out of you in front of Shultz or anybody else if you don't give it to me. Sometime before the show opens I'm going to call you to do Yoland's solo, I'm going to try and do it with Shultz watching, and if you're not set for that, God help you because I won't."

"Nick, you're wonderful to help me!"

"Not because I love you, be sure that's clear in your head. But because outside of today I never saw you work a poor performance or let down in a rehearsal. You got me believing in you. But listen kid, you nearly broke my heart today. Don't do it again."

"I won't. Oh, your lunch hour! Nick, you must eat."

"Clean forgot. Hold on, we're not done yet. Wait till I

turn on the light." He struck a match, but instead of moving briskly to the switch he held the flame, seeing her face come out of darkness. "So that's what you look like. Pretty nice, even with those eyes. Try cold water on them, sugar." The flame dying, he lit another, went to the switch and sent light flooding through the long chamber. "Here's fifty dollars of Mr. Shultz's money. Sign this—here's a pencil. Okay, now I give your I.O.U. to the business manager and that's that."

"Is this the pencil you dropped? May I keep it?"

He chuckled, pleased to hand it over.

She had something else in mind and hesitated, serious and shy. "Is it all right if I—if I bawl you out?"

His eyebrows went up, his face whimsical. "Do I rate a call down? Then give it to me."

"You shouldn't swear. I don't mean just at me. You shouldn't."

"Well, I never. That bother you? Okay, sweetheart, I'll watch it. Thanks for telling me. Now scoot. You go on ahead, I'll stay here and keep the lights on till you're up."

Diana started for the steps, but slowly, and on the third she turned about. "Nick, I want to ask you something else. Important." This time she gathered courage and her eyes were down. "What is lust?"

His answer was immediate. "Something that's got nothing to do with you and me."

She met his eyes. Slowly a smile grew between them. Then she turned, going lightly up the stairs. He saw the change that had come into the lithe, agile body and it was a kind of holy wonder thinking that he had the power to give her joy. He called after her softly, "Hey!" She faced about on the top step. "Once in a while—look at me. At rehearsal. I didn't mean you should never look my way."

She lingered briefly, smiling, waved and disappeared.

Nick switched off the light, made his way to a chair and sat on in darkness. Lust. . . . As if she didn't have enough to overcome already! To put that word into her mouth was sheer cruelty. How could anyone have the heart to hurt that girl?—anyone, let alone her mother. He thought back over their talk, wondering what he might have said to bind Diana to him, wondering too, how deep love went with her. Maybe it was the mark of rape, maybe it was just her youth, but he knew the love Diana consciously wanted of him was not the love of a man, the love of a husband, it was the love of a deep comradely friendship, intense enough in its own way and capable of strong emotion and fond tenderness. Something like, yes, like the way she loved her mother . . . as though—and she didn't know it—she was part way in the act of transferring that love to him. Still, he believed it had gone beyond that yesterday, Diana lying in his arms, and today, in the moment when they kissed and she had clung to him, yes, for that moment he had meant a lot to her, more than just a friend. How quickly she reacted to his influence, came back to happiness. If he could have her with him all the time. But now? Why, for a month he could not have her to himself, have the talks that set things straight and gentled her, have that intimacy of fondling and caress that healed the hurt and built the whole of love. If there could have been more than one afternoon. Lust! What would that woman do to Diana in a month's time? Well, Diana had fought for him, had refused to give him up for good, that was something. . . .

He leaped out of reverie, aware of time's passing, groped for the stair-rail and ran upward. People filled the stage, Shanley was walking to the table. His watch told him it lacked two minutes of starting time. He went up on the stage, called Tommy over and sent him out for coffee. He drank it while he worked. Once, wanting to put a mark on the script, his fingers went searching through his pockets for the pencil. Oh yes. He bent over to Shanley, asking for the loan of one, his lips twisted in a smile.

10

THE NEXT MORNING Diana again came to rehearsal with swollen eyes, and again the day after that, and then again on the third day. By that time Nick was ready to jump out of his skin. She was taking an awful beating and it was because of him. The slow heaviness had gone out of her, now she was as taut and nervous as a whipped thoroughbred. She worked the rehearsal, worked it too hard, and went on working upstage in the corners, practicing ballet turns until you'd think she'd drop; it looked as though she thought work was the only thing that would save her. But for all her youth, her radiant vitality, she was too sensitive, too high-strung, the strain showed and she was losing weight. He wondered, fuming, if that woman ever let her get a full night's sleep or eat a meal in peace. Sometimes for half a moment Diana would look toward him but her heavy-lidded eyes were clouded with such an intensity of unhappiness that it was heart pain to meet her look.

Why did she take it anyhow? Why didn't she flare up in rebellion? He remembered he had never seen Diana angry. But she must have a temper; no one with the fine mettlesome spirit she put into dancing could be lacking that. Nick thought, I'd like to see her get stinking mad, I'd like to see her go to town on someone, just once. She can't go on taking this from Mama, she's taking it too hard.

On the second day she got a break that came from Shanley. Shanley had an idea. Taking the wet unlit cigar out of his mouth, he talked with Nick; there in that scene after the Baghdad song, some girls in a bit of an Oriental dance. Yeah, said Nick, swell, and waited. Shanley's eyes roamed over the company and picked out Diana. "That girl. Ask her if she can set it."

Nick called her up and explained what was wanted; could she do it?

"Yes, Mr. Allingham. What music? How long? How many girls?"

Shanley said the same music as the song, two verses. "Have them enter upstage right and go off downstage left. Put yourself in it and a couple of others."

She was like an entrant in a race, aquiver to be off, her eagerness transparent, her look darting from one man to the other. "When—?"

"Do it now. Take them out in the foyer."

Nick asked what girls she wanted.

She was quick on that. "Elsie Maynard and Mattie Blake."

He summoned them. The three girls went fleetly, Diana at their head, and Nick wanted to sing. See now, it's not just because I'm crazy about her that I think she's good—Shanley picked her. Oh boy, the smart way she took the order. But something in that unguarded childlike joy smote him; she was too vulnerable, too open; you recognized a rare beauty in that glad innocence of spirit and yet it scared you, knowing the brutality of living. If ever anyone needed to be protected, cared for. . . .

In short time the three girls returned and stood together at one side on the apron, announcing by their presence that the work was done. After a minute Shanley said, "Let's see it."

Diana led the others to their entrance, stopping to give an order to the rehearsal pianist, "Slower than the song, please, like this—" She hummed, beating time, then turned to take her place with the other two. They went through it.

"Fine," said Shanley, "That's fine."

Fine? You're damn tooting that's fine. Nick was exultant. A swell formation and a pretty exit and she carried the whole thing off like an old hand. An artist, a little artist; she had the stuff.

He hoped the news of this accomplishment might ease

things up for her at home, but when she came in with those swollen eyes on the third day—

He waited until the afternoon rehearsal was over and then told Shanley, "I might be late turning up tomorrow. Okay by you?"

"Certainly, Nick. Take your time."

Mrs. Heaton, still in bed at eleven, called, "Come in," when the maid knocked.

"There's a gentleman to see you. Mr. Allingham. He's downstairs."

Ah! "Wait a minute, Mary. Make the bed for me, will you?" The woman was out of it, her white feet thrust into the pretty green satin mules Diana had given her at Christmas. She slipped on the matching satin dressing gown with the wide, loose sleeves, tied the sash tight and went to the bureau and brushed her hair—thank goodness it was freshly dyed! Her hands were trembling so she could not trust herself to do it up, besides, it flattered her, hanging loose, long and straight and glossy. She thrust in a comb on each side, looping it back from her face and recalled Diana as a child, playing grownup, sticking combs in her hair. Diana was still playing grownup, carrying on like a woman when she should have been a child!

"Anything else, Mrs. Heaton? He's waiting."

"He'll wait. Take that bottle off the table—throw it away, it's empty. Yes, and clean the ashtrays—and that glass, don't leave it there."

She drew rouge over her lips making them fuller than they were, smoothed powder lightly over face and neck and picked up the perfume atomizer—another of Diana's gifts. Her rings? She found them in the drawer and slipped them on, and Alf's diamond brought to mind another world, a Mrs. Heaton, mistress of a house, upstairs and down, beautifully appointed, smoothly and comfortably maintained, parlor maid and cook; Mrs. Alfred Heaton, one of the Heatons of Chicago. She caught at the faraway memory, establishing

176

identity with it, even as she went hurriedly to the alcove, opened a fresh bottle and poured just the right nip. She came out, scanned the room. "All right, Mary, that will do. Tell him to come up. Mary—" it was a favor to ask of a hard-working boarding-house servant "—show him up, will you?"

"Yes, Mrs. Heaton."

He had come. She would be able to see what sort he was, know better how to end this hellish business. This was the most important interview in her life. What chair to sit in . . . make him face the light. Now . . . steps approaching . . . Lord, give me brains to handle this. As Mary rapped, she called a musical, "Come in!" and as the door opened, glided forward to receive her visitor, the folds of jade green satin swirling gracefully with movement, her smile a touching thing, tremulous and sweet. "Mr. Allingham—I'm glad you've come! I've wanted so much to see you, to know you."

She wasn't what Nick had expected at all. He saw at once her charm, her poise, the femininity of her attraction, and knew the will that was set against him behind all this courteous grace of greeting. Taking the delicate pale hand she offered, he caught the scent of whiskey on her breath and was glad to have proof that this was the same woman who had come drunk and bedraggled to the stage door, making a fool of herself.

"We should have met before this, Mrs. Heaton. That's my fault."

She gave him a rueful look with the fragment of a laugh. "I'm afraid a lot of things are your fault now! Will you have a cigarette?" She took one herself, offering him the box. He accepted, lit hers—and found her eyes intent upon him. She swirled into a chair. "Do sit down. Really, I'm so glad you've come."

They faced each other from opposite chairs, taking measurements with a mutual respect for the other's fighting skill. She was a bit shaken by his ease, his bearing, the courtliness of his bow over her hand, and he was good-looking as the

177

devil and no fool. This was going to be difficult. Nick found her altogether amazing; he caught himself checking back on what he knew about her, wondering if he had got it all straight, if it could be true this was the creature with the unscrupulous ambition and the cruel domination. All right, she was putting on an act now—and it pleased him that Diana's mother could put on such an act and show to such good advantage—but surely some of this gentle wistfulness, this rueful delicate reproach came out of some tenderness within her. She had beautiful eyes, bewitchingly beautiful . . . but tricky, tricky as a fox's. He said, "Mrs. Heaton, I love Diana."

Her eyebrows rose in distress, she gently shook her head, her lips went on smiling. "Do you think you should—Nick?"

Looking at that face that certainly had known love, he asked quietly, "Should? Do you believe there is a 'should' about love?"

She dropped her eyes, her teeth biting on her lips. "For a man, yes. Yes, certainly for a man." She looked back at him. "You men are supposed to think for us, aren't you, even if we lose our heads?"

It was done so prettily, with such a charm of appeal, an intimacy established. He paid her the compliment of a smile. "I wouldn't be loving Diana if I wasn't thinking for her."

She went on smiling, almost to herself, her head turned, her eyes on the business of brushing ashes from the tip of her cigarette into the tray on the table beside her. "Diana tells me everything." She hesitated, repeated the phrase in a more sorrowful cadence. "How often I have said that! All her life. And it has always been true—until she met you. Now I must amend it and say, Diana tells me everything, but tardily, not always when she should. I think," she eyed him levelly, holding to her mask-like smile, "that I know better than the child what you have done to her. You knew her youth, her innocence. What right had you—" she hesitated as though the words were hard to say— "to take her alone, unchaperoned, into your rooms? What right had you—" she closed her eyes and shook her head before the awful picture "—to lie beside her on a couch and kiss her?" She opened her eyes, waiting for answer, triumphing over this thrust.

Nick's face was as much of a mask as her own. His tone stayed pleasant, there was no deviation from the courteous intimacy she had established. "Suppose we get this straight, Mrs. Heaton, then we can understand each other better. Diana isn't what's generally meant by 'innocent.' "

She was shaken out of her ease, gasping. "What do you mean?"

"What you think I mean. You see, Diana tells me everything too."

Appalled at this unexpected treachery on Diana's part, incredulous, the woman demanded sharply, "What did she tell you?"

Nick went on being easy, pleasant. "She didn't have to tell me a thing. I could see it in the way she behaved. Any man would have seen it if he tried to touch her. Diana had been with a man and it was a nasty business that left her scared sick."

Her composure gone, the woman rose, moving fitfully about the room. Nick rose with her, standing by his chair, waiting upon her mood. She stopped before him, demanding, "Did she tell you the truth? Did she tell you how she *would* do that thing and I couldn't stop her?"

He wagged his head at her; that line was no good. "You know Diana tells the truth."

Mrs. Heaton stamped her foot. "Oh, of course she does! What she thinks is the truth. But with her imagination—why she can make herself believe anything! Why, do you think that I would let her do a thing like that—"

Nick cut in suavely. "You've got her under pretty good control it seems to me."

The woman fell back into her chair. "Oh! Then you actually believe . . . you think. . . ."

"I'll be glad to listen to your version if you like." He was still pleasant, still smiling, but her attempt at deceit had

179

brought a steely note into his voice. "Want to tell me about Mr. Mowbray?"

Mrs. Heaton gave him an ugly look. "It's none of your affair. Believe what you like. If you do believe it, I shouldn't think you'd care to have a girl like Diana for your wife—a girl another man has had."

That hurt. Nick remained standing, delaying answer, making sure of himself. When he spoke it was without taking the cigarette from his lips, his eyes squinting through the smoke, paying back the flash of ugliness and cruelty with a sharpness of eye and tone. "I believe that kid works on the wires you pull and I don't like the way you pull them. We don't need to quarrel about it. You and I ought to be friends—for her sake. You want the girl to be famous? So do I. You want her to be happy? So do I." The cigarette was burning close to his lips. He crushed it in the ashtray and went back to courtesy. "Mrs. Heaton, I do want to marry Diana. What have you got against it?"

"Everything!" the woman snapped promptly, and her eyes looking up at him showed hate.

Hands thrust in his pockets, Nick walked away and came back. He told her softly, "Diana loves me."

Mrs. Heaton's laugh was brief, derisive. "Lusts after you, you mean. That's what you wanted."

He walked away, returned more slowly, took out his cigarettes and offered them. She pulled back with a shudder, insistent on enmity. He lit his own and retreated to his chair to lie in it loosely, eyeing the woman, trying to see how this might be directed. He thrust aside antagonism, repeating his question with patience. "What have you got against it?"

Mrs. Heaton tossed up her head. "You're not good enough for her."

"In what way?"

She had meant to tell him bluntly he was not a gentleman; that had been her fixed impression before meeting him; now she was not sure; something in his poise and manner, something in the way his eyes had narrowed, and in the

quietly spoken challenge of his query warned her to a some-
what more subtle answer. "I don't care to have my daughter
pick up your Broadway jargon. Diana is not a 'kid.' The
class of people that she belongs with do not speak as you do."

He drew on the cigarette and let the smoke idle from his
lips, his eyes on the ceiling. "Class counts, does it? Well, for
Diana's sake, I'll come clean. Ever hear of Arthur Allingham,
the concert pianist? Pretty big name, isn't it? Among the
biggest? He's my old man. My mother is the daughter of a
Polish count who wasn't poor. I don't care for the snob
stuff, I've done my best to duck it. I ducked out of a snob
school and took a course in the navy instead, and I've been
knocking around on my own since I was fifteen, and maybe
you wouldn't like all the people I've rubbed shoulders with
and found were decent human beings. But if class is going
to make a difference to you, I'll tell you this—the latchstring
is out for me any time, and I can take Diana into a house
where only the top-notchers are invited and they don't pass
up the invitation when it comes. That satisfy you?"

Mrs. Heaton did not answer. If what he said made any
difference to her she did not show it; if anything her hostility had deepened.

Nick sat up straight, urging with a sudden earnestness.
"Look here, I'm doing everything I can and this isn't going
right. I suppose I hurt your feelings, speaking too bluntly.
I only meant to get things straight at the start. I'm sorry if
I seemed rude. Don't hate me."

"But I do—quite thoroughly."

"I wish you'd tell me why."

"Because you want Diana."

"Are you going to keep her to yourself always?"

"She's mine."

"She's your daughter. But she's got a right to more in life
than you can give her."

"She's got her career."

"She's a woman."

"No, she's not, she's a child."

181

Nick conceded with a nod. "All right, but she won't be one always." Coaxing, he asked, "Mrs. Heaton, were you ever terribly in love with a man?"

"Yes, I was."

"Would you deny that to your daughter?"

"Yes, I would. Love? I haven't got over it yet—I'll never get over it." She was speaking with a bitter honesty. "When I think how that could break me, change me, make me into a person that I never was before, give me heartache to lie down with at night and heartache to rise up with in the morning, and to know that if I saw his face right now I would run to him like a dog that's whistled to heel. Do you think I want that for Diana?"

Nick lowered his eyes. "I'm sorry. You didn't hit the right guy and that's tough. But it doesn't follow that I'll break Diana's heart."

"You'll never get the chance."

"You prefer to do the breaking, then?"

"Breaking?"

Nick lost his patience. "Can't you see what you're doing to her? Can't you see you've got her so worked up she's just about crazy? She can't take much more of what you're handing out and not smash up. My God, if you love her, how can you do this to her?"

It was Mrs. Heaton's turn to speak coolly. "She's out of her head now. That's your doing. But what can a child her age know of love? Yes, I remember, I had desperate affairs at sixteen and seventeen, I thought I would die if I wasn't asked to a dance or I didn't get a valentine! That's adolescence, that's what Diana's going through. A year from now she won't remember you, she'll laugh when I say, 'Do you remember Nick?' "

"You believe that? You honestly believe that? Then you're wrong, terribly wrong." Nick answered back with the vehemence of a sincerity that abandoned every ruse. "Diana's no ordinary adolescent, she's an artist by temperament, and a girl who's come a long way from childhood—even if she's still a child in years. I never knew anyone to feel as intensely as she does—responsive, sensitive, she can't toss things off lightly, forget about them. I tell you she loves me. You can't hurt her the way you're hurting her now and expect to get away with it."

"You think you know my daughter better than I do?"

The cutting sarcasm went unheeded. "Some ways I might. I see the woman in her and you see the child. I know you're hurting her. You mustn't do this, Mrs. Heaton, you mustn't. She's got the makings of a fine woman. You mustn't destroy that."

They were both on their feet. "I want Diana to have a career. Nothing must interfere with that. I know the slow rot of a lifetime spent mourning lost opportunity! Diana's life shall be different from mine. I'll see to that. She'll have fame to make her happy. Don't talk to me about the woman in her. If it's a woman you want, find someone else!"

"You can't destroy the woman and not destroy the artist— it's one and the same thing with her. You've no right to possess her. Why do you put her through the torture of a choice? Stop what you're doing to her. You can't go on torturing her."

Breathing fast, small willful head flung up, Mrs. Heaton spoke through clenched teeth. "I shall until she promises me to give you up forever."

Nick caught up his hat from the table, plunging toward the door. He pulled up and stood silent, turning the hat in his hands, back to the woman, thinking was there anything, anything that he could say. There was a lot he wanted to say. . . . He turned about and managed a bow. "You might as well get used to the idea—you and I will have to learn to get along together. I mean to marry Diana."

"Not you or anyone."

Nick nodded and went swiftly through the door. Halfway down the stairs he checked himself—yes, there was something else that he had meant to say. He ran up the stairs and rapped on the door. He thought he heard her say 'come in,' but when he opened the door he felt he had intruded; Mrs. Heaton stood by the table in the act of pouring a drink. "I'm sorry, I—"

"Sorry?" Mrs. Heaton laughed at him. "You think I care?" She drained a glass that was a full third filled. "This goes on all the time now—because of you!"

Nick was pleading, "Look—I just wanted to say—you made Diana promise to cut me for a month. I want to give you my word—"

"Your word!"

He closed his eyes at the insult, pride sending anger smashing at his will. In a minute he went on, humbly, still pleading, "Yeah, mine, it's a good one, I never broke it. I give you my word I won't make a move to try to get her to break her promise—"

She laughed again, taunting, "You couldn't get her to!"

He took that, too. "You might think I'd try, that you had to keep at her. You don't have to. Leave her alone for a month and I will too. Let up on her, will you? Just lay off her for a spell—"

" 'Lay off!' Oh, what an expression for a gentleman! Really!"

Nick closed the door very, very quietly. He dove down the stairs, raging. Devil with the fox eyes, devil. I didn't make her budge an inch. Oh Diana, kid, oh, I bet I only made it worse for you! Oh honey, honey, why can't you run away and come to me!

But behind him in the room, Mrs. Heaton was in a turbulence of mind that surpassed his. The man was in deadly earnest, and he was a man, not just some silly boy, a man with a will of his own, set against her, hard as steel. The son of Arthur Allingham!—and Polish blood in him, that dark look of inner fire; yes, and for all his affectation of being a tough, he was quickened with pride, acute in perception, sensitive and keen. And young, oh Lord, young and handsome! What a man to have against you, fighting for your daughter!

And she hadn't been able to do a thing with him. . . .

Diana talked to him of Mowbray. Oh, where was Diana, the true, the loyal, that she could give that away! Oh, bad girl, bad girl, to speak of that!

The strain of the encounter had been great. The woman sank into a chair, pressing a hand to her head and all at once she was weak and trembling and confused. She began to whimper miserably, scared and alone, knowing that the fight must go on and she might lose. Trying to think back, she could not recall the things that had been said by Nick or by herself, it all jumbled, and she was going to pieces, shaking and whimpering alone.

Nick had gone straight home from rehearsal, striding stormily along the street, head down. Two more days of seeing the girl flit about the theater like a distracted wraith. She strove for invisibility far worse than when he had first noticed her, hiding away until the moment when work called her forth and then appearing in her place to dance with a spurt of zeal that it was pain to see, the sudden poignant intensity, rising out of misery, was an effort far too big for such a young thing to make.

It could not go on. It was an outrage on the most elemental sense of decency that Diana should be made to suffer so, that this cruelty should be practiced, could be possible. And that he must be a witness to it, unable to do a thing to help her. That devil of a woman. And she possessed Diana.

He found himself in his room, throwing open the windows to the soft restless air, over-warm for spring, promise-laden of oncoming summer. His coat hung over the chair, he stood motionless, sunk in tempestuous gloom, badgered by the sense of impotence to put an end to this.

And in two days she had not once met his eyes. The things her mother said were working in her.

A soft impatient rapping came on the door. He turned his

185

head to stare, knowing what it sounded like. It couldn't be. He crossed the room in a stride.

But it was. Diana.

"Look here—you can't do this. You promised not to come here."

There was a frenzied look about her, white and staring, all aquiver. "I don't care—I don't! Nick, let me in!"

"Steady, kid. Think it out. You gave your word."

"Let me in—you must! I've got to tell you something."

He stood back admitting her.

"It's you—I came to warn you—she's going to. . . . " Speech left her. Diana swayed against the wall, fear-choked.

"Easy, honey. We can handle this, whatever it is. You want to tell me something? Well, go slow, take your time. Since you're here you might as well sit down." He took her arm steering her toward the couch, professing a calm that was not in him.

But she had no time for sitting down and dragged back, pulling him to a stop. "It's you—she's going to ruin you if I don't promise never to see you again! Oh Nicky—!" She leaned against him with a dry sob.

He did not put his arms around her. "Sh, sweetheart, try to keep your head. Don't get upset like this. She can't ruin me."

She was not quieted, her excitement stayed. "She can! Oh, you don't know her! And now—she's drinking all the time, she never lets up, she's liable to do anything. She can say you ruined me—she can make people believe that."

He laid a hand under her chin and raised her face, assuring her, "That's only talk to scare you. Besides, you and I know different."

His apparent calm seemed stupid to Diana. Why couldn't Nick see the danger? "I tell you she'll go to the theater, make scenes in front of everybody. She could do that—when she's crazy drunk. Nick, you've got to look out for her!"

"She might try it—once."

"That's why I came, so you'll know, so you'll tell Joe not to let her in. Can you fix it, Nick, can you?"

"Sure I can fix it. Honey, won't you try not to let yourself go to pieces? Please—"

"I've got to go." She moved toward the door with that tense springiness that made him think of the lashed thoroughbred. "I mustn't be late."

Seeing her start to go away as wild and pitiable as when she came, a wave of feeling rose, and lifted on that crest he knew that promises no longer mattered, nothing mattered, only Diana. He went between her and the door, speaking grimly, speaking fast. "I can't take this, kid. Duck it. Marry me, marry me right now, don't go back. She can have me up for abduction or whatever it's called, but once it's done it's done and I'll look after you." He spread out appealing hands before her. "Will you do it?"

She flung her arms about his neck, pressing her lips to his. By that it seemed she had consented and a riot of joy swept over him. The exultance in her love, the shock of relief and triumph at this victory, were almost unbearable delight. He held the pliant, quivering body close, and the passion that had been so willfully held in check surged up, pounding in his blood. He strove to check it now, impatient to be off, to marry her at once, and made a stir to end the kiss. But at that Diana clung more tightly. He thought the wild desperation in her was an answering desire and held her tighter, his wits half drowned in this sudden flood of ecstacy. He ended the kiss to lay his cheek beside hers, murmuring, out of the certainty of bliss, "Oh, I want you so, I want you so!"

A madness had taken Diana in which she felt that she must cling to him, she could not bear to let go, to stand alone. She felt the coming of a kind of reined-in fury in his ardor and it was frightening to her and yet she welcomed it; to escape out of present pain, be stabbed by a fresh violence of feeling, would be to gain a new mixture of emotion more bearable than what she had been enduring. Let it be blinding and terrible hurt if only it came from Nick and held him to her and gave her some share of his strong self. All of this, without restraint of reason, came on the instant, and she answered back without pause, granting what he wished, wild and sacrificial and abandoned to him. "You can have me."

He managed to keep thought going, to force words through this delirium. "We got to go. We got to get married."

"No." Her reply was again quick, daft, in the same light, heedless tone. "I can't. But I don't care."

He threw off her arms and stepped back from her, gripping her shoulders, holding her at arms length, his eyes blazing. "We're going to get married."

Her white, distraught face was a blur before him. It seemed he saw her lips moving before he heard the words. She was saying. "No. That would kill her. I won't."

Anger took hold of him. "What do you mean by saying I can have you?"

Her eyes closed, her head lolled back. "I don't care."

He shook her, maddened by this pale martyr who stood in place of his love. "Are you crazy? Do you think I would?"

Her eyes opened. She demurred faintly at the shaking. "Don't."

"Marry me."

"I won't."

He pushed her away from him with a violence that made her stagger to catch her balance; he went raging up and down the room, pounding his fist into his palm, fighting to gain mastery over the tumult of passion and anger that possessed him. He was so maddened that he dared not look at her or speak, and plunged in between the piano and the wall, caging himself, having something between them, something to hold on to. And at last, keeping his head down, he won control and could trust himself to speak. "If you won't marry me, go home. I've got this thought out straight and I'm sticking to it. What you're saying is no good. You don't know what you're saying anyhow—you came in here so worked up you're not responsible for what you'd do. I wouldn't want it that way and you sorry afterward. I know your mother's given you some queer ideas, but they're not mine. I'll take a girl when I want one and the girl's willing, but I won't take you because that's

188

not all I'm looking to get from you. I want it beautiful between us and I want it lasting. Get it straight and don't pull that on me again or you'll drive me nuts."

No answer came from her. He raised his head and saw a shamed, drooping figure and he was dismayed lest he had said too much, perhaps made real to her what she had not consciously intended. "I didn't mean to speak rough, Diana. Maybe what I said sounded all wrong, maybe I'm getting mixed up. You know I love you?"

Dulled, subdued, she answered, "Yes, Nick," not looking up.

He went on gazing at her and it struck him that in every mood she had, his love mounted. To go to her now with tenderness. . . . But he did not dare. "So you can't marry me. Sure about that?"

"It would be—so final. It would kill her. I've got to look after her." Diana stretched out her hand to the door knob.

She was going. All at once the picture of Mrs. Heaton, glass in hand, stood before him and he heard the woman's proud taunt of power; she had said he could not make Diana break her promise—and Diana had broken it, coming here. Thrilling with alarm, Nick begged, "Let me go home with you. Let me face her with you."

Diana shook her head. "That would only make it worse."

He pleaded passionately. "Then lie, kid, lie, will you? Don't let her know you came here."

She looked across at him, confused and troubled by his counsel. "It isn't right to lie."

He leaned toward her across the piano, fingers interwoven in appeal. "Don't you understand she'll give you hell for this?—and you came for my sake! Lie, I tell you!"

She drew a heavy breath, resigned. "I can't lie. I'm no good at it anyhow."

He dropped his head, groaning, knowing this was true. Then suddenly lashing out, "Why do you take it? Why don't you ever get mad? Why don't you tell her to shut up and go to hell? Why do you—"

Diana threw up her arms, fending off the words. "Don't. She's my mother. I love her."

He said nothing. He heard the door open and then Diana speaking again. "Nick—you won't forget? Tell Joe."

"Sure. Thanks."

The door shut. The room was empty. He felt as dulled, as beaten as herself, and then it all came back on him, the longing for her and the maddening sense of loss, and he came loose from his self-made cage, thrashing about the room, more animal than man. He had sent her from him, he had said go home, and there might never be another time when he would have her in his arms.

The bigger hurt came with remembrance of that cowed figure by the door. In his imagination he saw her scurrying along the street, holding to her hard purpose, heading into certain misery with that kind of high, dogged courage which has no buoyant bravery but only the fixed intent of loving duty and does not count the cost and knows no guile.

Sure, she knew what she was in for now.

The passion in him sickened. He sank down in the armchair, filled with an emptiness that ached and throbbed. The soft, restless air, too warm, stirred in through the windows, a woman passing on the sidewalk chattered, laughed. Cars went by, the side-street traffic pouring into Broadway heavy as the dinner hour came on.

Diana, oh Diana kid. . . . .

"You're late." Mrs. Heaton sat facing the door, glass in hand. She had been watching the door like a cat at a mousehole. She pounced now, shooting out the accusation before the girl had time to close the door, and her eyes shone hard and merciless in a worn, haggard face.

Diana did not come on into the room. She shut the door and stayed against it, watching her mother's eyes, not knowing how bad this could be. She was late, full twenty minutes late.

190

The fact stood out. Dread of what was so surely coming robbed her of all defense and held her frozen.

"Why don't you take off your hat, stupid?"

Diana took off her hat and held it along with her purse.

"Where were you?"

Diana could not speak.

"Tell me where you were."

The girl's silence was not evasion or resistance; it was sheer dread that stopped the power of speech. But she looked steadily at Sue, trying by that to claim that, wrong as it might seem, she had done only what was right. Sue's stare was hard to meet, but she would not let Sue stare her down and so seem guilty.

The demand came again in the hard, even, expressionless voice. "Tell me where you were."

Cold fury gleamed in Sue's eyes. The hat slipped from Diana's hand and she made no move to pick it up. Oh God, take her eyes off me.

Again the same demand. "Tell me where you were."

The purse fell, flopping.

"Tell me where you were."

Like a cry, Diana flung out her arms across the door as though she felt that she were falling backward. She stayed so, pinned there, arms outstretched like a cross, meeting the stare of those gleaming eyes.

"Then I'll tell you. You broke your promise. You've been to him."

Please God take her eyes off—

"You little bitch. I'll fix it so no man will ever want to sleep with you." The hand holding the glass shot back and up and over. Diana cried out, ducking the glass that struck the door above her head and shattered. After it came the woman, hurling herself forward, maniacal. "I'll fix you—"

Diana grabbed at hands clawing toward her face. "Mother!"

"You're bad, you're bad." The woman wrenched and pulled to free her wrists. "Let go of me."

Sue had gone mad. Such things did not happen. Frantic,

Diana held her wrists, calling out to her. "Mother! Mother!"

The woman left off struggling. She announced with calm loathing, "You're hurting my wrists."

Diana let go.

Starkly, Mrs. Heaton asked, "Did you go to him?"

Just as starkly Diana answered. "Yes."

Blinking, the girl saw it coming and made no move to dodge. Mrs. Heaton struck her full force across the face, so hard that there were two blows, her head banging against the door. There was a dazzle of crisp, white pain and then a swirling blackness and then Sue speaking out of a swinging face that formed mistily, steadying. "I'll *make* you be good. I'll *make* you obey me," and Sue was walking haughtily back to the table, seeking the glass, forgetful that she had thrown it, and the pain was reverberating and Diana's nose was filling up as though she had a heavy cold.

Mrs. Heaton went into the alcove and come out with another glass. She filled it and sat down. "Wipe your nose. It's bleeding. You're disgusting to look at."

The girl bent down for the handkerchief inside her purse, so shaken that she could hardly get the purse open. This was not ordinary fear, not fear as she had ever known it. This was the hideous sensation of having come loose from the known, the certain. The impossible went on about her. Mother had hit her . . . Mother had meant to claw her face . . . 'Bitch.' Blood dripped fast on the floor as she bent over. She straightened up, holding the handkerchief lightly against the throbbing ache.

The woman drank and refilled her glass. Diana knew it was too fast even for now, time out of gear, one big drink on top of another. "You're a rotter, Diana. You gave your word and I believed you. You're bad. I can't keep you from being bad. I can't make you obey. Obey!" She broke into a derisive sob. "Papa told me years ago—you only obeyed me because you wanted to! Lord, it's a cruel joke on me that he was right and all the love I gave you means nothing now."

"No, no, that's not true, that's not true!"

Mrs. Heaton was beyond hearing her daughter; she was isolated in her grief, alone with it, lamenting in a heart-pierced marveling. "My baby. My beautiful girl. I have to strike her, strike her, trying, trying to make her be good."

The girl drew to her, beseeching. "Mother, please—dearest—" The handkerchief was sopping and bright red. Distractedly, Diana picked up her mother's handkerchief from the table and threw her own away. "Sue—"

Mrs. Heaton was up, fierce, drawing back. "Get away from me. I can't bear the sight of you. Don't touch me." She wandered up and down, her head in her hands, her teeth gritting. "This is hell, hell. I can't stand this. A ring of fire is in my head. What are we coming to? No, I can't, I can't endure it. This is too much." She saw her reflection in the mirror and paused before it. "Is that me—that hideous, mad, old woman? Is that my little girl, all bloody from being hit?"

Her daughter's voice came in a clear, ringing call across the room. "I love you! I love you, Mother!"

The woman let her hands fall, turning slowly toward the voice, peering with pale eyes that seemed to have no focus. "No. You don't love me. You wouldn't have done this to me if you loved me." She drew herself up in haughty grandeur, quoting, " 'Love is not love that alters when it alteration finds. . . . Love's not Time's Fool.' "

"Sue!"

Mrs. Heaton's voice rose shrilly. "No love lasts, not even yours. This is the end, the end! You'll have lovers—you'll never be anybody. Oh God in hell. *I told you what I'd do.*"

She was running, running, clumsily but fast—to the window, getting a foot on the sill, clambering up—rising—rising—

She screamed as Diana caught her, dragged her down. Scream after scream tore out as Diana lugged her, forced her, to the bed, got her upon it, held her there by force. Plunging and kicking and screaming with the full force of her lungs—there was nothing in the world but awful screaming and the blue mouth wide open. . . .

Mrs. Borden stood in the open door, one hand on the knob, looking as if she meant to turn and run. Diana shouted, "The doctor—get the doctor—Minelli—" The phone number came clear in mind, she shouted it over and over while Sue screamed and fought, plunging in her grip, and blood fell on Sue's blouse and neck.

Finally Mrs. Borden understood and went away.

11

THE DOCTOR had left, the trained nurse dominated the room; after the second hypodermic Mrs. Heaton slept heavily. Mrs. Borden took Diana down to the basement kitchen and gave her cold lamb and bread and butter and a glass of milk, and stood over her, seeing that the food was eaten. Then she led the girl upstairs to a vacant hall bedroom on the fourth floor. She turned down the covers and plumped the pillows. "Now go to bed like a good girl and don't fret no more. Your mother's being looked after."

The doctor had said 'delirium tremens.' . . . Diana did not know what that might mean. "Why does she have to go to a sanitarium, Mrs. Borden? Why can't we keep her here, and the nurse too?"

"My goodness, I can't have that crazy screaming in my house! Didn't the doctor say she belonged in a sanitarium? Of course, if your folks can't pay, there's Bellevue."

"Oh no! I can get money, I can draw advances on my salary. But to send her away. . . ."

"The doctor knows what's best. Now go to bed, the ambulance will be here early. Good night."

"Good night, Mrs. Borden. Thank you for everything."

"We all have our troubles, dearie. You did worry your mother, and she's got a sweet way about her, so dainty and ladylike, I always felt sorry for her even when she carried on. A mother's the most precious thing in the world and the good Lord only gives us one. You just be a good daughter to her and you'll live to be thankful for it." Pleased by the soundness of her good counsel, Mrs. Borden patted the girl's shoulder and went out, pulling the door shut.

Diana sat down on the narrow bed and for a long time stared straight ahead of her at the images that formed out of memory, so piercing in the heightened intensity of this catastrophe; the mother who moved lightly through the house at Frostburg, who tucked you into bed in the warm, quiet dusk of a slow evening, who was heard singing in the parlor below as you drifted into slumber; the mother who took you in her arms when you were hurt and coaxed you into smiling with a smile of her own; who explained all things with such a patient, gentle gravity; who took you to theaters, concerts, museums, and held your hand as you thrilled to wonder; a gay, pretty, young mother with a gallant air who laughed and sang as she walked down a country lane; a pal who confided all her secrets; a fragile, lonely woman, weeping over heartbreak. . . . Sue, lovable, a being like no other. And Sue had tried to kill herself.

Because of me. Because of what I did to her.

How could it be? How could it have come about?

Diana could find only one answer, the one Sue had given her; she, Diana, had been bewitched. It could not be that she in her right senses would have brought this suffering to her mother. Sue had said things that could not be denied. It was true that she had deliberately deceived her mother, that she had then refused to obey her wishes and that finally she had broken her promise. And all of this, knowing how Sue would suffer. Bewitched; there was no other explanation for such monstrous, bad behavior.

Bewitched by a man. A man who could say—why, only a few hours ago!—'Why don't you tell her to shut up, to go to hell.' He could tell her to say that to her mother; he could urge lying, even desertion.

Memory came of that afternoon when Nick had lain beside her and for a space out of time she had been wrapped in a magical daze of exquisite happiness, knowing through a slumbrous exultance the dim stir of a longing to be drawn wholly to him, absorbed in the spell he made, given over to its dreamlike beauty.

Bewitched. Illusion. See how far that spell had brought her —was it actually she herself who had clung to him in his

196

room tonight declaring wildly he might have her? That recollection brought a stifling hot shame. Yes, bewitchment certainly. All this evil was a spell that came from him because he was a man and wanted her.

And now a trained nurse sat by her mother's bed and in the morning an ambulance would come, take Sue away.

Suppose—suppose the trained nurse fell asleep—Sue woke—the window—

Diana was out of the room and slipping down the flight of stairs through the silent, night-darkened house. She listened at the door, eased it open so carefully no creak broke the silence. In the dim room with the shaded light the white-clad figure sat on guard beside the bed, looking up to give a nod of reassurance. The girl drew back, pulling the door shut as carefully as she had opened it.

But she could not go away; the night hours passing, the nurse might doze and Sue might wake. Diana stretched herself out on the stairs, prepared to spend the night upon them like a watchdog. To her tired body they were not uncomfortable, one step taking the weight of her head, another her shoulders, another her hips; but comfort was no matter; she would gladly have laid herself down upon a torture bed of spikes.

Grampa said, Look after her, look after your mother. . . . A white-haired man with a stern, kindly face and slow, deliberated speech; a good, wise man giving a good, wise order. Remorse swung into high resolves, the spirit of atonement grew and fixed, filling Diana with a sense of noble purpose in which thought moved sketchily; be good . . . work hard . . . get ahead . . . bring joy to her. . . .

A soft tread inside the room sent Diana spinning to the door, her heart in her throat. But it was only the nurse who shook her head in reproof at alarm. Diana went back to her vigil on the stairs. Lying there, all lifted up and held together by the glowing ardor of the redeeming good resolves, she watched the scurries of a mouse who came and went along the hall close in by the wainscoting, and her lids grew heavy.

An early riser on the top floor, coming down at six, found

197

the girl sprawled on the stairs, asleep. Carefully tiptoeing, he stepped over her body, but Diana woke with a start, gazed blankly after him, sprang up, hastening to the door.

She stood by when the doctor came, when Sue was wakened, the sanitarium idea explained; she heard Sue agree to it, drowsy, not caring what was done with her. And then Mother looked at her with a slow, faint smile and shut her eyes, and the men came in with the stretcher and carried her downstairs and into the ambulance and Diana stood on the sidewalk and watched it drive away.

Mother had smiled. It was a dim, faraway smile, but it was like forgiveness and a blessing, and all Diana's good intentions were strengthened by the gratitude and the compassion that made tears run down her cheeks standing there on the sidewalk, people hurrying by in the slanting morning light.

Mrs. Borden had come out to see the ambulance. "My goodness, crying at your age—where everyone can see you! You look a sight with that nose as it is! Come inside and have your breakfast and act like a sensible girl."

After breakfast Diana went back into her mother's room. It was a sad, heavy business being there, Sue gone for two weeks or three and no knowing how she would return. But Diana kept busy tidying the place, cleaning out the accumulated bottles, and after a while she bathed and dressed, making ready to go to rehearsal.

Nick came early to the theater, hung about the entrance, watching the busy street both ways. But every time he watched for her it was no-go. It came to five minutes of ten and she had not appeared. He went into the theater and she was not among the girls already on the stage, dawdling in talkative groups or busy with their limbering or lounging in the chairs. He went on to his place at the table and sat down sideways, putting an end to watching; elbows on the table, chin resting on the bridge of his hands, he looked out into the darkened auditorium.

And if she didn't come. . . . If he had to be stuck there, the work holding him, not knowing what had happened to her. ... I should have gone home with her, I shouldn't have paid any attention to what she said.

"Morning, Nick." Shanley slid into the opposite chair. "Nice news for you. Shultz thinks you're the white-haired boy. He's thinking about giving you the new Tod Lester show to direct."

It was great news, stunning. Nick realized that, even though he lacked the spirit to exult. "Started to cast it yet?"

"No. Won't go into rehearsal till August."

Diana was standing by the table.

Nick's glance shot up. He saw the mark of the blow and the sight of it gave him the feel of it so that his stomach sickened. He slid a hand up over his face, needing that shelter. Oh God, oh God. I can't look at her. That hurt; that must have knocked her flat.

"Mr. Allingham, I would like to have another advance."

It was a gag; she wanted a chance to talk to him. He answered from behind his hand. "I'll see you after rehearsal."

"Thank you." She moved away.

Shanley gave a low whistle. "Say, see her face? Somebody messed her up pretty."

Nick grunted, rubbing his hand over his eyes, needing a long moment more to be certain of impassivity.

Shanley asked, "Sleepy?"

"Yeah. Couldn't sleep last night."

"Warm," Shanley agreed. He pulled out his watch. "Well?"

Nick stood up and rapped on the table. The work started. He knew where she was standing. He wasn't going to look at her; he was so jumpy right now he hardly knew what he was doing. And there was a lot to do. Shanley was just sitting back, twirling his thumbs. And if Shultz had ideas about the Tod Lester show—that was a stunner—this one had better be good. Nick didn't know what the script of the Lester show called for, but any musical could use a dance soloist and a director had a say.

He didn't look at her, he wouldn't, but when the Roman

scene came he found himself gazing with horrified fascination at that damaged face, unable to take his eyes away, and again his stomach turned. Then he was hating her, hating her for taking it. A damned little masochist, likes to suffer. Sure, beat me up, break my nose, wipe the floor with me, mess me up so the whole world knows about it. She didn't have to take it, no one had to take a thing like that; she chose to take it. And if she thought that dull, sleep-walking execution of the dance was the best she had to give an audience—after the talking to he had given her down in the lounge—he had warned her—he had said what he would do if she let the work sag—

"Hold it," he snapped, stopping the number. Yeah, maybe she thought he was just kidding about the work, that what he said didn't matter. No, only what Mama said mattered. Well, if she liked punishment she could take it, and if she couldn't take it there was no use thinking about dance solos in the Lester show. A fine candidate for a solo she looked right now! "Look, you in the middle, maybe we got you up too early and you didn't wake up yet, and it's awfully mean, isn't it, but we do expect you to do your work when you come in here. Do you mind?"

As usual the bawling out brought every eye on the victim, watching with morbid expectancy for signs of that possible crack-up when a girl broke down, lost her head, cried or answered back. It was the standing out alone, the center of all attention, taking rebuke in silence before them all that made a bawling out so hard to take. Knowing that, Nick had cut it mercifully short on that previous occasion when he could not spare her. Now he dragged it out, drawling the words, pausing between them, wanting to lash her into some recognition that she had no right to let this happen, coming in banged up for everyone to see, messing along in the routine, not caring how she danced, making him so sickened just looking at her that he wanted to get up and walk out of the place. Whispering comments on Diana's bruised nose and swollen lips spread among the watchers, some noticing now for the first time. That goaded him. Had she no pride at all that she could appear among them day after day with tear-swollen eyes and now this?

"You did us a big favor to learn that routine. Please do us one more and try, try awfully hard to keep your mind on your work. You're not much on looks. You can't get by as an ornament. If you think you can dance, how about showing us?"

Diana stood poised and quiet, eyes on the floor, waiting for him to finish, as though nothing he said or could say mattered to her. She was not going to break down, not by a glance ask for mercy. And that goaded him still further. Only what Mama said could make her turn cry-baby. He kept her standing there a full minute before he spoke again and then his words came so quick and sharp that instinctively she jumped. "Snap into it! We don't want to find out we got a flop on our hands on opening night. Take it again and I want the best you got."

He finished, knowing with a cold, sobering shock that Shultz had come to stand a step behind him on the apron, square and squat, the beady little eyes shooting out from the massive lowered head, taking in everything.

So. Here it was, a showdown. He had done about the best he could to rattle the kid and break her nerve, and here was Shultz walking in to get an eyeful of the result. The anger washed out of him, his love leapt to the girl, words forming, spoken in mind—Come on, honey, forget it, show you can dance, put it over, you got to put it over. . . .

But Nick did not know how the fire of good resolves had tempered her ambition, how underneath the abstraction that had raised his ire lay a new forged steel of endeavor. It shone out bright and flashing as the dance began; Shultz was watching; Diana knew as well as Nick what that could mean in her career. She moved among the others, spirited and expert, outstandingly the best, astonishing in radiance, and when the group broke from the final tableau she had the poise to look at Nick, head tilted, smiling, asking prettily by that if the director was now satisfied with her.

There was shouting inside of him. Nick wanted to cry out Bravo and take her in his arms. He had not shown he knew that Shultz was there. Holding to that pretense, he turned to Shanley, asking innocently, "Okay if I try understudies?" and getting an assent, checked the stir that had set in for places in the next number. "Hold it. Go back on the Roman scene. I want the understudies in this—Miss La Tour in the song, Miss Heaton in the solo. Set? All right, give it to me."

It ran off like magic. . . . It didn't matter about Diana's swollen nose and lips, no, honest to God, the way she danced you wouldn't even notice. The sparkle, the seeming delight with which that lithe, slim, pliant body flashed and swerved, you'd think that dancing was new-found joy to her; it lifted you, you had to share in it.

The dance finished, Nick looked around at Shultz. "Oh. Morning, Mr. Shultz."

The heavy man laid an approving hand on Nick's shoulder. "Getting results, boy. Nice work."

"You get results when you got the stuff to work with," Nick said nimbly. "What you think of that kid? A natural, huh?" Shultz's eyes were on Diana, withdrawing among the others. Nick thought maybe he had never taken a good look at her before, mightn't remember what she actually looked like. He went on smoothly, "Got banged up in an accident last night, she was telling me before rehearsal. Sure looks a mess right now." All right, Shanley heard him. Shanley knew Diana had said nothing about an accident, but let that go.

Shultz inclined his head, indicating that there might be possibilities that would be judicially considered. But it was a point in Nick's favor if he could turn up talent for him; Shultz boasted of the stars he had discovered; it was his directors who discreetly pointed out the talent. He took Nick's chair at the table, exchanged words with Shanley, and after watching two more numbers, rose. He told Nick, "Come up to the office at five. Want to talk to you," and bore himself away.

Nick took out his handkerchief and wiped his face. He had been working hard, so had the company, a rest was in order.

He waved his hand for a break in the rehearsal and dropped into the chair.

Shanley winked at him. "An accident, huh?" He glanced over the disordered company, seeking Diana among those who were streaming over to the water cooler or back to their chairs. "Some accident. You sure treat 'em rough, Nick."

Grinning, Nick's eyes narrowed. "You wouldn't want to get wrong ideas in your head, Mister. I pulled that one on Shultz to give the kid a break she's got coming to her on the way she works. If you think that's my handiwork on her face you got another guess coming."

"Sure, Nick, sure, anything you say." Shanley stood up, stretching. "You sure did give her a break on that understudy gag. I just mightn't have thought of it, unless, of course, the girl meant something to me. Unusual, putting in under-studies at this stage. Say, you can get along without me in the back seat. I'm going out for coffee." He winked again. "I couldn't sleep last night either."

Nick let the pause run on. He wanted to meet Diana's eyes, to have that flash of momentary communication, to tell her You're great, you're tops, right now I'm giving you a hug and kiss for that, and oh boy, wait till you hear what's in the bag. How about a solo in the Lester show? Like that?

But though she sat facing him from the row of backstage chairs it was not easy to catch her eye. She was gazing in every direction but his. And then suddenly she was looking straight at him and he felt the shock of it, electric. There was no mistaking that look. It was hostile and intense.

Diana made her meaning clear. She opened the purse she had taken on her lap when she sat down, drew out a pencil, snapped it deliberately in two, dropped the pieces on the floor and spurned them with her shoe, kicking daintily. Then she leaned back, yawned, folded her arms, turned the hostile stare upon him and withdrew it.

If she had risen, walked across the stage and publicly slapped his face, Nick could not have felt more amazement, more shame, more hurt. The piece of business was an insult to his love for her. And the way she had done it, so coolly, so deliberately. Her mother could not have carried off that little bit of cruelty with more suavity.

But, getting the rehearsal underway again, he tried to argue an excuse for her, even though the hurt deepened. Sure, it was his pencil, the one that she had asked for, but this was a flare of childish petulance, paying him back for the bawling out; the bawling out had been a tough one. Anyhow, hadn't she fixed it so they could talk together with that gag about wanting an advance? He had himself in hand when he dismissed the company and stood waiting for her to come up.

But she came too promptly, not waiting for Shanley to rise and go. "I'd like to have an advance of a hundred dollars, if you please."

Why the hell hadn't she waited until he was alone. And the request, so airily stated, was exorbitant, ridiculous. "Come down in your figures." It nettled him that Shanley, departing, winked behind Diana's back.

"But I need a hundred dollars." She was as cool and imperious as a prima donna.

"You got an advance already, Miss Heaton." He lowered his voice. "Come out to the lounge. We can talk there."

She informed him flatly, no change in voice. "We can talk about an advance right here."

He sent her a quick penetrating look. "Are you in earnest?"

"I am. I asked for an advance."

This was bad, so bad that his hands, folding the script upon the table, shook. The stage had been quickly drained of life, they were alone upon it, though girls winding up the stairs could look down upon them and shortly the same girls, dressed for the street, would descend and look again. "Kid, this is no place to talk."

The cold, accusing hostility stayed in her eyes. "I don't want to talk to you any more than I can help."

He stepped back from her. That she could say that to him,

that she could say it so stonily, that she could mean it, cut so sharp and deep that pride came uppermost and he was answering with the same hard coldness. "The most that you can draw is fifty dollars. You can go to the box office and speak to Mr. Stern." He made the barest bow, courtly, heels together, and walked away.

She called after him, "Mr. Allingham—just a moment—please—"

Halfway across the stage he wheeled and made his formal bow again. "I am not the call boy, Miss Heaton. See Mr. Stern." He went smartly on and out into the alley where she, still in costume, could not follow.

He turned north, traveling at a rapid pace, going in that direction only because he had never gone that way with her. When he came to Fifty-ninth Street he crossed into Central Park. Walking on grass, passing through shade and sun and earth fragrance, he slowed down. He pressed through bushes and came onto a small rolling patch of lawn shut in by foliage and a shouldering mound of elephant-grey rock, open only to a roadway on the lower side; the place was deserted, he could be seen only by people glancing from swiftly-passing cars if they should chance to look that way.

He lay down on the grass, pleased to feel earth under him, to rest his eyes on the fresh spring green of myriad wind-stirred leaves, to gaze up at white cloud banners in a blue sky and a daytime moon made of cloud stuff. Below Fifty-ninth Street the city rose in a jagged wall, the tall buildings, many toned, white stone or grey or faintly pink or tan, methodical devices, ordered and symmetrical, a world apart from this lapse into earth ways where all about him was haphazard, undevised, the ground uneven, the growth random; old rocks bore the scars of glaciers and mocked at sudden shoots of stone and steel, man-set. Wind touched his hair, sun warmed his body; it was good to know again how lush and green and fragrant living growth of earth could be, that this went on, apart from all of man's invention and commotion and distress.

He pulled a blade of grass and bit it with his lips. So. . . .
It had ended. He had known all along that it might end,
his head had told him so, but never that it could end like
this, just mean and small and cold. Now there was no
looking back without this making a mockery of what had
seemed fine and precious; this made all that he had felt of
love a fool's illusion.

Hadn't she ever guessed the love he had for her? Hadn't
she known that it was something big that you couldn't kick
away like a broken pencil? Hadn't she sensed that it couldn't
end with petty insult? How could she do this to the love he
had given her?

He lay there wishing that the simplicity of anger would be
in him, that it would come, fusing him into mastery of this
degrading torment. But anger flamed in thin brief shoots
and died, the pain of love going on in the vacuum of bewilderment. How could she do it. . . . How could she end
it so. . . . How could she. . . .

He thought of the beauty in her dancing, the quality of
spirit that soared above the physical exuberance, a kind of
morning joy, the lyric joy that was like poetry and, like
poetry, stemmed out of elemental and enduring passion.
Nothing she did was trivial, superficial; music was in her
and took form in dancing. That self in her that danced had
risen and the rest had sunk. Well, wasn't that what happened
with most artists, why, as a lot, they were a disappoint-
ing set of humans outside of what they gave in art? As a
lot. . . . Not all of them; just because a guy played a piano or
painted a picture he didn't have to be a rotter. But mostly
he was. The all-consuming effort at artistic production
drained what energy there had been in the other selves.
Mining deep the facets of intuition and emotion, enwrapped
in mysteries, the self grew egocentric, feeding on that hidden,
secret intensity of experience that could make the common-
places of living drab and black and nerve-torturing. Yet out
of the immersed self-seeking came the revelations of the uni-

versal self, revelations of the tumult of hope and fear and joy and grief shared by humanity.

Diana, with the ugly swollen nose, had made the artist's effort at rehearsal, rising as the moment summoned, poised and victorious out of all the welter of fear and misery and sordid ugliness that had been raised about her; the joy she had expressed was not the easy-come, spontaneous joy a young girl might chance upon, it was a thing created in imagination, willed, art's illusion, art's mastery of human mood, art's insistent declaration. Diana was an artist . . . and a rotter.

Wise up to it, Nicky, you know all this, it's no surprise to you, you've seen artists before this. So there's your sweetheart for you—a brat of a girl who thought it smart to break the loven token and kick it on the floor, to cut you off with one snappy line, you, nobody, a sap not worth a decent exit.

A passing limousine, going slow, suddenly put on brakes. Nick, attracted by the screech, saw the car door open, a woman lean out, waving to him, calling, "Nicky!"

He spat out the grass blade, stood up, brushed himself off and swaggered down to present himself. "Hello, Mother." He kissed her hand.

"You lie in the park like a bum?" She was laughing at him fondly. "Get in, Nicky, you come for a ride. Mamma never sees you! She finds you—like a bum!"

"You know I am a bum. Nice people, bums." He glanced at his watch and smiled at the chauffeur. "Lo, Tom. Drop me at the corner of Forty-ninth and Seventh in ten minutes, will you?" He got in, settled in the seat beside his mother, linking his arm companionably with hers.

She was beautifully groomed, pleasant to look at, blonde hair turning to grey, a woman who had long since made her peace with fate, accepting life's pattern, facing days without resistance, laughing often and warm-heartedly; enjoying nice things to eat, a session at the couturiers, a drive in the park, a social gathering, her duties at the church. If there were times when Arthur was a beast, well, he was her husband,

and a woman held her position with a yielding grace and had the intuition, the worldly wisdom, to remain a successful wife.

She spoke to her son, addressing him in French. "Why don't you come to see me? It is weeks. I worry—naturally! And see?—I find you lying in the park."

He answered her in Polish. "I am in love." It was a nice language, you could say things like that. "And she does not love me and it is ended. She is a dancer, very beautiful, very young, it is possible she will be famous. But now it is over."

She accepted the change of language. "Oh Nickolas, I suffer for you! You must find another girl."

"I will never find one like her. I will never love anyone else."

"No, that is stupid! You are young, handsome, clever, and one of these days you will have sense. You will not say good-by to love. Only do not twist your mouth when you smile, do not let people see that you laugh at the world with the corners of your mouth turned down. You are too bitter, Nickolas. The world is a nice place."

"The sun is good and the wind is clean. People?—only a few are nice, and only nice for a little while."

"A few? That is a lot! What lasts? You dream too much, demanding what was never found—perfection. Come to see me. I will find you a nice girl."

"No. You will pick out a fat hag or a skinny wench—what matter to you so long as they are rich and of good family? No, Mother, I do not want any girl. Not for more than one night. Love, no. That is ended."

"You are not desperate? This is serious?"

"Extremely so."

"But this is terrible! You will not kill yourself?"

He pressed her arm affectionately. "I am only half Polish."

The car left the park at the Seventh Avenue exit and rolled south.

"You will come to see me soon?"

"I will come soon. But my life is the theater and truly I work hard, and already I have made some headway." The car slid in by the curb. "How is my father?"

"He is well. Here and away, of course. Nickolas, he would like to see his son. Believe me, I know."

Nick slipped out of the car. "Tell the old devil to go to hell, will you?—as a message from me. Good-by, Mother, my devoted salutations. You are looking beautiful. That hat becomes you." He closed the door and returned to English. "'By, Tom. Be sure they give you a raise now and again, and don't forget to strike for a night off."

Sitting at a lunch counter, having a cigarette with the coffee, Nick smiled over the conversation, smiled in the way his mother did not approve. But though it amused him now to translate the things he had said into English and hear their hammy melodrama, the talk had eased him; it had put Diana in the past, an experience to be regarded as part of one's personal history, not forgettable, but of a period, dated. It was pleasant to have seen his mother; yes, he would go to see her when the old man was off on a concert tour. Now there was an artist for you, an egomaniac with a temper that he never even tried to hold. And how beautifully he played. . . .

Brisk, swaggering, braced for any wisecrack about Diana that Shanley might have cooked up, Nick went out and along the street and turned into the alley.

Diana stood there, waiting for him.

He did not check his pace. She came to meet him saying, "Mr. Stern only gave me fifty dollars."

"Rules," he said, still moving, not looking at her.

She moved beside him. "I have to have more."

"Not my business. Rules are rules." He whipped into the stage door and left her standing in the alley. Well, that was the way she wanted it, wasn't it? And that was the way she'd get it.

But seeing Diana had brought her back into the present and he knew it would be a long time before he could even think of her without a passionate commotion starting up inside of him. To go on thinking of her when she had shown she did not love him was a weakness. Yet he was nagged by the question, what does she need money for? Her mother had some kind of income, her lessons were paid for. But she had said she had to have it, she had hung about waiting for him for an hour. No business of his. Forget it.

Easy to say. His will might give the command but his will was only a very small part of him and the rest was in upheaval. He could not by the most resolute determination check the wounding flow of love to her nor rid himself of the bewildering intuitive belief that she was his by destiny, nor could he deny the physical hunger for her that came like a fever, clouding thought. In a break in the rehearsal Nick sat back dully in his chair, his eyes wandering over all the young bold faces that had the look of invitation and experience. Some of these girls he knew from other shows and some from hearsay, knew which were kept and which were hunting for a daddy, some of them surprisingly pretty and trim and willing enough. And it made him sick to think of kissing one of them. It was Diana he wanted. It had to be love, it had to be Diana.

So he was a sap. He went into an elaborate bawling out of himself and kept it up, the work resumed. And in the end he was back at wondering why she wanted money and worrying lest she be in trouble.

He left a few minutes early to have a bite before going in to see Shultz. Coming down the alley a flash of familiar color caught his eye. That yellow dress was Diana's. She stood waiting on the opposite side of the street. Seeing him, she darted impulsively across. A taxi swerved, brakes jammed on. . . . Nick stopped short in horror. She just got by. And there he was, standing still, waiting for her.

He went on along the street. She tagged him, asking, "May I speak to you for a minute?"

He threw her own words back at her. "Don't talk to me any more than you can help."

That rattled her. It was a moment before she replied, "I shan't."

"I got to eat. You can spill it in here." He turned into a coffee shop. There were side tables, which meant sitting opposite, her face in front of him. He ordered coffee and a sandwich for himself not asking if she cared for anything, and she did not order. He lit a cigarette, glancing across the flame. The enmity was still in her eyes; it pleased him that, asking favors, that stayed. "Shoot."

She began, her voice low and steady and going on that way. "My mother tried to kill herself last night. I just managed to prevent it. She was out of her head, screaming, until the doctor gave her morphine. There was a trained nurse with her all night. This morning an ambulance took her to a sanitarium. I paid the doctor and the nurse and the ambulance bill and that has used up all the money from my mother's income and she won't get another check for two weeks. I don't need money for myself, the landlady will trust me, but my mother's bill at the sanitarium must be paid in advance. You say this isn't your business. No, it isn't, and I wouldn't trouble you if I had anyone to turn to. I can't ask the family, they mustn't know about this, they don't know she drinks. This afternoon I tried to find one of my mother's lovers, I thought he might lend me money, but I can't find him. Do you think if you would do me the favor of speaking to Mr. Stern he might make an exception in my case?"

Nick's hands were so shaky that he hid them under the table, the cigarette dropped, the food a waiter had set before him untouched. "Yes," he said, "I think so. Yes. You needn't go hunting up your mother's lovers."

"Thank you very much."

He wasn't looking at her, he didn't dare, love flooding in on him. "When do you need the money?"

"I should have taken it there today."

"Could you go tonight if you had it?"

"Yes."

"Meet me at six-thirty and I'll have the money."

"But—Mr. Stern has gone for the day."

"I expect to meet him in Shultz's office. That's where I'm going now." It was a lie about meeting Stern; better so. "Where will I meet you?" He had the queer feeling that he was still speaking Polish. "Not around Times Square where someone might see us."

She thought a moment and suggested, "Forty-second Street Library?"

"Yes. At the main entrance. Six-thirty."

"Thank you very much."

"Not at all."

He expected her to rise and go away. He waited, dreading that moment, knowing the pain of her presence was better than the loss of her company.

"Nick."

At the use of his name his eyes went to meet hers, and he was seeing it all again, the damaged face, the hostile stare.

"I think there's something I should say."

"Yes?"

"I hate you, Nick."

Somehow he was glad she had said it, said it straight and clean. "That's better."

She rose quickly and walked toward the door. He looked after the slender, easy-moving body, the swing of the golden skirt. Out on the street the sun lit her, then in a second, passing figures blotted her out and she was gone.

No, not small and mean and petty, no. This is tragedy to her. A sixteen-year old trying to act like a woman, standing up to handle what comes to her. She'll go on hating you, Nicky, you nearly killed her mother, that's the angle. Yet she had the pride to let you get away with saying this was not your business. . . . You won, Mrs. Heaton.

He pushed back from the table, the food untouched, went to the counter and paid the bill. Out on the street he scowled, not certain if he had fifty dollars in the house, and at this hour the bank was closed. Well, he'd get it somewhere; from his mother if he had to, and that would make her open her eyes very wide. He hoped fervently he had the money; he would hate to do a thing he never had done, and that was to ask for it.

But that was a small vexation in a vast trouble.

12

How strange and dreadful that it did not matter what time she went home or even if she did not go home at all; no one waited, no one received her. Diana had never been alone before and her aloneness was a desolation, oppressive and a little frightening. Always there had been Sue's head on the pillow beside her when she awoke, the business of each day carried on against the background of that companionship; her whole life entwined with her mother's, the intimacy deepening beyond the normal. To come home to the empty room where Sue's presence dwelt so powerfully, to pass solitary hours in silence, to go alone into the double bed and lie staring into the dark was like living among ghostly ruins.

She set herself to go through with it somehow, bad as it was. And it was bad, for now it was not the sweet mother of earlier memory whose image came to her, it was always Sue as she had been since this trouble started; the woman who stood over her as she lay sobbing on the floor, the woman who could hold her pinned against a wall in fright. She saw the ravaged face with the gleaming eyes and heard the curse of talk that flamed from the thin angry mouth and lived through the panic shock of that hideous screaming over and over again. But was it not deserved punishment? Was it not her own guilty conscience that was haunting her? It must be borne as penance.

And it would not be for long. The future lay just ahead, a new life all to be fashioned differently. At last Rod's final term of school was ending, early in June he would come East for good, the three of them would have a home together, an apartment of their own; mother's furniture, so long in storage in Chicago, would be shipped on. Grampa had written there would be a position waiting for Rod with a railroad in New York. Of course, as Sue had said, that could be thrown over once Rod started in to paint and be an artist, but for the present it was comforting to know that he also would be earning money and Mother would be able to have everything she needed.

The days were busy. In between rehearsing and the ballet class and the twice-weekly visits to the sanitarium, Diana hunted for an apartment, cheery, pleasant in layout and outlook, and at last she found one over on Staten Island. That made the trip in to work longer than she liked, but Sue and Rod would enjoy having trees about them and a view, something different from the noisy streets of Manhattan, and when she told Sue, sitting beside the bed in the sanitarium, Sue said that would be very nice. She said it in the new weak voice and with the new weak smile that had been with her since the morning she had been taken away in the ambulance, and Diana, hands held prayerfully against her breast, would smile and nod, yearning toward her with a devotion and a gratitude beyond expression. They talked little and the calls were brief, the nurse coming in to rout Diana out almost, it seemed, as soon as she had settled in the chair. Diana would come away in an ecstasy of high purpose, yet at night, sitting solitary in the long silence, Sue's presence moved about the room and always the force was evil and malignant.

Diana thought of Nick. It disturbed her that he should come so frequently to mind, that, worse still, there would arise an impulse in which she started up, wanting to go to him. He stood condemned for this disaster, the instigator of it; she had only to put the two images together, Nick holding out his arms to her and Sue gone crazy, screaming, to keep that feeling fresh. But with the first impact of shock lessening she had the sense to know she owed him much, and realized it was not Nick she hated but the evil consequences of his bad counsel. She wished with all her heart that it had stayed at friendship, that that friendship might still be hers, a joyful bond, innocent of harm. But there was no returning to that far-off time when Nick, seen only as a friend, had brought such happiness and ease to her. No, Nick had caused Sue's awful suffering; he must be thought of only as the director, Mr. Allingham, a hard director but a good one, a director Miss Heaton would try hard to please. And that was all.

But she was lonely, very lonely. A diary made some sort of company; she began one and turned to it fitfully in the long evenings. And then the last week of rehearsal came on, the theater claimed both day and evening, she had barely time for the dash home for the boarding-house dinner.

One evening shortly after she had come in and cast herself on the bed to rest for the few minutes before dinner would be served, and the flaming sunset colors were mounting in the sky and she lay thinking of nothing, the spell came back; she was lying in his arms, his dark head on the pillow beside her, his low voice murmurous with the giving of love talk, his lips coming to hers in the magic of his kiss, and the melting, drowsy, warm happiness that put time out of mind and dissolved all fret and wove beauty that was like music about her, came alive glowingly in memory. She knew she wanted Nick, wanted him urgently, and that his love was beautiful.

She got to her feet, scared, wrenching away from the danger of the spell, her eyes fastened on the window seeing Sue's body spread across it, clambering up. . . .

No. It was horrible to be feeling this. It must not be. Nick must stay put as Mr. Allingham.

But it had been love. . . .

She recalled the breaking of the pencil with remorse. She wanted to run to him crying out that she was ashamed of having done such a thing. And for the first time she recalled her promise to go to him when the month was up.

But it was not to be considered. By then, Mother would be home. To go to Nick and then return to Sue? Why, it would be the same horror starting up all over again. 'Tell me where you were.' No. It was not possible, promise or no promise.

But. . . . She could write to him. She could ask to be released from the promise, do it nicely. That at least she owed him.

216

And maybe, just once in a while when she was dancing, only then, she would let herself think . . . he said my eyes were beautiful . . . he said he loved me true. . . .

Nick came to curse the meeting with his mother. Of course there was no sense to that; it was Diana and not his mother who was slowly and steadily driving him out of his head, but he hadn't much sense left, and ever since that chance meeting in the park he had the queer, recurrent feeling that he was thinking, speaking in Polish. A part of himself that he had thought long buried had risen from the grave to jinx him. He found himself to be all the things he did not want to be, that he had set out deliberately not to be, that he had thought he never would be since he came to manhood; he found himself unstable, subject to impulse, taken by moods, imagination running wild, emotion turbulent.

Fits took him. He went night rambling, striding along deserted shabby streets, prowling by the waterfront, watching dawn come over the harbor. He took one of the chorus girls to a night club and danced dance after dance with her until the place closed, then thrust her into a taxi, gave her a bill for the fare and told her to scram and slammed the door in her inviting face, and that was no way to treat any woman. He sat down at the piano and was possessed, composing feverishly, not the Broadway stuff it tickled him to write, no, it had to be music for a dance, good music, and he could see her body gliding and twisting before him as the melodies emerged; and while that fit lasted he was all absorbed. Now if anything went wrong at rehearsal he was lashing out in excited anger and he could not snap back to being cool and collected, and this worried him most of all for this was work and pride demanded it be well done. But always there was that figure on the stage, day after day, getting in the way of his eyes, he had to be seeing Diana and the commotion starting up, his mind and body all on fire.

The last week came, day and night rehearsal, the whole cast in the theater, the influx of costumes and wardrobe

217

women and orchestra and full stage crew, and everyone on edge, in everyone the tension and the expectancy of opening night, the longing for the work to be culminated in a hit-success, a long run. And a prop wouldn't be there, a set of costumes had to be changed, the orchestration of a song was lousy, the ingenue had a scrap with the comedian, a girl was struck by a gelatine frame falling from a cradle light. A hundred and one things had to be straightened out and Shanley yawned, got up, went out for coffee. Nick buckled down to cleaning up one mess after another.

But there was one mess he couldn't straighten out—the mess Diana had him in. Okay, if it had to be a break, it had to be, but she could at least be human about it. He was leaving her alone, he wasn't asking her for anything, he wasn't bothering her, he wasn't going to. It was all washed up and he knew it, so why must she assume that priggish air? Her scrupulous aloofness, her painstaking and pointed avoidance of the barest notice of him was continual and maddening insult. There was no reason on earth why she should treat him with this contempt. There were moments when the wounding hurt ached and throbbed, moments when rage stood in him and he would have liked to shake her so her teeth would rattle, moments when the hot delirium would strike him blind and he would think that if he could not press her lips he would never be free of the destroying torment of wanting her.

Stepping into the theater two days before the opening, he found a note from her, a prim little note, dry and sparse, requesting release from the promise. Of course she was released! What did she imagine? That he would exact fulfillment of the promise after she had said, 'I hate you?' He tore up the note and threw the pieces in the alley for the wind to scatter. And yet as he plunged wrathfully to work he found he had been hoping. Sure, if he had ever meant anything to her, she would have given him those promised hours. To be alone with her in his rooms again. . . .

Shanley was coming to at the last moment. Now, with the finale tableau all set he had to get an idea. Nick sat back in his chair on the apron watching the man move among the lined-up cast, pushing one or another to a different place. Shanley came to Diana, laid his hand on her shoulder and stood reflecting. And Nick saw that Diana did not wince from the man's hand; she bore it with unconcern, her dread of touch effaced, so that when Shanley went on handling her, pushing her now here, now there, she even smiled at the man, head on one side in that birdlike way she had.

The devil of jealousy broke out in Nick. He had done this thing for her and some other man would profit by it. He went to lunch and choked over the food he tried to swallow.

It was worse in the afternoon. Yoland stayed out, delayed by a costume fitting, and Diana took the solo. Watching, Nick could have sworn there was the soft warm glow of love-dreaming in her eyes. That got him completely. He could not look at her, he had to find pretext to turn away and fight for mastery of himself. 'You can have me.' She had said it, he could hear her saying it. And he could have had her. Why hadn't he. Why the hell hadn't he. She would be saying that to someone else, not knowing any better, raised as she had been by that unprincipled woman who had lovers of her own.

That finished him. He knew, this show opened, he would have to duck and get away, there would be no directing of the Lester show; he would have to pass that up, much as it would have meant to him. Let Diana go after the solo and look out for herself. He could not stand up on the apron and have her there before his eyes, day after day. It was too much.

The afternoon rehearsal dragged to an end, the night rehearsal would begin at eight. Nick went into the prop-room to inspect the new urn for the Baghdad scene, another of Shanley's last minute ideas—the urn should be big, man-size. Well, it was; Nick told the property man the urn was right and paused to look about, checking once again on all the details.

The room was small and warm and smelt sickeningly of paint and glue. It was crammed, props stood along the shelves and about the floor. What a crazy museum of the imagination.

219

The ugly black masks used in the Primitive number hung in a row, eight of them and all alike; copies of an authentic African mask, they had the look of the original devil-magic in them. Scimitars for the Baghdad scene, the silvered blades gleaming freshly, were stacked together by the carpenter's box. The papier maché reproduction of a nude female statue that ornamented a pedestal in the Roman number stood upright in a corner. Rope garlands of flowers, crudely pink, festooned the upper shelves, beribboned tambourines were heaped beneath them. Nick looked at the large, earth-colored urn. He had the queer feeling that he would like to crawl into it, curl up in the dark and sleep. "Yeah," he said, "That'll do. Big enough."

The property man started out, going first.

Diana appeared at the door. "Did you get my message, Mr. Allingham?"

Message? She meant the note. What did it matter to her and why had she come to plague him! He regarded her in silent, savage enmity, seeing how she stood primly, wrapped in distance, yet with some quality of mettle as though she were aggrieved at not having received an immediate response to her silly little note and had come to demand the reason why.

The property man had gone by her and out the door. She stood waiting, just inside it. They were in a room together, alone.

Nick knew then what he would do. He knew it with a prescience that was a part of that submerged personality, newly come to the surface. The moment hung when he could have walked forward on the heels of the departing prop-man, left the room and the temptation that it held. He felt the moment come and knew that he would let it go, even while the illusion of decision lingered. But there was no decision; fate had this settled. She stood there, female, the destroying power, putting a challenge to him. It was ordained that obsession would be ended here and now.

"Your note? Yeah, I got it. Come in." He stepped by her, pulling the door closed, shutting her in without a glance to see who might be watching. She looked at him, surprised. "This in place of the promise." He spoke harshly, hating her for the thing he meant to do; it was her fault, she should have left him alone. "We'll have our talk right here and it'll be short." She had dropped her eyes, waiting, passive and aloof, and still there was that galling air of childish reprimand about her, coming to demand an accounting. The room was hot, the smell choking. He hurried on. "I spoke about you to Shultz for the solo in the Lester show. That'll go into rehearsal in August. Go after it, go up to the office and pester him." He finished, through with talking.

"Thank you. I appreciate what you do to help me."

Formal. To a stranger. He was wishing she would look into his face and see danger and get away, wishing it with a duality of being, knowing what was going to happen from the moment he had said 'come in.'

"I wanted to tell you something. . . ."

Her shy, momentary hesitation heightened his intensity to almost intolerable pitch; it could be endured, having her there, being certain of what was to follow even if the door opened and the whole world looked in.

"It's about the pencil. I'm sorry I was nasty. I didn't think."

He waited a moment longer. That was all she had to say and it meant nothing. Quickly, strongly, he laid hold on her, catching her so she could not break away. And it was happening; he had his kiss. She managed to turn her head, escaping from his lips, but she could not wrest free of his arms. It suited him that she was struggling with all the strength in her strong, active young body and was helpless, he could hold her tight against her will; but most of all it suited him that she was angry, not afraid; if she had been frightened he would have had to let her go. Nice and angry, beautiful in anger, sparkling.

Taken so completely by surprise, Diana was outraged. Of any other man she would have been instantly afraid, but this was Nick and he was being abominable just out of spite.

221

This was that side of him that showed up in rehearsal, the ruthless, hard-boiled, dominating nastiness that made the chorus girls hate him. Out of the sense of helpless indignity, of insulting capture, of an incredible and totally unjustifiable mistreatment, her anger flamed. To do this—on top of ignoring her apology! Twisting and pushing, she strove to thrust him off. "You let go of me."

He held her, frustrating her attempts, shifting his grip adroitly, anticipating every move she made, his mock smile cruel. "Mrs. Heaton's daughter has a temper. Always wondered if the cry-baby had one. Kept it stored special for me, didn't you? For no one else, just me. I'm the one who rates it. Swell."

"You let me go."

"Thought you didn't mind who pawed you any more. Letting Shanley put his hands on you—smiling at him!"

"You—you let me go, Nick."

"Oh, so you remember the name? Couldn't use it before, could you? Just 'Mr. Allingham.' My, you're a strong little cuss! And not strong enough, are you? You wouldn't have given me that kiss if I asked for it, and it was mine, you promised. I want one more before I let you go."

Both panting now, the tight struggle going on in the hot, smelly, crowded little room, the black masks looking down, the scimitars gleaming in the corner, Nick again shifted his grip, making it more secure, and his lips curled back, teeth gleaming. The force that had been breaking him, burning him with such consuming, wasting fire, making him nothing, despicable to himself, was belittled; he was triumphing over that humiliation.

"If you don't let me go, I'll—I'll—"

"Yeah, what'll you do? Go on, tell me. Scream and let everybody know? Go ahead, I don't care. You look nice when you get mad. Give me a kiss and I'll let you go."

"I hate you, I hate you!"

"Sure, don't I know it? You told me that before. You been

letting me see it for weeks. Nasty little female trick—hate the guy who loves you. Kiss me."

"I won't!"

"Yes, you will."

"I'll never kiss you—you can't make me!"

"Don't be so sure."

She flung back her head, eyes half closed, and spat insult directly into his face. "You dirty Polack."

The mock smile vanished. Blackness came over him, his eyes hot. He gripped her head by the hair and forced her face up close to his. "You won't say that to me."

She saw danger in him, yet her anger stayed, riding high above incoming fear, spitting reckless defiance. "I do say it. You're a dirty Pol—"

He forced the insult of his unwanted kiss upon her mouth, stopping the word, and then demanded, "Will you say that again?"

"You're a dirty—"

The silencing kiss was forced again. "Will you say it?"

"—dirty Pol—"

Again the enemy kiss cut her off. She tore free of him, trembling with rage. "You dare touch me again and I'll yell."

He made no move. Alive with hate, animal, intense, he spoke softly out of the hot blackness. "I could kill you."

Brave with fury, she stood her ground, beating down fear. "Get out and leave me alone!"

"No. I don't take orders. Not from you. You get out. I had all I want of you. You better go. Quick."

She whirled to the door in a step. Her hand on the knob she turned to spit out the infuriating words, "You're a dirty—"

A flash of movement and the tall dark figure was between her and the door, the knob no longer in her hand but his. "No. Not again. You won't say that." He was breathing fast, mouth open, lips drawn back, the veins in his temples pulsing. Murder was in him. It took all his strength to speak, speak softly, dazed. "If you open your mouth again . . . I'll put my hands around your throat . . . . You won't have time to scream.

223

Do you understand? I'll kill you. . . . Shut your mouth. Keep it shut."

In the heavy silence his breathing sounded. Outside on the stage, quick steps tramped by and were gone. Diana stood, unable to move, to go forward or back, watching with intent wide eyes, support of anger gone, fright large and swelling rapidly to panic.

"Good." He labored with the effort of talk, grasping at words and thrusting them out in the soft, blind voice. "Keep your mouth shut and get out of here. Quick!"

He swung open the door. Diana went through it in a streak. It shut behind her, separating them.

Inside, leaning against the door, the tension in him began to break. His whole body shook, his joints loosened, his legs would not hold him up. He went down limp, swerving on to the carpenter's box, passing into sleep.

But it was brief momentary nightmare. He wanted to get out, out of that stifling, box-like room, the heat, the putrid, stinking air. Black masks in a row grinned down seeing him suffocate, crawling, struggling to get out, gasping for breath of air.

He got onto legs that barely held him, staggered the step to the door, got it open, breathed. He went reeling, sense-dimmed, along the deserted stage, keeping to the wall, his hand upon it, and went on, crawling through the passage, not knowing Joe sat there, staring and astonished. He stumbled out the stage door and traveled drunkenly along the street, came finally to his own place and managed the key. He sprawled down on the couch and lay without moving, the blackness swirling over him.

If she had said it just once more—if he had been unable to get her out—

The darkness closed and settled. He was falling, senses gone, some abstract spark of consciousness sailing and tumbling, fading in the black smother as he fell backward into vacuum, a long, hideous, unending fall, the spark struggling against extinction . . . blotted out.

224

The ringing of the phone two hours later stirred him. He sat up in his own room, hearing the phone ring, not knowing what had happened or why he was there. He went to the phone.

Shanley was speaking. "Nick, you're late, it's eight-thirty. We're waiting for you. You all right?"

"On my way."

"Joe says you're drunk, says you went out of here drunk. Can you make it, lad?"

"Be on the job in five minutes." Nick slapped the receiver on the hook. He strode into the bathroom, dashed cold water on his face, combed back his hair. He veered into the kitchenette, caught up the coffee pot and poured black coffee standing over from the morning and drank it in a gulp. He patted his pockets, locating cigarettes, as he went out the door. A cab was passing; he signaled, running, jumped in for the four block ride and managed a few puffs on a cigarette. He still did not know what had happened, only that rehearsal was on and he was not there. But sitting on the edge of the taxi seat, it came back to him—

He had nearly murdered Diana.

So that could happen. A thing like that could come over you, take possession of you, drive you on and you would not know what you were doing. It could happen.

He was very sober coming into the theater, grave and quiet, setting about his work. Joe told Shanley afterward he never saw a man get sober so quick.

13

IT WAS a fresh beginning, a new life where there would be tranquillity and joy with a Sue who would gain back her health, a Sue who would have no more affairs, a Sue who would never drink again because the doctor had said it would kill her. Yet, as Mother explained, this new life was actually a return, a recapturing of what had once been, a setting up of old forgotten standards.

The three of them together at last, and Rod so full of celebration, the happiness of the reunion making clear how wrong had been the separation; now they were a family with a home of their own, even if it was only an apartment; all of Sue's furniture, dignified things, solid, beautiful pieces that spoke of background and tradition, evoked memories that, for Diana, went far back in time. The hedgerowed streets, frame houses with a garden front or back, and only an occasional apartment building, church bells ringing out in the quiet of a Sunday morning, were reminiscent of a small town and brought something of the feel of Frostburg. And Rod's coming raised up so many memories to be recalled, discussed. Being older than Diana he could share recollections with his mother in which Diana had no part. They talked much of the past; it pleased the woman to bring it back to mind, to link it with this new life as though there was a continuity, and what was done today was as it would have been in Frostburg.

They were going to be happy now. They were all agreed on that. That was as it should be.

Only—Mother was not yet herself. It shocked Diana at the outset to realize that Sue had not recovered fully; somehow she had expected her mother to come out of the sanitarium made over into her old self, and it was disturbing to find how invalidish Sue still was. Nervous, easily upset, often dejected, often irrational, one had to be wary, always keeping in mind avoidance of anything that might excite her. Well, Sue always had been different from other people, more sensitive, more temperamental, and never strong, so of course it was only natural recuperation would be slow.

Sunday evening, no performance, Diana finished washing the supper dishes while Sue and Rod sat on the back porch. It had been a jolly supper, Sue quite gay and in high spirits, and Diana hummed as she set the dishes on the shelves. Finished, she stepped to the screen door on her way to join them, and then seeing the two talking softly together, rocking chairs drawn close, Rod's shock of bright red hair beside the sleek copper one, Diana had the vague sense of breaking in upon conspiracy that she had felt once or twice before; it was queer and disturbing, but so vague that the impression was effaced at once by the glad welcoming they gave her. Rod, a slight youth, delicately built and looking more of a boy than a fellow of nineteen, sprang up to offer his chair; Sue gave invitation with a tender smile and a wave of her hand. Diana joined her, slipping into the chair as Rod settled on the porch rail. There was an interval of complacent silence.

From the back of the house the ground fell away to a steep incline, the next street two hundred feet below, then the narrow valley curved up with rows of small houses on the opposite hill, growing poorer and more scattered, with stretches of open field between. To the left, the hills piled, fold on fold, tree-mottled; to the right the valley ran down to the narrow, oily waters of the Kill Van Kull, rimmed with jutting uneven wharves like broken teeth in a comb, and beyond, on the level plain of Bayonne, industry crammed buildings close together and sent up waving towers of smoke. Over this panorama the afterglow of sunset lingered, the sky layered with rifts of cloud, lemon and yellow, flame-colored orange and purple-tinted pink.

Mrs. Heaton, watchful of Diana, crooned, "My little girl loves beauty."

Rod chimed in with his customary fervency. "She always did, Mother. I remember. She loved flowers so!"

"When she was two. . . . Two candles on the birthday cake—"

"In the nursery! Diana sitting in a high chair!"

The memory-talk went on between them and it struck Diana as a little odd, as though she was not present, or had died. She joined in, asserting, "I remember Rod's chalk drawings pinned all over the nursery walls."

Mrs. Heaton sighed. "You were such wonderful children, responsive to every influence I gave you."

Melancholy was creeping in. Rod slid to his feet asking brightly, "Who wants to go to church?"

But his mother claimed the evening with a pretty pout. "This is the one night in the week when I can have Diana to myself! You go alone, Roddy, I went to church with you this morning."

"But then Diana'll never go," he objected mildly. "She sleeps too late in the morning."

Diana volunteered, "I'll go with you sometime," and fell to wondering what church would be like. Church. . . . Sue standing up to sing and then a bottle rolling down a twisting stairs. . . .

But Rod had no such memories. He rewarded his sister's offer with a grateful and approving look, yet still he lingered, loath to leave his mother.

"Roddy," Mrs. Heaton teased, "You'll still be deciding what you'll do and church will be over."

He broke into merry laughter, admitting, "I do moon, don't I?" and bending down to kiss the woman's cheek, set off with his blithe bouncing step, waving a farewell to Diana as he passed into the house.

"There! Now I've got you all to myself!" Mrs. Heaton reached across for Diana's hand and brought it back into her lap. The two chairs rocked in harmony. The colors of the sunset faded below, blazed up above in a mighty arch. A woman in a house across the valley came out to shake a rug and went back indoors. A boy whistled deep in the street below. Mrs.

Heaton asked with a touching, childlike simplicity, hungering for response, "I *have* got you, haven't I, Dicky?"

Diana pressed her hand. "You've got me, Sue."

It was a moment for communion, intimate heart-to-heart
talk. So many big and stirring things might be said, avowals
and assurances. But Diana hung back, dreading the clumsy
damage words might do when this mood was so contenting.

But her mother ventured, skittish, ready for maneuver.
"Is my girl happy?"

"So happy, Mother."

The woman played with her daughter's hand, bending the
long flexible fingers open and shut. Brilliancy faded from the
sky, the mournful blues and violets of oncoming night deepened. Street lights came on in a row in the lower street, from
the scattered houses on the hill squares of yellow light glim-
mered. "My pal. It's so long since you and I really talked
together. We used to talk of everything. I love you so, Chick.
We must be pals always."

"Always, Sue."

Mrs. Heaton waited, inviting confidence, Then, gently,
deftly, "You loved him, Dicky."

"Yes." The reply came easily, startling and unexpected as
the subject was. But this was right, the old intimacy re-estab-
lished, nothing coming between them, nothing barred from
talk.

"Where is Nick now?"

"I don't know. He's gone away. Out of New York I heard."

"He doesn't write to you?"

"No. That's all over. I shan't see him again."

"Poor Diana. . . . He was your lover."

"No, he wasn't." Diana's chair stopped, she turned to look
at Sue, surprised. "He wasn't. No."

Mrs. Heaton's expression underwent no change. She went on
smiling ruefully, eyebrows upslanted. Slowly it come in upon
Diana that her statement was not believed, then, fast on the
shock of that realization came the greater one of knowing
she had been drawn out to speak of this by trickery; Sue had

feigned the old spirit of intimacy to gain advantage of her confidence. Expecting guile, not trust, it was not real to Sue. This was not the old communion but a cunning enemy maneuver. Diana contended against falsity, striving to set up truth. "Mother, I never went with him."

"You loved him. You just said so. And he wanted you. You went to his rooms that night." The gentle voice went on, speaking mournfully of wrong-doing.

There was one way out of this and Diana snatched at it. "Dearest, let's not talk about it. It's all over. Forget it."

"Forget it! Ugh, that sounds so cheap—slangy—like him. I see bits of him in you, in my lovely girl."

Sue's melancholy had deepened, her smile had faded, a nervous twang had come into her voice. Not knowing where the conversation might lead, Diana begged, "I do wish you wouldn't think about him. Really, dearest, you have nothing to worry over now."

"But I do worry. I worry all the time." Bitter sorrow showed on the woman's face that in this twilight gloom still looked so girlish and so pretty. "It's all my fault, Diana. I have done dreadful things when I was not myself. You must forgive me."

Diana leaned across to kiss her mother's cheek. "Oh, darling, that's so silly! I've nothing to forgive! Why, don't you know how much I love you?"

The woman's chair started up a rapid rocking, breaking away from the girl's. "No, no, you must realize they were dreadful, you must learn to know what's right and what's wrong." She spoke excitably. "Or how do I know what awful things you'll do next? If not that man, another."

This talk, so happily and easily begun, was rapidly going from bad to worse, out of all control. It was appalling to know that Sue's thought was running in this course. "Mother, don't you know I'm sorry for what I did? Don't you know I won't ever do it again?"

"No," said the woman with a passionate vehemence. "I don't know it. I worry all the time. I suffer every moment you're away. I'd like never to let you out of my sight."

Diana stood up before her. "Sue, I give you my word—"

"No, don't. Don't say that. That's like him, too. Don't speak to me with his words. I can't bear it."

The girl wrung her hands. "Mother, you must believe me. You must trust me. I tell you I have no secrets, I won't have any. Believe me."

"I wish I could, Dicky, I wish I could." It was said with anguish.

"You've got to believe me. I'll do everything I can to prove to you I mean what I am saying."

The chair went on at its rapid pace. "You'd better, Dicky, you'd better be good. Don't think that you can be a famous dancer if you're not nice to your mother. What you are shows in everything you do. People won't like you. You may kill me, but I'll haunt you. My ghost will follow you to the ends of the earth."

Diana's spirit entered into a vast desolation. Such talk was unreal, it belonged in the nightmare past, it had no place in this new life. Things happen, there is change, alteration in being, you advance—and here was Sue, far away, sitting back among the ruins, stirring dead and evil things. What could be said? It had been said, and not believed. A kind of wounding anger at the injustice in Sue's attitude, at her own helplessness to combat it, at the large misery that could go on and on for both of them, misunderstanding and distrust piling confusion upon confusion, made Diana cry out in protest, "It's not fair, Sue, you've got to believe me!" She dropped to her knees, taking both her mother's hands, putting an end to the hurried rocking. "Believe me. You must."

The woman peered straight into her face. "He had you."

"No, he didn't."

"Why do you lie to me?"

"I'm *not* lying!"

"Don't shout at me."

"Oh, Mother, Mother. . . ." Diana laid her head on the woman's lap. Mrs. Heaton gave her no fondling. The desolation spread about the girl. She saw, as it were, a road that must be walked alone, a road that stretched away and away with no promise of that turning point where it would join with Sue's path, bringing them together. She got up quietly and went back to her chair. A stir of warm air, the land breeze drifting seaward, flapped her skirt, fell slack.

Mrs. Heaton twisted a loosened wisp of hair in place and her hand stayed by her cheek in the old face-lifting gesture. "You'll have to be nice to me now," she warned, morose, "I've got something dreadful to face—change of life. They say it drives some women out of their heads. Age is so frightening, so ugly. To be withered, dried up."

This new idea roused the girl, bringing relief. It was reminder that Sue was not well, not to be taken seriously; it was an appeal for help. Strength of spirit was renewed by compassion; comfort came from giving comfort. Diana assured her mother loyally, "You'll never be old."

But Mrs. Heaton was not to be consoled. She went on murmuring gloomily. "To grow old. To know that you have failed in everything. Even in bringing up your daughter."

"You gave me love. Could you have given better than that?"

"And now you cast me off."

"I cast you off?"

"Yes, you do. You never ask my opinion, you decide things for yourself. When I think how you used to let me help you!"

"Dearest, you've been ill, I try not to worry you with details. There now, everything is going to be all right."

"So many things aren't right," fretted the woman. "Rod must give up that dreadful railroad work. I want my son to be an artist."

Diana thought of bills unpaid, of how this setting up house had added to them; for weeks to come she must pay back advances on her salary. If Rod threw up his job—"Wait, Sue. We're short of money now."

"See? You want to run things. Oh, we'd have plenty of money if it weren't for your incessant silly ballet lessons!"

"Why, that's absurd! You know they hardly cost me anything. I've got a partial scholarship. And Sue, I need technique, the more I study, the more I know I need it. I shan't be a finished dancer for at least another year of steady work. I'm lucky to have a natural limberness and strength and a facility for picking up things quickly. I've got a knack for turns, and that's lucky too. But I'll be all the better for keeping at technique."

"Then you're going to be a ballet dancer?" Peevish, taunting, spoken with nervous irritation.

Grown nervous herself, Diana answered with forced patience. "No, dear, I'll always compose my own dances and they'll be original."

"If you were a creative artist you wouldn't need to line up with a lot of empty-headed girls to be taught. Or is it an excuse to get away where I can't see you practice, where I can't help you? You studying ballet! Ridiculous. Give it up."

"No, Sue, I won't."

" 'I won't' . . . I wonder how many girls would answer a mother that way."

Diana was astonished. "Why, haven't I always—I mean—why, Sue, we're pals, I've always spoken to you—"

Mrs. Heaton nodded. "That's just it. It's my fault. I brought you up that way. And it doesn't work."

The new desolation returned, heavier than before, and with it a new uneasiness, a foreboding that the depths of trouble had not yet been plumbed. Sue was talking with that unreason that heretofore had come with drink, but this was frightening and strange because Sue was cold sober, and yet—not herself.

"Diana, are you ever going to be a great dancer?"

"Yes, I am."

"When? You should be famous now! You should be giving concerts, touring the world—and you're nobody, a girl in a group in a Broadway show!"

"But this is all experience. I still have to learn to dance alone before a big audience, learn the art of performance, how to put it over—"

233

" 'Put it over'!—and 'wow finishes,' I suppose. Give up Broadway and be an artist in the concert field."

"No, Sue, I won't." There—she had said it again.

Taunting, derisive, Mrs. Heaton baited her. "So you won't be an artist?"

"I will."

"You just said you wouldn't."

Diana bottled up an angry impulse to protest this heckling, irritated by unreason, the growing nervous misery of this unhappy, muddling talk. "Now Sue dear, you're twisting it. I didn't say that."

"Yes, you did."

"No, I didn't."

"How dare you contradict your mother!"

Exasperated and bewildered, amazed by the sharp, cross reprimand, so unlike Sue, the girl cast about for reason back of this. Change of life? Could it be that? It must be. Then patience and pity were required. "There, dearest, don't be upset."

But that also turned out to be the wrong thing to say. "Don't be patronizing, Diana. Try to understand I *am* your mother and don't act bossy and superior."

This was even more bewildering. Diana was dumbfounded, and by this time Sue was snapping angry.

"And another thing—Tear up that silly diary of yours. The idea of writing such morbid twaddle! You're not a poet."

"You *read* it?"

Mrs. Heaton's chair went off at a fast gallop. "You thought I wouldn't?"

"Why, but a diary—it's personal—"

"You see? You do mean to have secrets. Tear it up."

"No, Sue—" She caught herself in time and substituted 'please' for 'won't.'

"You told me a minute ago you'd have no secrets. Do you mean it or not? Are you going to do what your mother tells you, or are you going to be disobedient?"

Disobedient! "Why, Mother—"

234

Mrs. Heaton sprang to her feet. "Do as you're told! I've had enough naughtiness from you! You'll have to learn to behave yourself the way other girls do!"

Rod came quickly, unhappily, out upon the porch. "What's happened? What's wrong? Oh, you musn't quarrel! Sis, how can you make Mother so unhappy!"

The empty chair went on rocking. Diana sat still, staring up at the woman's figure, a dark blot against the starry sky. "No," she answered slowly, agreeing, all confused, "I don't mean to."

"She doesn't know any better," Mrs. Heaton said with a bitter sharpness. "She'll have to learn."

Time passing, day following day, Diana came to remind herself more and more frequently that Sue wasn't well. She gathered information on change of life as best she could; the grey-haired wardrobe woman had a lot of folksy lore, the elderly comedienne dropped hints. It did seem that this would explain Sue's behavior. In time everything would be all right.

But decidedly things were not right now. It was as though dark forces moved about the pleasant sunny rooms and Mrs. Heaton was possessed by their evil. Diana gloomily admitted to herself it made no difference that Sue did not drink, Sue could behave as badly sober, and there wasn't even the solace of blaming drink for what Sue said which made it worse. But of course, change of life. . . . Time, time and patience. . . .

But very shortly it began to seem that time would be no help. No, time made things rapidly worse, not better.

Rod helped; he wanted peace and joy and he conspired to build it, doing everything his mother wished with a passivity of devotion that even Diana, with all the ardor of her good intentions, could not equal. Did Mother want him to throw up his railroad job? He promptly threw it up. Did Mother want him to be an artist? He applied the color as she directed, scolding at his elbow. Did she mistrust the looks of the sedate young woman who walked home with Rod from prayer meeting? Rod walked with no more young women. He was a model son and still his mother fretted, finding fault, even with him. Rod smiled at her, fond and tranquil, blinking when she scolded, and went to his room to pray.

Diana could not match him. She did her best to grant Sue's wishes but on anything concerning dancing it was not so much that she would not give in to Sue as that she could not, the compulsion of her ambition was too strong. Give up her lessons? No Sue, I won't. . . . Give up her job? No Sue, I won't. . . . Let Sue tell her how to set a dance? No Sue, I've got to do it my way, the way I feel it.

And Mrs. Heaton wept and lost her temper and made scenes, quite awful scenes. Diana casts me off, Diana won't obey me, Diana doesn't love me any more, Diana is a bad girl. Her voice rose, shrieking out her anger and her grief so that shortly Diana dreaded meeting neighbors on the street. What must they think! Oh, she knew well enough what they thought—a poor distracted mother, driven frantic by her wayward daughter.

Rod, tremulous, reproachful, pleaded, "Why don't you do what Mother tells you?" And Diana, venting on him some small part of growing pent up exasperation, cried, "What good would it do?"

It grew worse, not better, rapidly worse. Mrs. Heaton's doubts about Diana were soon openly expressed; suspicion, starting in with hints and glances, flared into wild accusals. If any accident delayed the girl's return to home no explanation would suffice; Mrs. Heaton believed the worst, and Rod fled to a distant room, stuffing his ears and murmuring aloud to God for help while Mrs. Heaton told her daughter what she thought.

Yes, Rod knew his sister had been immoral and it was this sin that had broken his mother's heart and wrought such disastrous change in her. Now if they found themselves alone Rod would not meet Diana's eyes and talk limped and died between them.

"Roddy, don't think me bad. Mother is wrong. I'm not doing anything I shouldn't do. Roddy—*you're my brother*."

She said it only once. Mother wrong? How could he believe that? Besides, he heard her answer back, argue, and say 'I won't.' He told her, grieving, "If you would only pray. Try, try to pray."

But when the three of them were together and for Mother's sake there must be cheer, Rod found a way to meet Diana, to accept her; she was little Diana, the baby sister of long ago, the dear, innocent bright little thing who could be loved, admitted. He would call back that time, talk of it, make it seem as if that child sat in the room, and he would smile and nod happily at the grown girl, seeing only little sister in her. His mother loved that image too, there could be pretense of happiness while this game was being played. They even fell to baby-talk. "My little girl, all tired out! Cuddle up cozy on the great big sofa and go bye-bye while Roddy and Mother make nice, nice supper for the pretty one." And Diana would lie down and turn her face to the wall and wonder when, when. . . .

But it grew worse.

Mrs. Heaton was obsessed. The fear that she might lose Diana had settled in her. She had one fixed idea, that she must dominate the girl. Diana had deceived and disobeyed her once, Diana might again defy her. She had but to think of Nick, convinced that man had had her daughter, that all Diana's protestations were deceit, and she was roused, hate giving animation to her fear. It seemed to her that the girl moved airily about the rooms like some lighthearted visitor who might decide at any moment to depart. And if she went it would be as a thief, stealing away what belonged to Mrs. Heaton, what was flesh of her flesh, her own creation. How could such calamitous wickedness be prevented? How bind the girl securely?

Love had failed. The very qualities she had so proudly fostered in the child, now, in the budding woman, mocked and menaced her; independence, self-confidence, initiative, were seen as headstrong waywardness that held the threat of rebellion; the affectionate equality in which they had played at being pals led to presumption, lack of respect for mother-rule. It was heartbreaking to admit as much; Mrs. Heaton would lapse into spells of inconsolable grief, thinking of all the love that she had lavished on her daughter.

She swung out of grief, purposeful and domineering. The old ways had failed, a new pattern must be established at once, the pattern of the authoritative parent and the child who would not dare to disobey. Mrs. Heaton reverted to the way in which she had been raised, trying to speak as her father would have spoken, taking no nonsense from an unruly brat. She set herself to break what she had built, determined to remold Diana. To that end, she fastened on her daughter with unrelenting purpose; she nagged, mocked, berated with a merciless persistence.

Soon she had Diana utterly bewildered and as nervous as herself. Doggedly, the girl held to her best behavior, yet everything she did displeased her mother. Raised by reason, she tried to reason now, contending against Sue. Oh, it was all very well for Rod to beg 'Don't argue with her,' but how could she let Sue go on thinking things that were not so and which were making her unhappy? Diana felt that she must protest the wild assertions, she must strive against the false conceptions that were without foundation; she could not abandon Sue to the suffering these misconceptions caused without an effort to combat them. Of course she had to argue.

The woman grew more savage as she met resistance, not compliance. But Diana could not comply, not knowing what Sue wanted of her, and when her mother tried to make it clear Diana did not take her seriously; this was sick talk, no sense to it, something to overlook, be patient with. Under continual harassment, she marshaled her good intentions, striving to maintain a stoic calm.

It was the calm which most infuriated Mrs. Heaton. She would have none of it. It was the headstrong obstinacy that must be beaten down. She baited the girl until, stung to retort, Diana lost her head and answered back, her calm shattered. Again and again Diana thrust up her shelter, again and again

Mrs. Heaton smashed it down. The woman gave her no peace and the girl's emotional confusion deepened. She did not know what Sue was trying to do to her, and soon her mother had her so muddled that she did not even try to think; at sixteen much goes unquestioned, accepted childlike, as phenomena; to have analyzed her mother's behavior would have required more detachment than she possessed. She knew that Sue was not herself, but that enslaved her more, imposing tolerance.

She was no match for the woman. She was too emotional, too impulsive, and she cared too deeply what Sue said, while Mrs. Heaton with planned deliberation never ceased to lie in wait for her, setting traps with a cunning Diana lacked the guile to suspect. Diana's shelter soon grew flimsy. It grew easier for Mrs. Heaton to touch the girl upon a sore spot and make her leap to angry protest, it grew easier to turn anger into tears and tears into surrender; it grew easier to lure Diana into lulls of tenderness and play upon her heartstrings before rending her anew. Day by day the girl's resistance weakened and her nervousness increased and her longing for the brief lulls heightened. Unconsciously, she grew afraid of the woman, she lived in growing dread of her attacks, the sound of Sue's voice rising in temper brought instant attempts to placate her. There were times when a gleam came into Mrs. Heaton's eyes that froze Diana, filling her with a large, nameless horror; it wasn't Sue who looked at her. She would close her eyes, blocking out recognition of the change in personality that could not be admitted.

She soon knew better than to argue with her mother, to contradict or flatly say I won't. As Mrs. Heaton put it, Diana was learning. Winning ground, the woman felt her tactics vindicated, and if she had momentary qualms, Rod dissipated them, siding with her sorrowfully and bringing in a note of religious righteousness; it was wrong of Sis to answer back, to lose her temper, to refuse to do what Mother told her; Mother should punish her and make her be good. He was sorry for his sister, but he was not as sorry as he might have been; there was a comforting gratification in the justice that had brought the favored one, the one who always had usurped first place in Mother's love, to judgment.

The dark forces moved and gathered and it grew still worse. Mrs. Heaton felt no curb upon her power, she set no curb herself. The girl was helpless in her hands, Mrs. Heaton could have a scene any time it pleased her. She came to know a satisfaction in the persecution. It obsessed her with a strange excitement. It drove her on. She could not stop.

Using Rod's words, she told herself it was a righteous satisfaction. But it was other than that; it was release from the festering guilt of conscience, the hate Bob had predicted; proving that the girl was bad assuaged her. And it went deeper still; it was release for the emotional surplus that had no other outlet, all the woman's life now centered on the girl's; it went deep into the dark, unexplored, archaic regions of the self where power leads into cruelty and cruelty becomes a satisfaction. After a session that had gone through all the stages—Diana starting out with one more feeble effort to stay calm and calm had been shattered into anger and anger had been broken into tears and Diana lay sobbing at her feet—Mrs. Heaton told herself, that is the way to handle her, that is the way to make her mind, she won't dare to disobey me now. Oh Papa had known, Papa had been right; *she* had been switched when she was a child, and had *she* dared to disobey? Diana was only a child, an obstinate, naughty child; a few good whippings would take her down and straighten her out in no time. If only there was a man in the house, if only Diana had a father to handle her. Mrs. Heaton cried with vexation that she did not have the strength; in the state that she had come to she would have whipped Diana if she could. As it was, battling with the girl took all her energy; she went to church with Rod and grimly prayed to the Lord to give her more. Was she not triumphing? They had been in their new home but six weeks and already what a change! With incredible obstinacy, Diana had never given in on anything that

240

touched her dancing, but now for two days she had kept Diana from her silly lessons.

Then suddenly it came to an end. Diana turned on her. It was not anger, it was something more than anger; it was repudiation.

"Stop it. Leave me alone. You're acting like a crazy woman. You ought to be ashamed, Mother."

She made Diana pay for that. It led to the worst scene of all and there was one hideous moment when Diana thought the screams would never end and that she had killed her mother. It wound up with Diana as usual upon the floor.

But Mrs. Heaton was frightened. She could not forget the rejection in Diana's voice, she feared that she had gone too far. What if, with all her trying, the girl should come to hate her?

She went to bed, sick, drained of excitement, suddenly quite weak. Thin and small and fragile in the bed, she watched her daughter with scared eyes and spoke meekly, grateful for the trays brought in, the little favors done. She began to notice the way Diana looked, how thin the girl had grown, how nervous; some part of mother-love came back, pronouncing condemnation on herself, and she was confused, unable to think things out.

Sue was pathetic. Diana poured out love upon her. She saw that her mother hungered for it as she had hungered; she knew the joy of giving. And she saw, too, those recurrent moments when Sue forgot who sat in the room and the steady enigmatic stare of that remorseful face was beyond Diana's comprehension; she only knew it was suffering that cried aloud for pity.

Days passed and Sue stayed on in bed, brooding, melancholy, but giving back the smiles Diana gave, rising to faint cheer upon occasion. It was truce without parley, they were both too worn to enter into talk. Mrs. Heaton waived responsibility and let Diana handle everything. There was a lot to handle, the end of the month approaching, bills coming in on every side, Sue's income spent and only Diana's salary to make do for the three of them. But the girl managed somehow and saw to it there were dainties on Sue's tray.

There was peace in the house. Diana believed that her mother was getting well, that the menopause had passed and all the crazy torment with it. Her spirits started to rise.

Brother and sister drew together. Rod met Diana's eyes and smiled. There was much he did not understand, did not want to understand; loyalty to Mother held him fast, no censure of her could be admitted. But he knew that Sis had suffered and so should be forgiven, and it was right that tranquility and love should dwell in their home. Alone together at the dining table, they met each other with returning affection and talked with interest of the stage designs that Rod was sketching.

It did seem as though at last the new life was beginning.

The stage doorman stopped her. "Letter for you, Miss Heaton."

She knew at once. Nick. Who else would write to her? The envelope in her hands, she went on, hurrying up to her dressing room, immersed in excitement. The room gained, the door shut, she stood staring at the envelope, knowing the danger that was in it. Tear it up unopened? Pretend even to herself that it had never come? Impossible. It had to be read. It took so long to tear open the envelope—pull out the folded sheet—unfold it—

Dear Diana—

Forgive me. Please forgive me. You had a right to call me a dirty Polack. I was all wrong and I'm sorry. Don't think I'm going to bother you unless you want bothering, and if you do just give me the word and I'll book the act for as long a run as you say. I'll be at the Majestic Theater in Chicago for another week. It would be swell to get a line from you. Better stick the name of the show on the address—"Revues of 1928."

Keep your chin up. You're great. Been in to see Shultz yet? Talk sassy when you do. You're safe with Shultz if he thinks you're a virgin. He's that kind. That's why I never wanted any talk about you and me around the theater.

I love you,
Nick.

P. S. I make the humble suggestion that you don't take this letter home to Mama. Burn it up.

Joy caught her, smote her like a blast of wind, lifted her up and carried her sailing away to heights of song and dance and laughter and such high tumult that there was nothing you could do that would tell of it. The full, strong loverly spell of the man was with her, and the happiness that flowed out from him and gave her growth and being, and she was laughing, kissing the letter, pressing it to her breast, spinning around on one foot in a ballet turn, foolish with the overwhelming onslaught of this tremendous joy.

She stood still, settling gradually. The tumult faded. She was holding a paper in her hand that had danger in it. 'Leave men alone.' 'Tell me where you were.' 'Why do you lie to me.' A figure spread bat-like across a window. . . . A man at a door, barring escape, murder in his face. 'You won't have time to scream.'

Steps coming along the hall made her start guiltily, her heart starting up a rapid pounding. But the alarm was needless, the steps passed on, some dresser coming in ahead of time to mend a costume; it was still too early for the girls.

But it frightened her to hold the letter in her hand. It must be destroyed before some mischance gave it power to wreak harm. Suppose she were to put it in her purse, go home with it and Sue should—Yes, Sue did things like that, searching Diana's purse, her bureau drawers. Diana had come upon her, stealthily at work; it was enough to give you the creeps.

Heart still beating rapidly, she lit the candle used for heating cosmetic and moved to the corner washstand, the flame bending, protesting at her haste. Alone in the room, she felt no safety; it was as though Sue lurked, watching. She set the candle on the white tiling and read the letter once more.

When she came to 'I love you,' her eyes lingered, and in through apprehension joy swirled making a painful mixture.

It must be destroyed. Yet there was desecration in seeing fire crawl up the paper, curling it, turning it to fragile black ash that fell into the bowl and was washed away.

Nick had said to burn it. He was right. But . . . if he was right now, had he been right before? Had not all his counsel to keep the truth from Sue, which had seemed so wrong, been wise? Of course it had been wise. She had been a fool and a prig to condemn him for it.

Diana was learning; Mrs. Heaton had taught her much in the weeks of vengeful punishing. The girl knew better now than to tell her mother anything if she could help it. Sue would abuse her confidences.

On impulse she went out of the room and turned into the dark fly gallery that looked down upon the stage; she had stood in just such a place with Babe that first night she went before an audience. Since then how much had happened that was terrible to think back on. If only the procession of events would take on a different character, no more ugly memories coming to join in the train. If one shaped a right course . . . . Sitting down on a sandbag close to the rail, hugging her knees, she tried to put her thoughts in order. She was glad that he had written; it was enriching joy to know he loved her still, to carry that secret in her heart. Answer his letter? But say what? One line, just one line—I love you. But what tremendous and destroying storm could brew out of that, what rending passionate forces would again be set in conflict. Now, with Sue coming round, hope of her recovery cherished. . . . No.

Mrs. Heaton's power still held. Not the new power she had set herself to build with such a violence of will. She had indeed succeeded in making Diana fear her; the mere thought of Sue's displeasure made Diana quail. Yet it was the older power that bound the girl; she could not go against her mother's wishes because, loving her, she feared her own conscience if she did.

She loved Nick, it couldn't be helped. But that love must be martyred, dwelling only in memory. Diana sat on in the dim solitude, feeling the want of him grow until unhappiness became too oppressive. She stood up, shutting him out of her thoughts. Clearly, one right course was open to her and that was to dance, to give everything to that single effort, let nothing interfere. Dancing was not an activity that ran in a separate channel, isolated from the rest of living, it was the main current of her life, the current into which dreams, longings, all hope and all dissatisfaction could be poured; with that put first, life had a plan, a pattern, order.

To dance, to be in a theater, a part of all this that was about her, to go into the dressing room, make ready for performance, thought turning on the solo she was arranging for the coming audition of the Lester show—that was as it should be.

She would not write at all.

'Talk sassy.' She knew perfectly well what Nick's advice called for in the interview with Shultz. She should have gone in, smartly dressed, brisk and confident, speaking brightly and with assurance.

And she had not been able to carry it off. She had stood before that squat, forbidding figure, awkward and stammering, knowing that his beady eyes took note of her nervousness, her lack of poise, and of her makeshift attempt to freshen up an old dress. She came away hating herself, knowing she had looked like a nobody and had acted like one. Why, he would think she had no confidence in her work, that she had no right to ask for a solo! And the dance she had arranged was good, so good that even that grudging old man, the ballet master, forever thumping his cane in petulance with his class, had praised it, calling her the best of his pupils, the one who made the fastest progress in technical accomplishment, the one who 'had ideas' of her own. And he had composed ballets of world fame, his opinion counted.

But Shultz would never guess that. . . . Well, he had said she would be notified of the audition in about a week's time, and Mr. Aronstein, the director, would see her then and pass on her work.

And that too was a blow. From talk about the theater she had learned that Nick was back in New York; she had dared to hope it might be he who would direct the Lester show. Fretting over her failure in the interview with Shultz led to the fear of a second failure; suppose her nerves again betrayed her and she could not pull herself together even when it came to the audition; suppose before a strange director she was shaky, insecure, failing to do her best, and he should turn her down.

She was beside herself at the thought. She went over and over her solo, lengthened her period of practice after the daily ballet lesson, drove herself through hour after hour of physical effort, exhausting herself with renewed attempts at perfection until she limped, stiff and strained, every muscle aching, and warming up to start in on another session was a long and painful process. When she was not dancing she could not rest, could not relax; she stayed taut and jumpy, moody and distraught. She woke at night whimpering with nightmare, mumbled and wept in her sleep. She did not want to eat anything, food had no taste, it stuck in her throat. Nick came more and more into her thoughts. It was distracting to know that he was in New York, close by, yet lost to her when she had most need of him. Longing for him, she would lapse into dreaming spells in which she sought to recreate his presence in imagination, gaining a faint essence of the love and belief and strength he had to give.

Mrs. Heaton, up again and moving about the house in slippers and trailing negligee, her hair hanging loose—it was much too hot to dress, and why should she dress when there was nothing to draw her from the house?—knew that something was amiss. Diana was her occupation, she never ceased to watch, to study her. It was not only Diana's vivid changing face that she could read, but the quality of movement in her body; the way Diana stepped across a floor or sank into a chair informed her mother of her mood. So now Mrs. Heaton had to know what this was all about.

246

Diana told her in the barest detail. A chance for a better job was coming up. In a musical show?—yes, in a musical show. Mrs. Heaton sighed and shrugged. Oh, when would Diana quit the commercial theater and emerge as the celebrated artist? Ah, if only she would let her mother guide and help her!

At first Mrs. Heaton accepted the reason Diana gave, but then she grew uncertain. Such excitement over a triviality! Besides, there were spells when the girl moved with languor and her face was rapt and trance-like . . . just as though . . . yes, as though she were in love. The day that suspicion started up, Mrs. Heaton chanced to be in the living room, kneeling to take a book from the lowest bookshelf in the corner. Diana came meandering into the room and did not see her mother. She stood gazing at the piano, seeing Nick sit there, hearing his order, 'take it again.' Her arms stretched out and up in a sweeping gesture of almost voluptuous longing.

"Diana!"

The girl swung about in a sudden guilty amazement. And Mrs. Heaton knew—there was a man in this somewhere.

The truce was off. It began again, the railing, driving, ceaseless persecution. Diana must tell her mother everything. Frantic, the girl denied that there was anything to tell. But that gesture and that guilty start? Mrs. Heaton was positive her daughter was in love. Diana must tell her mother. She began upon the girl the moment she awoke, kept after her every minute she was home, waited up for her at night, dragged her out of nightmare, sitting upright in the bed beside her. Diana must tell. If Mrs. Heaton had been cruel before, the devil was in her now. In two days she had her daughter frenzied, close to the breaking point where no more could be endured.

Then abruptly, mysteriously, Mrs. Heaton called the truce. She became plaintive, even sweet. Diana thanked Heaven for the change, the audition right upon her and her fear of failure riding her to distraction. But somehow she could not believe in the reality of Sue's sudden gentleness; it was deception presaging some new and worse attack. Still, for two nights and a day she knew what seemed like mercy.

Mrs. Heaton had sent her daughter out upon some errands, quite a number of errands, and she was insistent on their execution. The dog-days of an early August hot spell had set in. The heat was sickening although it still lacked two hours of noon. Stepping out of doors the impact of the sun was instant. The brazen sky had the colorless, bright shine of metal, the hills were colorless, undefined by shadow, the harbor water was a smooth glare, the distant Manhattan spires quivered in haze. Diana hastened along the quiet streets resentful of this waste of energy; Rod could have done the errands, why of all days had Sue encouraged him to visit the museum? The audition might be called for tomorrow, all her energy should be reserved for that. Her legs and back were stiff and sore, they needed, she told herself, another good workout to be limbered up. She must hurry, get to the class, stay on, practice. Better still, go to the theater, practice there, spend all the time on the dance itself. . . .

Entering the relative cool of the house, she took the stairs quickly, thrust her key in the lock, pushed open the door.

Grampa was sitting in the living room in the blue wing chair.

Grampa. . . .

The unreality of his presence stupefied her. Then came the quick uprush of love, the love that had been solid since earliest memory, love bound up with deep respect, with pride in him. Her packages dropped, Diana ran forward with outstretched arms, crying out incredulous delight.

And the man put up a hand, stopping her; his sober time-scarred face was stern and his brown eyes pierced, strangely hostile, under the white-tufted brows.

It was—as though—as though he didn't know her. She hung before him, suspended. "Grampa. . . ."

"Sit down, young lady. I got something to say to you. Hattie, you'd best leave us alone."

Stupefaction doubled, the girl was aware that her mother had risen nervously from the sofa and was moving to the man. Mrs. Heaton laid her cheek against the stern, lean face that held to its one look of non-recognition.

"Papa, please don't be too hard on her, she's young. She doesn't realize."

The man nodded acknowledgment of having heard, his steady concentration on Diana undisturbed. Mrs. Heaton flitted quickly from the room.

"Sit down when you're told."

It was reprimand, severe, the girl slipped onto the edge of the nearest chair, staring at him without comprehension.

The heavy level voice went on. "I told you to look after your mother. Look after her, I said. You know as well as I do what you'd ought to have done. And you haven't done it. Your mother loved you, always treated you mighty fair. She's your mother and you had a right to think first of her and do your duty to her. And you haven't done it. Now don't you go holding this against her and saying as how she told on you. She's doing just what every mother does, she's sticking up for you right now, and I had to pull it out of her to get the lay of the land. You been a bad girl. What have you got to say for yourself?"

Diana's thoughts could not move. She did not know this man who spoke out of a family tradition that had come down from Puritan days, voice of a primitive and rigorous morality. She had never seen this man, head of the family, the authority, the lawgiver. She had known only Grampa, kind and grave and good and always loving.

Getting no answer, Luke went on in the same slow steady tone. "You answer me, young lady. Speak out and speak straight. Don't give me any sauce or I'll thrash the living daylights out of you."

This threat still further paralyzed her. That he could say

such a thing to her, that such awful shame and outrage might even conceivably be committed. . . . And this was Grampa . . . Diana could not speak.

He waited. "You got a right to have your say."

He meant to be just. Thought groped feebly. She was aware that he was giving her a chance to vindicate herself, that he would listen to anything she told him, that he would pass judgment upon it and he would be just. But what could be said? What, that would not sound like condemnation of her mother?

"You got nothing to say for yourself?"

What had Sue told him? Faltering, her voice small and thin, Diana begged, "Only—only that—you don't understand."

"What don't I understand?"

So much, so much—but it could not be told to him. Diana's eyes sank from his face and fastened on the gnarled hands gripping the chair arms. She was silent.

Luke took up the prosecution. "You been with a man?"

Her head dropped lower.

"Answer me."

"Yes."

"I don't hear you."

"Yes. Yes, Grampa."

"And you're not married to him?"

"No."

"You got nothing to say for yourself." It was judgment, final. "You done what no decent, respectable, well-brought up girl would have done. No woman that was a Fletcher would have done it. Nor a Heaton neither. You come of decent folks and you done it. There's no whores in either family. And you're not ashamed. You hold to worrying your mother."

"No, I don't."

"What's that?"

The thin shaky voice trailed on, "I don't worry her now, I'm not doing anything wrong. She just imagines that."

He was rising, slow, deliberate. His resolute plodding steps

250

advanced upon her, full of intention. She glanced up at the lean hard body and the severe set face and shrank in sick terror.

"You got your mother near crazy and you know it, and that's not imagining. I told you not to give me any sauce. Get up outa that chair."

She cringed further into it, helpless with fright.

The man caught her arm and yanked her to her feet, held her there before him. "Git up when you're told!" He released his grip on her arm and Diana, swaying, caught at the back of the chair. "Let go of that. Stand up on your own two feet and take what's coming to you."

The chair abandoned, Diana faced him, not knowing what degradation he might hurl at her. She was so sick with shame and fright that his face swam before her, her vision blurred.

There was another order coming. "Speak out straight and say you know you been a bad girl and you're sorry for what you done."

He must not think it—he must not believe—if it could be communicated to him that she was not bad—The power of speech gone from her, inadequate for this great emergency, she shook her head helplessly in the most feeble of denials, her eyes imploring him to understand.

Her silence vexed him. He warned, somber, "You'd best do as you're told, young lady. I'm going to give you a licking that you won't forget."

It could not be. It was not possible—he wouldn't—no—Diana gasped out appeal. "No, Grampa, no—I'm not a bad girl—I'm not bad—"

It was the wrong thing to say. The face that had been impassive in its severity clouded over with wrath, the brown eyes snapping. He turned from her and began methodically preparing for what was to come, taking off his coat, hanging it upon the back of a chair, unfastening his cuff links, rolling up the sleeves of his white shirt, slow and precise in all he did, while Diana, half out of her mind, went on begging senselessly, finding no other words to say but, "No—no—I'm not bad —I'm not bad—" until, ready to proceed, he turned his face

251

upon her and she saw the wrath still on it and spilled backward into the chair.

"I told you to get up outa that chair. I told you to speak out straight. I told you what to say. And you won't do nothing you're told. You been with a man and you're not married to him, and you got the sauce to tell me you're not a bad girl. You're just begging for a licking, that's what you're doing, you're just spoiling for a sound thrashing. Well, you're going to get what's coming to you. You got a lot coming to you for a long time back. It's gonna take more than one licking to straighten you out, but I'm gonna straighten you out if it's the last thing I do in life. Get up outa that chair!"

The command lifted her.

"Say you're sorry."

Hypnotized, she mouthed the words. "I'm sorry."

"Say you're a bad girl."

She found his eyes, and looking into them she could not say it. "No—no—I'm not—Grampa—"

His fingers went to the buckle of his belt, worked there, unfastening it, drawing the leather strap out through the loops. Diana, watching without belief in what was happening, came suddenly and terribly alive. It could happen—it was happening. She cried out shrilly, "No, you can't—you can't do that!"

His fingers paused in their work. "Why can't I?"

"No. I'm not a little girl! I'm grown up—I'm a woman—you can't."

It seemed that she had made him understand. He was threading the belt back into the loops, fastening the buckle. But there was no change in the wrathful face. "You think you're grown up. You think you're a woman and you're not ashamed. Well, I'll shame you, Diana, I'll give you what you'd ought to had when you were six years old." He took a step to the chair and sat down on it, the fingers of one hand clamping on her arm. "You just git across my knee and I'll show you if you're grown up or not."

She went numb. Out of a mounting agony of dread and

shame, her spirit came away detached, and all at once nothing mattered, she would take no part in this.

"I told you to git across my knee."

A wrenching, painful jerk sent her falling, sprawling across his lap, head hanging. Suddenly in thorough numbness a stabbing sentience shot and she was again hideously alive, having one clear vision of the picture of herself in that position, degraded. Then rage came. She would not speak to him. All communication was shut off. He did not exist. She would not even let him know that he could hurt her.

But she had forgotten pain. She did not know what this could be.

Luke struck with all the force and ire of righteous anger, and at that first astounding, smiting slap, Diana gasped and jumped. The second blow coming down on the pain of the first shattered the illusion that she could withdraw in spirit. With the third slap hurting worse than the second, rage crumbled, deserting her. She made a sudden wriggling effort to get away, and pain increased, the fingers of the hand that held her biting deep into her flesh. She made another desperate twist, getting her head up, and got a stunning slap across the face. She was caught fast, she could not get away, and the amazing pain was increasing, going on, and it could go on, she had no defense to set against him, her nerve going. She bit on her hand to keep from crying out, clinging to that shred of pride, feeling it swiftly crumble as rage had, knowing it could not long survive. Her nerve broke suddenly and she was crying like a child and calling out to him to stop.

He did not stop. A girl who had not guarded her virginity, who had no shame in the matter, a girl of decent folks, well reared, should know what punishment for that offense could be. It was not enough that she cried 'stop.' The wrath of punishing released, the hard heavy slaps went on, deliberate in purpose.

Pain mounting, all possessive, she was surrendered to him, committed to as much of this as he might choose to give. All control shattered, her submission was complete. She begged,

imploring him to stop, calling him by name, promising anything, anything, if only he would stop, unable to put a check
upon her tears, her cries.

And Luke did not stop until he had made sure that she
would recollect what that surrender felt like. Then the slaps
ceased, the commands came. "Git up on your feet. . . . Say you
been a bad girl. . . . Say you're sorry for what you done. . . Say
you're going to behave yourself and do what your mother
tells you."

She said it all. It was over. She tottered to the sofa to fall
face down, still weeping, still writhing; there was nothing left
of her now. She heard him moving about the room and turned
her head to watch in an animal dread of his approach.

Luke pulled down his sleeves and fastened his cuffs, mopped
sweat from his face and put on his coat. By then her crying
had died in exhaustion. He walked up to the couch and she
shrank, eyeing him in stupor.

"Do you now know what you'll git if you don't behave
yourself?"

She nodded, thinking that sufficient.

It wasn't. "Answer when you're spoken to! You asking for
more? I'll take the strap to you right now."

It was not over—it would never be over—he would take off
his coat, begin again—"Don't—don't—please—I'll be good—I'll
do anything—"

He had what he wanted. He nodded, satisfied, and walked
out into the hall, and Diana was listening acutely, straining
to hear him go. "Hattie!" he called, and quickly a door opened,
there was a rustle of skirts. The man's voice went on. "You
won't have no more trouble with her. She's learning. I'll give
her a few more lessons and she'll know what's what. Be round
tomorrow. I'm going back to the hotel now. You just tell me
if Diana gives you a word of sauce." There was the smack of a
kiss. The hall door opened and shut. He had gone.

Fluttering, fearful, Mrs. Heaton stepped into the living
room and looked at her daughter. Limp, tear-smirched,
rumpled, dulled with dishonor, Diana lay on her side, staring

back. Something stirred in her mind, something she wanted to tell Sue. She tried to think what it was. Oh yes—"I never told on you. I kept my mouth shut."

Mrs. Heaton's hand flew to her head. She spun, fleeing. Diana lay on, staring at nothing. The numb, dead feeling came back to her, but heavy and complete; nothing mattered. She said it aloud, speaking softly, "I don't care. Not about a blessed thing. I don't care." Fear tried to enter, warning of danger. Had she just sauced Sue. Sue would tell. He would come back, take off his coat. You sauced your mother. The belt. Be round tomorrow.

But tomorrow seemed remote. It was nice to feel that nothing mattered. If it would only last. Because she had sauced Sue and he would come back 'Talk sassy.' Who said that? She could not remember. It didn't matter. To stay numb. Not to care. To feel nothing. . . .

But then—

The dance—the audition!

She was up, unsteady, wincing, struck by a new and horrible alarm. What if she actually stayed numb, felt nothing. Without feeling she could not dance, and the audition—

I got to go to the theater.

She saw her purse on the table between her and the door and picked it up as she staggered out.

Theater—I got to dance—

'I never told on you. I kept my mouth shut.'

Diana's words had pierced Mrs. Heaton. The depth of love and loyalty in what the girl had said was a last goad in that repentance which had begun when she stood, ear to the crack of the door, hearing her baby's piteous cries. Stricken, she huddled in the armchair of her room. 'I never told on you. I kept my mouth shut.' Flat statement, uttered without reproach, and it was damning. Diana loved her. Diana had stood by her, and what had she done to Diana? She had summoned her father, knowing how harsh his punishment could be, she had planned it all, thinking she would know a satisfaction, hidden back of the door, hearing Diana get what she deserved.

What she deserved?

I have been mad, mad. How could I do this thing. To Diana. How could I. What demon possesses me. How many more times in life must I suffer fresh remorse. Everything I do is wrong, wrong. Will I never get straight. . . .

The clarity of her thought dimmed and she was in trouble and confusion, not knowing how it was that she should still be wandering astray, meeting fresh misery when all she had intended—

'I never told.'

Yes, she remembered; coming out of the woods with Chris . . . 'Dicky, don't tell on me.' Binding the child to that promise. And Diana had kept it.

Mrs. Heaton stood clear of the long delirium of persecution, knowing it had been wrong, the nagging and the scolding, wrong and futile. I don't care what she does, I shan't go after her again. Let her do anything she pleases, have affairs if she likes, I don't care so long as she keeps on with dancing.

She would go to Diana now, beg her forgiveness, become her ally, plan how Papa was to be managed, tell the girl what to say to escape his further punishment. I will not let him lay a finger on her ever again, he'll have to beat me first, and he won't do that. Yes, she would go to Diana, say it all—I have been mad, out of my head, I had forgotten what it was to be a pal. Forgive me, Dicky. We *are* pals and I'll stand by you, and I won't ever be cross again and you can do as you please. Just keep on with your career, that's all I ask.

Now. . . .

But Diana had gone from the living room. She was not in the bathroom. Nor in the dining room—kitchen. She was not in the house. Diana had gone.

Luke went along the street at his one pace, sorrow on his time-worn face. This came on top of everything else. Hattie didn't know yet about Nyrum. He'd have to tell her that, he'd have to say it straight. My son's no better than a swindler.

Heat came down from the color-bleached sky and up from the sweltering earth. He walked with his head up, his back straight, and that new, twisting pain setting in about his heart. He came downhill to the ferry house, boarded the boat.

Nyrum Fletcher, Luke Fletcher's boy . . . fine a young fellow as is, smart, a hustler, graduate of Harvard College. Why, Nyrum Fletcher?—his word's good on anything. Fletchers are old stock, honest folk, honest as the day is long. . . .

No, it don't go that way, never no more. Nyrum's word's no good on anything. Shouldn't be so that a lot of lawyers start poking their noses into a man's business, asking questions, calling for an investigation. Come to me to judge I'd give him jail. He was well raised. He knew what's what.

Ambitious. Too ambitious. Tried to be too smart. Seemed like ambition was the same as liquor and some folks didn't have the head to carry it, drove 'em crazy. Driving the whole country crazy. Everywhere men pushing, trying to get ahead, trying to beat the other fellow, bound to get there and not caring how. Ambition in Hattie, always worm-eating her, making her send Diana on the stage instead of keeping her to school. Ambition in Diana making her go wrong. 'Fling away ambition, by that sin fell the angels.' My son's a swindler and my girl's daughter is a whore. Lord God take me soon, let me come to rest.

The pain twisted tight about his heart. He had been warned and he was unafraid. He would keep on, pulling in harness, taking care of his load, doing his duty as it came to him to do, no matter what. Sobeit, Lord, when You're ready.

Crossing the lobby of the Biltmore, the slow marching steps halted as at an army command. He stood a moment straight, at attention, the steady eyes staring into eternity. Then he fell, face forward.

He was dead when strangers came in a quick closing circle, stooped to lift him up.

A soft, hurried rapping came on the door. The pencil that had been moving rapidly along the bars on the page of music manuscript came to a stop. Nick sat unmoving, bent over the table, no longer listening to the melody in his head but for the recurrence of that knock that he had thought never to hear again. The knock was repeated. There was no mistaking it. He was on his feet and striding to the door.

Diana yes. But so altered that Nick stared, shaken. Hatless, disheveled, the girl wavered, holding to the door frame to keep her balance, gazing at him with blurred eyes in a smirched, thin face with lips that trembled and let out a reek of whiskey.

If he had never had to see this. If he had the strength to slam the door in her face. But she looked at him, sick and beaten, saying in a whisper of a voice, "Nicky, help me."

"By God. You're a fine example of a mother's loving care. You're drunk."

"Please help me."

He was too sickened to be angry. "What can I do now?"

She took it her appeal had failed. Head sinking, she made a move to turn and go away, and at that wretched, miserable acceptance of rejection his heart turned over. He reached out a hand to draw her in. She flinched, blinking, as if she thought he meant to hit her, and flinched again in pain when his hand closed on her arm. He said softly, "Come in, kid. I'll straighten you out."

Her blurred eyes questioned, slid away. With an abject docility she went where he led, walking stiffly, unsteadily, across the big room, into the bedroom, through that into the bath. Nick filled a glass with tepid water. "Drink it."

She sipped and demurred. "Warm. Make me sick."

"Sure. We got to get this poison out of you. You keep on drinking that till you throw up." She drank it. Nick refilled the glass and pressed it on her. It was plain that she thought this unkind treatment but lacked the will to protest. "Boy, I never thought that I'd be doing this for you!"

"I'm going to. . . ." She wanted him to go away. "Disgusting."

"Glad you think so. I'm standing by. Go on, get it out of you." He stayed there, holding her head. "There now, you'll feel better soon. Let's get that dirty face of yours washed. You've been crying again." She held to the stand, weak, submitting to whatever came. He washed and dried her face. "Got a comb in your purse?" She nodded. He found it and combed her hair. "Now come out and lie down on the couch while I make you some coffee." He took her arm and she moved beside him, silent. "Say, what's wrong with your legs?"

She gave no reply. He stood watching the care with which she laid herself down on her side, her face twitching. He went into the kitchenette, started the coffee, came back to clear the table and set out cups and spoons. The sky was darkening for a thunderstorm, the air heavy and oppressive, the heat holding. He brought a chair over to the couch and sat there fanning her with a folded newspaper, waiting for the coffee.

She lay limp, unmoving, eyes shut, lips parted, her breath light and quick, broken now and again by a sigh of exhaustion; from time to time her muscles jerked and her face twitched. She was thin as if she had been ill; her wrists looked small and fragile. That was the familiar yellow dress; faded now and ripped at the belt.

This was Diana, the girl he loved; this was the girl who could dance with a delight that would put wonder in you. This wreck of a youngster, sixteen years old and drinking. It would be better to be sitting by her coffin; yeah, and easier, a whole lot easier.

He got up, fetched the coffee, poured it out. "Come and get it."

She started to rise at once; instant compliance told of brutal discipline, of spirit broken. He said, "Maybe you'd rather have it over there."

She would; she sank back upon her elbow. He brought the coffee things to the chair, turning it into a bedside table, wondering what hell she had been through. He pulled up another chair and sat facing her across the makeshift table. She sipped the coffee, not meeting his eyes, the cup rattling on the saucer when she set it down. Nick lit a cigarette. Elbows on knees, looking down at the floor, he asked, "How long you been drinking, honey?"

"I haven't been drinking."

He glanced up sharply. Her face, like her voice, was dull, and shame was written all over her, he thought that she was lying. "Came in here drunk, didn't you? You look like you'd been drinking for weeks. You're all shot. You can't even hold that cup steady. How come?"

She spoke flatly without emotion. "I was in the theater. I was trying to dance. I couldn't. I kept trying. Everything went black and I fell down. The doorman picked me up and he had a glass of whiskey in his hand and he told me to drink it."

"You only took one drink?"

"Maybe it was a big one. And my stomach was empty. I never had any before. Right away everything started to whirl and I knew I was drunk. I knew somebody would have to look after me. I thought you might."

"You never took a drink before today?"

"No."

Nick sprawled back in his chair luxuriating in relief. "Say, that's a whole lot better. I'm glad the sick pup knew where to crawl! You don't need to be ashamed about that, Diana, that's just an accident. Come on, get your head up. Give me a smile, will you? What's the matter, honey, can't you smile?"

She stayed dulled, spiritless. Her coffee finished, she laid her head on the pillow and covered her face with her arm. "Thank you very much for getting me sober. I'll go away in a minute."

"What are you trying to do to me, break my heart? Honest to God!" He moved the coffee things to one side and drew his own chair closer. It had grown very dark. Lightning flashed and a crackling boom of thunder came right on top of it. Diana gave a start.

"Honey! What's wrong with you? What are you scared about?"

"I never used to be scared." Her voice shook, she hid her face still further under her arm. "Not of anything. Not when I was a little girl. I danced in the thunder, I thought it was a grand uproar."

He put his hand on her arm to draw it down. She shrank from his touch, stiffening. "Aw kid, are we back at that stage? You're not scared of *me!* You got my letter, didn't you? You know I'm sorry for what I did to you. I won't do that again. Let me hold your hand. Why didn't you answer my letter?"

Again came the shivering light, the reverberating boom. Her fingers tightened on his, then tried to draw away. He held to her hand, repeating his question, coaxing, asking a third time, "Why?"

"Because I couldn't write you what I wanted to write."

"What did you want to write me, honey?"

In the dull, weak voice she told him, "That I love you."

Nick stared at her. "Say, look at me when you say that! Are you talking in your sleep? Maybe I didn't get you sobered up yet. Won't you look at me, Diana? Give me that line again."

She drew her hand away from his and covered her face. Nick slipped to his knees beside the couch and bent over, kissing her bare forearm, pressing that shelter gently from her. But she would not meet his eyes and a new fear gripped him. "Listen kid, you're all messed up about something

261

you're ashamed to tell me. Let's get one thing straight at a time. Now you don't like me to touch you. Is that my fault or have you got tangled up with some other guy?"

"No other guy."

The flat statement brought vast relief. "Okay, then it's my fault. Remember how you trusted me once? Well, I don't know what's going to come up between us or how it's going to hit me, I love you and that might make me go crazy again, I don't know. But I give you my word on this—when I start turning into a—a 'dirty Polack' I'll give you fair warning to clear out and get away from me. And until I do that you can trust me. How's that?"

She did not answer. Rain came down on the sidewalk outside with a hard smack, the cool freshness of it drifted into the room. He put out his hand to stroke her head and she blinked, tensing. "Honey," he begged, "Don't, don't do that!"

Her voice twanged, nervous. "I didn't mean to. I can't help it. I want to go away."

"Diana, you said you loved me."

She grew rapidly more agitated, her head rolling distractedly upon the pillow. "Oh, leave me alone—leave me alone—"

"Do you love me or don't you?"

"Oh, what does it matter—"

He put his hands about her face holding her head still before him, demanding, "Do you love me?"

"Yes, but it's no good, no good!" Her eyes flickered away.

He still held her head between his hands. "Wait a minute. You love me. There's no other guy. You're not a drunkard. That's a lot to start with. Why can't you look at me?"

She pushed his hands away, made a move to rise, and fell back moaning.

Quick, insistent, he demanded, "Sweetheart, please, what's wrong with you?"

"Oh leave me—"

"What's wrong with your body?"

She broke into dry sobbing. "Can't you see it doesn't matter, nothing matters—I don't care, I don't care about anything—" She was all at once near hysteria, thrashing about in a wild, feeble excitement.

Nick slipped onto the couch, lay down beside her, put an arm under her shoulders and drew the thin, taut body to him, holding it quiet. "Stop it. Don't talk. You've got to calm down. Listen to the rain. Ever go walking in the rain, feel it falling on your face? Smells nice, doesn't it? Feel that breeze coming in the window, nice and cool." The tension went out of her body, the wild energy quickly spent. "There now, that's better. We're going to get everything fixed up."

Her voice came in a desperate whisper. "You don't understand. I can't dance. I'm going to fail. I can't stand it. I'll die."

He went on speaking softly, stroking her. "You'd better tell me, honey, tell me everything. Just stay quiet like this while you talk. Maybe I can help you."

"You can't."

"Give me the chance. I'll do anything I can for you."

She stayed quiet, her face hidden in his neck; the moments went by. He thought his offer rejected. Then she was speaking in a low voice. "You *could* help me."

"Then I will."

"No—wait. Don't promise yet. It's a big thing to ask."

"Go ahead and ask."

Another period of hesitation followed. "Nick, you know how I am . . . I mean . . . if you and I . . . I mean if we . . . "

"Say it."

The words came in a rush. "If I was married I wouldn't be any good at it but—will you marry me, Nick?"

The question rocked him; he did not know what to make of it. He lay thinking, going back over what she had said;

she had told him that she loved him, but that wasn't the reason. "What do you want, wife-in-name-only stuff?"

"Yes."

"Will you come to me, live with me?"

"Maybe. . . . Maybe not."

He rose on his elbow looking down at her face. Her eyes still dodged his. "Why do you want it, Diana?"

"I can't tell you."

He sat up. "Sweetheart, maybe I'm asking a hard thing of you, but if I'm going to marry you I've got to know why."

Her face puckered. "Do you have to know?"

"I have to know."

"And then maybe you would?"

"Maybe I would."

Her hand reached for his and gripped tight and now she was looking straight into his eyes, telling it fast. "My grandfather's here and he shamed me, he made me say things no one would say if they had any pride or courage but I said them. He made me. I couldn't stand it. He hit me, like a baby, across his knee, hard, he wouldn't stop, he was angry because I'm not a virgin and I'm not married and he wanted me to say I was bad and I said it, I said everything he told me to. And it's not over, he's coming back tomorrow. He's going to hit me with his belt, and it'll go on and on because I'm not a virgin and I'm not married and I can't stand it I'll die. Oh Nicky please—"

"That's enough." Nick was on his feet, harsh and dark with anger. "I'll marry you and that's not doing you any favor—you know I want to. But get this straight—my wife isn't going to live with her mother, there's no 'maybe' about it, you come here to me. If I've got a wife I'm going to look after her and see no harm comes to her. You've got to come to me, Diana, you've got to let me be your husband. Now hold it—" He sat down beside her. "Don't get me wrong on that. If you don't want to go to bed with me I'll wait until you do, but I want you here with me."

"You said you'd wait. . . . " Diana strove to deal honestly

264

with this. "I wouldn't want you to expect—Nick, I might never—No. I never would—"

He raised her hand to his cheek saying gently, "Will you let me worry about that end of it? I'll marry you, Diana, without any promise from you, only that you come to live with me." But Diana was gazing starkly at nothing, fear and misery in her eyes. "Oh honey, don't you believe—"

She turned her staring eyes upon him. "The audition. I— There isn't time. I can't pull out of this."

It was good to know her fear was not of him. He smiled at her. "Think I'm a pretty good director? Will you let me handle you? Will you do what I say?"

She only looked at him, begging hope.

"You'll dance. You'll go to that audition. But you've got to take my orders. Will you?"

She nodded, eyes unmoving.

"Then here's the way we do it. Suppose you do get a call from Shultz in the next two or three days—don't go. Sh, don't get excited. I know all about those auditions, they'll last a week when they do start, and you won't lose a thing by not turning up on the first day. You're in no shape to give an audition, that's a fact. Your nerves are shot, your legs are on the bum and you're too skinny even for a dancer. But if you do what I say you'll be in shape in a week or ten days. Sleep all you can, eat all you can, and no practicing for four days at least. How hard you been working? How much of what's wrong with you is your grandfather's doing?"

"I was awfully sore before that. I'd been working hours every day, hard as I could."

"You've overtrained. Your muscles will tone up fine with a rest, and you let me give them a massage every day. Did you call your stage manager, tell him you're not working tonight?"

"Not working!" She was shocked.

Incredulous, Nick asked, "You didn't mean to try? Why, no stage manager in his right mind would let you step inside a stage door the way you are now." Her consternation made him shake his head and smile. "It's an awful thought, but that show can run without you. Even stars have to learn that sometimes. Getting set for this audition means more to you than missing a couple of shows. Now you've heard the orders. Are you going to take them?"

Her eyes had cleared, fear gone and hope shining feverishly in its place. "Yes, Nick. Oh, you're wonderfully kind and good to me!"

"Why, you've got the makings of a proper wife! May I kiss you, Diana?"

"Do you want to?" Anxiety came into the question. "Am I a nice person, Nick?"

That incredibly innocent, vulnerable quality in her struck him afresh. That she actually felt any blame upon herself for what had transpired in that cruel punishment was reminder of just how young, how idealistic she was. "You mustn't ask a thing like that. You are a nice person. That niceness is yours, no one can take it from you. Sure I want to kiss you. Every chance I get." He bent over her and pressed her lips, remembering with heartache how he had last insulted them. He kissed her cheek, her throat, her eyes, and came back to her lips for one more soft, lingering kiss.

Sitting upright, he stroked her hand, thinking. "Diana, this might sound like a funny thing to talk about to you, but we're going to be married and I want it all straight. When I was in Chicago and you didn't answer my letter I thought it was all over between us. And I had a girl. Well, I had several. But even though I thought you didn't love me I felt untrue to you all the time and I feel worse right now. I've loved other women, Diana, thought I did anyhow, but no woman ever meant a thing to me compared to you. I'm sorry I messed around in Chicago. Forgive me?"

The honesty of his intention warmed her to him and she twined her fingers with his, answering with shy constraint, "Don't be sorry. When people have things on their conscience it seems to make them cruel. If they're tormented they torment others."

266

"So I'm forgiven and I have nothing on my conscience. Say, you're feeling better now that you've got Mr. Allingham working for you. You almost smiled!" He glanced toward the window. "Rain has stopped. Well, want to get married?"

"How strange that sounds. . . . It isn't as though I were deserting Sue. . . . She's got Grampa. He'll look after her."

"Nothing on your conscience either, is there? You're a moral little cuss, Diana." Nick got up, lit a cigarette and paced the room. "Here's the layout—we'll trot off now and do the Mr. and Mrs. trick and throw a good dinner into that poor empty belly of yours some place along the line. Then we call Mama and tell her you won't be home tonight and why. Then I'm going to take you up to my mother's house and you can sleep there, stay there as long as you like, come down here and visit all you want to. My mother's a museum piece, honey, and the place is lousy with glitter, but she's sweet and she'll make a fuss over you. I think you'll like that plan better right now than being here with me at night and maybe getting scary ideas in your head. Now do I get your okay on all that?"

Diana had risen on an elbow and was thinking very seriously, her brows drawn together. Marriage. . . . It seemed so strange. To leave Sue. . . . Yet when her thought turned homeward it was not Sue she saw but a lean hard man who stood in the center of the parlor, taking off his coat and rolling up his sleeves. "I'll do it, Nick. There isn't anything else I can do, is there?"

He stopped in his pacing. "Well now, that's not exactly complimentary to me, is it?" He tried to speak lightly, pass it off as a joke, but his look was sharp and penetrating. Diana's brooding frown was not reassuring. "Sweetheart, I'm marrying you because I love you."

She wondered at the tension in him.

"I told you a moment ago that I had loved other women. Diana, I never asked one of them to marry me."

Confusion filled the girl; she did not know what point

267

he meant to make. Had she been wrong in asking this of him? "But—you did ask me once."

"I asked you. Because this can be what marriage means to me—real and lasting and important."

Diana forced herself to a sitting up position. "Nick, I didn't mean to be rude. I was just trying to be sure."

"Yeah, let's be sure. *Do* you love me, Diana?"

"I love you, Nick."

The simple ready answer sent him to her holding out his hands, helping her to her feet. "So! Here we go, honey. Say, your dress is torn—there at the belt. Slip it off. Won't take a minute to mend it." He went into the bedroom. "I got a needle and thread some place."

Diana's hands had moved obediently, unfastening her dress, but then they slowed, stopped. Nick came back to find her still in the dress and blood in her cheeks.

"Oh. Don't want to take off your dress in front of me?"

Embarrassed, she murmured, "Do you think I'm silly?"

"Yes, I think so, sweetheart, because I can see you've got a slip on and with that you'd be more covered than in a practice costume, wouldn't you? But go ahead and be silly, everyone's silly about something." He handed her the needle, dropped a kiss on the nape of her neck. "I'll go phone your stage manager while you're mending that." He went into the bedroom closing the door behind him.

When Diana called to him that she was ready, Nick came quickly and they started out, Diana leaning on his arm and limping stiffly. She felt his happiness and was gladdened and strengthened by it. She rubbed her cheek against his shoulder and smiled up at him.

Nick's plan went smoothly until it came to phoning Mrs. Heaton. Diana thought she should be the one to phone. But Nick persuaded, "Let me. The very idea is making you jump out of your skin. I'll say it right, nice and polite. For your sake I'll even croon."

So Diana waited outside the phone booth at the back

of the drugstore, twisting the strange ring on her finger, her heart starting in to hammer. Rod had answered, Nick was asking for Mrs. Heaton. Diana waited to hear him say 'Is this Mrs. Heaton?' and go on from there. But he wasn't saying it. . . . He was listening, not talking, giving brief responses, "Yes, your sister's here. . . . All right, I'll tell her. . . . " He hung up.

Frantic with alarm, she clutched at him, pulling him out of the booth. "My mother—what's happened—quick—"

His answer was immediate, emphatic, reassuring. "Your mother's all right."

Diana's eyes closed, her head rolled back, she swayed, about to collapse, and Nick's arm shot about her. But she rallied at once. Eyes flashing open, she demanded, "What is it? What's wrong? Why didn't you speak to her?"

"Diana, you've got to pull yourself together. Don't go to pieces like this."

She saw consternation in his face and gasped, "It *is* Mother!"

"I told you no."

"Then what?"

"Get set and hold steady and I'll tell you."

She made the effort, impatient.

"Your grandfather."

"Oh. What—?"

"Yes, I've got to tell you. Keep a hold on yourself. He had a heart attack."

"He's dead."

"Yes, honey."

She took it quietly and was silent. Nick got a cigarette lit. Boy, if it had been her mother. . . .

"Nick, I've got to be there now. I've got to go home."

He studied her before he spoke. "Think so?"

"I must. It's my duty."

"Give me a minute." He drew on his cigarette, considering. It was a surprise to him that she would want to go. He granted the claim of family at a time of death, but surely the treatment Diana had been given canceled that. But he saw how resolution had possessed and calmed her, how fixed was her intention. To oppose her now when she was overwrought, high-strung, near collapse, would mean tears and trouble, a bad beginning for a marriage. He told her earnestly, "I don't want you to go. I don't think you should. You're in no shape to take on any more loads."

"I've got to do what I think is right."

He smoked a moment longer, dropped the cigarette and stepped on it. "Yeah, I guess you have. But listen, Diana, we'll make it a brief appearance in the family circle." He took her arm and started for the door.

She asked, surprised, "You're not coming?"

He was even more surprised. "You didn't mean to go alone?"

They came out into Times Square, threaded their way across a crowded pavement toward a taxi. Nick helped her in and followed. The cab started.

"Mother will be awfully upset. She loved Grampa. If she saw you now. . . . No, I'd rather go alone."

"And come all the way back to the city by yourself tonight?"

They were far apart in understanding, each perplexed and disturbed by the odd statements of the other. Diana told him what to her seemed obvious. "Why no, I'll stay there tonight, I've got to look after her." A moment later she put something in his hand. "Here—keep it for me."

It was the ring. He held it in his hand. "Why did you do that?"

"I won't tell her just now. It would be too much of a shock."

"Diana, this isn't right. You should keep this. You should tell her now."

"Later, when she's not upset."

She seemed so certain what she did was right, answering promptly, giving no consideration to his words. Nick held the ring a moment longer, then put it in an inside pocket, making certain it was safely stowed. "Well, honey, I don't mean to start in bossing you. Only, feels all wrong to me."

They rode on in silence. The night had turned muggy after the rain, the drift of air caused by the car's movement was moist and lukewarm. Nick's foreboding grew; he wished he could be certain it was right to let Diana have her way, but her fright when she had thought something had happened to her mother showed the hold the woman still had upon her. Then it flashed into his mind that Diana had gone into marriage believing her grandfather would take care of Mrs. Heaton, counting that into her decision, and now. . . . Of all the lousy breaks.

Diana was speaking in an altered voice, grief sounding in the quiet tone. "He died thinking I was bad. I used to love him, he was good. How could he do that thing to me?"

Nick tried to fill her need, "He was old-fashioned, wasn't he? By his way of thinking what he did was just standard treatment for a girl who lost her virginity before she was married. I'd say what he did was a crime but I guess he saw it as a duty."

"Oh, I'm sure that's what he thought!"

"Yeah, duty can make people do some queer stunts. Like you going back there now." She was silent. "Diana, you clear out of there tomorrow. I'll be expecting you."

"I'll do my best."

The answer was not satisfactory, and she sounded remote, making him nervous. He asked, "Know your name?" She turned her face toward him, not knowing what he meant. He asked more sharply, "Got a name, haven't you?"

"Oh. . . . I wasn't thinking. . . . "

"Give it a thought once in a while, Mrs. Allingham. Keep it in mind you've got a husband."

"Yes."

Still remote. His foreboding changed into immediate anxiety, her indifference to his name was a slight that hurt. Well, he had another hold upon her. "Look here—what about

271

the director's orders? Does all this throw the audition out the window?"

"Oh no! Of course not."

Lucky for me, he thought bitterly. "Then you see me tomorrow, understand?"

"Yes, Nick, I will."

He went all the long way home with her. When they came in sight of the house Diana stopped. "You'd better not come any further. Mother might be watching out for me."

He took her hand, speaking very earnestly. "Diana, this is getting me. I don't like to let you go in there alone. I hate the idea. I don't think it's right. You ought to let me go in along with you and tell your mother that we're married. You ought to let me stand by you and face whatever comes of this."

"Please, Nick, I know her better than you do. She—she hates you. I don't know what the sight of you might do to her now when she's all upset."

He pressed her hand and dropped it. "All right honey, we'll do it your way. You and I aren't going to start in quarreling. Kiss me." She put up her lips dutifully, but he could feel her hurry to be away. "Good night, wife."

"Good night, Nick."

He watched her hasten up the street, turn into the house, disappear. He told himself reasonable things; she had been through a lot, you wouldn't expect her to be clearheaded in the state she was in now.

But he wished with all his heart that she had answered back and called him husband.

15

As her sleep thinned, awareness of some oppressive event grew upon her, confused and hurried her awaking. Diana opened her eyes knowing calamity had struck from some quarter. The sight of her mother's sleeping face brought recollection of her grandfather's death; on top of that came the shock of realizing what she had done.

Coming fully awake, she struggled to throw off a crushing sense of guilt, not understanding why it had come, unreasoned, unforeseen. She thought in words, telling herself it was not wrong to marry the man you loved. She did love Nick. She wasn't sorry.

But the heavy oppression could not be thrown off, and she was sorry, sorry and scared. Married. . . . The act stood, it could not be denied. Nick's wife. And she lay in bed beside her mother and her mother did not know. To have done it without telling Sue that she was going to. . . .

She had come home to find the old Sue that she so adored. Her mother's grief was real and it seemed sorrow had recalled her to herself. This woman who wept so quietly, holding to her daughter's hand, was not the erratic, hostile, dominating, sick creature who had made life a constant hell in recent weeks. Lying in bed talking before they fell asleep, Sue had spoken as she had not far a long, long time. 'Forgive me, Dicky. I've been unjust, unkind. I had forgotten what it was to be a pal. Do as you please, I'll never scold again.'

Here was the mother Diana had believed in with such dogged loyalty even when there had been no sign of her. Walk out of the house forever now when, after all that had been endured, Mother was herself again? Desert her when she was grief-stricken, relying on the comfort of her daughter's love? Go to live with some strange woman Diana had never even seen?

It was impossible—preposterous.

But—'My wife isn't going to live with her mother.' . . .

He meant it, he would be determined; he was a man, strong-willed, with an unfathomed, violent force flowing on underneath all his wonderful tenderness. But how could he be so unreasonable! Couldn't he see that Grampa's death changed everything? No, he couldn't; riding in the taxi he had made that plain. He expected her to rise up now and walk out of her home forever.

And if she did not. Oh, it would go all wrong between them! The beautiful happiness would be smashed. He would stand back from her, his face would darken and his eyes would squint and he would be harsh, even—it was possible—wild and dangerous.

Apprehension growing larger by the moment she could only cry out helplessly to herself, what have I done, what have I done! If only it were possible to be two entirely separate people—the daughter Sue thought her to be, the wife Nick expected. The two ways of life stretched before her, she could see herself fitting into either of them—when she forgot the other. And she wanted both with an equality of yearning that blocked solution. The more she mulled it over, the more impossible, the more disastrous either course appeared.

The audition. That seemed to give an answer that would at least postpone disaster. Surely Nick would grant her time till then, not force decision; he would know that work came first and must not be disrupted. The prospect of a respite even of a few days in which she could stay on with Sue brought hope. Time passing, surely the problem would come to have a different aspect, be easier to solve.

But what if even with Nick's help the days went by and still she could not dance, could not catch the spirit of it, her feeling deadened as it had been yesterday?

274

The idea threw her into panic. She wanted to leap out of bed on the instant, rush to him. . . .

There were duties to perform. Sue must be spared all she could. The funeral parlor must be phoned, arrangements made for shipment to Frostburg where the funeral would be. But all of that would not take up a day. The duties done, she would dash in to Nick, tell Sue work called her to Manhattan; it was work, really.

Nick. To go to Nick. . . .

Mrs. Heaton stirred. Her daughter turned to give the loving kindness of her solace to that sad awakening.

Diana stood looking at him, sprightly, gay, and Nick threw wide the door with a gallant, welcoming flourish. "You made it, kid. Swell. Good to be looking at you."

She entered, still walking stiffly, but her air frolicsome. "Oh, I had to come to the director!"

"To the director?" Nick closed the door. "Is that who I am? Just the director?"

She saw that she had blundered at the outset, his pleasure at her coming struck down. If only he would not be somber, probing; she wanted a lighthearted Nick, merry and unthinking. She put her arms about his neck and kissed him.

It was a child's kiss, brief, casual. Nick watched her move on into the room, lay hat and purse upon the piano, and at that distance turn to face him with another sprightly, too-bright smile. So, I'm the director. And you don't know how to kiss your husband.

She was chattering. "I had nine hours sleep. I ate a big breakfast. I drank a pint of milk at luncheon. I didn't practice a step. I came to you as soon as I could. Isn't that a nice report?"

By God, I'll mean more to you than the director. "Come here." She came readily, anxious to please, but in some doubt of him, her eyes questioning. Nick took the ring out of his pocket and lifted her hand to slip it on.

But she objected, trying to pull her hand away, speaking

without forethought. "Oh, no! I might forget and go home with it on."

"Home?" He was, as she had dreaded, somber. He put the ring on her finger, saying, "This might help you to remember. So you're going 'home?'"

She was ill at ease under his scrutiny; her smile a difficult thing to sustain. "Oh, darling, you didn't think I could get away in a day!"

Taut, nervous, her playfulness was a shocking falsity that hid some guile, some underlying turbulence. He was baffled by her intention to return home again. "What's making you so happy all of a sudden? You're not able to dance, you've got a funeral in the family, you had to leave your husband on your wedding night, and you come in here like a holiday to tell me you're going 'home.' What's the idea?"

She wriggled in discomfort, hunching up a shoulder, laying her cheek against it, twisting one arm about the other. "Nicky, don't be cross! You're always asking questions! Why should you think it funny I'd be happy coming here?" She ventured another of her brief, meaningless kisses. "Please don't look at me like that! Nick—can I work tonight? I hate to miss—"

"No."

"Oh. . . . When?"

"Tomorrow, if the stiffness lets up."

She roused out of disappointment with another show of make-believe, announcing brightly, "I brought my practice costume."

"Why?"

"So you could massage me, darling. Shall I put it on?"

" 'Darling,' 'dearest.' I never got so many nice names from you before. Only they sound like hell. Yeah, put it on."

She escaped from him with relief, flitting into the bedroom to change. Nick stood brooding, more heavyhearted, more troubled than he had ever been. He did not dare to be direct with her; Diana was too flighty in this nervous state, too close to breakdown; a straight-out demand upon her might bring the wrong response and cause havoc. What had happened when she went home? What tricks was Mrs. Heaton up to now that Diana should wish to linger in a home where she had been delivered over to such humiliating punishment, forced to stand up and whimper she was 'bad'? Besides all that—did marriage mean nothing to her? Or was she in so confused a state she couldn't think? His self-reproach at having let her slip back into her mother's influence was fierce; he should never have permitted her to go.

He heard the door opening and looked up. He saw that in addition to the blue-green slip of a practice costume, she had put on dancing shoes, and that she approached with a burning eagerness, marred by uncertainty of him. So—she wanted to dance. Thin, lamed, and muddled, that spirit still came up. He marveled at it, at her enduring zest, her recuperative power. He pointed at the shoes, asking, "Why'd you put those on?"

"Those?" She looked down at them as though she could not recollect. "They—they just go with my costume."

"You're forgetting one thing you told me yourself one time—you're bad at lying. No, you're not doing any dancing. I told you that was out for four days at least."

Pretense dropped, she begged, "If you would play for me —just a few steps—just enough to know that I can get the feel of it—"

"And that's why you brought your costume. Why didn't you say so? No."

"Nick—you're so gloomy!"

"And you're so gay. It was the director you wanted, wasn't it? Then take his orders. Lie down on the couch." Nick slipped out of his coat and slung it over a chair and began rolling up his sleeves. Then he saw that her face had gone stupid with fright. "What is it now?" He kept on with what he was doing. "I'm going to massage you. Every time you come in here you got a new collection of scares. It'll get so that I can't even sit down in your presence without reminding you of something awful. I'm not going to humor you, Diana, or you will turn

277

into a coward. Just now it's your nerves, but if you give in to them you'll become what you said you didn't want to be—a freak. How about it? Think you can endure the sight of me with my sleeves rolled up?"

She nodded, diffident but relieved and grateful to him, and her smile was true.

"You've got sense when you use it. Stretch out on the couch and let the director get his hands on you."

At this remark, the scare came back on her. This time she tried to fight it off alone. With effort, she went laggingly toward the couch, but came to a stop beside it, apparently unable to go further. "I never had a massage." Her voice was faint.

"So?" He followed her over. "Lie down."

She remained standing, wretched. "Are you going to put your hands—all over me?"

"What is this? Another attack of modesty? How much silliness do I have to put up with? You use your whole body when you dance, don't you?"

"Nicky, please. Don't be cross."

"Are you going to stop insulting me with your suspicions?"

"Why, is that what I'm doing?"

Her surprise was so innocent, such an honest, guileless thing, that his lips twisted, smiling. "Come on, honey. Trust me."

She lay down on the couch, submitting with docility, apprehension gone. Her muscles still painfully sore, she squirmed under the skilled manipulation of his fingers, he had to make the massage a light one. "There now, lie still and rest." He left her, went over to the armchair, and sat watching her.

She lay face down, her head turned toward him, eyes shut. The massage had relaxed her, she rested peacefully. After a while she opened her eyes and gazed dreamily at him. "I liked that."

"Come here."

She rose languorously, like one arising from sleep, and came drifting toward him without question.

"Sit in my lap. You can rest in my arms. My, what an obedient child! Sleepy eyes. Not nervous now?"

She lay against him, passive and content, glad to be in his arms, glad that he had grown gentle.

He fondled her, running his fingers through her hair, stroking her cheek, and won a sigh of deepening contentment. "You like me to caress you. See—these are the hands you didn't want to touch you. Nice hands?"

"Nice."

He kissed her lips. "Glad I love you?"

"Yes."

"Like me to be holding you, kissing you, loving you?"

"Yes."

"Who am I? Mr. Allingham, the director?"

She was flustered, not answering.

He kissed her lips again. "Now do you know who I am?"

"You're the man I love."

"Pretty nice, but the wrong answer just the same." He held the kiss longer this time. "Know me now?"

"Husband."

"Boy, I had to drag that out, didn't I? Kiss me, Diana."

She gave him her full, sweet lips and he pressed her closer, letting the kiss go on. Slowly, wonderfully, the change came, her kiss no longer a passive acceptance but a response. The response grew beyond all doubting and she was joined with him, the current flowing between them, rising steadily in power, sweeping on, the deep surge of the all-consuming happiness of love-born passion. Triumphing joy raced through the wonder of his amazement; in that one kiss, in what was actually a few short moments, he was finding what he had thought could not be found without long and patient seeking. That there was passion in her he had never doubted, but he had not dreamed that ardor could be drawn out so easily, freed from the restraints that bound her, stemming from the ugly, brutal memory of assault. The joy he felt, the longing for her which that joy so mightily increased, threatened to

279

become the strongest sensation he had ever known, a kind of suffering in which the craving to let go of all control and sink into the dark realm of blind emotion seemed of compulsive force. But he had lived through that experience before because of her, that time in murderous hate; he was warned by it, he knew the danger he was in to keep his head. The kiss broken off, he hid his face in her hair, forcing the mastery of thought. It was of Diana he must think. That his desire went far beyond hers he knew. Between that desire and the consummation of their marriage lay great difficulties for her. And it must be she who would make this marriage real; she must want it real, want it with a full awareness and a steady wish. This love was not for today or tomorrow, an affair that might go well or wrong. It was for always.

Did she know what change was working in her? Was she frightened by it? He raised his head, looking down into her face. Not frightened, not aware. Eyes half shut, she seemed to dream in some timeless spell of happiness that was not troubled by any foreshadowing of possible event. Not heeding that he, the giver of that happiness, had raised his head, she dreamed on, in his trust. No, what she felt now she had never felt before; there was nothing here that linked with fright.

There was need to penetrate that rapt dreaming, to break through to her, to move toward that perfect union which was so wonderfully close. "Sweetheart. Let me see your sleepy eyes. Why, what's making you so beautiful, so rosy? What is it, Diana? What's happening to you?"

Her eyes were soft, their gaze direct. "I don't know."

"And you don't seem to care. Honey, something's happened to you. What makes your voice so low and husky?"

"I love you.'"

"Oh. Think that might be it?"

"Yes."

"Who do you love?"

"You."

"Wrong answer. Now we have to start all over again."

"Yes."

"Oh, you want me to?"

"Kiss me, Nicky."

"Well, see if you can get the answer right this time." As his lips met hers her arm went about his neck pressing him closer. . . . And this was Diana, the scared child. . . . The kiss ending, he teased her coolly. "Well?"

"Husband. I love you."

"Sweet." Nick set her on her feet and stood up. "Go get your duds on."

She wondered at this abrupt termination. Loverly, gentle, was there some hint of mockery back of his enigmatic, smiling face? "Why?"

"Why not?"

She took his hand and played with it. "I like you to kiss me."

"I'm not going to kiss you any more just now."

"Why?"

"I want you to know what it feels like to want to be kissed. Then you won't make any more mistakes coming in here looking for the director instead of your husband."

"You're teasing me."

"I mean to tease you."

"Oh, you don't!"

"I do. I'm going to do my best to drive you crazy, and I'm certain that I can. I'll kiss you when I like and I'll stop when I like and you won't have a thing to say about it. Go get your things on."

She did not know what to make of what he said, only that the happiness and the warmth was still there between them, and so she was inclined to laugh, moving reluctantly away in compliance with his wish. He waited until she neared the door and was some distance from him. "Diana. Stop a minute."

She faced about, laughing outright. "Well, you do give orders like a director! It's no wonder if I get mixed."

"And having a director for a husband is a good thing for you, sugar. I stopped you to give you a good exit going

281

through that door. A fine, proud exit with your head up. Diana, you don't know yourself. You asked me something yesterday most girls wouldn't ask. You asked me to marry you without any expectations. Honey, you didn't need to ask it. You're no freak. You're as natural as they come. You're fine and strong and beautiful in love."

She had listened with increasing fascination, her eyes widening, her lips apart. Now that he had stopped, the full meaning of what he said came to her, and the color went out of her face. She went on staring at him and at last managed to get out the words, "How do you know?"

"Sweetheart, you have an idea passion is an ugly thing. It isn't. There was passion in you when you kissed me."

She hung a moment longer, staring, then turned in a whirl, bolting into the other room.

Nick walked over to the piano and sat down at it. His fingers on the keys stayed motionless, thought holding him. That scare was in her deep. It would recur the moment she thought he was attempting to force his love upon her. Build it, Nicky, build it like a work of art. You haven't got her yet.

Diana, getting hurriedly into street clothes, slowed to listen as he began to play. How wildly beautiful! What was it? The music began with a slow pulsing, barbaric beat of dissonant chords, accelerated, broke off, went into a minor key, the melody plaintive, mysterious, ecstatic; there was another quickening of tempo, then a break into a different rhythm, the fast tempo sustained, exciting, joyous, it went on to a prolonged climax in which the primitive beat came back. Diana thrust open the door, hastening to him with her brittle walk. "What was that?"

"Could you dance it?"

"Oh, I could, I'm sure I could! I felt it, Nicky, I wanted to dance!" She came beside him, hands clasped in delight, her face lit up. "What is it? It's like De Falla—only it isn't. There's a Slavic quality."

Nick was grinning. "That's the 'dirty Polack' in me."

"What? You mean—?"

"The name of the music is *Brief Rhapsody* and it's composed by Nickolas Aloysius Wladyslaw Blake Allingham, and you can't use it without the composer's permission." He stood up, lounging against the piano.

"It's a splendid thing and you must let me have it for a dance."

He mocked her. "You couldn't dance that. You're not brave enough."

"Brave?"

Out of relaxation, he moved with an animal swiftness, binding her in his arms. In an instant she was struggling, resistant. In the next instant he was back at the piano, lounging, laughing at her. "See? Scared of me. I've got to handle you with kid gloves, baby you. When you going to learn a man in love is nothing to be frightened of and take all his moods—all that's in that music—wild and strong and fierce, and love running through all of them?"

She cupped her hands over her face, turning from him, and at once Nick left off mocking. He came in back of her and kissed her neck and turned her into his arms. "Don't feel bad I said that. I'm only trying to help you be yourself. I know there's no mood I have you couldn't come to meet me with and match. I composed that seeing you dance it. It's yours."

"Oh, Nick! May I have it for the show? If—if I can get the job?"

"Sure, and cut out the 'if'." He raised her hands and kissed them. "Sensitive hands. If I saw the hands alone I'd know the woman in you. And you didn't want to wear the ring today. I had to force it on you. All right, give it to me, I'll be taking you out to supper soon, and I don't want you sporting that ring in public till you're living with me. But before we go, now that you're sweet and natural, sit down a minute and tell me what game you were playing when you came in here today." He motioned her to a chair and dropped back on the piano seat.

But Diana did not take the chair. She stood, running her

hand back and forth upon it, her mood rapidly changing, downcast.

"Come on, honey, don't tighten up."

She walked nervously a few steps away and came back exclaiming, "Why must we talk! I hate talk—trying to explain! Words are no good."

"We have to use words, sweetheart. Right now we have to. You came in here as false as a ham actor. Why?"

Her body swayed, arms rising high above her head, twisted together.

"Don't try to dance it. Tell me."

"Why must you ask questions all the time?"

"Yeah, questions you don't want to answer. Stop getting all worked up. Sit down."

She slid into the chair. It occurred to her a clever woman would know how to handle him, get what she wanted. Sue was clever that way. If she could be clever, like Sue. She put on a smile, coaxing, "Nicky, I haven't been in the park for ages! Let's go, before supper! Oh, do you know what we could do? We could take a boat—"

He shook his head gravely. "No-go, you're not changing the subject, I'm sticking to this. And I don't like your smile. It's false and it's new to me. When are you clearing out of your mother's house?"

Diana tried pouting. "Oh, Nicky, why do you pin me down? Nicky darling, you don't realize—"

"The act's a flop, kid, it's not your style." Eyes squinting, he spoke quietly, seeing how quickly she had grown taut. "And don't you call me 'darling' just to try and make a sap out of me. Be your honest self, Diana. I asked you—when are you clearing out of your mother's house?"

She flounced in the chair, winding her arms around the back, not answering.

"Got any idea the stay is indefinite?"

She jerked up from the chair and across to the table, played aimlessly with a magazine, flipping the pages.

"Can't be indefinite, sweetheart."

She turned on him, imploring, "Can't we wait until after the audition to talk about it?"

Nick went over to the table and got his pipe and came back to the piano seat to stuff it. "That's a week or more. And you say, 'talk about it.' And one of these days I open my door and you tumble in here such a beaten, broken mess I can't hope to straighten you out. No, Diana, there's nothing to talk about. I told you I was going to look after my wife and I mean to."

She came toward him, still imploring, desperate in her appeal. "You don't understand—you don't know—Mother—it's all different now—she's changed, she's herself, she won't scold me ever again—she's loving, sweet—"

"Getting all worked up won't help us get this straight." He pressed tobacco into the pipe, speaking mildly, though this was much worse than he had thought it could be. "Making every allowance for the state she's got you into, I ask you to reason this out with as much sense as you've got now. Can you remember that I married you on one condition—that you leave your mother's house? Can you remember why? You came in here yesterday the most heart-breaking specimen of humanity I ever laid eyes on. You didn't get that way in one day. You expect me to let you stay in her hands one hour longer than is necessary? Maybe you trust her now, I don't. People don't change overnight, Diana."

Diana gripped the back of the chair, striving to match his calm, but her voice shook and she was trembling. "You know I married you thinking Grampa was alive. Who's going to look after her?"

"Not my wife and you better get that into your head right now. Look after her! She's a grown woman, isn't she? She's got a son, hasn't she? And a husband if she wants him? And a mother? She's not an invalid, she's got an income. Diana, I told you my wife isn't going to live with her mother."

The girl beat her fists upon the chair. "Please, please, Nick, don't be so hard! Wait—wait till after the audition!"

Nick held a lighted match. "And after the audition?"

285

"Give me time, give me time to think! Why do you make me decide right now?"

He drew the flame against the bowl, puffing. "Honey, I don't like this one little bit. You're going back on something that was all understood and agreed to before we got married. There's nothing to decide now or after the audition, it's all been decided."

She gasped, "You're cruel, Nick, you're cold and cruel!"

"Yeah?" He took it with a bitter smile. "And yesterday you said I was kind."

Diana slid down on her knees before him. "Please—please—"

He got up, lifted her to her feet and led her back to her chair. "Don't do that. It's beneath you. Don't go down on your knees to me or to anyone." He stood by the chair, his hand on her shoulder. "Try to get a hold on yourself, will you? Try to use your head. You're a fine person, Diana, but you've got an obsession where your mother is concerned." He gave a pat to her shoulder and went back to the piano seat.

Diana began to cry. "Oh, you don't know her, you don't know her!"

"Sweetheart, I think I do."

She was up, weaving back and forth distractedly, the tears streaming down her cheeks. "No—you're like the rest of the world, you think because she drinks she's no good! But she doesn't drink any more—I tell you she's good, she's kind, she's sweet—that's what she really is! If you knew—"

"If I didn't know you I'd say you were an awful liar. But that's the worst of it, she can make you believe all that, and it's not true. She hasn't been good to you, she hasn't been kind. I'm scared to trust you with her, I don't know what she might do to you—"

Diana had gone down full length on the floor, sobbing.

Nick laid his pipe aside and went to pick her up. He held her at arms length, a hand on each shoulder. "You got to stop your tantrums, Diana. Stop it. Stop your crying."

"Oh, Nick, you're so hard, so hard! Oh, I can't think—I can't decide!"

"I guess you can't at that." An arm slipped about her, he again led her back to the chair. "All right, I'll give in to you until after the audition, and I'll tell you why. I think you realize you've got to get into shape for that, and getting into shape, you'll get a hold on your nerves and your head will clear and you'll begin to see things straight."

He returned to his pipe. Diana had stopped crying, and she stayed in the chair. He re-lit the pipe, watchful of her, trying to make out what she was thinking. "Don't get any wrong ideas in your head because I'm giving in on this. I'm just trying to be patient with you because your nerves are shot and I don't like to make you any more nervous than you are. I don't want to pull any caveman stuff on you if I can help it, I don't want to drag you off to my lair by force. That would make things bad between us, we'd be a long time getting straight if that had to happen. But giving in to you now doesn't mean I'll give in to you again, don't count on that. After the audition you'll go to my mother, or you'll come to me, whichever way you want it, but it'll be one or the other. You come under your own steam or I'll come and get you."

Diana had gone rigid. "You can't do that."

Quietly, between puffs on the pipe, Nick told her, "I will do that."

"You've no legal right to me. I'm under age."

"That's a nasty thing to say, sweetheart." His eyes hot and narrow, he went on speaking coolly. "If I'm willing to risk going to jail for marrying a minor, do you think I care about the legality of this? You're my wife, not because of any claim of legal property, but because you told me that you love me, because you asked for marriage. Maybe you don't take marriage seriously, but I do. I'm your husband and that gives me the right to look after you, and I'm going to do it. You'll come to me, or by God I'll come and get you."

Diana stayed silent, face down, her thin body hunched. Nick got up and walked the length of the room and back several times. "If you take that as swearing, I'll apologize.

You asked me once. . . ." The pipe laid on the table, he leaned against the wall, tall and spare and dark against the white surface. "Diana, did your mother ever tell you that I went to see her?" The surprise with which Diana spun around in the chair was an answer. "Yes, I saw her. When you were living in that boarding house. I know your mother. I know she has great charm, a vivid, forceful personality, a thousand endearing, feminine tricks. I think she could talk almost anyone into believing anything. She could make black so white it would shine in the dark. And she's a damned attractive woman. I don't know if she's forty or forty-seven, but she could still have her pick of lovers if she held off the drink. Yes, I know her. I know how she loves you, wants to keep you, and will fight to keep you. But I know it's because in you her vanity and her ambition live again. She's a thwarted woman who makes you her means of expression, and that way she fits right into a type you see a lot of among stage mothers. It's not of your good she thinks first, but of her own will to power, and Diana, she's proved that in everything she's done to you. Believe me, I wouldn't speak against your mother, I wouldn't try to turn you from her, if I didn't fear what she can do to you. I've seen what she has done, and that's enough for me."

Nick had come into the center of the room to stand braced, feet apart, driving his words down upon her with a passionate earnestness that held Diana motionless in attention. "She's sold you once. She'd sell you again if the chance came. Diana, if you lost your looks, if it was obvious you'd never be famous, her love would die. I'm proud to have a beautiful girl for a wife, I'm proud to have a wife who has the makings of a fine artist, but I tell you if you were nobody I'd love you still. If she does smash your nose, or gets someone in to beat you up, or break your spirit so you'll never want to dance again, I'd still love whatever there was left of you to love; I'd love the woman in you if Diana Heaton's name meant nothing on the stage. It's you I love, and that's not true of her. You told me I was cruel. You don't know what a cruel thing you ask of me. I can't stand by and see your courage beaten down, your loyalty abused, your reason fuddled, your body mauled, I can't, I love you too much. Today you came in here prepared to trick me if you could. Today I saw the bruise on your arm where your grandfather laid hold of you. Look at your hand—the mark of teeth is on it still! And you complained that I was gloomy! Diana, you've no right to ask me to endure this. You felt it was your duty to go home last night. I say you've got a duty to come here to me. You took me for a husband, you've got to live up to the bargain. Nothing you can say will make me change my mind on that." He stretched out his arms to her. "Diana kid, don't you know our love can be a wonderful thing that will grow and be a joy to us? You musn't let your mother come between us."

Diana went to him in one swift flow of movement and their embrace was strong and joyful. "Nick, I know you're good, you're fine, I want your love. I don't believe my mother is the dreadful person that you think she is, I don't believe it. I know she's got a side to her you haven't seen. But—if you'll be lenient with me, if you'll let me go to see her often, look after her even if I don't live with her, I'll come to you."

"Why honey, I'm not going to boss you! Go see her as often as you like. For your sake, I'll even be friends with her, if she'll let me. But live with her? No, not even for a night. Don't ask it."

"You said you'd wait till after the audition. Give me till then, Nick, it's—it's going to be hard, awfully hard. But I'll do it." Diana drew his head down to hers and held it there, kissing his mouth. Quickly the kiss came to life, having its own power over them, the passion rising, and for a long moment they were pressed together, their love affirmed.

Very gently, Nick drew away. "Enough, sugar. Let me be the director, will you? When I've got you living with me you

289

can maul me all you like. Not now. Look here, what do you say we eat? You're supposed to, you know. Let's go to some nice place, step out for a change."

She had clapped her hands together at the prospect of a celebration, but all at once turned dubious. "My dress—I'm not well-dressed enough. Not for a nice place."

"Well, I never. And you the prettiest girl in town and that little yellow dress doing things to your hair and skin so you're all golden. At that, though, you could do with some additions to the wardrobe." Slipping into his coat, he reached into his pocket and drew out a billfold, selected bills, and turning to her purse, opened it, inserted them. "A present for the wife. Not much. Enough to get a couple of things you might be wanting now." He handed her both purse and hat, smiling, "If I gave you too much, you'd hand it right over to Mama, I bet she's got you trained. When I get you to myself will you let me go to town dolling you up? Boy, that would be fun! You'd take dressing." He caught up his hat. "Set? We'll go to a cozy little French joint where they have sentimental music on the strings—the fiddler's good, by the way. And we'll hold hands between courses. You can do that there."

They went out arm in arm. Going along the street, Nick said, "Say—here's something important—my mother wants to meet you. Remember I phoned her yesterday, thinking you were going there? Well, now she knows I've got a wife, and I suppose we have to grant her the privilege of giving you the once-over. We're involved for tea. Wednesday at five. Jot it down in the date book, kid. Remember."

"I won't forget."

Dodging traffic at a crossing, Diana exclaimed, "You should have been a dancer!"

He made an impish face. "I can dance, smarty. I'm good at it."

"You move so quickly, so lightly—."

"So unexpectedly. All of which makes me a dangerous man,

doesn't it? Sweet kid, how you can blush!" He stopped short. "Want to go back to the house and kiss me again?"

She laughed, being bold. "Yes, I do!"

He led on with his brisk pace. "We're not going back."

She mimicked him. "So—we're not going back."

"Wrong answer. You should have said 'please Nicky.' That's going to let you in for a lot more rehearsing. Here's the joint, sugar, and I'm going to look into your eyes for five courses and you'll be sorry you didn't say the right words. Honey—you know I'm good for you? You're laughing, you're happy—" He shook his head in wonder, contrasting the Diana of today with the Diana of yesterday. "Can I do this to you? You must really love me."

16

DIANA WAS IN LOVE—Mrs. Heaton knew that for certain. The impulsive leniency of repentance waned in a day; no, of course she did not mean to let her daughter do anything she pleased, fall in love, throw her life away, what mother would? The question was merely how to manage her. Diana had walked out of the house without a word the day dear Papa passed away; Diana might walk out again and not come back. Mrs. Heaton could not forget the terror she had lived through, alone in the empty rooms, thinking Diana had been driven from her home, never to return. The experience prompted her to be more cunning in her domination of Diana, and the spell of leniency had made her realize the hold she had upon her daughter's affection. It might be best to seek by every means to make that hold more binding.

And it was heartening to see how responsive Diana was to this change of tactics. Oh, Diana was malleable, easily influenced, utterly guileless! Mrs. Heaton felt something like contempt for this girl, so open to emotional assault, so unquestioning of purpose, so unsuspecting of intent; Diana was not clever, and what mother likes to admit so grave a fault? But she was beautiful and young and possessed talent; once she came to her senses and let her mother do the thinking for her there was still hope for the career, it might yet rise to glorious heights.

Yes, Diana was in love with some unknown man and that was a trial to bear. But at her age it could be only puppy love; see how quickly she had forgotten Nick once he left town! When Diana's confidence was won all secrets would be told, then the two of them, like pals, would talk it over and that would be the end of that.

Mrs. Heaton exerted all her charm to win and hold Diana.

Event was not an ally, it was not easy to make home a cheery place right on top of Papa's going, and the first of the month had passed and still her check had not arrived, and everyone was so rudely insistent about bills. Besides all that, a tooth was bothering her. But she held to her role and drew encouragement from her daughter's ready sympathy for every ill. Diana loved her, there was loyalty in that affection; give her free rein for a spell and she would be won over wholly. What mother would not go to any length to save the precious child that she had borne and raised and loved?

Diana was two separate individuals, two distinct identities. Coming into Sue's presence Nick became a dream, a cherished dream but completely unreal. Sitting across the table from Sue was such a normal act that recollection of dining with Nick became fantastic. Habit picked her up at home and carried her along, and that was real. To recall in Sue's presence the things that Nick had said about her mother was to feel vile with treachery. To be sure Sue had done wrong things, but with Sue repentant, making amends, should those past errors be held against her?

She was going to Nick. She loved him. She must go to him. She would not admit that any other course was possible. Then Sue would move her hand in a familiar gesture, shrug, toss her head, say some fond thing that roused the old enwrapping intimacy, and Diana's heart would drop and she would stare at Sue not knowing how it was possible that she could ever dream of leaving her; the weight of guilt would come upon her spirit, crushing it.

It was all very well for Nick to make fine speeches, but he did not know her mother, he only knew the worst about her. There was a rare sweet quality in Sue that Nick just didn't know. If it were only possible to bring him here, let him see for himself this lovable, gentle, gallant little woman. . . . But no, that might not work at all; at sight of Nick, Sue

293

might change completely, grow hostile, angry, make a scene, and only prove his worst conclusions.

'Nothing you can say will make me change my mind.' . . . Oh, Nick, Nick, how can you be so stubborn and so harsh! Sue will die if I leave her. How could I go on living if I had killed my mother? Sue said it and it's true, her ghost would follow me to the ends of the earth.

Couldn't Nick see for himself how changed things were? With her new grant of freedom, Diana came and went as she pleased; she could have both things at once, long hours with Nick, her home with Sue. It was ideal. Why could he not be satisfied with that? Why must he demand an act that would bring such misery upon them all? It seemed to Diana that his male spirit moved with a restless, violent force and only destruction could follow on his willfulness. Why could he not see. . . .

But he would not see, and he was her husband and she loved him, and she must do as he wished and walk straight forward into doom and torment.

Her two selves fought together, first one on top and then the other, and despite the blessed peace at home, the elation of the hours with Nick, the joy of her returning confidence in work, the inner struggle grew until she felt that when the time ran out she would be incapable of doing anything, she would sit helpless, waiting to hear his steps sounding on the stairs, his ring at the door, knowing he had come to fetch her; and she would go on sitting there, without will, letting Sue stand up to him, leaving the struggle to those two, and whoever won it would possess her. The horror of that scene fixed in her mind. She dreamed of it at night. It came upon her with recurring fright. It must not happen. Nick had said he did not want to come and fetch her, it would make things bad between them.

But he would come.

Even in the hours she spent with Nick, illumined and idyllic as they were, Diana had the sense of doom impending. He had said that he would drive her crazy, and he had the power to do it, was doing it. He would take her in his arms at will, at will dismiss her, suave and mocking even while that steady glow of ardor flowed from him. Now there were moments when even to see him walk across the room sent riot through her, when the merest touch of his hand was enthralling, when a steady burning look from his eyes poured confusion upon her, when his kiss swept her into ecstasy where she had no being save the one he ruled. And he knew it, willed it. It was his deliberate intention, and he was experienced in love, master of its mysteries. And all of this went on because he was a man, wanting to possess her. And if he wanted that to happen, it would happen. The hour would come when she would be mastered by him, swept along in the compulsion of that overwhelming current that flowed from him with such magic power. It would happen. And how would it be with her then, knowing that nightmare of pain and horror and disgust?

Dread moved beside desire and even in her love for Nick, chaos stood and waited for her.

Nick rejoiced at the way Diana was coming out of the mess she had been in, catching hold upon her work. It had not been easy; she had thrown a few tantrums at the outset; twice she had pulled that trick of going down full length upon the floor to cry, quickly abandoned to despair when she had felt some lag in execution, some dullness in her work. Little as he liked that, he was not impatient with her when the intensity of feeling rose out of work; he had seen a famous conductor in rehearsal with a symphony break down and cry like a baby over some fault of rendition. The excuse of temperament might be abused by every bad-tempered incompetent who played around in art, but the fact remained that intensity of feeling was essential in artistic work and frequently quite childish outbursts would show up among the most outstanding workers in the field. Diana could dance, it was an instinct with her, and along with that she had the essential drive to work, to reshape, polish and perfect. She was gaining back needed weight, her muscles were growing supple, her confidence was returning. But she was still far from steady and she had him worried. She didn't talk about it, but he knew the coming break with her mother was on her mind and she was taking it hard, still taut, moody, nervous. She was going to be just about turned inside out when the break did come, and the tension and the moodiness would double and make her more unsteady than she was right now. Rehearsals going on, Aronstein might fire her, not knowing what she had to give.

Turning it over in his mind, Nick came to a decision. Late Tuesday night, he set out to hunt up Tod Lester, black-face comedian at six thousand a week, the foremost star in the Shultz array.

The desk clerk at the Astor said Mr. Lester had not come in yet. Nick hopped a taxi and started on a round of the hot spots. The hunt was easy, at most clubs Nick didn't even have to leave the cab, the doorman could tell him if Mr. Lester was inside. And Tod Lester was at the Low Down with a party.

Good so far. Better breaking in on a party than on a two-some. Nick strolled into the hot, noisy, dimly-lit room, crowded even in this August weather. The bar was at the end nearest the door and furthest from the band, a good place to talk. He spotted Lester's round, red face and sandy hair at a floorside table halfway up the room. Nick sauntered down a narrow aisle, sidled between tables and laid his hand on the comedian's shoulder. "Hi-yah, Les."

"Gob!" Lester rolled up on his feet and caught Nick in a bearlike hug. "You damn old fool, where you been? I been in town a month already and you never looked me up! Join, sit, have a drink." An arm about Nick's shoulder, he introduced him to the party, shouting to be heard as the band started up. "You all know Allingham, best guy in the world? Me and him scrubbed decks for Uncle Sammy and dodged the police in every port. Sit, Nick old man, what's holding you up?"

Grinning, Nick gave a nautical salute to the party with a "hi-yah" for the couple that he knew; eight of them, all show people, a friendly bunch. But he resisted Lester's tug on his arm, not taking the chair a waiter had slipped into place. "Hold it, Tod. Can I talk to you a minute? I got something heavy on the mind. Clear that and I'll join you. Come over to the bar, will you?"

"Righto. 'Scuse us, folks." He held to Nick's arm, wedging between tables, side-stepping dancers moving toward the floor space. "Say, Shultz told me you did a nice job on that show Shanley tried to duck. What you been doing since? How long since I seen you? I was in Hollywood five months and does that place reek! Give me Broadway any night in the year!" They came up to the bar. "What'll you have? I'm on gin-and-tonic, swell drink for the tropics. Do I sweat like a pig! Make it two, Steve. Only thing wrong with New York it gets hot and it gets cold. Someways Hollywood's got it all over New York. Say, that song you sent me is a wow. I'm using it in the show. Got any more like that? You got the real stuff, Nick, you're no 32-bar-chorus man that can turn out tin-pan alley stuff with twenty other guys standing round to help him put the tune together, you're long-haired, you ought to do a full score for a musical. Say, I got some songs I want you to look over. Listen—"

"May I cut in? You do the listening first and I'm your stooge for the night. Tod, I don't go around asking favors as a rule—"

"Aw, you're so afraid someone might think you'd ask a favor, you even drop your old friend flat!"

"Well, there's something I want you to do for me."

Lester ran a handkerchief up over his circular face and back over his thinning hair. "You know I will, gob."

"Shultz asked me to direct your show and I got involved in a heart-tangle and turned it down—"

"Well, I'll be—you louse, you, you—"

"Hold it. I changed my mind. I want to do it, Tod. But I

297

can't trot in and tell that to Shultz now, can I? Want to fix it for me?"

Lester ran his handkerchief between his collar and his thick neck. "That's fixed right now."

"He's got Aronstein, but maybe they didn't get to the dotted line. Anyhow, Shultz can shift Aronstein onto another show, he won't lose by it—only the joy of working with a good-natured slob like you. I know Shultz takes orders from you, and at that I guess you're the only one. Think it over, huh?"

"I said it was fixed, didn't I? I know Aronstein, he's all right but I don't want him. I guess I can have the director I want when I'm sinking dough into this. I heard you was a wow. Listen, it's too reeking hot in here. Stick around, I'll ditch the gang and you and me'll go over to the hotel. I got a piano there, we can run over some stuff. Righto? Wait here. I got to dance with that cute little dame once more or she'll call me names." He finished his drink in a long gulp. "Have another." He waved at the barman as he moved away. "On my bill, Steve. Come again."

Nick told the barman he wouldn't have another and leaned against the bar, humming softly along with the music. So that was that, all set. Good old Les, swell guy. It had been tough passing up the direction in the first place, Nick had hated to do it; to get the chance back made him happy. And now this business about Diana. . . . I'll have to go easy on her, handling rehearsals, drop a pin in back of her she'll still jump a mile. But she sure can pull out of things fast, she'll be all right when rehearsals get going and the work takes hold of her; it'll be a solo this time. He wondered what lengths Mrs. Heaton would go to, trying to keep Diana. That devil . . . the mask-like smile, the subtle, deadly charm, the whiskey-colored hair and those mysterious, beautiful eyes, tricky and yellow as a fox's. But something to her to have had a daughter like Diana and to hold that daughter's love the way she did. Maybe before that big love affair that went wrong she had been a different woman.

He wondered what Diana would think of his mother, happy at the thought of showing off his wife; the two women ought to get along well enough, they were both amiable in temper—yeah, both of them knew what it was to put up with bad temper in someone else. Maybe at that I got a lot to thank my old man for in the way of learning self-control. Self-control was coming in handy with this build-up of Diana's love. Just how much more can you take, Nicky, and keep the old bean working?

Why the hell didn't Les come along? The music was getting into him, making him restless. Watching the swirling, rhythmic figures on the dance floor he was thinking that Diana had never danced with a man; the poor kid had never been let out for one night's fun, the innocent fun most young girls knew, going to a party, dancing with a fellow. To dance with Diana; to hold that lithe body close, moving in rhythm. . . . Cut it, Nicky, don't pile on the agony, don't build up the scene until you've got the star. . . . She loves me. She never loved any man but me. She's as sweet and innocent as any virgin ever was. . . . She won't go to Mother's, she'll come straight to me. She wants me now.

He tried to turn his thoughts from Diana. Something odd in seeing Tod again, fitting into the old companionship. It made him feel the change in himself. Diana had done that to him, making him recognize a part of his personality he had been trying to ignore. *Brief Rhapsody;* he wouldn't have composed that kind of music if he could have helped it; the Broadway tunes were facile, safe . . . safe, that was it. Aim high and the fall is long and the world says the son of a famous man never reaches Papa's standing, and who wants to be a second-rate composer. Yeah, scared to risk it, trying to run away from yourself. And love made you turn around and write good music. And it is good, not second-rate. Now you know it's there, you've got to do it. . . . Face it, Nicky, you got the Polack in you, you're emotional as hell and full of music and you got to let it come out. Diana liked *Brief Rhapsody.* I'd like to do a ballet for her. . . .

Two men had drifted up to the bar, coming in close behind him. Their talk broke in upon his reverie. One was a dirty talker. He mentioned a girl's name, relating his conquest with detail and relish in a thin, clipped, sing-song voice. Nick shifted along the bar, out of hearing, disgusted. You low-down stinker. So her name was Alice Randolph, and she was a virgin, and you laid her, and now you're telling the world. Some guy ought to punch your face in.

This bit of nastiness added to the heat and noise, the nerve-assaulting blare and beat of the music, made him more restless, more anxious to get away. Then the band stopped and he saw Lester's burly figure toiling toward him through the crowd leaving the floor. In the comparative quiet the two voices behind him came close again. The other voice was doing the talking now.

"—so that's what she did. Well, you know how it is with a girl, Mowbray."

Nick spun around. There it was, the corrupt old body, the shifty, lascivious eyes, the loose obscene mouth. . . .

Lester slapped him on the back and Nick jumped, growling like an animal.

"Say, what—"

"Tod. Get a hold on me. Get me out of here. Get me out."

Lester saw the black, murderous face, the tensed body, and laid hold on him. "Start marching, gob. Here we go. Easy now, don't wreck the joint."

Nick was silent, only his body protesting. The bouncer saw what looked like trouble and sprang forward to give Mr. Tod Lester a hand. Between them it was done quickly, Nick propelled into the street and thrust into a cab, Lester ducking in after him.

Released, Nick thrashed and plunged upon the seat in the wild anguish of his fury, casting himself into a corner to smash his fist into his palm, flinging himself back, arms wrapped about his head, hurling forward to sway side to side, hands covering his face. "Why did I look—Oh God, Tod, why did I have to look--why was I fool enough to turn around--"

"Easy, Nick, this isn't a padded cell. Quiet down, will you?"

But Nick went on writhing, gasping. "Did you see him? Did you see what I was looking at? That--! He had the woman that I love--he had her--he stood at a bar and talked about it, he said her name--*I* know how he talked about her--"

"All right, all right, calm down. Maybe I ought to have let you take a sock at him at that. Why didn't you?"

Nick groaned, shooting out of a ball to lie stretched and rigid. "Oh, Tod, she's my wife, if I hit him there'd be talk--"

"Shut up, will you? Now you're talking wild and saying things you don't mean to say."

But Nick went on. "I don't care how young she was, how dumb she was, she had eyes, didn't she? How *could* she--"

"Shut up, Nick, you're raving."

"How *could* she! Sure I'm raving! This is one night I got to get drunk--I got to get into a fight--I got to beat somebody up--I got to get knocked out cold--I got to--"

Lester shook him by the arm. "You going to direct my show or are you going to do time in the brig? Come to, will you? You're not a kid in the navy any more. With a temper like you got you ought to know how to handle it by now."

Nick went limp and silent. After a minute his hands went searching through his pockets for a cigarette. His fingers came upon the ring and stopped there. Tod's right, I'm not a kid. I'm married. I knew all this. She came out with it straight, she never tried to put anything over on me. I just got to take it. . . . But the difference in a fact and getting the feel of it! The difference in knowing there had been a man who was a stinker and in seeing what a stinker that man was, and out of that imagination starting up. . . . Oh God, Diana, no wonder you're scared. What did he *do* to you, kid, what did he *do*--you, innocent, a child, sensitive. Oh, I ought to

301

killed him. But couldn't you tell—just looking? How *could* you —No. Stop it, Nick. Not her fault. Fourteen, Nick, only fourteen and that devil pushing her on. Forget it. You got to. She's your wife. You love her. . . .

Nick spoke quietly, "Say Tod, I guess I left my cigarettes on the bar. Give me one, will you? Sure I'll cool off. Just went crazy for a spell. Ought to carry you round as a bodyguard at that. Thanks."

"Boy, you snapped out of that quick when you made up your mind to!"

"Guess I always had a temper, but it never used to be as bad as this. Maybe it's love, I don't know." The cab drew up before the hotel and they got out. Grinning, sheepish, Nick asked, "Well, now that I busted up your party, mind if I go home?"

"Aw, come up for a while. If you go home to your wife the way you're feeling—"

Nick's grin turned sour. He didn't want Tod to know he didn't have a wife he could go home to. "Say, I spilled a lot I didn't mean to. Don't you spill it, will you? About the marriage. It's a secret."

"I never heard a word, gob. You were talking in your sleep. Aw, come up for a while. Have a few short ones."

"Thanks, Tod, I'll do better without it. I'll be around tomorrow or the next day. I got a couple of songs you might like, nice and sobby and a twist. Say Tod," he held out his hand, "I'll work for you on the show and give you all I got."

"I know that, Nick. I'm counting on you."

The strong handclasp fell apart and Nick swaggered up Broadway, going home. Lester, looking after him, thought, that was a neat trick the way he pulled out of that, he was all set for damage on a big scale. Boy, he's got the killer in him and I guess he knows it. Aw hell, why do all the decent guys fall for a gal who plays dirty?

Diana had said she would come in around three-thirty so they might have time to spend together before going to his

302

mother's, but it came to be four-thirty and still she had not arrived. Then the phone rang.

"Nick, you'll have to excuse me, I can't come."

It was a moment before he could say anything. "Diana this is a date, it's important. You can't break it."

"I know, I'm sorry, but I have to. Mother has an abscessed tooth and she's in awful pain. I have to take her to the dentist."

"No-go. Your brother can take her. Keep your date. My mother is expecting you."

"Nick, I can't."

"Don't tell me that. You could if you wanted to. You're going to get me all messed up if you let me down."

"I'm sorry, but—"

"I was polite to your mother, you might be polite to mine. I tell you I want you to come. Will you?"

He waited for an answer. And then, insistent, "Nicky, I *can't*. I've got to look after my mother."

He was furious. Almost choking on the words, he managed to sound pleasant. "If you can't, you can't. See you tomorrow. 'By, honey."

It had to be swallowed. The audition was set for tomorrow. Her grant of time at her mother's house was running out and he must do nothing that would throw the advantage to Mrs. Heaton. He must help Diana face the audition, he must pull her through the break with her mother, he must give her all the help he could and let no trouble come between them that would give her cause to waver, to be uncertain.

Yeah, go ahead and make me into your pet door mat, wipe your feet on me, I'll take it. I'll take it all and call you 'honey' just to get you in my house. But how much did she love him anyhow? Not enough to do the one favor he had asked.

Nicky, she married you to get out of a spanking. You knew it, you just didn't want to pretend you knew it. You've got a wife who isn't alive to what love means. She's not staying awake nights eating her heart out for you, you sap.

He set out grimly to face his mother alone, to make the best apology he could, knowing she would think this very strange indeed and would make use of the advantage of having him alone to cross-question him about his wife. His wife? Did he have a wife or didn't he? He hadn't got her yet. 'Peter, Peter, pumpkin eater, had a wife and couldn't keep her. . . .'

17

DIANA CAME to him early the day of the audition. She was regretful over the broken engagement without having any idea how much he felt it; how much he was smarting from his mother's freely voiced comments on this strange marriage where a husband did not have his wife; what a night of wild misery he had spent with the thought of Mowbray coming again and again to plague him.

Nick was glad that work came uppermost, engaging them. He played for her to dance and she was in fine shape, though he wished she were less tense. Then, practice over, he told her the news—Shultz had engaged him to direct the show.

"Why, then I'm giving the audition for you!"

"Not quite," he warned, still sitting at the piano. "For Shultz and Lester too, and Lester has a say. Tod is a friend of mine, I could put in a word for you, but that's something I won't do. It's no good to you if you have to get a job on pull. If you can't get it on your own, why kid yourself? Lester doesn't know you mean a thing to me and I'm not telling him. Do I have to?"

"No. I'll do my best and if that's not good enough I'd like to know it."

"That's the ticket. Now let me give you a couple of ideas. Sit down a minute. Don't try too hard, don't let them see you're trying. Go out and do your solo as though you had lots more where that came from. One thing about an artist, you always feel no matter how much they give they have a lot more back of that. And another thing, you're going to be nervous right up to the last minute. Take that for granted and don't let it throw you. Don't think because your mouth goes dry and your legs shake you're done for. That nervousness is what you work on, it's the sparkle that lifts your work and makes it come to life. The kid who never had stage fright hasn't got a thing to give. And when you do get going, don't let anything take your mind off what you're doing for one single second—if you do, something is bound to go flooey. Suppose you do make a mistake—keep going and don't think back on it; your thought has got to be a jump ahead of what you're doing, once it drops behind you're in for trouble. The time for thinking over mistakes is in the dressing room when you come off. Bawl yourself out in there all you want to, but never on the stage. But it should never be that you go into the dressing room knowing you could do a whole lot better on a second try—think of that before you start; there's no second chance in an audition or in a performance either. Now, Diana, we're going at this as if it were the one job in the world, and it isn't by a long shot, you'll have bigger jobs than this coming along. And if you should mess this up today, you'd learn by it. Some successes are built out of an accumulation of failures, and they're mighty sound successes. So maybe I shouldn't be making this seem so important."

"Go on, Nick. What you say helps me."

"Well, there's one other thing—the difference between the way a star steps out on a stage and some green kid. The star is used to applause, she takes approval for granted. She knows when she comes out that she's loved, and that gives her assurance and a warm feeling for the folks out front. She knows how to handle them, and they know she knows, and that makes it all smooth. Now if you can come out there the way you would if you had just taken five curtain calls, if you can put that over, kid, and with all the fire that's in you when you dance, why, I know I don't have to pull any wires to get you set."

"I'll try. I'll remember everything you said." She came across the room to say good-by. "Thank you, Nick. Thank you for everything. You've helped me so! Nick—I'll come to you this evening."

He had risen beside her. Silently, he drew her close for

306

a farewell kiss. This evening. She had said it without a word from him to prompt her. He had done everything he could to win her, and here was reward, and it was heart's-ease for all the pain of love. The kiss was short, time running out. He told her briefly, "I'll come back here after the audition. Call me if you run into any trouble. Yeah, I knew I could count on you, Diana. But listen—put your mind on the dance now. Get going."

The dance was hers. She had won it. She had gained the rank of soloist in a big Broadway show, top notch of its kind. Diana Heaton, solo dancer. . . .

Out of an agony of stage fright she had somehow managed to grasp and hold control upon herself, not muffing anything. A glance from Nick when she had finished, the merest glint in his eyes, had been like applause from a full house.

But hadn't it been a help to have him there on the apron, one of the three who stood in judgment! She had almost felt him pull her through the dance. He would be as proud and happy as she was herself. Now she could walk on air. She could—if only—Sue. . . .

Diana hastened home, heading into that scene with Sue which she so greatly dreaded. She had no clear idea that what she meant to do was right, only that it must be done—something must be done, even if it was the wrong thing. Better to blunder straight ahead and let the heavens come down upon her as they surely would than to sink into torpor waiting for Nick to come and drag her from her home. She was resolved to act, to be one person only, Nick's wife, admitting no promptings from that other self, Sue's daughter, to weaken and betray her.

But that resolve was like a foreign substance introduced into the chemistry of her being which put all other elements in conflict; around that fixed resolve turmoil seethed and rose as she neared home. The intoxication born of triumph over her success in the audition was a strength she had counted on to carry her along; it went quickly, leaving her flat and grey and quaking. Mounting the steps, doorkey in hand, she felt the last of her courage drain away, leaving a gutted hollowness inside. No matter. Things could be done without courage, with teeth chattering and darkness in the mind, once a course had been laid out. You just went on.

The living room was empty. Voices came from Mother's bedroom. Why in there? Going with unslackened pace along the hall she felt Nick's presence go from her and lost that self that was his wife. But there could be no turning back. She pushed into the room.

She halted in the door, checked by the surprise of seeing Sue in bed, Rod in the chair close by, their faces woebegone. "What's the matter, Sue? Are you ill?"

At sight of her daughter Mrs. Heaton sat alertly upright. "No, I'm not. The audition, Diana, did you—?"

"I got the job." It was something to be able to give Sue that news, cushion the shock of what was to come. Diana slid into the chair nearest the door. "I'm going to do the solo in the new Shultz show."

"Solo! Why, you never said a word about a solo! You only said a better position, that's all you said! Dicky, is it true? A solo in New York?"

Diana nodded. She had not foreseen how Sue's joy would work upon her; it was like the seizure of a powerful undertow pulling her out beyond her depth to flounder, fighting off drowning.

"Dicky! My winner!" Alive with incredulous delight, Mrs. Heaton held out open arms. "Oh, my baby, come to me!"

Until Sue's excitement died down, no more could be said. Diana moved forward. Her mother's arms closed about her, she was pulled down on the bed, her head against the lacy nightgown covering her mother's breast, scenting that vague flesh fragrance known before memory became a conscious thing.

"Ah, ah, ah! I knew you had it in you! And to think you kept it a surprise!"

Rod piped up, joyous, reflecting Mother's mood. "You

always said she would be somebody. Why, I remember when she was only six—"

Mrs. Heaton cut him short. "Rod, make us some coffee, do! I'm sure Diana would love a cup, she's probably exhausted!"

"Yes, Mother." Beaming happily on the scene, he went springily from the room.

Rod disposed of, Mrs. Heaton rocked her baby, crooning a lullaby. Out of the store of long forgotten things the song came back to Diana and now the words seemed dire with prophecy.

> "Sail, baby sail,
> Out upon the sea.
> Only don't forget to sail
> Back again to me!"

The current swept her along and she was drowning in it; she was only Sue's little girl, eyes shut, hearing the sweet musical voice, knowing the warmth and fragrance of her loved mother and the safety of her arms.

Mrs. Heaton turned her daughter's face up to her own fond doting gaze to say mischievously, "Your hair didn't smell of the smoke from a man's pipe when I held you in my arms to sing that!" Again she pressed Diana's head to her breast. "To think that once I could carry you in my arms! I was always lugging you about, even when you grew to be a great lump of a child. Mama used to say I was like a cat with one kitten! Oh, my precious! And now you're a great, big girl and it's all coming true, you will be famous! My baby. . . . "

I cannot do this thing to her. Nick, you don't know what you ask of me, it's too cruel. I cannot smite her down in all this bloom of hope and joy.

But you must, it's too late now, you can't prevent her knowing. Nick will come through that door, he will say you are his wife. You took the lock off the door, you gave him the right to enter, you destroyed the safety of this house;

you have destroyed your mother. Tell her, tell her what you've done. No. . . . in a minute, give her time, let her have her coffee. . . .

Mrs. Heaton led on, becoming direct, wanting to know how this miracle had been performed. True, this was not all she hoped for; the goal of Diana, the concert artist, world famous, lay ahead; but she was practical enough to see the value of a solo on Broadway and her hope for the future was uplifted. Released from the embrace, Diana sat upright, held on the bed by her mother's handclasp, answering questions about the audition, what dance she had done, what Mr. Shultz had said, seeing, while they talked, how Sue's hair, hanging long and straight, always gave her the look of a quaint, pretty child, thinking how small and thin and white Sue's hand was, how fragile in comparison with Nick's. How could Nick, with all the strength he had, need her as this frail, aging, childlike little woman needed her strong daughter. . . .

Mrs. Heaton played coyly with Diana's fingers, eyes downturned. "Dicky, you—you didn't have to be nice to any man to get your solo?"

"No, Mother, I got it on the level."

"I'm so glad." She said it heartily and knew she should say it, yet in the background of her thought she was not gladdened; if Diana had won this solo without connivance the guilt of Mowbray was made heavier, for the futility of that was proved. Stealing a glance at Diana, seeing how worn, harassed, the girl appeared, she came quickly to the belief that Diana feared to tell the truth, that there had been a price to pay. Consideration of the matter was shut off; Diana had her solo—that was what counted.

Rod came in with the coffee. Diana rose to let him place the tray where Sue could serve. Returning to the arm chair by the door, her eye was caught by newcomers on the bureau —Grampa's bible, Grampa's copy of Shakespeare; they recalled the day his suitcase had arrived from the hotel and Mother had shut herself up alone to sort his things, to store them away; her eyes had been swollen when the task was done. She had lost her father whom she loved, and now. . . .

Diana sank into the chair, accepting the cup Rod passed to her, accompanied by his approving smile; Sis had done the right thing, she had made Mother happy. She sipped the coffee, knowing this interlude would shortly end and that her treacherous pretense of being one of them would dissolve. Her mother went on chattering happily, re-telling Rod the things Diana had told her. The moments speeding, resolve began to drain away as courage had; better to sink into stupor, await Nick's coming, than to assume responsibility for this act. Don't do this thing. Say nothing.

Nick. She seemed to rouse herself at the last possible moment, clutching at the last fragment of resolve before it slipped away. Do it. You must. She forced her thought on Nick, fighting to carry out her promise to him, having some instinctive sense that if she failed in this a part of her would be forever damaged, and that what Nick came to claim would not be worthy of his love. She tried to summon his presence, saying his name, calling out to him, while she sought the words with which to begin. Mother, there is something I must tell you. . . . Too slow, frightening. Mother, I'm married. . . . Abrupt, cruel. Dearest, don't feel bad, I'm. . . .

The cups were empty, the interlude was over, a silence had come. It was the moment. Now—

But it was Mrs. Heaton who spoke first, sending a regretful glance to Rod. "I'm afraid we'll have to tell her."

His face went glum. "I suppose so."

It came back to Diana that she did not know why Mother was in bed, why they had both appeared so downcast. Something was astir. Inquiry offered respite, another deferring of that dreaded moment, the sound of her own voice speaking out. Still, to let resolve slip, go through the agony of gathering it again. . . .

Mrs. Heaton twisted a strand of hair and bit on it, announcing plaintively, "Dicky, we haven't any money."

Such a statement might legitimately claim one's attention. Diana asked, "What do you mean?"

"Just that. You know I've been wondering what possessed Mama not to send my check. I've written and I've wired. Today a letter came. Show Diana the letter, Rod."

Rod produced it and Diana read,

Dear Hattie:

I have not forgotten you as you accuse me of doing and I do wish you would not send me so many wires collect. Your income was only an allowance your father chose to send and I do not see my way to continue it now that he has gone. You have often written of what fine prospects Roderick and Diana have and I trust they will assist you now as is their duty. If you should ever be in need you can come to your mother for you know she will share her last crust with you. I greatly miss my beloved husband. He had a beautiful funeral.

Your loving mother,
Lucy T. Fletcher.

"Isn't that spiteful?" Mrs. Heaton cried, "Last crust indeed! I'd sooner starve. Oh, if Papa knew this! But—what will we do? We've only got your salary."

"No, Sue, it's worse than that. I've quit the show to start in rehearsing with the new one. I won't be drawing any salary for five weeks or six."

Mrs. Heaton gasped. "Diana! Why do you tell me such frightening things? Oh, I can't bear this! What happens when people haven't any money?" She began to whimper, her eyes round and scared.

"There, dear, of course we'll manage somehow. Rod—?"

But the more they talked, the darker grew the immediate outlook. Rod had already tried and failed to regain his position with the railroad, and if he did succeed in quickly finding work it was unlikely that he would earn enough for three, and of course Diana could not give up the solo. And the

312

bills! Good heavens, the bills. . . . Diana was appalled to realize they could not hope for credit anywhere. Advances on her salary could of course be drawn again, but not enough to keep them going through the weeks to come.

Mrs. Heaton wailed, "Dicky, Dicky, what will become of us? You must think of something! You must look after me!"

"Yes, Mother, don't you worry, I'll look after you." All at once Diana realized she need no longer struggle on with her resolve, a deferment had been gained; she could not tell Sue now. Eyes closed, she sat quiet, feeling relief settle upon her, the scattered parts of herself starting in to re-assemble. Walk out on Sue when Sue was penniless and frightened, crying out for her daughter's help? Unthinkable. Surely that was plain enough even for Nick to understand.

But—Nick must be told. This new turn of affairs must be explained. Go to him—the sooner the better. For a second the notion came that Nick might help in this emergency, and in a second was dismissed; no, he would not help—had he not said he feared that she would give his money to her mother? Well, some way out would be found. Diana stood up. "Mother, I've got to run into Manhattan but I shan't be long."

Mrs. Heaton wiped away tears with her hair, staring, "You have to go now?"

"Yes, dear, but I'll hurry right back. And don't you worry. I'll look after you."

She went out, braced and resolute, all of one piece. Her duty was plain. Nick would see that.

Nick sprang to open the door, seized her strongly, swung her up in the air in a great circling sweep that caught her like a whirlwind, then while she was still gasping, she was locked tight in his arms, his lips covering hers.

And she was pressing her hands against his chest, pushing to be free.

He thought that he had startled her and called himself a fool for having given her alarm, and at once his grasp lightened, his lips drew away, while joy stayed wild and plunging in him. "You came, kid, you came to me!"

"Wait, Nick, I came because I said I would—"

He had to kiss her again. "I knew you would, sweetheart, I knew—"

"Wait, Nick. Let me speak. I'm going back."

His arms dropped slowly to his sides, he retreated a step, peering into her face, his mouth opening, a pucker coming on his forehead, so bewildered, so dazed, that Diana could not look at him; she had to turn her face away.

That movement told him it was true—this was loss. He went backward from her, turned and went on, traveling to the far end of the room, coming to a stop facing the window.

Diana's heart was aching as she had not guessed it could. Faltering, she pleaded, "I have to go."

She was just beginning to wonder if he had heard her when he asked, unmoving, "Now?"

"I must."

It was another long moment before he asked, "For good?"

"No, no, just—just for a little while—just until the show opens. You see—"

"Then go."

"Nick, I want to explain. Mother—"

"Go."

"Please, I want to tell you. I—"

He turned in a flash, savage, black with rage. "Get out. I told you I'd give you warning when to get away from me. I'm giving it right now. Get out of here—quick."

She knew him—the man of the prop-room. With a stifled cry, her fist against her mouth, she fled to the door. The door opened, escape assured, she wavered, crying out appeal. "Don't, Nick, don't! Please let me—"

"Get out. I shan't come after you. Will you get out of here? God damn you, go!"

He had started for her, swift and wild in fury. Diana jerked the door shut behind her and sped along the hall, breaking into sobs. She came out into the street, still running, still sobbing, oblivious of oncoming people who stopped to gape after her; oblivious until street traffic at a corner stopped her flight, and then she knew that there were people looking. But she could not stop her sobs. She pulled out a handkerchief and tried to hide behind it, but strangers drew about her, their number growing, and she was ringed and trapped on a city street with no escape to privacy.

A woman's voice asked, "Can I help you?"

She was a public spectacle and she could not stop her tears. If only she could instantly cease to exist, sink away. She held the handkerchief over her bowed face, speaking toward the strange voice. "Will you—get me a cab?"

The cab came. Someone opened the door. A man was asking, "What's wrong with her?" Another said, "She ought to be looked after." Then the same woman asked, "Will you be all right?"

Diana lowered the handkerchief and saw a blurred ring of faces. "I'm all right. Thank you." She stumbled into the cab and told the driver, "South Ferry." The cab started up, she lay back in the corner, sobbing without restraint. The future had gone black. Nick did not love her any more.

Every now and again the driver turned his head to look at her, and at last he commented, "You're taking on some, young lady."

"He—he doesn't love me."

"Oh well, you'll get over it."

"No, I won't, ever."

'Sure, that's the way everybody feels."

The talk had checked her sobbing. Then she remembered cabs cost money and every penny from now on was precious. She dried her eyes. "You'd better put me off here."

"Didn't you say South Ferry?"

"Yes but—I can't afford it."

He reached a hand to the meter, turned it off and kept on going. "Live on Staten Island? Going home to your folks?"

"To my mother."

"Well now, that's the best place you could go. I'll take

you down. No trouble. I got a girl about your age. Nineteen she is. How old are you?"

Gratefully Diana carried on the conversation; it was stupid and it meant nothing, but somehow it helped to settle her, this new suffering sinking to a lower depth to lie solid and heavy on her heart, but surface calm at least regained. She shook hands with Mr. Gleason when they parted and thanked him for his kindness and agreed that his advice was sound, she would try to forget.

On the ferry she sought the seclusion of the ladies room and lay down upon the couch. The room was hot and smelled sickeningly of disinfectant. The throb of engines below deck put everything in an unending shiver so that even her body quivered.

It was over. Nick did not love her any more. He would not come to get her. . . . 'God damn you, go.' . . .

18

NICK FOUND HIMSELF in the very jam he had meant to escape when he turned down Shultz's offer to direct the Lester show. Again he would have to stand there on the apron and have Diana before his eyes day after day, and he knew what havoc that could work on him. If it had been hell before, how much more so now that he had gone so deep in love, and with the mockery of marriage on them. There wasn't the wildest chance of ducking this; he had asked Lester for it as a favor, he owed Lester what he had promised —the best he had to give. Besides, there was Shultz.

That Shultz should have offered him the job in the first place had struck Nick as a lucky fluke; the old boy had just taken a fancy to him, that was the only way it could be explained. Not that Nick wasn't sure he could make a fine job out of it, but he was young and relatively new to the work, and the Lester show would be a big, lavish thing that well-known directors, old men in the field, would have grasped at. Shultz had been amazed and angry that Nick had turned the offer down, he would not have consented to take him back except for Lester's pressure. Nick knew if he again behaved erratically he would be all washed up with Shultz, and for that matter with every other producer, for the gossip would go up and down Broadway. No, he couldn't duck this time.

Then he must cut Diana out of his thoughts completely, he must give her no more consideration than he would give to any other member of the cast. The moment he permitted himself to brood upon her, to watch her face and guess her thoughts, he would be open to a thousand emotional attacks, no longer master of himself or of his work.

Diana must mean nothing to him. There must be no meetings, no talk, nothing of either love or hate, no relenting from the strictest professional behavior. She was the dance soloist, he was the director. That was all until this job was over.

He held to it, ignoring her as best he could, and it grew easier as the pattern became established though he knew some difficult moments in the first few weeks, for Diana did her utmost to break in upon him. For a time she merely looked at him, and when by chance or by necessity he met her eyes it was as though she called his name and kissed his lips. Then she played tricks to make him notice her, standing in the passage when he entered, walking conspicuously across the stage before rehearsal started; he even suspected her of upsetting the water cooler on purpose. She had come to him for an advance on the first day of rehearsal and he had given her a note to the business manager. Before the week was out she came again, asking for his intercession that she might draw more. He granted that, though it was on the side of leniency. But when she came a third time, still wanting money, he informed her, as he would have informed any other member of the cast, that he could do no more.

The work was absorbing. The complete production created in imagination, he built toward that end, and the conception grew as detail of color and movement and effect were worked out. From the outset the prospect was exciting, a good book, good tunes, good people to work with; the result could be a smart and lively show full of delight and laughter. And Shultz liked what he was doing.

Outside of work upon the show, music was coming to him as though once started it would never stop. Along with the serious stuff, the light tunes came, one idea upon another, and some of them were riotous; the best of these Lester snapped up and put into the show; *Peter, Peter, Pumpkin Eater;* Lester thought it was a howl and Nick smiled sourly, knowing that queer relief that comes of turning pain into a form that has identity separate from its origin.

One night, going through old papers in the table drawer in search of some production notes once jotted down, he

318

came upon a diary that he had kept when he first left home. He flipped it open, read a line at random. The words stunned him. He read them again, went slowly on for half a page, went back, re-read. It was incredible; he could not believe that he had ever written in such a vein. He looked at the date; he had been sixteen at the time. But there seemed to be no connection between the boy who had written those words and the man reading them. His feeling was one of mortification; the diary closed, he stood, head down, trying to recollect the boy, wondering if he had actually been the senseless, conceited, self-pitying fool that writing showed. Sixteen; why, he remembered how much a man he had then thought himself to be. . . . One thing was plain—in ten years' time he had come into a different existence, forgetting the world that boy had lived in. Sixteen—Diana's age. . . . And he had sworn at her and kicked her out. . . . His face grim, he tossed the diary back and shut the drawer with a slap, shaking his head. Then, resolutely, he directed his thought upon the problem that had been in mind.

But at work in the theater, there seemed to be no end to the number of things she could think up to come to him about. She wanted to be excused from afternoon rehearsals; that was possible for the present. Then it was *Brief Rhapsody;* she wanted that. He held his answer, knowing what it would mean to him, hearing that music go on in rehearsals. But he had said that she might have it, if she thought it would do better for a dance than what she was now using he could not very well refuse. So he granted that and spent two nights in orchestrating it.

Her work was unsteady, she seemed to flounder with it. He tried to think, as a director would, what he could do to pull her into shape. But this was dangerous ground and he decided it was better to wait, trusting that she would get herself in hand. The change came, he saw her steady, begin to take hold, then shoot ahead; that made it harder than ever to stay impersonal, to bottle up the pride he felt in her.

And still she would not let him be. She found a moment

when he sat alone at the director's table, rehearsal over, people going from the stage. "Nick, I want to speak to you."

He kept his eyes on the script spread out before him. "Is it anything about your work that I can help you with?"

"No, it's not that."

"Then I'm sorry, Diana, I don't want to talk to you." He turned over a page of the script and in a moment she moved to go away. Then he permitted himself one deviation. "Diana."

She turned back.

He looked up with tired, quiet eyes. "Don't forget your name."

She looked at him, uncomprehending. In an instant passion flamed in him and in another instant he had it smothered. "I said, don't forget your name, Mrs. Allingham."

She took an impulsive, repentant step closer. "Nick, I want my ring."

"No."

"It's mine."

"No. You've got no right to wear it, you're not a wife. All you've got is the name. Take care of that, it's mine." He stood up, folding the script, tucking it under his arm, looking at her as though she were a long way off and he had no curiosity in the object.

Again she said, "I want to talk to you."

Again he told her quietly, "I'm sorry, Diana, I don't want to talk to you."

She went hurriedly away.

It had to be like that. The momentary flare of passionate feeling that he had so quickly checked was a warning reminder. He did not even permit himself to speculate on what it was that she might wish to say to him. He had a job that he was honor bound to carry through and he was going to do it.

Diana walked south block after block on her way to Greenwich Village, the addresses the girls in the ballet class had given her tucked in her purse. They had assured her, scoffing, that posing was just work, you grew accustomed to it, and the men you worked for were a decent lot, nine times out of ten they didn't bother you.

Well, it was work that could be fitted in with rehearsals; little as it paid it would mean getting by until the show opened. There might be other ways of earning money but if there were Diana could not think of them and something must be done at once. Sue wandered from room to room whimpering with worry, and now Rod, after a spell of frenzied, unsuccessful searching, had come down with influenza, adding to the worry and the bills.

But to take off all your clothes and stand naked before some strange man's stare. . . . The thought of it was sheer suffering. To walk steadily forward into that experience required resolute determination. Only the sense of responsibility this emergency had imposed made it possible. She was the breadwinner; Sue must be looked after and Rod taken care of.

She had a sober sense of growing up; tomorrow would be her birthday; she would be seventeen. At seventeen one can no longer be mistaken for a child. Growing up . . . but the process seemed to go on and on, no end to it. . . . It was not easy to grow up; you were always realizing that you had done the wrong thing when you had meant to do the right. It was not only right, it was necessary to look after Sue. Yet—it had been wrong to break her promise to Nick.

Nick . . . it was impossible to think for long of anything without Nick coming to mind. She crossed through traffic, went on along the street, unmindful of the city, seeing Nick standing by the table on the apron, coat off, tie removed, his white shirt silhouetted against the dark of the empty house, a wiry figure filled with driving energy, his face somber, his eyes grave, his manner just as authoritative as it had ever been, but different, oh so different! A new patience was in him; you no longer sensed the whip-crack when he gave an order. Yet his power had grown. Quiet, impersonal, demanding, he got and held the best efforts of the company and carried them on to more endeavors.

But when it came her turn to dance it seemed that he withdrew that power, that she was there alone, unsustained. Had it been imagined that once his presence pulled her through a dance? There was no such strength to draw on now, she had to find strength within herself. That too was part of growing up; the effort put forth, gains made, you came to take a joy in work that you alone were mastering. But to have lost his love. . . .

Now, sharply, she could evaluate that loss, realizing for the first time how abnormal life with Sue had come to be, how shut in they were, without friends or family. The relationship with Sue, once all-satisfying, fell so far short of her need for human companionship that sometimes her thought idled among memories, seeking some contact. Father . . . there was such a person, somewhere. Was he actually the no-good that Sue had always made him out to be? But sometimes he must think 'my daughter.' . . . He had written once. And his letter had not been answered. The Heatons . . . why, there was a Grandma Heaton she had never known. Well, that was how it was, a pattern shaped. Yet it pleased her to nurse the notion that if it had been Father Sue had summoned he would not have struck her, somehow he would have understood, there would have been talk.

Talk. To be able to meet understanding. Where? Not with girls her own age. Lonely as she had been among the chorus girls, hearing their dirty stories, she was even more constrained with the girls in the ballet class. Nice girls they were, most of them, coming from decent homes, leading quiet lives. They could chat about boys, talk easily, romantically, of the possibility of love, and Diana, listening, was an outsider, having no insight into a virgin's thought, for she had not reached the boy stage when she had ceased to be one. It made her shy to be among them and so far removed.

Yet she tried earnestly for friendship even so—and came upon another barrier, astonishing; one that held the threat of an enduring isolation. The things she wanted to discuss, the things she said, appeared to startle and alienate her companions. She could not make it out; here were girls who made dancing their profession yet they never thought largely on what dancing was or could be; to them it was steps, well executed, and there thought stopped. 'But how is form in composition achieved?' Diana questioned, 'Can it be worked out in movement as it is in music? Are there principles not yet discovered, or is it only a question of feeling, a sense of rhythmic wholeness?' Girls stared and walked away to practice entrechats or fouettés, and agreed among themselves that she put on airs. They had modest little ambitions, yearning prudently; their reverence for fame amounted to abject denial of any claim to hope, and that puzzled Diana; it seemed feeble and cowardly not to assume the way was open for those who strove upward. But her zeal, her frank intensity, was interpreted by the others as bold conceit; she sensed that and was hurt by it, and felt a large loneliness press in upon her.

It had been possible to talk with Nick. He never thought it odd that she should work out movements of her own; he understood ambition. And often when he played for her he made some comment from a musician's point of view which opened possibilities, enriched the dance. He lived in that bright world of live emotion, thought blown up into a flame, knowing the ordeal of ever seeking to turn feeling into form. *Brief Rhapsody;* it must be a good dance; it would have to be.

Now it was she who suffered at the daily sight of him, who made a study of his face, trying to fathom what he thought or felt, who knew desire, who lay awake at night, heart hungry for him. For all the confusion in which she had been floundering, pulled one way and another, she had been moving steadily toward union with him. This break had put no stop to that urge; frustration brought increase of yearning. Impelled, she strove to thrust aside the barriers he raised, and as he met each attempt with a fresh check, his being cold, remote, her longing for him grew more fixed and more distracting.

323

Plainly, he had ceased to care. What did he mean by his reminder that she bore his name? Not to disgrace it. What an insulting thing to say. Yet . . . how would he like it if he knew the woman he had married was going to be a model, take off her clothes before a man? But did he care what happened to her? No. He did not.

Eighth Street, MacDougal Alley; old buildings, glass slanting in the roofs. At the first address an elderly Italian said wearily that he wanted no models. At the second, the ringing of the bell went unanswered. She went on in a hurry to the third. Suppose no one wanted a model.

A trim, bespectacled young woman opened the door. "A model? Come in please, I'll take your name."

Only a secretary, making a note for future reference. Diana followed her to a hall desk.

Up from a corner armchair rose a big man, curly grey hair about a face that had once been handsome. He advanced with an inquiring frown.

"A model," explained the secretary, speaking loudly.

"No, she's a dancer. I've seen her some place." The man's voice boomed. He turned his puzzled look on Diana and then a smile of almost boyish charm lit up his face. "I have it, that show at the Shultz Theater! Sure, seen her dozens of times. Come to pose has she? Give her my address, I can use her. What's your name, dancer?"

"Speak up, he's deaf," murmured the secretary.

Diana had to say it twice.

"Come tomorrow," the man bawled.

The need to shout making it all the harder, Diana offered, "I'd be glad to work today."

He scrutinized her for a moment, then his hand went into his pocket and fished up an untidy roll of bills. He handed her one, apparently at random. "Don't go working for any other flibberty-gibbet, you're hired. Come tomorrow, one o'clock, two o'clock, A.M., P.M., all the same."

He had understood she needed money. In a flurry of embarrassment and gratitude, Diana took the bill and the address the secretary had jotted down, backing to the door, calling out, "I'll come at one—noon."

" 'By, dancer!" He waved his hand like the best of friends.

Outside, she looked at the bill. Twenty dollars! Was it a mistake? Why, they said posing paid only a dollar an hour! She unfolded the slip of paper, read his name. Harold Barton? Was he one of *the* Bartons? Weren't they related to the Vanderbilts or some such family?

She put the money and the paper in her purse. Now she could go home to Sue and say 'you needn't worry' with more than just the intention of cheering her.

Posing might not be too awful. . . . He was kindhearted, friendly. His smile was nice.

Barton's house, iron railings at the stoop, white woodwork at doors and windows, suggested solid family wealth passed on from preceding generations. A Filipino answered the door, down a curving flight of stairs another one came running. "Modah? Upsta's, please."

Diana followed him up. From some place came a most ungodly screeching—what on earth? Parakeets! A vivid cluster of the tropic birds were on a rack in one corner of a long, low-ceilinged room. What color! Green walls, orange divans with yellow cushions; a huge glazed jar the color of lapis lazuli with a still fountain of gladioli mirrored on the shining black floor. Tropic, lush, the room had beauty, bizarre, original, and a simplicity about it, too. Long windows opened on a walled yard and gave a passing glimpse of feathery green boughs swaying in a soft breeze. Those raucous birds!—but he was deaf.

The guide led on into another room, monastically bare. Barton in a purple dressing gown was the only splotch of color against a grey wall. A few white statues gleamed under the diffused, cold brightness of a skylight; there was a model stand in the center of the room.

So he was a sculptor; she had been hoping he might chance to be an artist, wanting a model in costume. The big man

325

waved a greeting and gestured toward a screen. "In you go —let's see your hide."

Behind the screen she undressed quickly; the faster this was done the better; it was like plunging into icy water, once you hesitated, nerve would go. But when she had removed her clothes she found speed hadn't helped. She had to struggle to summon resolution to emerge head up and poised.

Barton's booming voice filled the room. "Diana, you said your name was? 'Queen and huntress, chaste and fair, goddess excellently bright.' Know old Ben? Ah, the Elizabethans, they were the boys! They knew how to live. You ought to know Ben Jonson with the name Diana stuck on you like a label."

He spoke like a gentleman; there was hope he would behave like one. Diana came quickly around the edge of the screen and stood tautly, head up. Barton tilted his head, appraising her; he looked and judged her as a man might judge a thorougbred.

"Glory, what a figure! Diana it is. Get up on the stand. I can't begin to do you, you know, I'm only an amateur who gets a kick out of trying. Girl, you're beautiful."

It was work, just work. It could be endured.

Mrs. Heaton did not like it, she did not like it at all. Diana had not thought she would. She had delayed telling her mother for over two weeks and then somehow it had come out.

"You—a model! Posing in the nude! Oh, how disgusting! Who is this man you work for?"

"Well, he's really very nice, Sue, he—"

"Oh Lord, you're not in love with him, are you?"

"No, of course not! Why, he's an old man!"

"An old man? That makes it even more disgusting! How did you come to know him?"

They were together in the living room. Rod, convalescing, sat alone sketching on the back porch.

Diana told her. "And he's a big bug, Mother, he's Harold Barton."

"Barton? Harold Barton?" Mrs. Heaton gazed at her daughter with amazement that quickly filled with excitement. "Do you mean to tell me it's Harold Barton that you're posing for? Why Diana, this is the chance of a lifetime!" She was on her feet, sweeping back and forth in delighted agitation, trying hastily to put the whole picture together. "Let me see—he married someone and something happened—yes—oh, this was years ago! It was in all the papers. He settled a fortune on her and she made a fool of him running off with a jockey and he divorced her. Yes, that's it . . . Harold Barton. . . ." Well, this certainly changed everything. She stopped before her daughter demanding, "Is he in love with you?"

Watching her, Diana had grown anxious. Excitement was not good for Sue; it led to scenes and no telling what. No doubt it was the recent shock of money worry that had unsettled Sue and plunged her back into that nervous instability in which the least thing set her off into a fretful nagging or a railing tirade. As in those weeks of persecution, Diana gloomily admitted to herself that there were spells in which Sue sober could be quite as hard to handle as Sue drunk. If only Mother were not quite so temperamental. She answered soothingly, "There, dear, you're building this up. I'm sorry that I told you."

Mrs. Heaton stamped her foot. "*Is* he in love with you?"

Diana shrugged. "Oh, he likes me."

"How much money has he given you?"

"He pays me a lot more than most models get." She gave her mother a placid smile, hoping to draw her into a quiet mood. "He wanted to give me more but I told him I didn't need it."

Mrs. Heaton cast herself into a chair. "Fool, fool! You've the chance of a lifetime and you don't know how to play your cards!"

"Well dearest, I couldn't just take money."

The woman lifted her hands to heaven. "You can't take money! Isadora Duncan was offered Madison Square Garden as a gift and you can't take money! Good Lord, what a girl!"

Nettled, Diana challenged her. "What is it that you want?"

Mrs. Heaton studied her daughter and shook her head in doubt. Such an honest simpleton. She leaned forward urging more quietly, "For the Lord's sake, Diana, try, try to be smart. There are a million girls in New York City who would give their eye teeth to be in your shoes just so they could have money to spend on clothes and jewelry. You're an artist —or trying to be—you need money for a career! Tell him about your work, your ambition. If he likes you, if he wants to help you, there's nothing wrong about that. Why, he might even marry you!"

"Marry? Why, I don't love him. Besides, I told you he's an old man."

"You said he was nice, didn't you? Well . . . Anyhow, he can help you."

"I'm getting ahead on my own, aren't I?"

Mrs. Heaton all but lost her temper. "A solo in a Broadway show! Is that the limit of your ambition? Oh, you'll drive me mad! You must give concerts, tour the world with your own company, have a symphony orchestra to play for you, appear in all the capitals of Europe—" She waved her hands at the futility of expressing the grandeurs that could be. Very earnestly she warned her daughter, "For heaven's sake don't mess up this chance."

Diana tried to be reasonable about it. "I don't suppose there would be anything wrong in letting him back me as an artist if he wanted to, but I can't ask for money."

The woman smote her head with a groan. "You can't ask."

"No, Sue, I can't."

Mrs. Heaton pulled herself together. This was going to require skill and cunning, but it was important, oh Lord, it was important. This was no wild shot in the dark—everyone knew who Harold Barton was. She put on a smile and her manner became winning, intimate and confidential. "Dicky, my pal, you certainly need a mother to help you! Of course I didn't mean that you were to hold out your hand and beg —a clever woman wouldn't have to *ask*. If you can make him like you, and let him know what you want, why, that's all there is to it!"

Seeing that Sue's excitement had died down, Diana's anxiety went with it. It was a relief to have Sue sit and talk so pleasantly, without that nerve-rasping antagonism. She smiled back, agreeing, "Nothing wrong about that, I suppose. And besides, I don't have to make Hal like me, he likes me anyhow."

"Hal? Is that what you call him? He must be very interesting. I always think older men are. I should think you'd be flattered that he takes an interest in you. But of course he must see how unusual you are." Mrs. Heaton was quite chummy. Diana was listening to reason, Diana was malleable, she would do as her mother told her if only. . . . The woman was thinking lucidly and in lightning flashes; this was adventure with promise of rich reward. "Dicky—" she hesitated, pouting, winsome, "—I said I'd let you do as you please but —Chick, you're not having an affair with anyone are you?"

"No, Mother, I'm not."

Mrs. Heaton sighed with sincere relief. It was true then as she had begun to believe—that puppy love had died and Diana was wholly hers to mold and to direct; if Diana had fancied herself in love she would have been obstinate, rebellious. Still, Diana was not clever, guidance must be subtle and indirect. Mrs. Heaton shifted in her chair with an air of changing the subject. "Are those your best shoes? You really need another pair. And you've had only one new dress in ages. You're so unselfish, you never think of yourself. Chick, can't you afford some new duds now? What fun we used to have shopping together. I always loved to dress you up so you'd look stunning!"

The suggestion caught Diana's fancy. It certainly would be nice to have more than one presentable dress. Nick always noticed how a woman dressed. He wore smart-fitting things

329

himself. If she were to pass before him stunningly costumed. . . . "Yes, I think we could afford it, Sue."

It was a small victory but it lifted the woman's spirits. She reverted to the main thing; after all there was no time to be lost. "Has he invited you to dinner, to the theater?"

Diana admitted that he had.

"Why didn't you accept?"

Her daughter smiled at her; she could not keep from saying, "Well, after all, dear, you did tell me to leave men alone. If I stayed out late—"

"And you took me literally!" Hope racing high, it was possible to answer gaily, turn the matter into a joke. "Why, certainly accept his invitations! With a man like that—" Mrs. Heaton heard Rod stirring on the porch and rose actively, reaching for Diana's hand. "Come in the bedroom where we can chat like pals, just the two of us. You must tell me all about him. Do you see him every day? What does he talk about? Oh, I do think older men are so much more interesting!"

19

THE SHOW was coming along fine. It had shaped up smartly and now with only three days to go before the opening it was riding smooth through each rehearsal. The company dismissed for the day, Nick lifted his coat from the back of the chair, slung it across his arm and went over to Lester's room to check on the way Tod wanted that new bit of business in the *Peter, Peter* song.

The star dressing room opened on the wings and Lester was lolling in the door looking out upon the stage. Nick glanced over his shoulder to see what Tod was looking at and saw Diana had stayed on to practice by herself. A hand pressed against the prop-room door, she swung one limber leg high front and back with a brisk movement like a pendulum. The bright red of her practice costume against the green of the door made Nick think of parrot colors, barbaric, tropical. She had come up amazingly in the last couple of weeks, steady and vivid and alive; *Brief Rhapsody* was a strange, wild dance, sensationally beautiful, and she put it over with a sock.

Lester, leering, jerked his head toward Diana. "Say, how you got her figured out?"

Nick brushed by him into the stark, bare room, as yet no make-up on the shelves, no costumes hanging on the walls, a bleak cell having that dead feeling that only a place can have which has known color and excitement. He laid his coat on the shelf answering tersely, "I got other things to figure out."

Lester dallied a moment longer, his eyes on Diana, then shut the door with a laugh. "The way she carries herself around here, nice and quiet and modest, wouldn't you set her down as a good kid?"

Nick had dropped into one of the two chairs that stood as though by habit facing the mirror along the shelf, and was lighting his first cigarette after four hours of steady work. He held the match, still aflame, shooting a sharp, quick glance up at Lester. He asked coolly, "You got any reason to think she isn't?"

The burly comedian flopped into the other chair. "Gob, the women can fool us every time. Know who she's running around with? Hal Barton, the old playboy who's had every show girl he could make up and down Broadway for the last twenty years."

Nick lit the cigarette and drew on it, his eyes on Lester, steady and intent. "Where'd you get that bit of dirt?"

Lester waved his hand good-naturedly. "Listen, Nick, I don't pass around all the smears I hear, I only hand out what I collect myself. She was out with Barton last night, they were at the opening of that new show at the Alvin. You know Barton, he's always got a box to himself and some dame along with him, and last night it was our sweet little dancer."

"Les, you're a decent guy about talk, but this is one time you're straying. I don't believe it."

Lester's round face was simple with astonishment. "Why should I say it if it isn't true? I tell you I saw Diana Heaton in Barton's box, and what's more they went over to the Low Down afterwards, and I saw that too, nobody told me."

Nick was on his feet with such sudden violence that the chair fell backward with a clatter. "Tod, it isn't true."

"My God, Nick, have I bust in on something? Are you and that girl—? Say, Nick, you aren't messing around with *her*, are you?" He sat staring up at the straight, tense figure in horrified bewilderment. "Why, Nick, she's not your girl, is she? Nick, you told me you had a wife—"

"Girl be damned, she is my wife."

Lester got up heavily. "Oh, for God's sake, Nick—I didn't know—I wouldn't have—Nick, you know I'd bite my tongue off—"

Nick whipped up the chair and set it on its legs. He threw

down the cigarette and crushed it with his foot. "It's all right, Tod. I just know Diana. I know she's clean and decent. You got to let me call her in here now and put it to her in front of you."

Lester was panicked. He pawed Nick with beseeching hands. "Don't do it, gob, don't. Let it ride. Don't do that."

Nick pushed his hands aside. "That's all right, Tod, I won't hold it against you. You just got to let me put you straight." He started for the door.

Lester dragged at his arm. "Gob, *don't*, *don't* ask her in, will you listen to me—"

But Nick had opened the door. He called across the stage. "Miss Heaton, will you come in here a moment, please?"

Lester whined at his shoulder. "Don't ask her. Pass it up, can't you?"

Nick held the door open, watching the approach of the bright-clad, bare-armed, bare-legged figure, and for the first time since rehearsals started he was looking at the woman, not the dancer, seeing the beauty of her body and her face, recalling the ardor he had roused in her. Suddenly, without apparent relevance, he was troubled by an impression which, when he had received it, he had ignored; yesterday, encountering her in the street outside the theater she had been smartly, richly dressed.

Diana stepped into the room and Nick shut the door. She stood, pleasant-faced, looking inquiringly from one man to the other, quickly aware that this room held trouble, but her poise maintained.

Nick said, "Sit down, Miss Heaton," and leaned his back against the door. Diana chose the chair furthest from him and sat waiting, meeting Nick's steady, searching gaze. Lester, making no attempt to hide his agitation, rolled up and down the room like a bear in a cage.

Looking into her eyes, Nick saw she was a woman, not a youngster, her eyes more beautiful and more mysterious. That childish look of open frankness was not there; and yet

333

they were true eyes, the gaze direct and fearless. "Diana, I've got to ask you something."

Lester, going on with his restless movement, growled, "Aw, stow it, gob."

Neither of them heeded him. Nick asked, "Where were you last evening?"

She answered simply and without the slightest hesitation. "I went to the theater."

If an explosion had occurred there in the small, close room Nick could not have been more shaken than he was by that glib admission. What Lester had told him he had been certain was impossible, it did not fit in with the Diana that he knew, and believed he knew so thoroughly. Time seemed to stop as he struggled to collect himself, go on; but then it was without a sign of the upheaval that had occurred within him; his face impassive, his eyes never leaving hers, he spoke as steadily as before. "Who did you go with?"

Mettle had come into her. She sat erect, her eyes unwavering, and answered with a cool hardness to match his own. "I went with Mr. Harold Barton."

Lester, turning and returning between the two motionless figures growled a pleading, "That's enough now, gob, that's enough. Drop it."

Nick threw him an answer, not taking his eyes from Diana, "No, I won't. Diana, why did you go with him?"

Her answer was quick and pat. "Because he asked me to."

The strain was showing on Nick, his impassivity was wearing thin, his nervous tension increasing. He clasped his hands, arms thrust down rigidly before him, and he spoke more slowly; to form a question was a labor, each word groped for and considered, but he still spoke quietly. "Don't be a kid. You know what I mean. What is he to you?"

"I work for him."

Lester, worn out, straddled the chair between them, his eyes moving from one to the other. He was sweating, the smell of it was in the room, an animal smell of fear.

Nick had the next question framed. He altered his position, his hands behind his back, his fingers locked. "What do you mean by 'work'?"

Now Diana stood up, holding her head high; she wanted to be on her feet to answer this one. "I pose for him."

Nick did not understand. "You what?"

"I pose. He's a sculptor."

She stood queenly, unflinching, and Nick could not believe his mind was working. "What do you do?"

"I told you."

A girl in a simple little yellow dress in need of mending starts to unbutton it, stops, her face aflame. . . .

"You stand up naked in front of Hal Barton? You?"

"Easy, old man," groaned Lester, not liking this.

But Diana held to her unflinching pose. "I had to earn money."

Nick ran his fingers through his hair and got them down and again locked behind them. The passion that he fought to master rang in his voice and his words came faster, unconsidered. *"You?* Will you stand up naked before me if I pay you a dollar an hour?"

Lester warned, urgent, "Keep it clean, gob."

Anger blazed in Diana's eyes and she answered hotly, "He pays me more than that!"

Legs spread, Nick braced himself, arms folded, and his voice stayed steady even with the ring in it. "What does he pay you?"

"He pays me a hundred dollars a week."

Silence fell, electric, Nick taking his time with the next question. They were all very still. "What does he get for his money?"

Diana snapped, "That's an insult!"

Nick's words came fast on hers. "Don't you want to answer the question?"

"You've no right to ask it!"

"I've no right? Have you forgotten again? Is it too big an effort for you to remember that you've got my name? I told you to take care of that! I asked you—what does he get for his money?"

"And I told you! I told you that I pose for him and that's what he pays me for it!"

They were both speaking fast and high, one retort coming on another.

"Just for standing naked. A hundred dollars a week."

"Nick, you're low, you're nasty, you're contemptible!" She was quivering with anger.

"Does your mother know?"

"Yes, she does!"

"I get it. She approves, of course?"

"She approves!"

Nick strove to hold himself, but it all piled up on him, Mrs. Heaton's unscrupulous ambition for her daughter, her influence over Diana, Barton's reputation with women, the passion in Diana that Nick knew he had aroused and left unsatisfied, and, most damning, her admission that she had been naked in the man's presence; if Diana was the girl that he had known and loved, she could not have taken off her clothes before a man, and such a man. But she was not that girl; there was a new, defiant self-reliance in her, bold and assertive. Yeah, and she wore expensive clothes and flaunted herself before the night-club crowd. With Barton. After he had reminded her she was his wife. There was no escape from one shattering conclusion. Nick told her, "You're a liar."

"And you're a dirty-minded fool!"

Nick started for her, not fast and not alert, but dazed and blind with the wounding pain of his fury. Lester was up, blocking the way, gripping him in a powerful hug. "She's telling you the truth, Nick, you got to believe her!"

Diana raged up close beside them. "Let go of him, Mr. Lester, I don't care what he does to me, he can't say that! Let him go, I'm not afraid of him!"

Lester pressed Nick back against the wall. Nick did not seem to be aware of him but only of Diana and that something had got in his way. He strained against the pressure, struggling to get free, his blind eyes on the girl. "You're Hal Barton's mistress."

"I'm not! Don't you dare say it!"

Lester, using all his strength to hold the man, argued shrilly, "She said she wasn't, you got to believe her!"

Diana danced beside the two straining figures in a rage. "Let him go, let him go!"

Lester yelped at her, "Don't you know what he'll do to you?"

"I don't care, I'll hit him first!"

"You're Hal Barton's mistress. You go to bed with him. I'll choke the life out of you."

Lester did not know if he could hold Nick much longer. "For God's sake, will you two elemental beings cut this out? Act civilized, will you? Nick, you got to—Miss Heaton, will you get out of here?"

"No, I won't." Fists clenched, her face thrust up to Nick's, Diana poured out her anger. "I've taken his dog's orders since the first day I knew him. 'Come here'—'lie down'—'kiss me'—'get out.' I've had enough, I won't take any more—"

Nick closed his eyes, moaning, "Make her stop, Les, make her go 'way."

Diana fumed on, "Yes, make me go 'way! You made me love you, Nick, you said you'd drive me crazy and you did, and then you flung me a dog's order to get out. You won't let me talk to you, you won't give me a chance to explain, you don't care what happens to me—"

"Make her stop, Les."

"You treat me with contempt and then you call me in here before Mr. Lester and say I'm a liar and a whore. Go on, break away from him, Nick, I'm staying here until you do. You can't scare me any more, I don't care what you do to me, I don't care! Mr. Lester will you get out of here and leave the two of us alone? I'm Mrs. Allingham, I've got the right to talk to him. You get out—"

Something was happening to Nick. His head had fallen

337

limply on Lester's shoulder, his body was heaving in great wrenches, awful, deep-throated gutteral noises were breaking from him. Nick was crying and the tears were rolling down his cheeks. "Les—God's sake—make her stop—make her stop—"

Lester led the drooping, wrenching body to a chair and Nick fell into it, his hands covering his face.

At the door a small voice spoke flatly. "I'll go. But I'm not a liar nor a whore." The door opened and shut.

Lester stood behind Nick, a hand on his hunched shoulders. "You're a crazy fool, gob. You got a swell little wife and you don't know it."

Nick wrestled with the unmanly fit that had taken him. He got the sobs checked in a minute or two. His hands fell loose in his lap, his head hanging. In a shamed, leaden voice, he asked, "Tod, do you believe her?"

"I do, and you're a damned idiot if you don't. Look at the way that she stood up to you! Nick—she gave you what was coming to you."

Inert, head still hanging—"But you know Barton."

"All right, say he's on the make the way he always is, but he hasn't got her yet if I know anything."

"Think I made her so mad she'll run off to him now just to spite me?"

"Well, I wouldn't know that, Nick. You were pretty nasty."

"Did she go yet? Look and see."

Lester opened the door. "No, she's just going, she's picking up her things."

"Ask her to come back."

Lester raised his voice. "Miss Heaton, please—just a minute."

She came quickly, the fire still in her, and stood in the door, looking at Lester. The crumpled, unmoving figure in the chair spoke on in the same leaden voice. "Diana, I apologize for what I said."

She made a start to go. Lester put out a hand, detaining

338

her. "Make it up, will you? Can't you see how he feels? He's said he's sorry."

Nick went on. "Tod, tell her to quit going around with him, tell her it'll ruin her reputation. Tell her—I'll give her all the money she wants."

Diana broke from Lester's hand. Nick heard her running fast across the stage. Lester closed the door. "She heard you. You said everything right. Give her time to cool off." He went back to the huddled figure and gave Nick a hearty slap on the back. "Straighten up. Think you're the first man ever cried over a woman? Pull out of it."

Nick laid his arms on the shelf and put his head on them. "Yeah. Give me time, will you? I'll come to in a minute. Boy, this has got me."

Lester went out and shut the door. He called and the stage doorman came hurrying along the passage. Lester gave him a bill and told him what he wanted, and stayed outside the dressing room until the man came back and handed him a bottle and two glasses. Then he went back into the room. Nick had not moved. He set the glasses on the shelf and poured two drinks. "This is coming to us. You're a strong guy to tussle with, gob, you got me wore out. Well—old times—"

Nick jerked himself upright in the chair. He took the glass and drained it, and faced his friend, trying to grin. "Well, what do I look like with my eyes swollen? Pretty girl?"

"I'm partial. You look like a swell egg to me." Lester flopped into the chair beside him, offering his cigarettes.

Smoking, Nick sprawled back, eyes on the ceiling, his legs stretched out. "Never cried in my life that I can remember, and I took some awful wallopings from my old man when I was a kid. That girl can turn me inside out. You know, I been wrong in this. I kept away from her since rehearsals started, we'd had so much trouble I was scared what she could do to me, and I wanted to make the show good for you. So I let her stay on at her mother's. But it was up to me to look after her, Tod, she's only a kid, she doesn't know her way around yet. She wouldn't know what it meant to be seen with a guy like Barton. I'm to blame for this mess."

"Well, you apologized."

Nick got up and paced the room. "She didn't forgive me. She ran away." He stopped before Lester to confess, "Yeah, I apologized. But I only did it to be on the safe side. Honest, I don't know. Maybe she is going with him."

"Aw, gob—!"

"Tod, some things don't fit. That nude stuff. If you knew how shy she always was, scared of a man—no, I can't get it."

"Nick, she's your wife and you got to trust her." Lester moved to refill the glasses.

Nick checked him. "Thanks, no, not for me. I want to keep the brain as clear as I can, I'm not through yet." He slid back in the chair. "Tod, it's a good show, isn't it?"

The comedian reached under his chair to rap his knuckles against the wooden legs. "Swell. Riding pretty."

"Not much to stew over now, is there? Well, I'll do my best to stick with it, but I can't let this go. Maybe tomorrow you'll see me out there doing my stuff and maybe you'll be minus one director and one dancer. I'm going after her, Tod, I'm going out to her mother's house and get her. I got to have her with me."

Dismayed, Lester begged, "Why can't you wait for a while? She's sore on you now. You'll just be heading into more trouble. Wait."

"I can't. I'd go nuts not knowing where she was. Maybe I'm letting you down, Les, and you're the swellest guy in the world, but I got to do this."

"Well, if you got to." Seeing the pain in Nick's eyes, Lester entreated, "Don't go off half-cocked. Come out and have dinner with me first. You'll be steadier if you have food in your belly. You don't want to do anything crazy."

"Okay. But I'll walk out on you as soon as I've eaten."

Lester poured two drinks. "We'll have one to the show and that'll just set us right."

Nick poured half of his drink back into the bottle. "To the show—and you." They stood up to drink the toast.

"Gob, I wish you wouldn't do this thing. Don't go after her."

"Tod, I can't take this any longer. She's got to sleep in my bed tonight."

> " 'Out upon it, I have loved
> Three whole days together,
> And am like to love three more,
> If it prove fair weather.' "

Barton boomed the words, smiling across the dinner table at Diana, and waited hopefully for a response. But her young face, framed between the silver candelabra, stayed grave. Breeze from the open windows bent the flames and sent shadows shifting about the long room. He wanted to break in upon her reverie and win back companionship, but her silence reminded him of the wide gulf between them; he was old and stood in danger of youth's ready judgment. Love makes a fool of a man, time he learned that. His thunderous voice rollicked on. "It's more than three days, it's more than three weeks. 'If it prove fair weather'—Note that—it's conditional. And right now the sun is setting in a cloudy sky, it's coming on to rain. Even you, 'chaste and fair, goddess excellently bright,' can't make the sun shine forever."

She smiled absently, making him nervous. The Filipino slipped about the table, refilled the coffee cups and vanished in shadow.

Barton fidgeted with a spoon. "Have a nice time last night?"

"The play was good."

"And the club was no good. No fun sitting with an old man who can't dance. You don't get enough of dancing, you were dying to be up and at it with that band, I know. So we turn domestic and dine at home. You don't want to go out with me any more."

She was silent. The mellow light bent and danced, moving the shadow.

"Like me? I could learn tricks." He tossed the spoon and caught it. "Sit up and bark for favors." He swallowed the coffee in one draft, pushed the cup aside and bent forward, arms crossed on the table. "I think old Herrick was wrong in that poem. I'd like you if it poured cats and dogs. A penny for your thoughts."

She glanced across at him. "Not for sale."

He heaved up and rambled over to a window. The wind was rising, the boughs in the yards tossed. He pulled the window shut. "No. Not for sale. That's where you have me cringing. Ever hear that about it's being harder for a rich man to enter Heaven? True. My heaven is the Mohammedan one. Glory, they had it right! Lovely and adoring females!" He came back to the table to snuff a candle wick, flicking at it with his fingers. "Angels and harps!" he snorted. "Ever hear of such foolery? What do I want with harps? I'm no musician! Ah, but Diana, it's hard for me to enter my heaven —the females start to slaver at the mouth when they see me coming. The girls have got me so I put my hand in my pocket when I touch my hat." He went on flicking at the wicks. "I've been a fool about women all my life and I've paid my way, and maybe I'm a bigger fool than I ever was, but I think you're different, and by the Lord Harry, it's a big difference. I think you like me."

"I do. You've been nice." The need to shout reduced her to telegraphic brevity, but her smile was warm and kindly.

"You like me." He took his seat again. "But am I getting anywhere with you?"

She stood up. "Don't say that."

He was on his feet, speaking under compulsion, uncertain of result. "I want you. I want you here in my house all the time day and night for as long as I can keep you. I know you'll hit it up with some young rascal one of these days and I'll never see the swirl of your skirts again, but you haven't any beaux dancing attendance on you yet, and maybe I could make you happy for a time—"

"No." She walked away from the table, across the dim room and on into the next one.

Barton followed, bawling, "Don't go. What are you going for?"

"For good." She came into the hall where her things lay on the long polished table. "Yes, I like you, Hal. You've been nice and I haven't. I never told you I was married."

"Married? Well—where's your husband?"

"We're not—living together."

"Then—"

"No. I love him."

Putting on her hat, she saw his face in the mirror, saw that it was old and sad and filled with loss. She turned about and put up a hand, pulled down the grey curly head and kissed him on the cheek.

His smile came, boyish, charming. "That was a nice thing for you to do."

They were shaking hands, moving to the door.

"Good-by, Hal. And thank you—lots."

"You did like me." He said the words in triumph.

She nodded, smiling, and went out into the street.

He filled the door, shouting after her, "Come back anytime you change your mind!"

She waved farewell and went on, hurrying, seeing the menace of oncoming storm. Thunderheads reared high in tumult blotting out the fading sunset colors; below them a massy band of darker cloud rolled, wind-torn, advancing. The line squall struck the street and Diana clutched at her hat, dust in her face and the cool smell of rain. She went still faster, hoping to reach the subway before rain fell.

'A penny for your thoughts.' . . . Such gloomy thoughts.

. . . A proud, violent man broken down into woman's tears, humbled to apology. I did that to him, I stood and taunted him when he was held there, helpless; he'll never forgive me, I'll be always hateful in his eyes. And he could believe that I would lie to him, that I would be untrue.

It was all broken now, hope gone forever. And yet it didn't seem to matter what Nick said or did, her love for him lived on.

The rain came and Diana ran fleetly for the subway.

20

R OD PAUSED in his reading aloud to count the intervening seconds between the flash and the thunder. "My, it's very close."

Mrs. Heaton, lying in comfort on the sofa, cushions piled high behind head and shoulders, remarked absently, "Don't be a scared-cat, Rod, it's so silly. Go on."

Rod resumed his reading from Emerson's essay on *Compensation*. " 'Crime and punishment grow out of one stem. Punishment is a fruit that unsuspected ripens within the flower of the pleasure which concealed it. Cause and effect, means and end, seed and fruit, cannot be severed, for the effect already blossoms in the cause, the end pre-exists in the means. . . . ' "

His voice ran on, wavering when the stab of light plunged and the thunder cracked, and Mrs. Heaton let it run, unheeding, her thoughts upon her daughter. It had been well after three o'clock when Diana returned last night and that was hopeful; now again tonight the girl was off to spend another evening with him. Oh, there was no doubt Harold Barton was eager and in pursuit. But Diana! Such a moody, difficult girl, too dreamily astray in her own inner world, not shrewd. But beautiful; beautiful enough for any man to prize, and young. . . .

Young. A faint smile played about Mrs. Heaton's lips, thinking of that handsome doctor who had taken care of Rod. Sour grapes indeed—what did youth know of all the sportive play of love a woman knew? Could youth judge a man and draw him out and call the tune and make him dance? Diana thought her mother old, passé. Ah, if only

Diana could be taught to use her charms and make the most of them. Still, an older man might find naïveté attractive.

Into her reverie Bob's image came and lingered. How stupid to have dropped him. How stupid this whole attempt at a return to a Frostburgian past. It was Diana who had brought her mother into this backwash of a suburb and plumped her down to vegetate and mildew. What had she, Mrs. Heaton, in common with the dull-spirited stuffy old frumps seen in church and on the streets, a narrow-minded ignorant lot who held her in suspicion for no better reason that that she looked young and pretty still, attractive to a man. Bob. . . .

But no. Her concentration must remain upon Diana, her own life sacrificed to the girl's. Diana had proved she could not be trusted to run her own career.

Career. All at once Mrs. Heaton's spirit left the room; it was away up in the top balcony of the Metropolitan Opera House. The lights were dimming, the curtain was going up. A woman was coming out upon the stage to sing.

To sing. And high in the balcony a little old woman who was nobody at all sat and wept and knew her heart was broken. Because it could have been, it could have been. . . .

Rod's reading stopped. "What's that?"

The key was sounding in the lock.

Diana? At this hour? Mrs. Heaton came out of her dreams with an abrupt jolt. Something had gone wrong.

Diana looked in upon them. "Hello there! I'm simply drenched. Isn't this a dreadful storm? I'll have to change everything I've got on." She disappeared, going toward the bedroom.

Mrs. Heaton rose to follow. Surprised, Rod asked, "Don't you want me to finish this?"

"Read it to yourself. I read it all when I was young."

He was troubled by her going. "You'll stay in there and talk—"

"Goodness! Scared of storms at your age! Say your prayers

or play the piano—one child is enough to fret over at a time!"
She deserted him.

Diana had removed her dress and was pulling the rain-soaked slip over her head. Mrs. Heaton shut the door and listened at the crack, making certain Rod had not trailed her. "Well?" she demanded, her tone conspiratorial.

Diana hung the dress in the closet. She wished Sue would leave her to herself once in a while. To be followed about the house, questioned and advised incessantly, told what chair to sit in, what book to read, what dress to wear, what words to say, had become increasingly irritating; it was an aggravation to be so set upon by mother-love, so continually dominated. Tonight of all nights, Diana would have liked to be alone. But now, Sue probing, there was bound to be a scene, a bad one. Poor Sue, it was so childish of her to have let her expectations run so high, she would be wild with disappointment. Diana sighed, pulled herself together and smiled at her mother with compassion. "Sue dear, I've left him."

Mrs. Heaton was aghast. She advanced to the bedrail and clutched it for support. "Diana! You haven't left Hal Barton? Don't stand there smirking like a half-wit who doesn't know what she's mumbling! What on earth do you mean?"

The conciliatory smile abandoned, Diana sat down and began peeling off her stockings, saying simply, "I had to, Mother."

Mrs. Heaton drove distractedly about the room, not trusting herself to look at this maddening creature who went on so placidly changing her clothes as though nothing mattered but that. The woman came to a stop and forced herself to watch the girl with a rising fever of exasperation. "Why did you do it?"

Diana fetched her old shoes from the closet and stepped into them. "I'm sorry, dearest, it just didn't work out." She knelt before the bureau, taking a fresh slip from the drawer. "I had to leave him because tonight he said he wanted me to live with him."

347

Mrs. Heaton perched on the edge of the bed. "Did he ask you to marry him?"

"No."

"Did he offer you money?"

"No."

"Had you let him know you needed money?"

"No, dearest, I couldn't do that."

With each negative response the woman's fever rose. She thrust her fingers into her hair and pulled at the roots. "Diana, how can you tell me these things *placidly?* Don't, I can't endure it. Will you tell me what in heaven's name you did get out of him?"

"Get out of him?" Diana frowned. "Why, it was a decent human relationship."

That sent Mrs. Heaton plunging head down into a pillow, her teeth grinding. But she emerged in a moment, unbeaten, and took charge. "Stop moving around, distracting me." She was up, pushing the girl, still only in her slip, into the armchair. She stood over her, going after the facts. "Is Barton in love with you?"

Diana answered mildly. "Dearest, what difference does that make now?"

"Have you slept with him?"

It was certainly provoking to be attacked with such insulting questions, first Nick, now Sue. But you wouldn't expect Sue to be anything but excitable. Patiently, Diana answered, "No, dearest, I have not."

"Did you leave him or did he kick you out?"

The girl flushed. "I left him."

"And he didn't want you to go?"

"Now Sue—"

"Did he or didn't he?"

"No, he didn't. What difference—"

"Well! There's still hope then!" Mrs. Heaton dragged a chair close and sat down in front of her daughter, trapping her in the chair. "Diana Heaton, I will not let you throw away your future. This means too much to your career. You must go back to him."

"Go back? No—you don't understand. He wants to sleep with me."

Mrs. Heaton tossed her head. "I understand well enough. After all you've done, is *this* the time to turn pernickety?" She bent closer with a fierce whisper. "Diana, do you yet realize who Barton is? Do you realize he's a millionaire several times over? Don't you know that he can make you famous?"

The girl recoiled from her, shrinking deeper into the chair. This willful greedy face with the hard bright eyes, this evil whispering, this was not Mother or Mother had gone mad. She answered slowly, "Mother, I'm not a prostitute."

Mrs. Heaton's cheeks flamed as though they had been slapped but she made no withdrawing move and her eyes grew brighter, harder. "You're not an artist either if you can speak like that. You don't need to use dirty words. I'm your mother and I'm telling you what you must do for your own good. This is your chance. You shall go back to him."

It was true, Sue meant it. Something large and fundamental in the background of Diana's thought crumbled and fell, sending up a whirling, thundering debris in which ideas leapt and crossed chaotically. That the thought of Barton's money had acted as a stimulant to Sue's ambition had been plain enough; Diana knew why Sue had dressed her up and urged her to go out with him; but that Sue's ambition could conceivably go to this length had never even crossed her mind. She had long since come to believe that Sue, like herself, looked back on the Mowbray business with remorse; she had taken Sue's apparent reformation, with all her counseling to leave men alone, as indication of sincere repentance. Now Nick's prophecy shot into mind, 'she sold you before, she'll sell you again.' Love for her mother sprang up in contention— this demented creature was not Sue. Diana tried to reach past the fixed, evil mask and speak to Sue, to summon her. "Long ago—you came out of the woods with Chris. You told me love was beautiful and natural."

349

Mrs. Heaton hissed at her. "We're not talking about love, you little booby, we're talking about your career!"

Diana closed her eyes, insisting, "Mother, you know it isn't right to go with a man you don't love just to get money out of him. You know that."

Mrs. Heaton's temper worked free. "You pick a queer time to prate of right and wrong!" She was up and swirling about the room. "God in hell, that I should breed such a commonplace, dull-witted little fool! 'Right and wrong!'—leave that to mediocrity! What of the famous women who have come to power, who have been raised by kings to stand behind a throne and rule it? Did they cower before a conscience?"

Diana had risen also. "Stop it, Mother. This isn't you that's talking! You don't mean what you're saying. You're asking me to sell myself—to go through what I went through before."

"Is there water in your blood? How can you hope to be an artist? The first essential of an artist is freedom—freedom that despises all convention. You're a fool!"

"Artists are fools, fools and dreamers pursuing an ideal, true to it, creating a world that's noble, beautiful—"

"Bah! How far do they get with that alone? Mozart lies in a pauper's grave and Poe starved in a garret! Is *that* what you want?"

"Don't, don't be Shakespearian!"

"Well, *he* said it—'conscience makes cowards of us all.' To win fame and recognition you must have money, power. How many of the great have bought their way to fame?"

Diana writhed in protest. Mother—this was not Mother. "If I tell you that to sell myself to Barton would be torture and degredation would you ask it still?"

Mrs. Heaton wound her arms about her head in the extreme of exasperation. "Do you think that all I care about is your having a good time? What do I care about your wanton pleasures with a man? You think if you go crazy about some young nobody that makes it right? Can't you understand that this is your career, that I want you to *be* somebody, you chicken-livered little moron?"

350

Diana sang out one last appeal, calling to the deep self of that lost woman. "Mother, Mother, don't you love me?"

Mrs. Heaton caught the bedrail in both hands, swaying in her wrath. "No!" she screamed, "not what you've become! I loved what I thought you were, what I thought you would be! I loved the baby in my arms, flesh of my flesh that I placed hope in! I loved the little girl that held such promise! I loved the smart, beautiful young woman I thought would be a winner! But you're not my daughter any more, you're not the girl I made and loved, you've destroyed her! Love you? You're an utter fool, dull and stupid and without ambition! No, I don't love you, I hate you, I hate you!"

Hate flowed from the bright, wild eyes and from the thin colorless lips, hate filled the room and all the force of evil gathered in it. Realization of complete severance and its large pain transfixed Diana. Sue stood there, demented in her suffering, and it was not possible to reach to her by any honest word of love or pity; nothing could ease, could break through, that wild, stray, angry grief that was so foolish, so pitiable, so demolishing. Sue had escaped, no tie remained to draw her back, she was beyond recalling.

The urge to get away, escape out of this evil, seized Diana. She moved swiftly to the closet for a dress. Rod was knocking on the door. Neither of them heeded that. Mrs. Heaton followed on her daughter's heels. "You shall obey me."

Diana gave no answer. Wriggling into the first dress that came to hand, she stepped around her mother, heading for her hat upon the bureau. Rod, still knocking, implored, "Mother, Mother!" Mrs. Heaton moved beside her daughter. "You shall do as I say!"

Rod broke in, his small face livid, agonized. "You mustn't quarrel so! You mustn't say such awful things! Diana, don't make Mother angry!"

Diana picked up her hat from the bureau and then Mrs. Heaton knew—the girl was going from her. She screamed, "You shan't! You shan't leave me!" She went between Diana and the door. "Where are you going?"

"To the man I love and you can't stop me, to Nick Allingham—if he'll have me."

Mrs. Heaton was beside herself with rage at the shock. Nick—and she had thought him long forgotten—while all the time—this devil of a daughter—"He shan't have you, never, never, I'll never let you go—I'll follow you—no—you can't do this to me. Rod—Rod—don't let her go—she's going to a man—"

But Rod was in a corner praying, his face screwed up, his head shaking. "Merciful God, stop them, stop them. Blessed Jesus—"

"You can't prevent me, Sue. He's my husband. Let me by."

"*Husband?* No—never, never, you're mine!"

"Jesus, show mercy to us—"

Diana ducked and feinted, trying to get by the mad creature holding the door.

Mrs. Heaton's voice rose high. "Don't let her go, Rod! Don't let her get away! Tear the clothes off her!"

But Rod had gone down on his knees. "Mighty God, save us—"

Mrs. Heaton clawed at Diana's dress and tore it open from top to bottom. "You shan't leave your mother—you'll have to trample my dead body—ah, ah, ah, and all I want in life is your success!"

Diana made a dart. Mrs. Heaton shrieked, whipping up a fist and striking out. Diana ducked and the blow went over her head, carrying away her hat. She was out of the room, fleeing along the hall. After her came a whirlwind of scuffling movement and outcry, Rod's arms about the woman, dragged along by her furious energy. "Let me go. I'll kill her."

"Mother, Mother, in the name of Christ—"

Diana whipped out the door, sped down the stairs, went speeding along silent, night-darkened, rain-swept streets. Blocks from the house she pulled up, gasping for breath, the panic of her flight spent. Without a hat, without a purse, her dress torn open, she leaned against the wall of a building, alone on the deserted street, rain pelting in her face. The moments went by as she stood, gaining breath.

Out of the past, a lovely woman dressed in white, dazzling against blue summer sky, her copper hair aglint in sunlight, came strolling down a country lane, singing for the angels. . . .

She's dead. Dead a long, long time. . . . Was it Chris that killed her, was it drinking, was it Mowbray, or was it that she never did the thing that she was meant to do; was that death inside of her from the time she gave up singing, always eating her away. . . . She was good and she was beautiful. I loved her. And she's dead.

Diana walked slowly on in the clean driving rain.

Nick told the taxi man to wait and skipped across the pavement to the door, ducking in from the heavy rain. Tod had kept him longer than he liked and this search might go on. If Diana were not here. . . .

He meant to keep his head. He knew he must. Danger was alive and working in him, suspicion an enduring pressure that could not be shaken off; that force could sweep him headlong back into blind fury once his grip on self-control went slack. He did not mean to ease his grip for half a second, control kept uppermost in mind. Only, it would have been better if he could have done what Tod said, let it ride, wait. But that he could not do. It was an added suffering to feel that at a time when everything depended on a cool, clear head, he should be afflicted with stupidity; it seemed to him his thought was slow and fumbling while his body wanted to move fast and strong, and ugly images could flash across his mind with lightning speed. He tried to take shelter in the protection of that wise, hard-boiled personality which had served him well, knocking about the world—until Diana came along; he tried to say 'So what,' knowing that along Broadway a man bowled over by his wife's unfaithfulness would stand out as a sap, a butt for ridicule; fidelity was more unusual than infidelity, and a wise guy—But it wouldn't go. Realistic as he had schooled himself to be in all his thinking, balanced by an accurate perception of the life that went on around him, such thinking would not fit Diana. He simply could not believe that she would be untrue to him. Neither could he believe that she would stand naked before a man. Yet that was fact, admitted by herself.

He came up the stairs and rang the bell. There was no answer. But he had seen lights in the windows. He rang again —again.

A slight youth with a shock of bright red hair and a pale frightened face opened the door—Rod. Nick nodded and pushed past him into the hall. Then he saw the woman seated in the living room. He saw her eyes first, bright, gleaming eyes in a set, vicious face. Somehow she did not fit in with the quiet, old-fashioned elegance of the furnishings. No money? They might have tried to sell that mahogany table before trying to sell Diana. An open whiskey bottle, large size, stood on the table; Mrs. Heaton had a glass in her hand. What was this talk about having stopped drinking? Had Diana lied about that?

He advanced into the room. "Good evening, Mrs. Heaton."

She went on eyeing him in silent, intense enmity. Then slowly, deliberately, she changed in posture and expression, shifting smoothly into a gracious, cruel satisfaction. "Good evening, Mr. Allingham."

Rod hung by the door, apart from them.

Nick spoke quietly, watching the fox eyes. "Diana is my wife, Mrs. Heaton. I've come to get her."

"My daughter, fortunately, is not here."

"May I make sure of that?"

"Certainly. Roddy, show the gentleman—" she stressed the word with subtle nastiness "—through the apartment. He will want to look in all the closets and under all the beds."

Nick followed the speechless, frightened youth from room to room; a home, pleasantly, tastefully furnished. What cruelty could these walls tell of; what tyranny, what brutal subjugation could go on within a home. He came back to

Mrs. Heaton with Diana's hat in his hand. "She has been here. She was wearing this today."

"And she has gone out again." Mrs. Heaton had lit a cigarette and was smoking with relish. "She dresses to go out in the evenings." The woman blew smoke toward the ceiling. "Did you look to see if her nightgown was in the house?"

Nick spoke slowly, steadily. "Where is Diana, Mrs. Heaton?"

"Mr. Allingham, why are you hunting for your wife?"

"I'm asking where she is."

"Don't you know?"

"Would you care to tell me?"

Mrs. Heaton flicked ashes toward a tray. "Really, it's not the sort of thing one cares to tell a husband."

He stood in the center of the room, Diana's hat still in his hand. His manner was even more suave, more courteous than when he had entered. "You're having fun with me, Mrs. Heaton. You may. I'm here to find out where my wife is. Do you know?"

She nodded and went on nodding gleefully. Nick turned to the unhappy youth hovering in the corner. "Maybe you'd better leave us alone."

Rod slid quickly away. Mrs. Heaton took no notice of his going. Nick studied the woman. Drunk or sober? He could not tell and perhaps it did not matter; even a crazy woman might speak the truth. "Where is Diana?"

"She's with Mr. Harold Barton."

"Now?"

"Now and for some time past. I wonder that you didn't know."

"Did she go to him tonight?"

Mrs. Heaton refilled her glass with a steady hand. "She goes to him every night. Tonight was no exception."

"I think you're lying, Mrs. Heaton."

The malice of her smile grew gay. "You *think*—but you don't know, do you? Well, here you are, seeking your wife, ringing people's doorbells and looking under beds! Mr. All-

355

ingham, what did you have to offer my daughter? Mr. Barton can give her a fortune."

Nick shook his head at her as he would have with a child. "Barton's a poor catch, you wouldn't get your price. He got stung once. He's not handing out millions any more."

That angered her. Temper spotted her cheeks and brought the viciousness back into her face. "What a fool you are! Barton is in love with Diana!"

Love? He had thought of Barton as a Broadway type, willing enough to spend freely for his pleasure but too much of a rounder to get tangled in love for any girl. But Diana would be something new to a man of Barton's type, and if it was love. . . . She would be more amenable to wooing than to a money proposition. He tossed her hat away from him, saw it light on the sofa, slide to the floor; he did not pick it up. He looked back at Mrs. Heaton. "Is Diana Barton's mistress?"

The taunting smile came back. The woman nodded and again her nod continued, the affirmation repeated with satisfaction.

Softly, almost to himself, Nick said, "You're so false I wouldn't know what you looked like if you told the truth. And you're getting one hell of a kick out of handing me that line. I'd like to know why."

Mrs. Heaton swung one leg across the other and dangled it back and forth. "I've always hated you. I'm glad some other man has her, a man who can do something for her."

Nick turned to go away.

"Surely you're not hunting further?" Mrs. Heaton asked sweetly, "Surely you don't want to be her fancy man on Mr. Barton's money? Oh, I forgot—you don't mind having a woman another man has had. There was Mr. Mowbray, of course, and you knew about that. Cuckold!"

He swore beneath his breath and wheeled around and stood baffled by those tricky yellow eyes. If he could catch her lying. . . . "Mrs. Heaton, would you say Diana is Barton's mistress if I told you I might kill her if I believed you?"

The woman sprang up, agile with hate. "You wouldn't dare!"

Nick insisted, *"Is* she his mistress?"

The question fuddled her; she was uncertain how to answer. She became cunning. "And if I say no?"

"For Christ's sake, tell the truth for once in your life. You know whether she is or not, don't you?"

Mrs. Heaton was trying hard to think. "Yes, I know."

"Well, *is* she?"

The woman bit on her lip, hesitating.

"Is she Barton's mistress?"

"Yes."

"Now you're lying. Why should you want harm to come to her if she's doing what you want?"

Confused, Mrs. Heaton broke out in the petulance of a bad-tempered child. "Who says she's doing what I want! She's a stupid little fool who'll throw herself away for pennies when a fortune might be hers!"

Nick took a step back, sickened. Pennies. . . . That fitted in with Barton's spending, with Diana's unworldliness; it explained the woman's hatred for her daughter. Then it might be true. . . . It seemed as though it might be true. . . .

He found himself outside in the hall and going downstairs at a fast clip. He awoke with alarm to the realization that he had left the apartment without knowing it. Slow, Nicky, go slow. Think what you're doing, think. Remember—you *don't* know. And if it's true, if it's true—

He stopped on the stair. Yeah, if it's true. You take it then, that's all, you take it. You have no right to harm Diana no matter what she does. Just—don't touch her, don't put your hands on her. Sure you might—you know damn well you might—and you're not going to. Keep your head, Nicky.

But Mrs. Heaton had not made it any easier. The hot darkness swept across his mind in waves. He went on slowly, descending the stairs, his hand on the rail, checking hurry. He had to go on, though. And the next stop was Barton's house.

21

DIANA HAD ASKED one of the gatemen at the ferry house if he would lend her a quarter. That had paid her way on the ferry, the subway, the bus. And finally she had come to a big house and asked admission there. Rain-bedraggled, hatless, in shabby shoes, holding the torn dress about her as best she could, she had presented herself to that exquisitely groomed woman who wore blond-grey hair plaited around her head like a crown.

Nick's mother had made her welcome with a warmth, a perfect courtesy that was as soothing as balm; Diana had been accepted with affection. She had known the comfort of a warm bath, of having a maid dry and brush her hair, she had been given a fabulous, gossamer nightgown and a long robe of ivory satin, and she had sat talking with the woman in a high-ceilinged bedroom, all white and gold and gilt and crystals, with heavy drapes of red brocade about the bed and windows, while now and again Nick's mother rose and tried to reach her son by telephone. But there had been no answer and at last the woman kissed her cheek and said good night and went away.

Diana had gone to Nick's door and knocked and waited; now, late as it was, he still could not be reached. Had she been wrong in coming here? He might not ever come to claim her. Did he love her? Did he hate her? Was it only pride that made him care what happened to her?

She turned out the lights and walked to the window that looked down on Central Park. The storm had gone by; a full moon showed between drifting clouds. How magical the still trees, the glitter of a pond, a mound of earth heaving up to form a hill above lesser hills; how sweet would be the smell there after rain. . . . Walking in peace through a dark, silent grove, a bough disturbed would spill rain spatter still upon the leaves. She looked southward where above the city towers the glow of lights lit up the clouds, brightest over Broadway, her world and Nick's. What was he doing in that world now, where was he, was his thought on her?

She left the window, crossed moonlight lying on the floor, took off the robe and laid it on the chair beside the bed. It was good to lie down between fresh, cool sheets, to invite sleep's erasure of heartache.

Diana came out of sleep feeling that she had been summoned. Eyes opening, she recognized the strange room and remembered how she came to be there. A Fifth Avenue bus groaned by in the street below; the house was still, moonlight had shifted along the floor. There was no sound or stir and yet she felt a presence in the room. Had someone said her name? The feeling grew upon her so that she sat up and looked around.

Nick!

He sat in shadow, silent, his long body sprawled in the chair between her and the door, his eyes upon her. He made no move and gave no greeting and she did not know what force was in the room, what violence of love or hate. It was enough that he had come; she pressed the pillows up behind her, resigned to wait for whatever he had brought, knowing a dreamlike peace in the fact of his presence.

"Were you in Barton's house tonight?"

It was hate; the hard voice told of anger held; the demand gave indication of another siege of questioning. What had brought him into this quiet room at night if he felt only hate! Still, he had come to her; if through any patience on her part. . . . "Yes, Nick, I was there."

"Did you tell him to leave town?"

"Leave town? No, I didn't know he had."

"Might be a smart idea to tip him off to duck right now, mightn't it, with a husband on the loose who might get an idea to hunt him up? What took you to his house tonight after I told you to stop going with him?"

"We had made an appointment for dinner. I kept it, then I left. I told him I wasn't coming back." So Nick had been to Barton's house. . . . Diana was glad he had not found Hal, that there had been no ugliness between them. But why had he gone? Nick's apology in the dressing room had made her believe that his suspicion ended there; she could not understand the hostile energy within him now. Was it lasting anger because she had been seen with Barton, because she had posed?

"Come here."

So cold, so harsh; an order spoken as to a dog. No man should speak so to a woman; not to his wife. She hesitated, considering protest, and then fell back on patience, hoping this wrong spell would pass, that he would grow gentle, be himself. Certainly a man was a strange being. She pushed back the covers and stepped out of bed, going without fear toward that unmoving enemy presence, waiting in the shadow. But a few steps forward brought her into moonlight and she stopped, drew back, aware the filmy nightgown was no covering and that he looked at her.

"Why don't you come to me?"

"Yes—in a minute—" She reached for the robe beside the bed.

"Why should you cover yourself before me?"

This was too much; it made her angry with him. "You needn't think that posing makes a person shameless! If you can't see the difference between doing a job that has to be done and—and—" She could not find the sleeve of the robe.

"Between getting paid for it and not getting paid."

The robe half on, she paused, unhappiness welling up so big there was no place for anger. "Why must you be unkind?"

"Isn't it a queer thing if Hal Barton can look at you and your husband can't, even with a nightgown on?"

She was slow in tying the belt about her waist. "Nick, my mother's income stopped when Granpa died. We owed money, no one would give us credit. Rod wasn't working and then he fell ill. We had no money for food. I didn't think you'd like me to do that, I didn't want to do it myself, it was awfully hard to do. But I couldn't think of any other way to earn money."

"Why didn't you tell me this before?"

"Have you forgotten that you wouldn't let me speak to you? Why wouldn't you, Nick?"

"Have you forgotten that I told you to come here?"

Unjust, unreasonable, unkind; how could he be so hateful! Diana went toward him, weary with unhappiness. As she approached, he came quickly up on his feet, tall, straight and tense. She stopped short with a quick-drawn audible breath; he wore a dressing gown.

"So. I'm still the toad you shrink from. I'm supposed to come into my wife's bedroom dressed for the street or she'll faint in fright. Ever see Barton in a dressing gown? I saw one in his studio tonight, bright purple, in the room where you took your clothes off."

Her voice shaking, Diana begged softly, "Don't, Nicky, don't be like this."

There was no relenting in him. Strange to her, the slim monk-like figure stood silent, all enemy, and she began to be afraid, cold creeping in to press upon her heart and suddenly she wished that she were not alone with him in this dark room in the strange big silent house. She put out her hand to him as she had done before when she had need of his kindness and did not know what words to say. But though she held her hand, waiting, he did not take it. Her hand dropped; she was more hurt by this rejection than by his insults, and the cold gripped tighter on her heart.

He moved from her, going into moonlight, coming to a stop beside the bed. "Come over here."

Fear leapt higher, all possessive; she thought her knees would let her down, that she must sink into oblivion.

"I want to see your face. Come where it's bright."

Relief gave her strength to move, to go toward him. But all that was going on was nightmare, the hope of love ebbing. She came within three feet and stopped.

He took a step closer, his eyes fixed on her upturned, moonlit face. "Diana, tell me the truth." His words came with a slow, labored effort, all the force of the man behind them. "Don't be afraid of me. I won't harm you if you'll only speak the truth, whatever that may be. Lie now and you'll destroy us both." He paused, gathering fresh energy. "Don't try any tricks for God's sake or you'll get me so muddled I won't know what I'm doing. Make it clean and straight." He had to pause again. "Were you Barton's mistress?"

She gazed up at the dark face, stunned. That he could still think. . . . After he had apologized for thinking. . . . Oh, what did anything matter now! "Why Nick, I told you this afternoon—"

He cut across her words warning, "Go slow, kid, and get it right. Your mother told me that you were."

Diana gasped. "My mother? Why—why that's not possible! My mother told you that?"

"Your mother told me tonight that you were Barton's mistress."

Diana fell back against the end of the bed. "That's not my mother, Nick, that's a fiend who's taken her shape. That she could tell you that. . . . Well, you'll believe her, won't you? You said she could make black so white it would shine in the dark, and that's true, everything you said about her was the truth. My grandfather believed her, you will too. What mother would make up such a lie about her daughter!"

The hard level voice drove at her. "I'm waiting to hear you tell me it's a lie."

Diana turned from him in a whirl, winding her arms about the bedpost. Grief rose so strong that she was free of fear, despising it. "Then go ahead and wait for I shan't say it! Why should I have to tell you twice that I am innocent? Why must I go on protesting when you won't believe what I've told you? What could I say to drive this idea out of your head? I have no proof to offer you—only my word, and that's not good enough for you! You want to believe this thing—and she's helped you to, she's cleverer than I am, she can beat me—

she's done it now!" Diana faced about, her back against the post, her head flung up. The vibrancy in her voice increased, her words came faster. "Oh Nick, what's the use, what's the use! No—it doesn't matter any more—the ones I loved all came to hate me—Mother, Granpa, you—You don't need to make me any bargains to get the truth! I don't want to live. How could I live, how could I dance, if there was only hate and no love anywhere? Go ahead and do whatever you want to do to me, I shan't beg for your belief! Believe what you choose—believe I slept with Barton, believe he paid me for it, I don't care, I'm as innocent as the day I met you and I love you but it's no good now and I'm sick to death of being questioned. You want to kill me, that's what you came in here to do. Go ahead and get it over with, I shan't fight back, I want to die. Go ahead—I'll make it easy for you—I'll say the words you want to hear, I'll keep on saying them—I was Barton's mistress, I was Barton's mis—"

"Stop it, kid. I can't stand it. You said enough. Forgive me if you can."

There was silence in the room. Nick said again, "Forgive me, Diana. Please forgive me."

He waited until it seemed that she would never speak to him, and then, low-voiced, she asked, "You believe me?"

His reply was quick. "I believe you. You said enough."

Again silence came between the two unmoving figures and then Diana was speaking steadily in the low voice. "No, maybe I haven't said enough. Forgiving you won't make things right between us because there's no equality. You claim the right to ask questions but you don't feel obliged to answer any. When I asked you why you wouldn't let me talk to you you passed up the answer. You ask to be forgiven now. But you asked that this afternoon. Why did you apologize then if you didn't mean it? Was that honest? But you expect honesty of me. How do I know when you'll throw Mr. Barton in my face again and start in with a fresh set of questions? And you're very rude to me sometimes. Oh Nick, you've no right to treat me this way! You treat me like a child. Maybe that's all I am, maybe I do make mistakes, but I'm your wife and you ought to respect me."

"I rate the call down. I'm glad you gave it to me. You've got as much right to ask questions as I have. I didn't let you talk to me because you could get me so messed up I couldn't do my job. Apologizing this afternoon was a lie. I was scared to lose you, that's all I can say about that. I've been wrong about a lot of things, all the nasty talk and the bad temper. But look here, Diana, you've put me through a lot of hell and if you hadn't been a child you'd know it. One thing you're wrong on—I didn't come in here meaning to do you any harm. I had my mind made up I wouldn't touch you—that's why I wouldn't even take your hand. I've been through this thing before with you. Today wasn't the only time I wanted to kill you. You've got me so I know I have to watch myself, and I've got sense enough to know that I've no right to harm you, no matter what you do. I've been fighting this thing for hours, and if you had come out straight and said you'd been with Barton I meant to walk right out that door, and God willing, I think I could have done it. About my treating you like a child, well Diana, I'm a man and I've knocked around a lot. I've had more experience than you've had, all kinds of experience, and I'm a good bit older than you. But if I act bossy I'm only trying to get things straightened out so you'll be happy and that'll make me happy too. But don't forget, there were times when I gave in to you and it only messed things up worse. Once we get set there won't be any bossing, there won't have to be. It was your mother got you twisted. A mind like hers would get anybody twisted. But you can see things clear enough when you get away from her, and you've grown up a lot, Diana, just recently; it shows in your work, it shows in everything you do. You're not a child any more and I'm not going to treat you like one. About respecting you, God knows I do, and for all the wild, nasty things I've said and done to you I'm sorry, sorry enough to try hard to keep from doing them again. I mean it when I ask you to forgive me."

Happiness was stealing back; it had come within reach.

Diana told him promptly, "I'll forgive you if you forgive me. Oh—that does sound like a child, doesn't it?"

"It sounds all right to me."

She tried to make out his face, not understanding why his tone remained grave, unchanged. Why was joy lacking now? Why did he not put out his arms, give her his love? "Nick— you *know* I wasn't Barton's mistress?"

"I know it."

She waited, wondering what was wrong, why he stayed somber. "But—you don't love me the way you used to?"

"I do love you. More than I ever did."

"Then . . . why are you so strange?"

She saw his hand go into the pocket of his robe, take out something. He picked up her hand. She felt the ring being slipped on her finger.

"Diana, the way things are we're all mixed up. We're married and we're not married. I've got to break a promise that I made to you. I told you that I'd wait until you said you wanted me. Kid, I can't hold to that, don't ask me to. Maybe I'm acting bossy now but maybe I know better than you do what's right for both of us. You've got to let me be your husband now."

After a still moment with no life in it, Nick waiting, getting no response, he took a step closer and his hands went to her belt, became active there, untying it. That movement informed her; he was resolved; resistance would be a futile, ugly thing. She stood frozen, knowing it was right that he should have his way, but knowing that it should be Nick, tender, loverly, and not this grave, gloomy man. Her heart sank lower and lower and her fright deepened. Making no opposing move, she begged in a whisper, "Don't Nicky. Wait. Please wait."

He remained the stranger, not unkind, but distant, somber. "Don't make a fool of me, Diana. I've waited long enough. I meant it when I said I'm not going to treat you like a child any longer. You called yourself my wife a minute ago, didn't you? This is no disrespect to you."

The knot had come untied. The robe was drawn away and tossed upon the bed. Nick stood looking into her upturned face and the long moments went by. Then with a spin he had gone from her, far over by the mantlepiece, his arms flung out along it, his head buried in his arms. "I can't. You're only submitting to me. You're scared to death of me." He broke out in sorrowful passion, "Oh Diana kid, why can't you want me when I want you so! What have I done to make you dread me! No woman ever shrank from me but you!"

Her heart leaped up at this return; this was not the cold stranger, this was Nick. Her voice small and shaky, she asserted, "I do want you."

"You don't, you don't, you're sick with fear—you're shaking like a little animal that knows it's going to be killed! Oh, loving you makes a mess out of me! Why do I have to care, why can't I do what any other man would do, why do I have to love you so! Oh damn you, kid, why do you do this to me!"

Diana's voice had sunk to the barest whisper. "Nicky, I said I wanted you. Don't shame me now. You can't deny me. I want my husband."

He seemed to listen to that whisper long after it had died. He came away from the mantlepiece, drifting, stopped. The moonlight caught his face and showed the longing and the incredulity. "What are you saying, kid? Do you know what you're saying?"

She loved him; the love grew big, full of tenderness; he must not suffer. "Yes, I do. All right, I'm scared—forgive me, I can't help it. But that doesn't mean. . . . Oh Nicky, take me in your arms and kiss me and tell me that you love me and help me to be your wife!"

"Diana! Do you want that?"

"Nicky—please—I do."

He came toward her, holding out his arms.

She went swiftly to meet him.

He was wakened out of sleep, hearing Diana gasping in

terror. "Nick—Nick—put on the lights—put on the lights—"

His hand flew to the switch over the bed. The room lit up. Diana lay on her back, rigid, eyes glazed with fear. "Is she in the room, Nick, is she in the room?"

"Honey, no one's in the room but the two of us. Wake up, you're having a nightmare." He bent over, kissing her cheek.

Diana clutched at him, awake and still in terror. "My mother came in that door. I saw her. She came here to the bed. She lay down between us. I couldn't reach you. I was dying, I was turning cold."

"There, sweetheart, you're dreaming—" Nick ran his hand along her arm. The flesh was icy. He felt her other arm; it was warm. One side of her was warm, the other was like ice.

"She lay against me. She was cold. I was turning cold. It was death."

"Honey, you've got a wonderful imagination, even in your sleep." Nick smiled, stroking her, soothing her, drawing her close. "Know what? We'll have to get the habit of you sleeping tight in my arms—like this, see? Then no bad dreams can come sneaking in between us."

She clung to him, her fear slowly dying down. "Nick, you're *sure* she isn't in the room?"

"Sweetheart, I locked that door when I came in. It's a funny habit I picked up as a kid, sleeping all sorts of places."

Her head buried in his neck, she told him with a sob, "Oh Nicky darling, I'm afraid of her!"

He turned her face up to his searching, worried eyes. "Diana, this doesn't mean you're sorry that you left her?"

"No, I'm not sorry, I couldn't go back, never, even if it wasn't for you! But she said she'd follow me, she said she'd haunt me, she said she wouldn't let you have me. There's a devil in her."

"Don't go medieval on me, sugar." He kissed her lips and smiled a rich rejoicing. "I got you now."

She came slowly into his joy and was a part of it. They gazed at each other, dazzled, silent in marvel. Then, out of sheer happiness, Diana laughed softly. "Darling! I'm sorry that I woke you up."

"Are you? I'm not."

"No—I'm not either. Put out the lights."

"Say, who's giving the orders?" He reached up to the switch; dark night filled the room, the moon gone down. "Any more orders?"

"Yes. Kiss me."

"Oh, now! Think I need to be told?"

They woke early and had breakfast from a tray brought up to their room and placed upon a table beside the open window. Finished, they idled in content, luxuriating in the grant of time before the intense activity of the day claimed them. Nick lay in his chair, his back against one arm, both legs swung up over the other. Across from him Diana was curled up, legs tucked under her, the folds of ivory satin spilling to the floor. Joy was in her, she contained it; it seemed to shine from her with a clear, steady light. Nick thought that to lie there looking at her, the way she was now, was to have the best that life could offer. To give her rapture, to share in it. . . .

"Nicky, I feel as though music were playing and it would go on and on. Is it the music in you? Will you work it out so I can dance to it? Oh, I'm so glad that I'm a solo dancer now! I shall make up dance after dance and I'll put into them all the things I never can say. Shultz will give me more to do in the next show, won't he? Perhaps two solos, or a long ballet. I want to work out something splendid, something big. I never felt I had so much to give before."

In her outspoken joy he saw again that unguarded quality in her, a kind of innocence, an eager and unwary zest that soared out of idealism, an unworldly thing, beautiful to see; and yet, as always, he was troubled by it, knowing a twinge of apprehension for her. It wasn't that she lacked strength to surmount the odds that came against her, it was that she could not foresee them, and so each trouble that arose brought fresh pain.

He reached out to the tray and helped himself to a cigarette. "Sweetheart, you're so full of dreams and decency I wonder if you have any idea how hard an adventure you set out on when you picked the theater to work in."

"I don't mind if it's hard. I love it so."

"You're feeling good about having a solo, and you've got a right to feel good about it, it's not beginner's luck with you, you've worked to get where you are. But it's only in the success stories that making good on one job sets you pretty for the rest of your life. From now on you'll have to fight to keep your place and fight harder to get a better one. Luck might be with you, but you can't count on that. You might be in for ups and downs for some time before your name sticks with the public."

Lightheartedly, she asked, "Trying to scare me?"

"Doing my best. You know, honey, a lot your poor crazy mother has been trying to stuff in your head is slick stuff, judged by what passes for success. You'd have to be blind not to see how many successes have been bought. But there's no recipe for success. As many people fail by trying to play smart and dirty as by sticking to the decent rules, and I hate to think of all the pretty kids who have it in their heads that the road to success is paved with mattresses. Sure, there's a mattress route, but to win that way you've got to be just naturally a rat who won't stop short at anything. The rats get there, don't think they don't, but there's a lot like you who can't compete. You haven't got the thick skin and the cunning and the lack of conscience."

Grown serious, she answered, "I'm glad I think you're right. No, I'm not what my mother would call a clever woman. But Nicky, you don't mean that only rats succeed?"

"No, I don't. I said there was no recipe. But you're going to run into some pretty slick rats and sometime a job that you're in line for may go to one of them. Don't let it throw

369

you if it happens. Keep plugging and take the disappointments as expected and you'll come through. There now, did I make the way seem long and hard?"

Diana shook her head. "I won't mind if I do hit the ups and downs. I'll keep plugging."

"Yeah, I think you will."

Their eyes met, the look held and a smile grew out of it. A subtle movement ran through Diana's body and she was murmuring, "Darling, darling, did I tell you that I love you?"

"That's something you have to keep on telling me." He craned his neck to see the clock on the mantle. "Oh, lots of time! Nice to dawdle, isn't it? We won't have much time for that the next two days. At that, we better hang out here until the show opens, then we can hunt up a pumpkin shell of our own."

"Don't. I hate that song. Besides—it's not applicable. 'Peter' has his wife."

"And he means to keep her."

Breeze stirred in, sweet with the smell of morning. She glanced out, seeing how fine a summer's day it was and then, recalling last night's storm, broke out in sudden dismay, "How am I going to the theater? My dress—it's torn. I can't be seen in that!"

"My mother has an eye for detail, sugar. I bet she's been on the wires since the stores opened, ordering special deliveries for you, and I hate to think how dolled up you'll be walking in to rehearsal. Yeah, Shultz is going to be around today, and if he gets an eyeful—Please keep your ring on, will you? Then I can ask for a raise on the strength of increased upkeep."

She was laughing, pressing the ring to her lips, asking, "May I?" and rocking her body in delight at the excitement this would cause among the company. To let it be known that she was Nick's wife! And then, thinking again on her torn dress, "How *could* my mother do a crazy think like that! Tearing my clothes!"

Still lolling, arms behind his head, he studied her before he spoke. "Don't you know, honey? She is crazy."

Diana's look became a stare. "Crazy?"

"I suppose it's been gradual."

"You mean—you believe—you think my mother's insane?"

"Never occur to you?"

"No. . . . Oh, you're wrong, you're wrong!" Diana started to her feet. "Why, she's always been different from other people, she's nervous, temperamental, she acts dramatic—but that's Sue!"

"Think so?"

The quiet query made Diana sink slowly back into her chair, the astounding idea, at first so instantly rejected, coming upon her with the shock of revelation. That would explain so much, those hideous weeks of persecution, the unreason and the cruelty, the sudden inexplicable changes from one humor to another, the disturbing sense that Sue was acting drunkenly when she was sober. . . .

Nick swung his legs to the floor, coming upright in his chair. "Honey, don't go all white and scary on me. Wouldn't you rather know the poor woman isn't responsible for all she's done? Wouldn't you rather think your own mother wouldn't act like that if she was in her right mind?"

Diana's look was shuttered and defensive. "What makes you think it? How do you know? How can you tell?"

"Diana, don't act as if I were attacking her and you had to mount guard." Nick came around the table to stand beside her, running his fingers through her hair. "I'm sorry I said anything if you're going to take it this way. I thought you had the idea yourself, with all your talk of fiends and devils in her. Why, I've called her crazy half a dozen times and you never took me up on it."

"You really think she's insane."

"Well, honey, what do you think?"

"But—what caused it? Was it—did I do it to her?" Diana cried out in distress, "Oh Nick, it's all my fault!"

"Well I'll be damned." He sat down on the arm of her

chair, his hand on her shoulder. "She's an alcoholic, isn't she? Is that your fault? The asylums are filled with alcoholics and that's where she's been heading for a long time. I don't say she'll get there—"

The full horror burst upon Diana. She pushed his hand away, springing up and drawing back from him. "No! They mustn't get her! They mustn't put her in a cell! They—"

"Diana, I didn't say—" He advanced toward her but she backed away.

"That *would* drive her mad! To be locked up, brutally treated by strangers! No, no, it can't, it mustn't happen to my mother! Nick I've got to look after her, I've got to—"

He had closed his eyes, his face uplifted, calm with suffering. "Don't, Diana. Don't say it. If I hear you tell me now that you're going back to her, it's me that you'll drive mad."

She was still. He opened his eyes and saw that she stood bowed, the fingers of one hand spread across her face. He turned to the window and looked out, seeing nothing.

Behind him, her voice sounded brokenly. "What can I do?"

"There's nothing you can do. You can't cure her. You can't make her happy." He heard the swish of the satin robe start up, go on; she was moving swiftly, restlessly about the room. He waited, then her voice came again, low, resolute.

"There *is* something I can do. I can keep them from locking her up. Would you let them put your mother in an insane asylum?"

He turned around, picked up his package of cigarettes from the table, turned it in his hands, examining it, seeing how the stamp was torn. "I didn't say that she would grow so much worse that she would have to be put away. But if she should grow worse, what can you do? Make her your work in life, become her constant attendant, never let her out of your sight, sleep beside her every night, humor every wish you can, oppose her when you must, endure all the torment that she puts upon you, give up your dancing, give up your husband, give up all thought of any life of your own—do all that and

372

still you can't be sure of doing any good at all. You may be the one who makes her worse, without you she may quiet down. Or you may be the one to break, and break more terribly than she—you can see her walking through locked doors right now. And how are you going to play the nurse and earn the money to support her? And if she does get worse you won't be able to handle her, they'll take her from you anyhow. That might not ever happen or it might not happen for five years or ten. What would you have gained by the sacrifice of those years? What would you have lost forever?" He laid the cigarettes on the table, straightened a spoon, looked at the cigarettes, picked them up and put them in the pocket of his robe. "Diana, it's time to dress and go to the theater. I've got to shoot along ahead of you. My things are in the dressing room. I'll let Mother know you're ready to dress and by the time you've had a shower she'll be along." He started across the room.

"Nick!" Diana made a movement after him, stopped, uncertain. "Aren't you going to kiss me?"

He looked at her with the tired, faraway eyes that she had seen before, returned and gravely kissed her on the cheek. "I won't have lunch with you, Diana. Nor dinner. I want to keep my mind on the show. I'll get back here as soon as I can after rehearsal tonight, but Lester may delay me a while." He went to the door, hesitated. "Please do me a favor. Don't wear your ring. I don't want to be congratulated on my marriage now." He went into the next room, shutting the door behind him.

No, he hadn't got her. Not even now.

The big house was silent, empty, no one in it but the servants, and by now they would be asleep; Diana paced back and forth in the bedroom, wishing that Nick would come, wishing that his mother had not had a social engagement that took her out, that she could have had the woman's company while waiting for him; it would have been so good to talk with her. How strange marriage was! To be plunged into a close, living intimacy with a man, his male nature still unknown; you could love a man with all your heart and know he loved you too, and yet you could not tell what way his mind would work, what shape his moods would take.

She had come straight back to the house when rehearsal ended at ten-thirty, expecting that Nick would follow shortly. But the hands of the clock had moved to eleven-thirty, twelve, twelve-thirty, and still he had not come, and with each half hour, her loneliness increased, her apprehension grew, so that now she was no longer able to sit still. What could it mean? Surely Lester would not keep Nick so long, surely Nick would not permit him to. Unless . . . suppose Nick chose to stay away. Could that be possible?

All day long and through the night rehearsal he had remained shut up within himself, immersed in work, not giving her one momentary, communicative glance. That power he had of complete emotional detachment was beyond Diana's fathoming; it chilled her, starting up alarms, one troubling supposition following another; suppose he were to remain severed and impersonal; suppose anger gathered behind that impassivity; suppose he might again be rude, harsh. That could not be endured, not now, not when the full dignity of wife was hers.

Or—suppose—some accident—crossing a street, a car coming fast—

Why didn't he come. If only he would come. Nearly one o'clock. . . .

She had grown overwrought and close to tears when at last she heard his steps. He was running up the stairs, coming briskly along the upper hall, hurrying to her. She ran across the room to snatch open the door, fling her arms about him—

"Sorry, Diana, Lester—"

Her arms about his neck, her lips put up to his, excited, joyful, full of celebration at his coming, she was in an instant transfixed, starting back from him; in that instant he had become loathsome, unbearable.

374

"Hold it, kid. I know what's getting you. Give me a chance—"

Her hand leapt out, slapping him across the mouth.

His face did not change expression. It was as though the blow had not been struck. He closed the door and stood looking at her, asking, "Do I rate that from you?"

"You've been drinking—I can smell it—whiskey." Arms about her head, she swayed, stamping in rebellion at intolerable grief. "You can't—you can't—Oh God, not you—"

He gripped her shoulders and held her straight and motionless before him. "Have you ever seen me drunk? Do you think everyone who takes a drink is a drunkard? Did I slap your face when you came to me smelling of whiskey, unable to walk straight? Don't you think you might have given me a chance to explain? I had two drinks with Lester and that's liable to happen anytime that I'm with him. I'm not drunk. Do you think you've got a right to slap my face?"

She heard him open-mouthed. Remorse came as swiftly as had her furious grief. His hands dropped to his sides, she remained as he had held her, unmoving before him, looking into his face. Her mouth closed. He saw the muscles in her throat moving. Tears came into her eyes and rolled down her cheeks and still she did not move or make a sound. She had stood before him once before like this, unmoving, eyes fastened on his. His memory went back to the day when she first came to his rooms and had stood so straight and still, answering the hard questions he had put to her. Only now she was a woman, crying in silence.

He leaned his back against the door, took out a cigarette, lit it, smoked, waiting. Her silent grief went on, the tears traveling down her cheeks, her eyes not leaving his. She did not have the words to speak.

The cigarette half smoked, he said quietly, "That's enough. You're sorry, let it go. I can take an awful lot from you, even a slap in the face—once, anyhow. I guess you feel bad enough not to get the habit."

She answered with the same quiet. "I didn't know that I was

going to do it. It just happened. I hit my mother once. It was the same. I had no intention of doing it."

His lips twisted in a smile. "Why, that almost gives me even rating with her, doesn't it?" He drew out his handkerchief and offered it. "Forget it. It's only a minor incident in the long procession." He moved on into the room, dropping into the chair by the window.

Diana wiped her face and followed him. She sat down on the floor at his feet, her arms laid across his knees, her face turned up to his.

"That's a funny place to sit, honey."

"Let me. I want to."

He stroked her cheek, his smile bitter-sweet, his eyes sad. "It's late and we're both tired, we'd better turn in. Diana, you have a lot on your mind you want to stew over. How about my leaving you alone? I don't want to be breaking in on your thoughts. I'm going to sleep in the next room tonight."

"No. That's wrong. You belong here."

"I don't know, kid, I don't know, but whether I do or not, the show opens the day after tomorrow, and it would be kind of a help if you wouldn't pull any knockouts on me till I get the job done."

"I'm not going to. All day I've wanted to come close to you, to kiss you, to tell you how I love you."

His look was quizzical, affectionate. "Think you do?"

"Let me talk to you. I know it's late, I don't want to trouble you—"

"Will your talk trouble me, honey?"

"No—I didn't mean that. I want you to know I've thought it out. About Mother. And I'm going to do the thing my husband thinks is right."

He turned the ring that she had put on her finger since coming in. "Don't duck your conscience. You have to do what you think is right, not what I think."

"It's right to stay with you, to be your wife."

"Diana, I don't want to be living with a martyr."

"No, Nick, you don't understand. I love you. You come first."

"And you're even willing to do wrong for my sake? No, it's a swell effort, but if you're going to feel haunted—"

"I do feel haunted, but I know that isn't right. I'll get over that. You've got the power to drive out devils, Nick."

"I wish I knew I had." He shook his head. "But this morning—this morning, Diana—you could still feel she had a claim on you."

"Nick, you must realize—if it was someone you had loved all your life, whose flesh had a fragrance, a touch unlike any other's, who had given you so much of love and beauty, given you life itself, who was once sweet and fine and full of patient, kindly reason, who had grown frail and pitiful and aging, easily scared, easily hurt, someone who looked to you for help, someone maybe no one else would help, someone the whole moral world would condemn and turn away from, and if you thought that person could be set upon, locked up, further hurt and scared and broken, and it was your own mother—"

Nick shifted in his chair. "Oh, don't, kid. I get it."

"No, darling, you don't. I'm trying to make you see how I could feel the way I did this morning. But I've thought it out, I know you're right. I can't help her."

He laid his hand over hers. "Diana, you mustn't go by me. I've been thinking this out too, all the time that I was working. You had the wisdom once to say that a person with something on his conscience wasn't pleasant company. You've got a conscience, you've got the makings of a feminine version of Raskolnikoff. If you have any idea that you're not doing your duty by your mother, that feeling's going to grow on you. I've done my best to take you from her, but if you think she needs you now, go to her, I won't do anything to stop you. I'll give you a divorce so you won't feel I've any claim upon you. The day must never come when you'll turn on me and tell me that because I loved you, you did wrong."

"It won't come. Honestly, if I thought I could help her, I'd have to go to her. Maybe that's wrong, but it's the way I'm made. But the night I left her I knew that nothing I could say or do would make her act like herself, like the person she used to be. And you're right, I make her worse. And you're right again—I couldn't take it, I'd break down. When I think of the scenes that went on for days, and how she seemed to get a satisfaction out of making me suffer, when I think of the hate that was in her that last night, and how she'd be going at me right now if I was there—no, I'd wind up screaming. The tragedy is—I want to help her and I know I can't. I've tried. I'd be a fool to go on trying. No, Nick, there won't be anything on my conscience that will come between us."

"Come up on my lap, sweetheart. It sounds as though you had it all thought out straight. You know, I thought afterward I should have told you—I mean to look after her myself."

"Would you? I mean—keep an eye on her, do whatever can be done. I'll support her, but—"

"No, I'll do that, too. If I've got a wife who stands by me I'll do the best I can for her mother."

"I'm standing by you."

They discovered they were shaking hands and broke into laughter.

"Strangers, huh? What about that kiss you said you'd been holding in all day?

She moved to kiss his lips, caught the scent again and wavered, then forced herself to put her lips on his, and in a moment there was only the strong spell of love rising, joining them. Nick drew back his head, smiling, content with her. "That's better. I'm not going to eat peppermints to humor you—that would be too much like lying, the way I look at it. And look here, honey, one of these days you're going to have a drink with me. Yes, you are. I don't want a wife who's a coward about anything, or a fanatic, either. A drunkard's a weakling. You're not one. You have no reason to be scared."

"You shoot so many things at me, Nick. I have to think them over. . . . Oh—it's late and you *are* tired! You must go to bed."

He grinned happily. "You said that like a real wife. You almost scolded me."

"Well! Aren't I?" She had answered gayly and then recollection overtook her and she laid her head against his shoulder, mourning, "Nicky, how could I do that thing to you! How can you forgive me?"

"Sh. You forgave me when I did worse than that to you. Maybe love helps us to know ourselves, at that. I never knew what a mess I could be until I started to love you. We're both emotional, emotion is our business, music and dancing and theater, and we work at tension. But we had to learn how to direct emotion in our work. We can learn how to do it in our love." His seriousness departed; he made an impish face. "You keep on talking about that and I'm going to think you're boasting about what you got away with."

Laughter came easily. Diana slipped off his lap and stood up, assuming a mock severity. "I told you to go to bed."

"Oh boy, I don't get a chance to give the orders anymore." He sprang up; about to put his arms about her, he checked himself, demanding with a sudden earnest gravity, "Look here, Diana, *have* I got you now? Is there anything more your mother can pull on us to break it up? Is there any angle or twist I can't see coming? If she was to kill herself—she might, you know."

"I told you the mother I loved died years ago. I told you there was nothing on my conscience. You've got all of me there is. I'm not Mrs. Heaton's daughter. I'm Mrs. Allingham."

He caught her strongly in a flash of movement and she flung back her head, laughing and exultant, unafraid. He swung her up in the air in triumph. "I've got you and it's for always!"

Diana's protest was a laughing one. "But darling—put me down—you're tired!"

"Tired? Me? When I have you? Oh, honey, honey, you don't know anything about love yet!"

Music sounded through the silent house, rising from the room below, flowing with entrancing skill. Over Nick's face a rapt look spread. He set Diana on her feet. "That's Arthur.

That's my old man. *Carnaval.* He's playing that for me!" He looked at her, happy and amazed. "Can you imagine that? He must have just come home and Mother told him we were here. He means it like a—a blessing, he means it for a welcome. We have to listen."

"I want to listen."

Arms about each other, they stole out of the room and along the hall to the head of the stairs and sat down there, letting that gay, rollicking music fill their hearts. With Diana in the crook of his arm, Nick was beyond grudge-holding; it was a surprise to him to know how good it felt to be given that gift of art as welcome for his home-coming.

Her head against his breast, eyes shut, Diana made her pledge again—to dance, to go on and on; this joy, this beauty, imposed a loyalty that could not be betrayed.

22

THE BARE, deserted stage, lit only by the dim, single bulb of the pilot light, was drab and stark and ghostly in the silence, the empty auditorium a vast gloomy hollow of darkness, yet to Diana, first-comer for the final dress rehearsal, the place lived, holding the vibration of the spells that had been wrought there out of color and music and movement and the play of fancy, all the stirring mystery of theater in the vast, empty gloom.

Bearer of the first small flash of color in the grim grey place, bright red and pale flesh, she worked alone, spinning, circling, weaving designs in movement, melting one into another, designs fashioned out of dreams, out of the insatiable hunger of the soaring spirit and out of endless toiling hours of discipline. But, as she worked, intently striving to attain a sense of satisfaction, a confidence that would rest solidly upon the knowledge that she was in trim, prepared to give the best she had, it seemed to her that a force, malignant, evil, gathered out in the darkened house. She could have sworn that Sue sat there, eyes fixed and gleaming, chanting curses. Never dare to face an audience. My ghost will follow you. She strove against the force, defying it, persisting in her efforts, and while she worked, slowly the theater took on new life, others coming in, preparing for rehearsal. A stage hand strolled through the stage-door passage, trotted up the stairs. A violinist, arriving early, went below to practice. In the prop-room a carpenter hammered on a faulty brace. The wardrobe woman, precious keys in hand, toiled upward. Feet sounded along backstage corridors, voices called and answered, life rising in the theater, coursing through its veins. Diana slipped away, mounting to her dressing room as men grew in number, overran the place, hauling at ropes, setting canvas, lashing and hammering like sailors heading into weather, knowing how their ship could sail in a fine breeze, knowing too how she might founder in capsizing gusts. The asbestos curtain slid down; deep-tinted radiance burst from an array of hanging spots and was answered by a sudden luminous glow of bunch lights. From the orchestra room came mounting bedlam of discordance.

In the dressing room Diana stood dejected, vexed with herself. Why had she been unable to throw off the feeling that Sue sat watching. To be haunted so.

A tap came on the door and Nick stepped in. She tried to face him with a smile but the attempt was fleeting; he could see it was pretense.

He put his arms about her, not saying anything. She was ashamed that he had found her in this mood. "Oh darling, why do I feel like this! It's so stupid, isn't it? Don't pay any attention to me."

He looked at the watch on his wrist. "Go on, talk it out of you."

She sank into a chair, her arms over the back of it. "Why don't you bawl me out? You're the director, you've got a right to. You know I was awful at rehearsal this afternoon."

"Pretty lousy," he agreed cheerfully, lounging against the wall. "You're letting the nerves get you. That's natural, coming up to the opening."

She reached for his hand. "Nick, she was sitting in the house a few minutes ago, I felt her. It's like a heavy weight crushing me so I find it hard to draw a long breath." She pressed his hand, exasperated. "It's not conscience, it's not reason! I called up Rod, I told him there was a check in the mail, that there would be every month, I told him what you said, that you could get him a job in a scene-painting studio. What more could I do?"

Nick patted her hand. "Listen sweetheart, you've been under a nervous strain for a long time and right now you're under another. Don't forget it isn't easy to stop loving anyone, and a mother has a powerful hold, any mother, not to mention how the one you had fastened on you so the wonder of it is that you're as normal as you are. But I'm not worried because you do a bad rehearsal. You've got the stuff, kid. You're going to give me a swell solo tomorrow night. Aren't you?"

"I'll do my best."

"That's good enough for me."

"If only. . . . Why do I feel she's in the theater right now?"

He gave her hand a final pat and dropped it. "I got to shoot. Now you talked about it, forget it. Watch that opening on your dance, attack it more." He blew a kiss from the door and stepped out.

To have the full of his love. . . . Diana rose in active resolution and began preparing for the rehearsal.

Nick took it with a wry smile, perched in the corner on Lester's make-up shelf, his legs hanging. "Well, a lousy rehearsal means a good performance. That's what they say."

Lester was a depressed hulk, more grotesque in appearance than in any of his comedy costumes; his face still black but his wig removed, a narrow line of white edged his tousled sandy hair. "Boy! Even I was punk!"

Diana, still in costume, not wanting to muss it by sitting down, shifted from one foot to the other, admitting unhappily, "I think I never danced so badly in my life."

Nick shook his head at the ceiling. "Tod, can you think of anything else that could have gone wrong? That drop curtain jamming made a wreck out of me. And that dim-wit on the cradle light! Why, he's had that cue for the last three weeks! Not to mention that we got a straight man who goes ga-ga if he goes up in a line! Shultz has gone home to try and figure out how come he ever hired me."

"Sure was a jinx on the show tonight." Lester had an alarming suspicion. "Suppose we got a green kid in the chorus who whistles in the dressing room?" He picked up the rabbit's foot that lay among his make-up articles and toyed with it gloomily. "I *started* to speak the tag line, but I caught myself in time. And I knocked on wood everytime I said the show looked like a hit. Say Nick, can you dope out something on that dialogue ahead of the *Peter* song? Gob, I felt it sag and die on me, they'll sit on their hands if I give 'em that tomorrow night. You can fix it, Nick. Give me a few minutes, will you?"

"Sure. Run over with you to the hotel right now. How about it, sugar, want to scoot into your clothes and come along, or shall I tuck you in a cab for home?"

"I'd like to stay and practice for a while."

"You overdo the practice stuff. I mean it. A rest'll do you more good."

"I won't stay long, Nick. I just want to go over the opening a few times."

Disapproving, he conceded. "Hold to that. Don't work more than half an hour." He slid off the shelf. "'Scuse me, Les, I got to kiss the wife before I let her go."

But Diana thought the kiss too brief and protested, mimicking the director. "Take it again!"

Lester guffawed. "Atta girl! Get back at him, remember how he's been going after us! Aw, you're doing the kissing! Say, don't forget—you're both stepping out with me after the show tomorrow night. We're going to have a party."

Diana clapped her hands in delight. "A party! Oh Nick, will you dance with me? I'll wear my evening dress! I never had an evening dress before, I never danced with—"

"Hold it." Nick cut in sourly. "We didn't put this show over yet, and if tomorrow's anything like tonight we're going to have a funeral instead of a party. Come on, Tod, stir. 'By, sweetheart. Don't work more than half an hour, understand?"

"All right, I promise."

Coming out of Lester's room Diana found the stage again swept bare, only the pilot light burning. She stopped, arrested; out of the corner of her eye she could have sworn that she had caught the stir of a figure in the dark passage leading out behind the boxes.

More nerves, imagination. She put down the strong impulse to turn back to Nick, to tell him. He would be sick of her nonsense. The momentary sharp alarm denied, she went on across the stage and up the stairs to her dressing room, going by locked empty rooms, the rest of the cast gone home.

Taking off her costume, it occurred to her that she should have told the doorman she was staying on; Joe might switch off all the lights. But he was supposed to check over the dressing room keys on the rack, make sure that everyone was out, he would see her key had not been turned in. Besides, he would have to wait till Nick and Lester left and by then she would be in practice costume and on the stage.

She wondered if she should stay on. . . . Her inclination had gone. But it seemed the right thing to do. Well, a few minutes, anyhow. She took off her costume and hung it up with care and then was caught up in admiration for it so that she lingered, running a caressive hand over the smooth, bright panels of silk. To be a solo dancer . . . to have a dressing room all to one's self. She draped the muslin sheet protectively over the costume, and then all at once she was standing motionless, listening.

Someone was walking up the stairs.

But no one would be walking up the stairs at this time. . . .

Now there was silence. If this was imagination—She was wishing passionately that she had told Nick she would go with him, wishing it with such a sudden craving of panic fear that she made a start to snatch up her slip. But again she stood tense, listening, every nerve thrilling.

Diana Heaton, you're a fool and a coward and that imagination of yours—

Someone *was* coming up the stairs, moving stealthily along the corridor, approaching. Diana stood rigid in the fascination of complete terror. The steps were outside the door. The knob of the door was turning. The door was slowly opening.

Mrs. Heaton faced her daughter.

Diana saw two things in the same instant—the gleaming eyes with the bright blind stare of hate and the revolver that pointed straight at her.

The lights in the dressing room and corridor went out. Diana threw herself forward to clutch, to overpower—Sue was not

385

there. The space where she had stood was empty.

She came out of a trance of cold horror knowing she must move. It seemed she knew that for a long time while she was standing still; there in the door, she was a target once eyes grew accustomed to the dark, enough light from the flashing street signs would glow through the frosted panes at her back in the dressing room to show her outline, the pitch dark of the corridor was safer—even though Sue waited for her in that dark.

She got herself into motion, slipping out and sideways along the wall, her back against it, her hands held before her chest ready to clutch at contact. Away from the door she stopped, straining to hear some breath, some rustle that would tell where Sue was. She heard nothing but the thundering rapid beat of her heart. But Sue was some place close. At any moment Sue might touch her.

Some power of reason functioned through the stupefaction of her terror, contending against the craze for shrieking, headlong flight. She was aware of many things at once, that Nick was no longer in the theater or the lights would not be out; that Sue knew where the stairs were, she had just come up them; that Sue, cunning and crafty, would be between her and the stairs, waiting for a blundering betraying move; that Sue might have seen her slide from the door and know just where she was, that right now, revolver pointed, Sue was waiting, just dragging this out, getting enjoyment from the suffering she had visited upon her daughter, taking her time about finishing it; why else was there no sound from her?

Escape—get away—the fly gallery—catwalk on the backwall— stairs on the opposite side—

She began to shift gradually along the wall, pressed flat against it, tensed to grasp at the first murderous touch, the shriek in her throat choked down. She traveled so slowly that movement became a drift across inches, her bare feet sidling, making no sound. With a tremendous gathering of will she forced herself to stop, to listen. Then she was again edging along, throttling the mad impulse for speed that all but burst control. In the hideous slow monotony of that creeping flight in the blind dark her mind wandered. She was in Nick's room, his black head on the red pillow, his voice murmuring, 'Easy, kid, easy. Go slow. Slow does it. Keep your head.'

Her bare shoulder blades signaled that the entrance to the passage into the flies had been reached, the wall turning at a right angle. The blackness gave way; dim as the light on the stage was, a faint glow showed the mouth of the corridor opening into the fly gallery. She got around the corner. It was more tremendous a strain to go slow now, escape so close. But even bare feet running would make a patter. She held to the agonizing pace, came to the opening, made another right angle turn. Cold metal slats were underfoot. She was clear of the corridor and in the flies.

She stopped dead, just around the corner, waiting to hear any stealthy rustle of pursuit, in readiness to pounce if a figure came drifting out beside her. But there was nothing, no sound, no apparition, and for a moment that was intolerable, as though all this were imagined and she must run, screaming.

The flies were narrow. Two steps would take her to the rail. Hand upon it, she could travel faster. There must be no tripping over the shadowy heaped up rope spilling down from the pins on the rail; there were lumpy things in the darkness that must be avoided, stepped over.

She got to the rail. She was groping along it, going faster, the speed drive urging her.

Something gave under the touch of her hand, fell, iron upon iron, clattering. Out of that clatter another started up—high heels striking fast along the corridor.

Diana turned to face her, too far now from the entrance to make a sudden seizure, no longer hidden in the dark. Sue would get her. She saw the figure emerge, running clumsily but fast—too fast—her shoe catching in a slat—her body slanting forward—gone out of control, impelled in one direction—

Diana yelled, scrambling to save her. "Mother—look out!"

Mrs. Heaton dove head foremost, plunging out under the guard rail, diving into air, falling slowly, spread-eagled.

Diana crouched, arms wound about the rail. Her shrieks rose, went on and on, blotting out reason and the knowledge that thirty feet below her mother lay in a motionless heap.

Nick stepped out of the bedroom. Lester stood up from the hall chair, went to meet him. "How is she, Nick?"

"Sleeping."

They turned into another bedroom, the door standing open, no one inside.

"Asleep because she's all drugged up." Nick sat down on a small sofa of brocade and gilt, his mother's taste carried out in every room. He leaned forward, his elbows on his knees, his face in his hands.

Lester edged into a place beside him, put an arm about him. "Diana's all right, Nick. She wasn't hurt none."

"Just driven crazy."

"Say, it's only natural she'd carry on."

"Joe said it took all his strength to make her let go the rail. He said she'd been screaming steady for half an hour. She didn't stop until the doctor plugged her full of dope. How do I know she won't start screaming when that stuff wears off?" Nick clasped his hands and let them fall between his knees. "I've only one thing to hold to—she seemed to know me, she wanted me to keep her in my arms, she didn't turn against me. But she wouldn't stop screaming. You couldn't talk to her. It wasn't Diana."

Lester patted him with an awkward, heart-felt attempt at consolation that shamed him for its inadequacy. "She'll get over it. She'll be out there dancing pretty one of these days."

Nick stood up. "Oh, I don't care about that—what do I care?—if she's—if she's only right in the head! I haven't got her now."

Lester turned his head away from the quiet agony in Nick's face. He gave up the hopeless attempt at solace.

"No, she won't dance, she won't ever want to, even if she pulls out of this. She'll never see backstage again without remembering her mother had to pick a theater to make an exit."

Nick moved toward the door. "Go home, Tod. Get some sleep. I've got to go back in there, I've got to be with her if she wakes up."

Lester thought of something he might do. "The place downstairs is lousy with the press, they'll grab me when I go down. Give me a line on what to say, maybe I can drag 'em out with a lure of a hot inside story."

"They've got the story, and won't it be sweet! Was there ever a mother who did wrong in the eyes of the public? What'll Diana's name mean now? The girl who broke her mother's heart!"

"No, gob, you're forgetting the gun. 'Beautiful Dancer Attacked By Murderous Maniac'—that's the story. Where'd she get the gun? Give me the story, I can put it over right."

They were walking slowly back to the bedroom where Diana lay. "Belonged to Diana's grandfather. Her brother knew it was in the house. He missed it tonight after his mother went out, he knew his mother meant to kill Diana, he came here, trying to find me. The police have his story. That's what clears Diana."

"Where's he now?"

"With my mother. He's taking it quietly, praying. Seems he's religious. Do what you can with the press, Tod. My father's working on them, but you can do better."

They had come to the door. "Gob, I'll go down like honey and they'll stick to me like flies. Say—honest—this is one time I sure could pass up the publicity. Understand?"

Nick nodded and eased himself into the bedroom.

Diana lay on her back as he had left her, light brown hair curling out on the pillow, framing her mild, sleeping face. Nick stole to the chair beside the bed. He sat there, his hand laid lightly over hers. How young, how innocent, how beautiful she looked, no mark upon that tranquil sleeping face to tell of all she had been through, you'd think she'd wake up eager, smiling. If she was broken now . . . if what she had dreaded might be her mother's fate—'brutally handled by strangers . . . they mustn't get her, they mustn't put her in a cell.' . . . How easy it had been to talk of asylums, thinking he could understand the way she felt, but now that it was someone that he loved. . . .

Oh honey, I let this happen to you. You had the premonition, no, the common sense to see it coming, and I called it nerves, imagination, and left you unprotected—me, who promised to take care of you. . . .

As though she heard him talking, Diana's head rolled toward him, her eyes opened, looked into his. Nick leaned closer, smiling love and reassurance, his clasp on her hand tightened. He saw remembrance come, changing her face into a mask of tragedy.

She must not scream—"Diana kid, I'm with you."

Her fingers gripped full strength on his, her eyes shut, but her lips stayed pressed together. A struggle was going on within her.

If only she would not scream. "Hold tight, honey. You're all right now. I've got you."

The struggle was subsiding. She opened her eyes. "Don't sit there." Her voice was torn and husky but low, almost calm. "Lie beside me."

He was disordered with the onslaught of hope and joy. If she could stay like this, be herself. He rose quickly to take his place beside her.

"You can't sleep with your clothes on."

"I'm all right, honey." He took her in his arms. "I don't want to sleep."

"You must—the opening." She had closed her eyes, lying limp and nerveless in the comfort of his embrace when all at once her eyes flashed wide in terror and she was crying out, the words rising in a shriek, *"Don't put out the lights!"*

"No, no, I wasn't going to."

The outcry had unsettled her, the struggle came back, her face working, her breath short and fast, her body tense. Nick held her close, joining in that struggle. "There, kid, you're all right, safe in my arms. Be quiet now. Rest easy." He went on soothing her; rigidity left her body, her excitement died.

The low, husky voice asked, "You can sleep with the lights on?"

"Sure, But I don't want to sleep, sweetheart. I want to see you sleep."

"Yes. I've got a show to work tonight, haven't I?"

He did not know how to answer, gripped freshly by the fear that she was not herself and all this quiet talk was only fooling him.

"Nick, I'm going to dance tonight."

"Sweetheart, don't talk now. Go back to sleep."

"Nick, you must let me, you must help me."

"Diana kid, please—"

"All right. I won't talk now. But if you'll stand by me I can do it."

. "Go to sleep."

Obediently, she closed her eyes, and then he was troubled, remembering—"I didn't mean to give you an order, Diana, I didn't mean to be bossy. Maybe I've got the habit, giving orders all day long, maybe I forget myself and give orders to you when I have no right—"

"It's you. Don't change. Go on giving orders. I'll tell you when I don't like them."

It was Diana; it was reason; he had her. He lay still while joy came up like a fountain playing, rising and rising and going on and on.

Drowsily, she murmured, "If you'll help me, Nick."

"I'll give you everything I've got."

The show was sailing; applause broke out where it had been counted on, where its absence would have been crushing; laughs came where they had been planted, and some where there had been only a hope; effects drew a many-voiced mutter of approval. In across the foots poured that sustaining, vitalizing current of acceptance in a steady flow that lifted every member of the cast to joy, to higher effort, sureness and a sense of triumph. The ingenue, colliding with a chorus girl in the wings, embraced her with a generosity of affection;

Lester, exiting with a comedy jig, continued the jig on his way to make a change; Shultz came to stand by the tormentor, hands in his pockets, rocking on his heels, proud of his property. And Nick was everywhere overseeing all that went on, giving the job that alert intensity of concentration that was habitual with him, but for all that, his heart was with Diana in the dressing room upstairs.

He went up at intermission. She must not try to do this thing, she must be stopped; it was too hard, she might get halfway through with it and then break up. After all, Shultz and Lester had to be considered too, he was responsible to them for what might happen. As for the public it was all right, the papers had got the story straight, the sympathy was with Diana; Nick thought grimly that Mrs. Heaton had given her daughter publicity beyond the dream of any press agent.

Turning into the corridor he saw Diana had not closed the door of her dressing room. That small detail gave him a further insight into the depth of the shock she suffered from; he could imagine why she had not closed it, fearing to see the knob turn, to see the door open.

She was made-up, but not yet in costume, her towel about her shoulders over her practice slip. She faced him in the calm of exaltation, yet he took note that she had left her make-up candle burning as though she could not trust the lights.

They met, body to body in a strong clasp, spirit joined.

"How's it going over, Nick?"

"Pretty."

"I can feel it here."

"Diana, don't do this. You don't have to. Sure, you're going on with your dancing, but it doesn't have to be tonight. Honey, let me put the understudy in."

"Nick, let me work."

"Please don't ask it. I got to think of the show."

She moved back a step, standing on guard over her costume, pleading, "I won't fall down on you. Please."

"Sweetheart, there's a power in you, but you're putting it

392

to an awful test. I don't know where you're getting the juice to run on, but I'm scared for you."

"She gave me beauty that I've got to cherish and preserve. She failed in everything. If I fail now her failure is beyond redemption. You can't understand. I'm not talking about the woman you knew. I'm talking about the mother that woman destroyed, the mother that I loved. That woman tried to destroy me too. If I fail now she will have succeeded. And my own mother wouldn't want that. Maybe that sounds like crazy talk to you, but I know I'm right in this, I mustn't fail."

"It's not failure if you give yourself time to build up. You're only human, Diana. You're acting calm and holy now—you get down there, your nerve may go. It's dark back of the drop curtain where you've got to stand before it rises on you. Go to pieces there and I won't have time to stick the understudy in. I'm the director, kid, and I say no."

Her tranquillity was shaken by the warning, but she did not accept his decision. She held out her arms to him, pleading with a more fervent urgency. "I know what I'm asking of you, Nick, I know it's a big thing to ask, but you've got to take a chance on me. Don't you see it's evil and madness and hate that's rising up to try and stop me, it's terror and screaming and living it all over again and again? I've got to beat it or it'll beat me. I've got to prove that love is stronger than hate and more lasting. If I don't, I'll be defeated too. Please, Nick, give me the chance. I won't fall down on you."

He could not oppose that plea. "Okay, kid, I'm counting on you not to let me down. It's got to be a good show all the way through."

The call boy was coming up the stairs, crying out the second act.

"Be with me in your love, Nick. Be standing there knowing I can do it. Give me everything you've got the way you said you would."

Her eyes shone, there was a glow about her; if she could keep to that pitch—"You can do it. Just hold steady and remember every trick of art you ever learned. Keep your mind on that and keep it cool. I'm with you."

He went out, striding fast, running down the stairs. Away from her, he was at once smitten by what he had done in giving his permission. Were they both crazy? Well, it was done now. The overture to the second act was playing when he came beside the stage manager at the tormentor. "Miss Heaton's going on. Watch it for a quick curtain if I say the word." The man was gaping in a way that made Nick wonder at his own sanity again. But he went on, quick and sharp, forestalling comment. "Shoot over to Lester and tell him to be set to go on ahead of time if he has to."

"But—Mr. Allingham—"

"You heard me. Snap into it."

The man hurried across to give the message.

So—that was that.

The act started, one scene running on into the next with snap, precision and speed; an uncanny speed it seemed to Nick, knowing the show was heading straight for a spot where it would pass out of his control and into the unknown. . . . Suppose that power in her ebbed, suppose she went to pieces out there in front of the audience, screamed, started a panic—

No. I got to be with her. I got to be thinking that I know she can.

But it came to the number ahead of Diana's and she had not come down into the wings. She should have been there, set and ready. Maybe the collapse had come upon her while she was still inside her dressing room. If she didn't come in another couple of minutes, he'd have to give the cue to cut her number. He saw Lester ready in the opposite wings, watching him, hoping maybe he would cut it, expecting him to. Well, if she wasn't here. . . . He picked up the buzzer to signal the cut to the orchestra pit and he was wishing that she would not come, that he could end this now. Then, in a flash, he was remembering that she had asked his help, was counting on it. He sent his love to her, calling. Come on, kid, on the set. You can make it. Lively, kid, lively. . . .

Diana was coming down the stairs, walking slowly like a sleep-walker. She would have to move faster than that, she had to be dead-center when the curtain rose. She was passing the spot where Mrs. Heaton fell. She was going smoothly on, passing into the darkened wings.

But she was not in her place and the ingenue had come off from a second bow.

Nick snapped at the woman. "Take another." She went on again, glad to milk an additional hand.

That gained Diana six seconds; by now she would be in her place. Yeah, standing in the dark. Nick gave the cue, the music of *Brief Rhapsody* began, the drop curtain was going up, the lights dimming to one blood-red spot center stage, picking up the lone figure.

She was there and in the opening pose, and everyone back-stage who was at liberty to do so was crowding into the wings to watch with greedy, morbid curiosity; another legend of the theater was being made—a girl dancing on a stage where her mother died the night before.

The opening movements of the dance were slow, the lithe body yielding with reluctance to the compulsion of that primitive beat. Nick had seen her build that mood until it gripped. . . .

She was not gripping now.

The sweat broke out on Nick. Diana was on stage, making the right movements with nothing behind them. It was as though death had come into her.

Did she know it, know she wasn't putting it over? Would she grow rattled, fumble, forget the routine? How bad could this be?

Lester was watching. Shultz had gone out front to watch.

If only she stayed with the routine, that would be something. But couldn't she *feel* that massed absorbent force of audience?

Come alive, honey, come alive, you got an audience out

there, give them something, kid, don't let the show sag, you can do it, kid, come on, put it over.

The dance stayed dead.

The music changed into the slow, wild beauty of the second theme and with the change, Diana's spirit stirred and woke. Feeling charged her movements, emotion lived in them—and it was grief that she was dancing with a passion of nobility. Grief—and it fitted, it was right, and Nick was spellbound.

The lights were creeping up, magenta in the foots, an amber spot shooting down from the cradle, the barbaric colors of the costume taking on depth of hue, mingled oranges and reds and purples, swinging silk panels about the slender, white body.

Grief . . . and she danced it with a power that gripped and held.

The music changed to the faster beat and Nick's spirit moved with hers and felt what must come now, and saw it come, true and strong and with a magic power he had not known was in her; this was bravery, the courage that could come out of grief, the soul's celebration of its triumph. The crescendo rose in the music and she rose above it, dancing in splendor, coming into the full joy, electric, meeting the audience, carrying them along with her, picking up the brilliant, hypnotic, prolonged spinning of the finale—a wow finish. . . .

The applause broke twenty seconds before the final pose; it grew, thickening, solid and steady, and a slim young figure stood alone center stage, poised, acknowledging the praise, taking it as a friendly, expected courtesy, but with a pretty grace of pleasure, bowing, bowing. Instinctively, Nick counted —three. . . four . . . five curtains.

The cues went out for the next number and Lester went on. Nick slipped away to meet Diana coming into the wings and found himself to be exhausted as he moved, exhausted but in such high elation that for the moment Diana put all else from mind. That the show was on, that there were others in the wings, did not matter, he had to take this wonder of

396

a girl, this damn fine artist, in his arms; he had to walk beside her to the stairs, he had to stand and watch her mount them.

Then the show claimed him and he went back to work. Lester had them rolling in the aisles.

The curtain came down for the last time. All the concentrated, nervous energy, the vibrant, glad excitement of more than a hundred people, spilled out. They were laughing and chattering and calling back and forth as they jostled, hurrying to be away, out into that other world beyond the theater, bound for parties, celebrations, privileged and special beings to whom the gods were merciful, having given them a hit to work in.

Diana came down the stairs in a white evening dress like a bride's, her wrap over one arm, American beauties filling the other, and above the flowers her face shone with a serene, proud radiance. Nick left Lester, advancing to meet her. They drew aside from the stir going on about them, the stage hands still at work.

"Heavenly."

"I did it, Nick, I proved it, didn't I? You gave me your help. I'm—I'm safe now."

Lester came on them, boisterous. "Diana, you're great. Five bows, I counted 'em, and just before my scene too! You sure warmed 'em up for me! Come on the two of you, I got it fixed right, private room at the Astor, our own band, a gang from the show and Shultz, just ourselves, a family party, no press allowed."

"Tod, you'll have to excuse—"

"Aw gob, what are you talking about? Do her good. You got to unwind after an opening, haven't you? Ever hear of anybody who didn't unwind? Say, can't you see she's all dolled up? Diana's coming."

She slipped an arm about Nick's waist, looking up at him to say, "I think we should go, Nick."

"Honey, you got to get some rest, you got to think of yourself."

"Mr. Shultz will be there, Mr. Lester wants you to come, you're the director and you're expected. You should go, it's part of your job. And I want to go along because I'm part of your hit show and I'm proud I didn't fail. For a half hour, Nick?"

Lester answered. "Righto! Nick, you got a wife with sense in her head. May I—?" He kissed Diana's cheek and then managed to get them both inside his hug. "Be with you in a sec— I got Shultz parked in my room—wait till I—"

Nick called after him, "Meet you there, Tod. I got a car waiting." He took Diana's wrap and placed it about her shoulders, smiling at her. "Seems I don't get a chance to direct what's going on. Maybe I don't need to, huh? But one thing certain, I'm going to see you tucked in bed within an hour."

"In your place, Nicky. I want to go there. It's a nice pumpkin shell, it's big enough for two."

He was pleased. "So you didn't fall for the gilded palace?"

"Your father and mother won't mind? They've been sweet —but we've got our own lives, haven't we? We belong by ourselves."

"I think we do at that, sweetheart."

Diana looked down at the roses. "Mr. Barton sent me these. It was nice of him to do that. He knows I'm married, he knows I love my husband." She laid her cheek against the flowers. "I'm glad I have them. It was for this she made me—that I should come through a stage door with roses in my arms."

Nick stood looking at the flowers. It was Diana's mother who had died. . . . You lay flowers on a coffin, you act decent. "Diana, you want her to have those now?"

Her eyes flew to his, surprised; quickly through surprise came gratitude to him for having thought of that.

Nick nodded and took her arm. They went briskly through the passage and stepped into the waiting car. He held her in

398

his arms and and kissed her lips as the car sped on, making its detour to deliver the flowers to the dead woman who had once been Hattie Fletcher, filled with an innocent dream of fine starry things beyond the ways of ordinary Frostburg folks, beauty and freedom and art, a career in far splendid cities.